RAPTOR'S REVENGE

RAPTOR'S REVENGE

Second Edition

Jim Malloy

To order additional copies of this book, contact:
Xlibris
844-714-8691
www.Xlibris.com
Orders@Xlibris.com
828787

To Maria, the love of my life. Who cheered
me on and watched my back.

CONTENTS

BOOK ONE

chapter 1

"I KILL FOR God once more," he whispered low.

As Thomas gazed over the silent valley, it seemed a veil of doom coated the mist of morn. Awake for a time, restless and anxious, he felt uneasy with a tickling dread this battle would be different. Something this morn would change his life. He was sorry he ever met that haggard old crone warning him of danger striking from behind. She looked every bit a humped old witch when she pulled on his cuff.

"Black art hags be damned," he huffed and shook himself, chasing the thought away.

Turning, he sniffed the damp hanging thick and looked slow toward the distant hill. No morning lark broke the silence as timid shafts of sun glistened over dawn crusts of frost.

The long valley, shadowed quiet, lay waiting for the day's dying and he sensed its scorn knowing its blood-watered grass would rise again, leaving no memory.

Standing hard in the breathless air, his eyes lingered against the ghost-colored sky knowing the enemy arrows would find their flesh. He smirked, certain Lady Death diced with Fate's Snicker for the power to decree the victor before this sun's zenith.

His eyes lifted as the amber sun cracked over the edge of the land and the curved valley slowly appeared before him. Lazy night mists hanging low swirled like wispy spirits sneaking sly, hiding from the day like their vampire kin. Again, thoughts of the netherworld shivered him as winter chills hit his bones, aching old wounds. He grunted, shifted his weight, and pulled his cloak tight with another deep breath, fogging the crisp air.

Trumpet blasts ripped the silent dawn, snapping his thoughts. Reveille, he hated it. Even the sun obeyed the call as its first glow caused the war camp to come alive with the familiar groaning, cursing, and clanking of troops. War-horses rustled, stomping against the tether as they whinnied their hunger with a snort, shooting jets of steam like old dragons with no more fire. He watched bushed sentries drag back to camp worn from the hoary night as his stomach growled from the warm smells of the morning fare drifting by.

With a last chilled shiver, he turned back as the sun melted the spirit haze, warming the plain to an Ireland green. He was surprised it was still so lush and thick this close to Christ's day. This morn would be the final battle before winter camp, then three full moons of much needed rest before the next campaign.

Wandering back to his group, he was keenly aware of the legions preparing for battle and felt blessed God favored him bigger than most. It stood him well since joining the crusade six winters past. He was just fourteen.

Thomas Michael Fallon was tall and skinny then, with strong arms from beating black-red iron in his father's smithy. But as time drudged and his height grew, he vowed a different course as he watched his father's tiring stoop and final step to the grave. So when winter bit under a harvest moon, he left to join the crusade.

As water boy, he hauled bone heavy water for two turns of winter for troops before and after battles. Always a pace behind the padre, he weaved between groaning and dying men begging for salvation, pouring many drops into mouths of soldiers bleeding their souls into the earth. As moons passed, the water skins, lead heavy, made his muscles iron tough and at sixteen, he was ready to kill pagan infidels. Eighteen campaigns since formed him battle hard with scars to prove.

His squad was hustling awake when he returned. Twelve good men and some would die today. The veterans groused at the routine of breaking camp while the fresh replacements stayed quiet with their fear.

"Good morn, lads," he greeted, knowing the worth of keeping spirits high.

Chris turned with a sleepy growl, "Watcha so happy fer?"

Chris was with him the longest, toughest of the lot, Irish like the rest. The command always kept Irelanders together, being Catholic and all. Over the seasons, he learned Irish squads were sent to the front more than the rest. It pissed him but made him and his lads' fierce fighters and was a point of pride. When an Irish squad strolled about the camp, no one dared cross their path except maybe another Irish troop. But that was rare, except when sotted, because they knew their bond of blood and stuck together.

As he readied, he looked over the rest. They were thick, the lot of them, and he was proud. By blood and death, they earned their badge of the toughest unit under the king's flag, willing to fight to the last man.

A trumpet blast sounded from the hill, signaling the call to arms. The rustling clamor of the camp rose as the sea of troops formed into battle groups. Men yelled and dust clouded against bugle blasts and rumbling drums.

"On me, lads," Thomas ordered, leading his squad to the center of the line. To the rear, jogging bowmen, a thousand strong, sounded like flapping birds splitting equal to the right and left flanks. Behind them, two thousand armored horse cavalry with lances three men long, waited, ready. To the right, on a low hill, the king's knight and escort took positions to direct the battle. Runners, trumpeters, and flagmen at attention awaited orders to relay messages to wherever needed. Scores of mounted knights, shouting encouragement, whipped through the ranks on war-horses directing the various fighting groups.

The men cheered the pomp as wild-eyed battle horses with stiff-bowed necks and flowing manes high stepped to their own tune. Slick sheens covered their hides as they champed and frothed the bit, huffing proud, with chests thick as bisons. Tail stumps, standing stiff as flag poles, sprouted from haunches so mortar hard arrows couldn't pierce. Their riders, armored Knights of St. John seemed born to their steeds, prancing their gallant flourish. Bright coverlets and sashes with thick colors waved soft in the still morn proclaiming holy truths and brave deeds, declaring them invincible, bequeathing courage to all. They were a wonder.

With the turmoil circling him, Thomas called his men to huddle, reminding them with a stern look to stay in sight at all costs. Catching each eye, he knew just eight were left from his original squad and four just added this week were yet untested in battle.

"Darby lad, whers yer cod?" he asked.

Darby glanced down nervous as a flopping fish. "I ferget it," he said, blushing bright.

"Too late now, . . . least ya got yer sword."

The others muffled a chuckle.

Another trumpet blast brought complete silence through the ranks. Only jingling tackle and shallow whispers of prayers broke the eerie hush of ten thousand. At the same time, Thomas almost felt the internal click as his mind and body centered on the battle. Embracing it like a sultry lover, he looked across the narrow valley toward the pagan enemy. His body warmed as his heart turned cold foreseeing the killing of the godless infidels before him. With shoulders hunched, his eyes grayed under narrowed brows waiting for the trumpet march. His men sucked his energy to their bones, standing solid, ready to follow his lead.

A helmet taller with heavy arms and shoulders, Thomas looked fearsome fitted with black breastplate and silver metal helmet. Below that, a black leather face guard, stitched with thin steel rods covered his face and neck, showing only silvered cold eyes. A mantel of laced steel plates with the Irish ensign, stamped special, guarded his shoulders.

Thick bull leather armor strapped to his arms and legs had an oiled shine. Spiked metal-toed sandals invented by him were mounted in salted leather that was boiled, formed, and dried metal tough, matched and the steel spikes strapped to his elbows. His leather codpiece was pulled snug with leather strips instead of linen laces. He wanted no mistakes there.

Two long daggers, one at the waist, the other in a sheath strapped to his calf matched the double waist high broadswords that sat heavy, crossed on his back, in leather metal sheaths oiled baby soft. The last, a narrow metal shield, heavy thick with a snap release, allowed a quick twist to protect the length of his back.

His gear finished with a small flask of lemon water and strips of boiled cloth for any wounds. Past trials taught him fast attendance cleaning a wound and stopping the flow could determine life or death.

Every foot soldier's first weapon was a broadsword near a man tall, needing most times two arms to swing. Double heavy, one blow with a claymore blade was usually plenty to cut a man down. Thomas, blessed with his left as good as his right, paid the armorer to shorten two swords a notch more than waist high. He tempered them himself, sniffing the steel, sensing time and flame perfectly. Then, under a witching moon, both were hand-honed for many turns of the glass with ballads of battles won to teach the steel its purpose.

Thomas could wield two the same and soon won the nickname, *Blade*. No other could match the fury of his whirling swords, one balancing the other, moving faster than any eye. When clanked with another, those close swore the metal near sang like a devil's angel.

Many times he tried teaching his men the way but their one arm was never as smart as its mate and all lacked the strength to handle both. However, he ordered they wear spiked sandals, elbow guards, water, and cloth strips.

God's army waited silent as the early sun watched, gold, behind them. Another slow trumpet blast and the rattle of the marching drums signaled the advance. The troops, as one, started moving slow forward, each with his own fears and sins, watching the enemy grow before them. Blade became detached, eyes zeroed, waving his men to follow.

A second trumpet, hard and sharp, blared.

Knight's mounted escorts, galloping up and down the ranks, kept order, spurring them on. Next, drums beat a quick step cadence and the sound of marching men and metal filled the air.

Blade forgot the count of battles past and long forgot he joined to fight for God. He fought now to stay alive and some day return home to Ireland. He wondered a moment if his mother still lived.

"Cover me back, Blade," his man Chris yelled.

"Aye, and you, me," he shouted back remembering the old hag's prophesy.

Trumpets blared again and drums quickened the pace. The enemy started taking shape, advancing as one. Its worm-gray line undulated like a snake poked here and there with bright banners marking positions. Blade and his squad jogged forward with the rest, the dust and sweat mixed in a pungent smell of fear and hate.

Blade's temples pumped as his body warmed to the pace. Lessons learned hard taught him to stretch his muscles before a fight to give easy movement, a clear edge against an enemy stiff from cold wet mornings. He felt strong, powerful, invincible.

"Spread yer ranks," he ordered.

His men quick moved one body length apart giving each space to wield his sword. Blade, sensing the air whispers, glanced above and spotted the arrows slicing toward their ranks.

"Ready for shafts, lads," he yelled.

As one they raised their shields in front of their bodies and ducked behind to block the incoming arrows. When the first volley slammed into their ranks, the peppering clatter sounding like hail, bounced off bucklers with screams and curses, marking notice, some found their mark. Blade turned around checking his men, knowing another salvo would spray them before meeting the enemy.

"Heads up now, lads, ther be more," he barked.

Another hail of arrows slammed down and a yelp, close, rang out. Blade turned, seeing a white shaft stuck deep in Finn's thigh.

"Chris, check Finn's leg, snap it, keep moving."

Chris fell back and in a practiced move, cracked the arrow at the skin.

"Can ya go on, Finn?" Chris asked.

"Aye, get on wi ya," he hissed through clenched teeth as he limped forward, taking position with sweat and curses pouring out of him.

Chris returned to his post with a nod to Blade. With his squad still together, Blade turned head on to face the enemy a stone's throw away.

"Ready now lads, for God and England, no quarter," he shouted.

Trumpets blared the final charge against thundering drums and the crusader hoard, roaring their battle cry, stormed full run into the enemy ranks.

For Blade, time slowed. In one smooth movement, he swung his shield to his back and drew the other sword. His eyes faded silver cold as his blades cut a swath before him. Enemy eyes turned to fear watching comrades die at their feet. He seemed a giant titan wielding magic scythes, marking their fate. His machine-like moves, in concert with his men, annihilated the godless souls. Clanging metal and whooping war cries muffled curses and dying screams. Blade, plowing forward, sensed all in slow motion. Swirling his tongue, he tasted metal blood mixed with muddy dust stirred thick in the still air.

Forging ever forward, he concentrated on the infidels' eyes, watching them change from hate to viewing their own death. A grunting gurgle turned him to see Finn buckle to his knees with Saracen steel through his throat.

"Josh, to your sword!" Blade yelled.

"Aye," Josh said, twisting smooth, stabbing Finn's killer through the heart.

Time raced and stood still. Blade, down to nine, closed ranks not knowing the fate of the other two. Slick bloody grass thick with bodies covered the killing ground. He glanced left, the line was not faring well, a wedge was cracking.

"On me, lads," he bellowed, drifting over to fortify the gap.

Chaos reigned as each squad fought its own war. Unending booms and clanks as one soldier smashed against the other with raging screams and curses, mixed with entreaties to God. Blade, tasting his sweat, saw friend Paddy fall and his blood lust flared. His blades slashed deep, fresh with hate, cutting through armor and meat pushing ever forward. Gulping deep breaths, his arms, dead tired, kept swinging, cutting, hacking, killing.

Suddenly, a man as big stood before him. Uniformed total black with a half mask the same, his eyes centered on Blade, cunning and glint sure, boring black hate. Raising his sword to end Blade's life, Blade, sensing the move, dodged as the infidel's steel slashed whisker close.

His eyes turned silver cold as his blades cut a swath before him.

The two backed and squared, locking eyes, forgetting the battle around them. Blade with his two modified claymores and the Turk with a hatchet blade curved like a crescent moon in one hand and a dagger, a half man long, in the other. Locking eyes, both forgot the battle surrounding them.

Time slowed to a snail's pace in Blade's mind as the first flurry of banging steel and straining grunts gained no advantage for either warrior. They backed, sucking hard for breath. Blade's eyes narrowed, glaring at the bull-like man with marble black stare. Sensing his confident smirk beneath his mask, Blade knew what he must do.

Standing a lance apart, he snapped his shield free and sailed it sideways like a skipping rock. It skidded, stopping flat a man's length from the Moor as Blade, huffing his chest full, stood tall, arms spread wide, and howled. Then, wild-eyed, he charged fake crazy with a banshee battle cry.

The infidel smirked knowing a temper lost sealed your doom.

He crouched knee-low, steel ready, waiting for Blade's death as Blade knew he would.

A tick before contact, Blade dropped his sword points to the shield and jumped, using them to vault over the Moor's head. In one motion, he twisted in the air and landed on his feet, facing his enemy's back. Surprised, the moor twisted around to late as Blade's swords hacked cruelly down both shoulders, sinking deep in his chest. The Moor, with arms slack, felt his bones crunch and his lungs suck raw air. His fate known, he looked at Blade with a snarl of admiration before crumpling to his knees in death.

Suddenly, a rank of distant trumpets sounded retreat and the infidels turned and ran. God won the day.

The crusaders stopped in their tracks and watched the troop of cavalry thunder through the fleeing pagans with heavy hoof and lowered lances, completing the slaughter.

Blade and his men slumped as their pumped blood ebbed, leaving lead heavy arms and numbed wounds. Looking over the carpet of dead covering the battlefield, Blade slowly led them to the rear, looking for his missing men. Stepping over the bodies, a dying Saracen, behind him, rolled with a final breath and swung his scimitar one last time, slicing Blade's Achilles heel. Blade yelped and twisted away, collapsing to the ground as Chris, jumping forward, ran his sword through the enemy's chest.

"Where'd he hit ya?" Chris asked.

Blade sat up and pressed the wound closed with his hand.

"Me foot, it don seem bad," Blade said, wrapping it quick with a cloth. Finished, he clasped Chris' arm, pulled himself up and fell over with the first step.

His foot failed to work.

The old hag foretold true, this morn would change his life.

CHAPTER 2

ANOTHER DULL DAY with these giggling girls, sewing and giggling, sewing and giggling, tis all they do, Elizabeth thought. But, I guess I should feel fortunate, I'm warm, safe, and in comfort. But tis boring, boring, boring. If only I could see the padre's books again or even better, Simon's collection of black volumes. I wonder where they are kept?

Simon, the palace seer, stargazer, writer of visions, and reader of horoscopes, held King Henry's ear, enjoying the power of a favorite. Moving silent through the castle on slippered feet, he haunted the halls like a ghost, a spirit divided, for he was often seen at different places at the same time lurking in shadows, cowled in a black robe. Wide-eyed witnesses, swearing over the cross, stilled doubters of his sorcery. He smiled, enjoying their fear, fostering his spirit power at every opportunity.

Heavy browed with black eyes buried deep in his skull, he was an unknown race but trusted by the king. His foretelling trances as he stood, arms wide, staring at the heavens, always bore true. The king's decrees were always measured against Simon's second sight. His treatment to all was as ice and Elizabeth wondered why he treated the women of the court with such disdain, as nothing, and wondered about his male desires. Greeting all with a vile look or a sardonic grin, she thought the worst. All were afraid to dare gossip, sensing his dark heart and finder of secrets.

Elizabeth, just thirteen when she arrived at court, was tall, thin, and gangly. Her quiet personality gave the appearance of being aloof and unfriendly, which did not help trying to fit with the other young ladies at court. So, she usually was charged to the governess to assist with the king's daughters, Princess Mary and Princess Elizabeth. Enjoying that time, she formed a special bond with young Elizabeth. Perhaps, she thought, because the young princess was marked a bastard and shunned like her. The child's mother, Queen Anne, was beheaded for treason. But also, she supposed, they shared the same hair color and same name. But truth be, she would rather not be at court.

Her Irish father, commanding the king's red army, recently lost his life in a heroic battle defending the crown. When the king honored his service, he offered a boon to her mother, fortunately, in the presence of the palace court and her mother dared to plead her favor to place

Elizabeth in his service. It was a brazen act, blushing him to anger but he could not refuse without losing face. An Irish girl at court was unheard of and his approval would sure cause a stir through-out the palace. But, king he was and so it would be. He would correct the matter later.

So here she lived with eleven other young women close in age, all English except her, all Protestant except her, all wealthy except her, titled *ladies-in-waiting.*

Outwardly, the others acted cordial and civil but Elizabeth was friendless, believing the Irish a lower class and excluding her from their inner circle of gossip and games. So, she kept mostly to herself busying her mind with music and poetry much to the consternation of the queen who recognized her future beauty and quick mind. Observing how the other young women treated her, she realized Elizabeth would have to win her own battles. The palace circle, forever cruel, was the test but she sensed Elizabeth possessed the inner strength to best them all. It would be an interesting tug.

Enjoying time alone, she loved exploring the palace castle. Wandering around the maze of corridors, she became lost several times among the countless residences and reception rooms, not counting the walled village. She enjoyed strolls around the great keep with its rich furnishings of tapestries surrounded by thick gilded moldings. One wall held a coned fireplace, higher than her, with a black stoned hearth highlighting a white marble mantel carved with hunting scenes. Beneath lofty vaulted ceilings, a dais at the opposite end served the king and queen's throne draped in a backdrop of purple velvet with the royal coat of arms, embroidered gold, high center.

Then there was the dining hall and of course, her favorite, the library. Each hollow corridor, guarded by stiff sentries, served the captain of the guard and who, for coin, secretly served the interests of Simon.

At dark, black tarred torches angled off wrought wall brackets speckled the hall with eerie light. Elizabeth imagined the hollow suits of armor seemed like steel ghosts. On gloomy days they appeared to spirit talk as drafts whistled through their armor. Stationed still, the cold made the metal creak and squeak. If one stared close, you could actually see them move, making her shiver, thinking they might come alive.

But usually, the palace was busy with servants and pages everywhere, racing about, seemingly in a contest of sorts with stewards keeping order.

After mastering the palace, she explored the outer baileys encased by proud turreted walls encircling many different village areas. Each served its purpose as Elizabeth's nose wrinkled with mixed smells of manure and animals of various types. Tart metal, sizzling from flaming forges, glowed before dunking, then hissed, protesting the temper as it singed the air. Fortunately, fresh fruits and vegetables balanced the aromas along with fresh bread from huge brick ovens, domed to even the heat. Tinkers and beggars were few but she watched with wary eyes, no trust there.

Although most lanes were cobbled, she had to tiptoe often, holding skirts kitty high to avoid the slop and puddle traps. Creaking wagons, both hand and horse, mixed with hollers and curses, crowded the lanes setting a busy mood under awnings and signs declaring wares of this and that. She liked it here.

The gatehouse sported not one, but two portcullises. The massive grills, metal sheathed, were the first line of defense if an attacker breached the moat and drawbridge. It seemed an impossible feat to Elizabeth as she viewed the hundreds of arrow loops shaped like Christ's crosses covering every angle from the towering pilliard walls. These plus the wall walk with protective hoarding, allowed defenders to rain boiling oil and heavy stones on the enemy below. She felt very safe.

Today's sojourn brought her to the base of the outer wall looking straight up to the bastions. Her neck ached spotting the watch turrets with their craggy crenels, like giant's teeth, reaching to the clouds. Excited, she climbed the endless circular stone stairs, finally reaching the ramparts with legs wobbly and puffing for breath. Once there, though, she leaned, her waist against a crenel and gazed out to forever.

Here, with the whistling wind, she fancied the most. Pulling her cloak tighter, hugging herself, she looked out at the world as far as she could see, imagining adventures bawdy and brave. Today was extra fair with clouds coasting below. The cleared land circling the castle was shaded black-brown to gold in organized squares of wheat and readied earth. Villagers and animals, tiny as ants, moved slowly about keeping a safe distance from the heavy woods.

The forest, from this high, with gusting breezes, caused treetop waves casting every hue like an emerald sea. She smiled remembering ghost and goblin tales in the haunted Sherwood Forest. Fables around the evening fire caused the wide-eyed young ladies to squeal and sign the cross, believing sure, the cost would surely be your soul if caught there after dark.

She wondered if wee people haunted the forests in England with their mischief as they did in Ireland. Every forest had fairies, but wee people, she wasn't sure. With a dreaming sigh, her eyes lifted and looked out to the end of things and the forever sea of Kendal green.

But Elizabeth held a secret. Her purpled eyes burned dark with anger at the way her sisters treated her and she took satisfaction in knowing she could read and write. She also studied numbers and could draw with some talent. She kept these skills secret being warned by her mother it was unseemly for ladies to involve themselves much in men's affairs.

Elizabeth remembered her mother was distressed discovering the house servant, Aglio, tutoring her in secret. Aglio, a freed Greek slave abandoned in Ireland years ago, was schooled in the arts, mathematics, languages, and traveled the known world and its seas. When her father rescued him, Aglio pleaded to be taken in his service.

Elizabeth thought him to be the oldest man in the world. At first glance, his stooped shoulders and leather skin, thick wrinkled, gave him a frightening look. But after spinning his tales and looking into his wise soft eyes, she felt safe and comfortable. He nicknamed her Becky, when alone, and instructed her in Latin, French, Spanish, and Greek. She learned her numbers but liked geography best. Understanding how different lands fit together circling the oceans stirred her spirit, especially when connected to his storied adventures. In addition, he taught her poetry, philosophy, and different religions with some sounding sacrilegious and forbidden, making it more exciting.

Elizabeth quickly figured the routine of the castle and devised a plan to smuggle books from the king's library. She smiled cocky thinking how simple it was as she carried a fresh bouquet and boldly approached the guard protecting the hallway, telling him she was instructed to display them on the center table in the library. Suspicious at first, he allowed her to pass. Once inside, it was just a matter of placing the flowers on the table, grabbing a book, and slipping it under her skirts. She thought she was very clever even though at first her heart pounded and hands trembled.

As dawns turned, her visits became routine and the guard looked forward to a pretty young maid cheering his day. Elizabeth added insurance by bringing the guard a sweet treat glazed with a coy smile. But as seasons passed, she became more aware of her desirability by the stares of young swains so she stopped the treat, relying on flirting smiles to ensure safe passage. She enjoyed this power.

Elizabeth, now seventeen, was tall with slim female curves and natural movements, both soft and regal. Fair as pale honey, but not too much so, highlighted eyes of violet summer pansies matching waist-long hair of burnished gold. Her look drew a fast male eye and clearly set her apart from her sisters. Their resentment and envy grew but she learned to ignore their veiled comments and was quick to turn mean remarks in her favor. She walked sure, head held high, determined not to let them know her hurt inside.

Mentally, however, they were no match and finally ceased their jealous effort. During those seasons, Elizabeth secretly read and reread most every book in the library. In fact, she even managed to sneak two of Simon's secret books hidden in an unlocked desk. At first disappointed to discover writings about why people acted in a certain manner, she decided to try some of the techniques on her sisters and young bachelors. Seeing the results, she now understood Simon's ability to manipulate others to maintain power and influence. She disliked him even more.

Elizabeth kept her own counsel but was observed closely by the queen. By this age, the ladies of the court were promised or became a courtesan, except Elizabeth. The young men of the court lacked the confidence to pursue her and those that tried, received polite rebuffs. Elizabeth could not fathom why her sisters would get so flustered and excited about male attention. She tried but it just didn't work. She was beginning to believe her studies were a secret curse and all suitors, both young and old, were uninteresting and boring.

The queen watched with interest and wondered.

A new spring bloomed and the annual May Day celebration brought forth a beautiful morn. A moon's planning transformed the dreary winter garden into festive shades of the rainbow. Bright banners and flags hung about colorful smelly booths packed with fruit and foods of every kind. Mutton, pork, rabbit, venison, along with several types of fowl, including lark, covered one table. Piles of manchet, cheat, with plenty of bran covered another.

Squeezed in between, pyramids of apples, pears, peaches and quinces with imported oranges from Spain, her favorite, were stacked scary. Then, of course, herbs and spices were separate but sat next to sallets of chicory, marigold leaves, and asparagus. At the far end, dates, nuts and seeds covered in sugar, plus gingerbread, her other favorite, were temptingly spread by colors. The chief steward also imported some rare chocolate to compliment the beer, ale, and cider. The palace table was truly admired and the king's steward puffed proud.

The aromas mixed perfectly as she strolled, admiring. Wheels of cheese, in all yellows, surrounded white butter and clotted cream with lightly salted and sweet pies cuddled in perfect crusts. Finally, keels of bread and platters of tarts, eggs, and honey-lathered confits, watered every mouth.

Nature's winter trash was swept or burnt away leaving fresh smells of new life in the air. All types and shapes of people in clothing hard and soft mingled with screeching children hoping not to miss a thing. There was peace in the land and news the king's crusaders were soon returning from their triumphant foreign war.

The warm sun made Elizabeth feel especially fine. Everyone seemed the same as the celebration started with troubadours strolling and strumming their lively tunes. The palace court mixed and mingled, laughed, and joked about events and gossip. Women toyed and men preened while food and drink flowed.

Enjoying the happy festives, Elizabeth stepped back against the garden wall to catch her breath. She snuggled against the scarlet roses, savoring the fruity aroma, content to watch the celebration from a distance. She enjoyed observing people and smiled at the flirting mastery of the finely dressed women of the court. The young men, no, all the men, she decided, were oblivious to their wiles.

Suddenly, a scream jerked her attention to the king's table. The queen was standing, bent over, leaning on the table with one hand and grasping her throat with the other. Her open mouth and bulging eyes told all she was choking. Someone started patting her on the back as Elizabeth ran toward her, pushing others aside that were gawking helpless. Turning blue, the queen gasped for breath as Elizabeth shoved the man patting her away, ripped the buttons from her tight neck collar, and jabbed the heel of her hand against her chest. The crowd gasped in shock. She struck the queen again and a chunk of meat flew out her mouth. Elizabeth heard her deep breath bring life back.

Immediately, the queen's attendants moved in and escorted her inside away from the others. The palace guests, hushed for a moment, finally realized Elizabeth saved the queen's life. Then, the chatter began with everyone talking at once, praising her and reliving the event. Elizabeth nodded, quickly acknowledging their regard, and left to join the queen. Rushing with skirts high, she entered the room finding a cluster of women hovering over the queen, all talking at once. With the ladies clumped together, the room was stifling with perfumes of every blend.

"Good heavens," she said, raising her voice, "Pray, step away, give the queen room to breathe."

The startled women backed away, shocked at her impudence, daring to speak to them in such a manner. Ignoring them, Elizabeth sat on the edge of the lounge and lifted the queen's wrist to check her pulse. At the same time, she took note of the color of her skin and breathing, silently thanking Aglio for teaching her some knowledge of the medical arts.

The circle of women, angry at her boldness and familiarity with the queen, whispered their complaint. No matter, Elizabeth thought, the queen would be well.

Next morn, rumors and gossip afresh, Elizabeth was summoned to the royal's rooms for a private audience. After graciously thanking her, the queen interviewed her for a time and when she emerged, Elizabeth was appointed the queen's confidant and attendant. The palace court fairly roared with gossip, wonder, and complaint. *And she was Irish too.*

As summer drifted, Elizabeth's stature and reputation grew while she continued to dream of her books' adventures and far off places. Although pleased with her position and busy with her charge and daily ministrations, she was lonely.

One eventide, standing alone on her balcony, her mind wandered as a tickling breeze brushed against her hair and filmy gown. Feeling the velvet night hug her, she sighed, gazing dreamily at the spotted heavens circling the crescent moon and whispered, "I wonder what my future will be?"

chapter 3

THE WINTER WAS pleasant, much better than Ireland, Blade thought. *Espana* felt like God's land as the army regrouped and mended from the last campaign. Troops cheered when the king's commander announced they would be relieved and return to England after one last liberating sweep on the plains of *Mordo el Polvo*, fifty leagues south. This last skirmish was expected to be of small consequence compared to their last great victory before winter camp.

Rumors were rampant. The knights of St. John held Malta. The Ottoman Empire was stalled by God's blow. The Turkish Sultan, Suliman the Magnificent, was stalemated at Rhodes by the miracle knights blessed by God. Indeed, the legends of Jean Parisot de la

Valette, the Grand Master, inspired all fighting under the cross. All hail, Charlemagne. But now, with relations strained between Catholic Spain and Protestant England, it was time to return home. Let the Spanish deal with the Turks. England's forces would return victorious and proud. Spirits were high.

Blade no longer remembered his home. Nine earth's turns had passed and fighting was all he knew. He wondered what would happen after the crusade. What work would he do? Where would he live?

Shortly after arriving at winter camp, he was summoned to the commander's tent to evaluate his injury. His heel mended but left a permanent limp that stilled him from marching to the tune of the battle drums. He stood, worried, still on crutches, before four king's knights who would decide his fate. He knew seriously wounded men, no longer fit, were cashiered to find their own way home.

A fast conference and vote decided that Blade, because of his legend reputation, would be assigned to the archers of the king's guard to train with the longbow.

Disappointed, Blade understood he could fight no more with his foot soldiers and decided to give it his best. After the first day, he looked forward to the training and a moon later, off the crutches, he proved he had a good eye backed up by long strong arms and shoulders. Blade was determined, worked hard, and after two moons was most good as their best.

After a few suns turns, he noticed the men spent all their training with the bow, ignoring their other weapon, the halberd. If ever overrun by cavalry, this horse-long pole with a spike and cleaving blade could save their life so he decided to teach them the finer points of its use. With his fighting reputation, in a half moon, confidence and morale was bettered. The master bowman observed Blade's action with favor.

One early morn at the ending time of winter camp, Blade was awakened by a dream. His mind conjured a stronger bow designed to shoot further than any other. Hustling up, he went off alone with a sack of food, water, tools, a couple of long bows, and a handful of flight arrows. He selected the bows from the best yew from the north rather than beech or elm and the longest ash arrows crafted by the bowmen of Cheshire. After finishing a full moon of practice, he preferred bowstrings of flax over linen and took an extra length.

Alone on a silent hill overlooking the valley, he watched the yellow sun creep over the distant plain as the smell of peat, drifting on the breeze, announced a rich dawn. Taking a deep breath, he settled under the shade of a wide oak enjoying the beauty of the valley. Looking aloft to the clear sky, he noticed a morning hawk circling, sailing slow on the wind, shopping for the best to eat. As he watching curious, the hawk suddenly seemed to stop in the air, staring at him. At that moment, Thomas felt a force surge through his body, a special kinship connected his spirit with the hawk. He shivered, welcoming the brotherhood as he watched the hawk vanish in the glare of the sun.

Thomas, feeling renewed, wondered the meaning of what occurred, finally deciding it was beyond him. Back to the present, he bent to his task.

He first placed the two bow staves side by side but separated in the middle by a hand-sized length of wood a knuckle wide. Then, he laced the two bows together from top to bottom with thin cut leather. Next, he strung both bows with the two flax bowstrings and with another strip, wound the strings together a hand's length long in the center. Finished, he held a single fat bow, extra wide, with a gap between the two staves capable of resting an arrow.

"Now to see if it works."

Sitting down, he placed his feet on each side of the staves, nocked the arrow, rolled on his back, and pulled the bowstring with both hands, full back. The tension, hard and tight, used most of his arm and leg strength, but it pulled smooth, allowing the arrow to be stretched full to the barbed arrowhead.

Releasing with a strumming twang, the arrow shot forward double the force and disappeared from sight. Frowning, he realized a problem. It was no good shooting an arrow so far if one could not be accurate. Taking a rest, he plopped on the cushion of cool grass pondering the problem as he absently watched swollen clouds pass by.

If only he could shoot arrows at the same angle and the same power every time, he mulled. It was known the length of arrow pull against a tested bow set the distance but how does one keep the arch the same for every shot?

Blade jumped up. He had an idea. Excited now, he cut four straight branches waist high about a finger round. He measured, cut, and stuck two sticks in the soft dirt and taking another, laced it to one allowing it to slide up and down. The fourth was tied across the tops of both, ending with a stick more or less horizontal to the ground. But, by sliding the two laced side by side, either up or down, he could change the angle of the horizontal stick. Now the trick was to line up the arrows to match the chosen angle of the stick before shooting. With a little practice and a good eye, he figured the arrows should drop just about the same place every time.

"Now let's see how this works."

Blade shot five arrows at the angle of his device and walked forward to see where they landed. After some distance, much further than the normal bow, he searched around but couldn't find them. Looking around, puzzled, wondering their fate, he glanced further and spotted some sticks poking up through the grass. Trotting over, he laughed aloud finding the arrows grouped within three arms of each other at least two furlongs from the spot he loosed them.

The next sun was an exciting time. Blade demonstrated his double bow and his target guide to the knight commanders, the archers, and anyone else who wanted to watch.

"I have never witnessed such a feat," the commander said.

The expression of the others said the same.

"Your name, Bowman?" he asked.

"Thomas, Sir Knight."

"Your Christian name?"

"Thomas Michael Fallon," he answered, standing tall.

"Well, Thomas Michael Fallon, you be Irish then, eh?" the commander said, noting his pride.

"Aye, Sir!" Thomas stood straighter.

"I am told you are also named Blade among the men. Why is that?"

Blade blushed slightly as the knight Bowman spoke up. "Because of his prowess with two swords, my lord, he was the best swordsman in infantry."

"Ah yes, . . . now I recall."

He turned to Blade and stilled, making a quick study.

"Well Blade, also known as Thomas Michael Fallon, your feat here today warrants recognition. As of today, you will be your knight's squire and train our archers with your new bow."

The task started immediately, fashioning the bows and crafting the new target guides, now made of metal, able to fold, and portable. The complete unit was pressed into service to complete the job and although all was on schedule, supervising the effort left Blade exhausted with a few hours sleep each night.

At the next moon's turn, the crusaders prepared to break camp when scouts reported a large infidel army moving toward them a quarter moon out. They judged the hoard at thirty thousand strong with animals big as ten horses pressing the march without cannon, scorching the land before them. The scouts, wide-eyed, described beasts with long noses that touched the ground and ears big as wagon wheels. Most had armored baskets strapped to their backs holding four archers and were supported by horse cavalry to thick to count.

This was dire news and an immediate war counsel was called. Blade attended because of his new position as squire but stood quiet in the rear of the command tent. One knight after another proposed various courses of action and after much debate, two conclusions were drawn. The first; to stay and fight, would result in defeat but their valor would be remembered. Second; to retreat and possibly escape, returning to England in shame. The room quieted as all contemplated the choices.

"How would their great army fare if they had no commanders?" Blade thought aloud from the back of the tent.

Everyone turned and stared, some dismissing him, others thinking his question foolish, the rest angry that one in his position dared to speak. Blade blushed.

"What is your aim, Blade?" the king's commander asked. "The answer is clear. The army would panic and route."

Blade cleared his throat. "With your leave, Sir Knight, I have an idea to kill all or most of their greater commanders before they attack. As you say, without their leaders they will be confused and panic."

"Speak up lad," he said with some reservation. "Lay out your plan so we may decide its merit."

Nervous, Blade, feeling every eye, pushed his way to the map table. Using the tip of his bow as a pointer, he cleared his throat. "Sir, we keep our camp where we are. The infidels can only attack across the open plain because of the steep hill behind and on our flanks. The devils, knowing our strength, will be arrogant in their expected victory."

Blade became more confident pointing to both hills, sensing interest starting to build.

"These two hills on opposite sides of the battlefield are the only outposts where their commanders can direct the combat."

"That is obvious, squire, tell us something we do not know," an impatient knight criticized.

Blade nervously held up his hand and continued, "They know not the range of our double bow. If we but measure the distance to these two hills before the battle, we can use a thousand archers to shoot as one and cover both rises with a blanket of arrows."

He took a breath.

"Feeling safe at that distance, they will be without shields. Three quick volleys would most kill or wound all their commanders causing surprise and lack of leadership in their ranks."

The command tent fell silent. No one even coughed as they stared at the map table. Blade started to panic. He should have stayed silent.

Blade quickly added breaking the hush. "This will put three volleys of five hundred arrows on each hill by a ten count and . . ."

The room erupted. Comments condemning and praising the idea bantered back and forth.

The king's commander raised both arms and called for silence.

"By the saints, tis a wild plan," he said, locking eyes at the table. "The distance would strain the talent of the new bow," he turned his eyes to Blade. "It is not yet battle tested."

Low murmurs of agreement filled the room.

"But by the heavens, the other plans are not worthy and no one proposed a better strategy," he declared, glancing around the room.

The master Bowman stepped forward "Pray, Sir Knight, the plan has merit. My archers are up to the task. Let us give a show to prove."

He paused in thought.

"We will be ready in four suns."

Blade breathed a sigh of relief for the support but panicked about their ability to prove the plan in only four suns. Twice that would hardly be enough.

The rest started muttering and whispering for and against.

The king's commander pounded the table, stilling all. Looking at Blade and his commander, he gave his order. "Sirs, you have three suns. More would hinder our chance of a successful retreat if your plan fails… Three suns, no more."

The test went well. Blade's plan worked. The commanders agreed and preparations were made. Five hundred archers were assigned to target each hill. They would shoot three volleys on command five counts apart, blanketing both hills with three thousand arrows.

It was judged that over two hundred high and lesser rank commanders would be stationed on the enemy hills plus bands of flag bearers, drummers, and runners to relay orders to the advancing army. A launching field was measured and laid out to match the enemy outposts. Target guides were mounted firm in the ground, each angle measured by three in square ranks a short arm apart, creating a grid, ensuring uniform coverage of the killing ground.

Tests shots were conducted and Blade personally instructed every archer. He ordered all to rub ashes on every arrow shaft to match the morning sky. The last task was dipping the arrows in a toxic poison captured from the Saracens in the last campaign. Blade cursed the order but realized it was necessary to insure any arrow's scratch caused a quick death.

The morn of battle was dull cast and cool. Blade studied the sky knowing the arrows would be near invisible. The crusaders, ten thousand strong, stood restless, watching silently as the enemy horde formed on the opposite plain. It seemed their masses were endless. The gray beasts, stationed in front ranks, were covered with harnesses of double leather and metal shields. As scouts reported, four archers perched in armored baskets on the animal's backs could shoot down at the crusaders at close range. For their protection, twenty to thirty lancers circled each beast. A prisoner, captured yestereve and tortured, named them elephants from India and as they thundered to position, Blade thought they looked like living castles. Behind the trumpeting gray wall, thousands upon thousands of foot soldiers formed at the ready.

The rumble of the pagan army trembled the earth as clanging and dust clouds filled the air. Trumpets sounded and drums beat to quarters while commanders took the expected positions on the two hills. The entourage of flag bearers, trumpeters, and runners crowded in position around the commanders, flaunting arrogant with slow bold movements, savoring their expected victory.

The Master Bowman and Blade watched from a small platform a man high. "I wish we could see their smug faces," the Master muttered.

"We will when they are dead," Blade answered, turning to the archers.

"Ready your bows, breath deep, with steady hand . . . . Remember, fire only on the green," he boomed as squad sergeants at arms walked among the grid, repeating the order. A thousand men sat down as one, placed the bows around their feet, nocked their arrow, and fixed their position with the target guides.

Suddenly, the thundered din of the enemy stopped and silence sucked the air. The infidels waited for their commander's order to attack while Sir Death watched from the heavens.

To divert the pagans' attention from the arrows, the center of the crusader army, six thousand strong, began chanting. When the enemy's eyes centered on them, Blade raised the yellow flag signaling all archers to make their pull to the arrowheads.

Five counts later, Blade yelled "fire", dropping the green flag.

A sucking whoosh filled the air as a thousand arrows, pulled to their barbs, left their bows. Yellow flag quick again, green flag dipped, and another thousand drops of poison rain filled the air. Another five counts and the last sticks of death sliced through the sky.

The first arrows slammed into the enemy command like needles from hell with devastating results. Most were dead or dying as the second curtain of poison sealed their fate. The third was the *Coup de Grace*.

The crusaders' cheers matched the enemy's cries of alarm watching their commanders die before their eyes. Wide spread panic and confusion spread through their ranks like wild fire. Truly the crusaders commanded arrows from hell. Blade redirected the bowmen to arch their arrows over the elephants, lobbing them into the pagans' legions. Terror and hysteria quickly spread and the army routed, fleeing the valley.

The confused elephants sensed their master's panic and stampeded in all directions slinging off archers and trampling everything in their path. Their trumpeted fear eerily announced their death march as they crushed the bodies of the barbarians.

The crusaders cheered and Blade was a hero.

As usual, as the sun moved low over the earth, squads were dispatched to inspect the killing ground to survey and report. As they spread out, Blade found himself at the far edge approaching a small copse of olive trees. Mindful of his sliced heel, he stepped careful, with bow strung, between the mess of equipment and bodies ever alert for wounded enemy who could still kill. As he remembered the sword slash across his heel, suddenly, a muffled clicking sound whirled him around, letting his arrow fly. A dying scream answered the shaft's mark. Advancing cautious, he spotted the arrow buried in the chest of a Saracen woman. Bending, he looked closer when a screeching noise erupted under her body causing him to jump, grabbing his knife. Heart pumping, Blade rolled the body over and found an angry infant.

His men laughed and Blade turned red staring at the screeching babe wrapped in a swaddling cloth. It somehow survived the horror of the morn protected by the mother, a camp follower trampled by the retreating army.

"Well now, Blade, whatcha find there?" one asked.

"Kill the sniveler and be done," another added.

Blade, confused, picked it up and held it straight out, stiff armed. As soon as the baby felt Blade's grip, it stopped crying and returned his stare, confusing Blade even more.

"It sure smells like dung," he joked, suddenly aware of the baby's fragile dependence and determined survival.

Feeling guilty for killing the mother, he couldn't bring himself to kill the infant. It deserved a chance so he decided to take it back and give it to a camp follower. Walking along, cradling the babe, he felt awkward and protective at the same time, especially with the teasing of his comrades. Finally, temper flaring with a belly full of jibes, he quieted them with a hard stare.

At camp, the doxies turned their back declaring it a heathen better dead, even with bribes of gold. Angry at their excuses, he finally found a temporary berth after doubling his cost. That done, he returned to duty, mobilizing the army west to the coast, and home.

After a quarter moon, it was clear the camp tarts were neglecting the baby. At the next village they passed, he took leave, determined, and finally found an older man and woman willing to take the baby boy for a handful of gold. Speaking was difficult, neither understanding the other, but with much gesturing, pointing, and face twisting, he finally struck a bargain. As best he could, he thought they might be Basque, a mountain people, living in a small village named *Cima Verde*. They seemed kindly, with several of what he supposed were grandchildren hanging on their legs. After they pointed to a nearby church, he figured they were Catholic, a bonus. With a breath of relief and a clear conscience, Blade gave over the baby and coin. As he turned to leave, the old couple started rattling in their tongue, gesturing excitedly, pointing to Blade and the baby.

Blade, past due and in a hurry, thought they wanted his name. "Thomas Michael Fallon," he shouted over his shoulder as he trotted away, afraid they might break the bargain as he waved, smiled, nodded, and stepped his pace.

After a distance, satisfied and relieved with his good deed, he returned to camp.

CHAPTER 4

LONG GOLD TRUMPETS blared and bronze bells bonged their hallelujahs announcing the victorious crusaders, King Henry's own. Rested and renewed, the polished warriors marched proud and sharp through the castle gates to the cheers and hurrahs of its citizens. The planned moon-long festival would rival the best, welcoming the soldiers back after six winters. Shimmering bright banners and skinny pennants of every color fluttered with the rhythm of parade drums. Women in their finest hung from windows and balconies shouting their pride and invitations as the men strutted by. Wild children and excited dogs yelled and barked, getting underfoot, as they jogged alongside the parading soldiers. It all seemed a blur as family and friends hollered at their recognized men. Cheers, tears, and laughter, mixed with song and music caused a deafening racket, proving everyone's joy. In step with his squad, Blade stood tall as he filed past the wide balcony, limping, but keeping pace with the rest.

King Henry and his queen stood to honor their brave soldiers filing by, four abreast. Elizabeth, to the right of the queen's elbow, watched wide-eyed, dazzled by the fanfare. She had never witnessed such a celebration. Her indifference a week ago changed to excitement as she joined the reveler's spirit.

Watching the soldier's tromp by, her eye caught and was drawn to one taller than most, unique because of the noticeable limp he fought to hide. A battle injury, she guessed as her attention was lured back to the festivities.

After the parade, the men were dismissed to enjoy and celebrate as they wished while the king and queen's entourage retired to the castle keep. Blade, after toasts and back slaps of good wishes, slipped to a quiet corner of the inn and watched comrades enjoy family and friends. Alone with no family and feeling sorry for himself, he started drinking more ale. Tavern wenches, sisters of camp followers, flirted for his attention without success. Although seeking them many times over the seasons, tonight he wished for something more.

Life's toiling waited while the whole region celebrated the festival. Blade roamed about curious at the whole affair. For the first time, he saw dancing dogs, bear baiting, and cock fights. It seemed bells from every belfry forever clanged with people jumping and dancing to flowing flutes and excited drums. The smells of cinnamon, licorice, and ginger filled the air while troubadours and mimes competed for favor. Dogs yapped and tots of all sizes laughed and played in their own world. Pennants and flags painted the sky with flaps of rainbow colors while drums rat-tat-tatted to bangling tambourines. With all this, Blade still felt alone among the fury and missed the order and discipline of the army. He went in search of some peace and quiet.

When the moon grew by half, the fanfare ebbed. He was surprised to receive orders to attend a ceremony to receive with other nominated soldiers special recognition from the king. Nervous and dreading the day, he was uneasy mixing with the castle court. A soldier since fourteen, it was all he knew. But an order was an order so he oiled his weapons fresh and cleaned his uniform. Still unhappy with his look, he purchased a new black cloak with red silk lining for too much coin. It was softened by a slice of ermine at the collar to help hide his well-worn uniform. Suiting up before a looking glass, he stood huffing his chest, deciding he looked bonny good.

The next noon, he mingled in the palace corridor with a score of others in uniform, all finely outfitted in their regimental best, all holding officer rank. Blade, embarrassed by his rag-tag look, wished he could be gone. As he seriously considered the thought, the double doors to the reception hall swung wide and the palace guard motioned them forth. Filing down the center isle, the court musicians struck a spirited march. Blade hunkered in the middle trying to blend in and turned beet red when the room full of well wishers hooted their appreciation. Feeling awkward like a pig on a pole, he sucked a breath to calm himself as they reached the opposite end, and with a signaled halt, faced the throne.

Standing tall and broad with metal bright and leather cloth uniform, his swords crossed on his back and fancy cloak made him stick out like a lad in a nunnery. His stern look sealed the tip as he thought he would rather fight ten men than be here.

Blade cursed silent, but calmed as he glanced around the crowd. His eyes settled on the raised dais seating the king and queen. The assemblage was crowded with attendants, squires, and advisers of every stripe with the ladies-in-waiting standing a pace to the rear. The stage was complete with a jester dwarf curled quiet at the foot of the throne like a loyal pup. Lace and pomp, mixed with perfume, filled the air and tickled his nose, causing shallow breaths. He wished he were not here.

The king stood and the music stopped, hushing the room. Blade's attention, however, was drawn to a young maid to the right of the queen. Like the other genteel women, she wore a straight gown of soft yellow hiding her soft curves, creating the mystery of desire. Tall and slight with golden-red hair and purple eyes, she mesmerized him as he openly stared, barely hearing the king's crier. Suddenly, her eyes met his with a questioning look, causing him to blush and quick turn away. Did she smile at him a bit? Feeling his body flush, he felt her eyes on him and dared not look back.

Elizabeth smiled to herself catching the big soldier staring at her and watching him turn apple-red. She couldn't resist making him squirm by returning the stare, daring him to look back. Her gaze reaped benefits noticing his brawny build in his warrior uniform. He looked ready to fight with the crossed swords mounted high on his back and knives strapped to waist and leg. His cape added the only finery to his rough look in direct contrast to the rest of the stately dressed company. He did not look very happy.

A womanly voiced minister broke her spell by announcing the names of military officers. As each stepped forward in front of the dais, the court crier recited an act of triumph or chivalry as the king's attendant presented a badge or medal. Some, with murmurs from the gathering, were bestowed lands and castles depending on rank and feat.

"Thomas Michael Fallon," the minister hailed.

Blade looked up and strode around the group to the dais smartly as he could, struggling to disguise his limp. He was not going to let some wench cause him grief.

Goodness, Elizabeth thought, tis the soldier I noticed at the parade. She wondered why he would be with this group. Fallon must mean he is Irish.

Her questions were answered as the crier boomed, "Thomas Michael Fallon. You are recognized for your service to God and your king in twenty battles with infidels, leading the front lines and being severely wounded many times. Also, for your design of an improved longbow and battle strategy that defeated the largest pagan army ever assembled.

For these brave deeds, you are awarded the king's cross and promoted to captain in charge of the palace guard."

A king's attendant stepped forward holding a crimson pillow, presenting the silver medallion to Blade.

"Your badge of office and emblem, sir."

Blade was stunned. It was all he could do to keep his mouth from dropping open. Captain of the Guard? Was this possible? He turned to his king and bowed. "Thank you, my liege," he said, picking up his prize and marching smartly back to his group. His mind raced. *Captain of the guard! Captain of the Guard! For one of my station? I cannot believe it.*

The rest of the ceremony was a blur.

Elizabeth stared back with a different look.

The next moon turned quickly as Blade's duties were outlined and he toured every nook and cranny of the palace and castle grounds. His stern nature hid his misgivings as he realized the extent and magnitude of his responsibility. He discovered weaknesses in security and quickly established his authority by issuing orders ensuring the protection of his charges. The challenge was daunting but exciting.

Blade inspected from the slimy moat to the highest parapet, including every turret, tower, and the strength of the gatehouse. Even the many baileys and bastions received his strict attention. Walking the hallways, he discovered the corridors, and the hundreds of rooms worse than a twenty-league forced march. At first a labyrinth, he soon learned the swiftest path to get anywhere in the walled area. He found he had the talent and was proud of his accomplishments. He loved it.

Demonstrating his weapon skills, he trained all his guards the same, furthering his reputation. As word spread and praises grew, he focused on becoming familiar with the movements of everyone in the palace. Although his manner was rough and hard, he gained allegiance for his thoroughness and efficiency.

Greeting everyone with respect, he was impressive in his new uniform of black-blue with silver thread topped with a bloused white collar. The hammered silver medallion pinned to a scarlet sash across the chest, worn by him and his men, made them proud and professional. He kept his old boots, shined bright, a remaining comfort from the wars, plus the weapons that protected him all those years. His men carried light rapiers with dagger and shined breastplate subject to daily inspections. And, woe to the guard not reflecting Blade's image off their chest, for failure meant a week's duty high in the chilled tower through the witching hour.

*

Blade soon learned her name was Elizabeth, passing her often with others in the palace halls. He always greeted her with a short bow and "my-lady" that blushed him every time to his dismay. He just couldn't make sense of it. No lass ever affected him this way. He knew she was Irish and the queen's favorite plus how she saved the queen's life. Beautiful and proud, she always passed a friendly smile toward him and he found himself thinking of her often, plotting different ways to cross her path.

Moons passed and duties became routine. There were several notable characters about but the strangest he met was Simon, the king's advisor. Blade's attention was drawn to him by his unusual nature. His gracious manner in the royal's presence contrasted with his snappy meanness with others. Haughty and over-proud, he seemed also sneaky and slick. With his political tongue, sure a mountebank, Blade decided he could not be trusted.

He was set further on guard by Simon's conduct toward him. Faking interest, Simon involved Blade in general conversations with oily questions about his duties and guard assignments, declaring he, like Blade, was concerned with the royal's safety. Simon hinted special favors for his cooperation on some minor matters but Blade's dedication to duty allowed for no variance. Blade at first was flattered by his interest but soon suspected other motives and vowed to mark him close.

Another, a sure enemy, was the captain of the guard he replaced and Simon's pawn. Rumors reported said the old captain, when full of wine, made mumbled threats feeling sorry for his lot. Blade humphed at the rumor, thinking the two spent too much time whispering in corners.

One day on a stormy mid-noon, Elizabeth was off on another sojourn to the library with a flower vase fluffed full. In a hurry, she rushed around the corner and crashed into Blade.

"God's breath!" she gasped, almost dropping the flowers.

"Pardon, my lady," he said, grabbing for the juggling vase, his beefy mitts ending up covering her soft hands.

"You startled me, sir," she declared, at first frightened, then miffed, and then tickled, giggling at his awkward look.

Blade jerked his hands from hers and blushed, returning her smile. Waiting for a planned chance meeting, he hoped to impress her with his gallantry, not frighten her to death. Relieved to see her warm smile, he turned brighter. Seeing his blush, she decided she would tease him for the scare.

"Pray sir, is this how you formally meet a lady?"

"Nay, mi-mi-lady, my pardons."

"Well, I suggest we start over. Your name sir?" Her eyes smiling.

"Thomas Fallon, ... your servant, mi-lady," he said, quickly composing himself.

"But everyone calls you Blade, why is that?"

She already knew his warrior history. In fact, for reasons she could not explain, she knew most of his past by asking seemingly casual questions of others since the first day he looked at her.

"Tis just a nickname, mi-lady," he said, starting to relax.

"Alas, it makes you sound mean. So I will call you Michael," she said coyly, making him wonder how she knew his middle name.

Enjoying his momentary confusion, she quickly added, "My name is Elizabeth, confidant to the queen," she remarked in a serious tone, not wanting him to think her too young.

Sensing her intent, Blade, liking this banter, returned her smile and looked deep into her impish eyes.

"And my lady is so formal," he said, "I will call you Becky."

Becky's eyes opened wide and her face flushed. "I must go now," she said as she hurried past him, vase in hand, feeling him stare after her.

Hearing her dear friend Aglio's pet name used by Thomas made her feel warm and wobbly all over. No one had called her Becky since she was a child.

This will take some thought, she mused. What is he up to? Is he just teasing or does he like me? Why should I care if he likes me or not? He really makes me angry. He is not like the others. One does not know his thinking. He certainly is not like the other young swains trying to impress. In fact, instead of making him blush, he is now making me blush. He really is starting to vex me. He thinks he's so smart but two can play this game.

Two more seasons passed. Becky and Thomas became friendly foes bantering and tantalizing each other in a continuous mating game neither knew. Each would contrive and scheme different ways to baffle the other, taking turns with riddles and verse, tormenting and teasing, pretending fake indignation. Then, when alone with their thoughts, both giggled and blushed. Evenly matched, over time, they cemented a bond of trust which soon would be put to the test. Two more seasons wore on.

*

After her chores, Becky went looking for Thomas. She had him this time. She spent hours planning today's sport to best him and she couldn't wait.

As she passed one of the anterooms, she overheard Simon's voice in Spanish and paused, surprised he could speak a foreign tongue. In fact, she remembered him insisting he spoke no other language, declaring it would be traitorous to our own God's English.

She stopped by the doorway pleased to hear a foreign voice she could understand. As she pretended to arrange flowers on a nearby table, her body stiffened at what she heard. Simon was giving directions and orders of betrayal. Did she hear correctly? *An order to assassinate the king and queen on the morrow eventide and place the king's foolish son on the throne.* Maybe she did not understand Spanish very well anymore. It had been such a long time since Aglio's lessons….. No, she was positive she heard true.

Now she understood why Simon was always pleasant and solicitous to the king's son. But why was the Spanish envoy in England now? Well, she thought, it seemed suspect that Simon was planning to control the throne through the son and plotting something black with the Spanish.

As those thoughts raced through her mind, Simon and the two envoys suddenly exited the room and spotted Becky arranging the flowers.

Eyes narrowing, Simon's suspicion boiled as he moved quickly toward her and pushed close, sneering, saying in Spanish, "We will kill this whore also."

He stared sharp for any sign she understood.

Chills climbed her back as her fingers squeezed white around the vase. Terrified, throat dry, she forced a pleasant expression and nodded to the gentlemen, trembling to her bones. Time stopped in complete silence as he stared, wondering. Finally, he turned away, satisfied she had not understood and marched down the hall, cape swirling and boots clacking cocky across the marble floor.

Shivering uncontrollably, her knees shook weak as wheat realizing the import of the plot. She did not know what to do. Because of Simon's power and influence, no one would believe her, especially hearing the treason in Spanish, which she wasn't supposed to understand.

Who could she turn to? . . . Blade!

Walking quickly as possible, she searched all over trying not to attract attention. Frantic and out of breath, she finally found him conducting inspections in the lower halls. As Blade was giving instructions, she grabbed his arm and pulled him to the side. His guards were surprised at her boldness approaching him in such a manner, but she did not care. Still shaking, she led him to a private alcove talking so fast she made no sense. Blade saw her fear and grabbed her shoulders, begging her to slow down.

Taking a deep breath, she poured out what she heard and saw. Blade listened close, asking what she thought were a million questions. Why was he so calm? But then, his manner caused her to slowly relax as they started deciding what to do. Both agreed Simon's power and position would protect him from any tale that they might relate. He would just deny their accusation and go to ground and strike at some future time. Becky and Blade decided it was best to expose the plot by catching Simon and his henchman in the act.

Finally, after weighing different plans, they decided Blade would form a group of trusted guards and create a diversion at the time the assassins would strike. Since they knew the time, they would fake a fire with lots of smoke creating panic in the palace and confuse the traitors, allowing Blade and his men to capture them in the act of the conspiracy.

Meanwhile, Simon was plagued with the image of Becky just outside the room where he met the Spanish envoys. It was possible she did understand Spanish and clever enough not to react to his taunt. Over the many seasons, he observed her with interest knowing she was different from the rest. Also, he resented her attitude toward him. With a low curse, he decided not to risk the coup and move on his plot early instead of striking at dusk. He had struggled and suffered long for this moment and would not risk failure.

As a secret Spanish agent, he passed a dozen winters plotting and acting the wizard to gain position and influence. Now, finally, it was time to strike. The king and queen would be assassinated and replaced with his twit of a son, Prince Edward. Young Edward was clay in his hands and Simon's mother country, Spain, would once again be the sole world power and forever grateful to him and his family. As a reward, their family's wealth and influence would shape the world forever. No, no chance would be gambled, he thought. I will advance our attack to mid-day and the queen's favorite will die by my hand.

That night a traitor's moon glazed the sky. Sleep was impossible. Elizabeth paced her balcony imagining every possibility that could happen on the morrow. The still night, casting a haunting pall, caused her to shiver believing Simon was most likely a warlock knowing their every thought and action. Just then, a flutter caught the corner of her eye and she whirled around to see a swarm of bats flit and twist in the gossamer moonbeams.

Frightened, she ran inside and latched the door, feeling a heavy dread fate was scheming dark. Scooting deep under her blankets, she prayed and prayed, beseeching God. Finally, she drifted asleep with wild dreams of sneering goblins.

The next day just past noon, Blade and Becky met with collected cloth and oil to create smoke but little fire. They reviewed where they would station the guards plus the role Becky would play protecting the queen. As they huddled whispering in a nook, Becky, from the edge of her eye, spotted Simon and guards walking quickly down the rear corridor leading to the King's quarters. Normally not unusual, their furtive movements caused her to suspect the worst. She told Blade and he told her to run to the queen's quarters and move her to locked rooms next to the king. He would follow Simon.

Blade raced down the hall, turned the second corner, and spotted a score of his guards, holding scabbards quiet, moving at a slow trot following Simon towards the royal chambers. Blade chilled as he cursed, knowing their intent. Simon was taking the long route, less traveled, to avoid being seen. He hoped he could intercept them before they reached the king's rooms.

Racing through the hall, he prayed the two sentries standing post were alert and not part of the plot. Hoping for the best, Blade whipped around the corner just in time to see the two unsuspecting guards stabbed from behind.

Blade howled his outrage and charged forward bent on killing every one of the foul blaggards. Sliding his steel slick from the scabbards, his mind clicked cold, promising their death.

Surprised, the shocked assassins swung to face their enraged captain, fanning wide to encircle him. Blade hacked and sliced, quick killing three. Howling his war cry, the remaining nine now knew the truth of Blade's reputation. Simon quick slipped to the rear and grabbed one of the frightened guards, yelling, ordering him to shoot Blade with his crossbow. At the same time, the rest of the guards regrouped forcing Blade's attack to slow. He pushed forward, cursing their death.

Hearing the clamor, Becky peeked from the side door to see what was happening. Seeing Blade's attack, she glanced toward Simon in time to spot the crossbow aimed at Blade.

"Michael, watch out!" she screamed, hearing the twang of the bowstring.

Blade twisted toward her voice, swinging his sword across his chest as the bolt struck his steel, ricocheting off, striking Becky on the side of the head. He froze, watching the arrow slash into her beautiful face. As she collapsed in death, he turned and faced the killers, his scream of revenge echoed through the castle as he stalked forward, blades mean, killing them one at a time. In a blood rage, Blade howled his battle cry cursing their souls to hell, showing no mercy, relishing the fear in their eyes as he cut them to death. He moved steady, slicing and slashing, holding one eye on Simon as he swore his soul to Satan, promising the pain of all devils.

Simon's arrogant eyes changed to desperate panic as he retreated, trying to escape this inhuman warrior hunting him over the bodies of his cohorts. With the last guard dead, Blade, with shoulders hunched, stalked sure toward Simon, backing him against the cold stone wall.

Then, Blade stopped a sword length from his prey, taunting, calmly enjoying his task, wanting Simon to know his death. Simon fell to his knees pleading for mercy. Blade stilled and cocked his head, staring at Simon, trying to understand why. Simon looked up with tears, reaching out with both arms, beseeching.

"In the name of God, please spare me," he wailed.

For a moment Simon thought he might be reprieved. But then, he saw Blade's warrior soul in his cold blue eyes and devil's smirk. He watched in horror as Blade's sword circled high and slashed down as an ax, felling his arms to the marble floor, sheared clean at the elbows.

Shocked, Simon stared at his stumps, disbelieving, as he watched his blood squirt with each heartbeat.

His eyes slowly rose to meet Blade's cold stare and heard his hard whisper, "Watch yourself die, traitor . . . Say hello to Satan."

Then, Blade turned and walked away as Simon's screams slowed to whimpering sobs of fear and a slow death.

A crowd quickly gathered as Blade's loyal men moved in and took command. One grabbed Blade's left arm and stopped the blood flow from a deep gash across the upper muscle. Standing in a trance, he allowed his arm to be bandaged as he silently asked God for Becky's life.

Becky was still alive but suffered a serious injury. The shaft entered the side of her face with such force it exited through her upper jaw. Attendants stopped the bleeding and carried her into the woman's quarters.

The Two Spanish envoys, staring at Simon's bloodless body, stood at the rear, shocked, suddenly fearing for their heads. The youngest starred at Simon's bloodless body propped against the wall, fighting bravely to hold back his tears.

Suns turned as facts of the failed coup filled the palace. One of the traitor guards, hoping for salvation, survived long enough to confirm Blade's account. The king's son was an innocent dupe and since Elizabeth could not testify to their conspiracy, the two envoys were banished to Spain relieved to still have their heads. Loudly protesting their innocence, they left the court with fake indignation already inventing new lies for their Spanish king.

A half-moon passed and Blade's continued pestering about Becky's condition was shooed away by the matrons nursing her. All he knew was she was still alive and he loved her. When the bolt found its mark, his mind finally accepted what his heart long blessed. He prayed to God. He beseeched God. He promised God anything and everything. Not caring what others thought, he fretted and moped about showing his feelings for the first time.. Moons dragged until finally the matrons sent word she could receive visitors the next morn.

When Becky opened her eyes, it took a moment to remember what happened. With the side of her face wrapped in a light bandage, her nurses helped her recall the events. Suddenly, she burst out, "What happened to Michael? Is he well?"

The nurses glanced at each other surprised at her only question about the failed coup. And who was this Michael? Seeing the nurse's confusion and failure to answer, Becky thought the worst.

"Michael, is he hurt? . . . My God, say he is not dead!"

Her questions flew so fast the nurses looked perplexed, suddenly feeling sorry for the captain of the guard who was the only man showing interest in her welfare.

The senior matron finally stepped forward and tactfully answered, "My lady, the Captain of the Guard named Thomas has been constantly at your door truly worried for you. Perhaps this Michael is not aware of your state."

Elizabeth paused, collecting her thoughts, then realized the confusion and asked in a calm voice, "Is the Captain of the Guard well?"

"Yes, my lady," the matron answered. "Just an arm wound."

Elizabeth smiled, wincing in pain, feeling relieved and suddenly wonderful. Then, she took pity on the confused nurses and explained the Captain of the Guard's middle name was Michael. Their surprise turned to giggles realizing the connection and in the same breath, concluded with knowing looks, Michael and Becky must be lovers. They assured her again he was in good health and very concerned for her.

Elizabeth relaxed back on her pillows, happy, but wondered about Michael's attention toward her. Maybe he loves me as I love him, she dreamed. No, no, he treats me like his sister. Oh well, at least he is not badly hurt.

The nurses, chatting all at once, started preparing her for Michael's visit. Becky learned he killed all the assassins, including Simon, and how her warning saved his life. The king and queen were safe. Blade and Becky were heroes.

Wondering why she was getting all this extra attention, the matron said, "The captain will pay his respects mid-morn, my lady."

Elizabeth suddenly remembered the bandages on her face and asked for a looking glass. The cotton dressing covered her wound but she was pale and drawn. She looked a fright.

"Saints, he must not see me in this state," she cried.

"My lady, please leave it in our hands. When the captain visits he will see a vision."

They propped her against fat pillows in the canopied bed. Lilacs and fresh linens brightened the room as morning light squeezed through narrow windows. She looked radiant in a yellow silk dressing gown with her burnished-gold hair falling soft past milky shoulders.

The nurses stood back admiring their handiwork. The rest was up to those two.

The time came with Michael nervous as a minnow. He paced, carrying a bunch of flowers, feeling clumsy and unsure of what to say. He practiced all morn but still had a thick tongue. Finally, he knocked lightly on Becky's door. A nurse answered with a smile, led him to Becky's bedside and quickly retired. Michael was speechless seeing the bandages covering her cheek but managed to reach toward her with his flowers. She was beautiful and her happy smile caused his serious look to melt.

With a returning grin, he found the words to ask how she was faring. His eyes watered seeing the difficulty she had telling him she was fine. The next moment he was on his knees beside her, declaring his love, thanking God for her life and swearing his protection forever. He babbled on, filling Becky's heart full with love, thrilled he felt the same. Michael looked up to see big tears of joy as she wrapped her gentle fingers around his hard hands. They silently gazed into each other's eyes knowing words were no longer necessary.

Four suns later Becky's bandages were removed and she saw the horrible scars that ruined her beauty. She cried for days refusing to let Michael visit her. Her nurses became alarmed at her depression and passed their concerns to Michael. Upset and frustrated, he barged into the room and ordered the nurses away as Becky covered her face, crying. Michael kneeled at her bedside and tenderly moved her hands away. Sobbing, Becky let them fall, trembling with fear, resigned to Michael's rejection feeling his eyes on her disfigured face. Michael lifted her chin, seeing only the woman he wanted and as she lifted her eyes to his, she felt his unconditional love as he pulled her into his arms.

The castle buzzed with gossip as the king and queen discussed a suitable reward for their loyalty and bravery. Because of his injury, Blade lost some mobility and strength in his left arm plus the expected cruelty of court would surely make life miserable for the scarred Elizabeth. Also, unfortunately, they were both Catholic and Irish without title.

In a rare private audience with the king and queen, the problem was solved with their special request. The royals thought it much less than they deserved but granted their wish.

So it was that Becky and Michael were granted their boon with the blessing of the monarch. Married in a quiet ceremony, they left the palace and settled on a farm in a green valley of hope.

BOOK TWO

CHAPTER 1

WwwwWWWWAAP C R A C K ! W w w w w W W W W A A P CRACK! The two whips snapped as both olives flicked from the branch.

"Ha haa, got em both," he said aloud to no one.

Shadowed trees marked the age of the day as Jamey pushed his goats through a low meadow toward the last hill home. As he cracked his whips, nipping the stragglers, he spotted a large column of dark twisting smoke coming from the farm. Sensing trouble, he ran toward the black cloud, charging up the hill. When he topped the mound, huffing, he froze at the altered world before him. The fire's last burning lit the fading sun with an eerie glow of bouncing shadows making it look unreal, a bad dream. Shuddering, his body turned cold as his racing mind rejected what his eyes saw. Stumbling forward, he ran toward the bodies of his family scattered on the ground.

Sliding to his knees to his father's side, Jamey shook him as he looked up through blurred eyes at his mother and sister crucified before him. His stomach bile rose seeing them hung naked and disgraced, nailed to the rough crosses, dripping thick blood. Dazed, he moaned as his grief settled deep. Finally, he stood slow with shoulders slumped, his mouth slack. The strange taste of new death coated his tongue, like licking metal, a blood taste. Numbed trancelike, without thinking, he gently covered his mother and sister and wandered around in a stupor, time ceasing, not knowing what to do. He seemed not in his own body, standing aside, paralyzed as he beheld the bloodbath.

"Why wasn't he doing something?" he screamed without sound. "Do something, you, you. Don't just stand there," his mind answered, "What, what do I do, tell me. What do I do, please tell me."

Then he spotted his two brothers a short distance behind his father laying face up, covered in rotting blood. He turned back and looked at his father, bent on his side, curled and hog-tied. As Jamey stared in disbelief, he spotted the black pool of blood mud by his chest.

Jamey screamed from the deepest part of his soul filling the fiery air in a wail of despair. He collapsed unconscious to the ground and lay there, unmoving. As the damp night passed, his mind, blocking the horror, dreamed how this was supposed to be a fine day. He hurried home anxious to boast his new skill with the whips to his father and dumb brothers. He had practiced since his twelfth year and with one in each hand could snap the head from any dandy at ten paces. Each crack of the whips exploded the flowered tufts into the wind like smoke from tiny cannons.

Fourteen and now a man, tending the herd was his task since eleven. Although still young, his father depended on him so his brothers could help with the heavy work. Every morning for the first weeks, he left, driving the small herd over the hill wearing a brave smile, waving to his worried mother. Out of sight, tears welled knowing he would be alone and afraid. He missed his mother and sister terribly at first plus his brothers, laughing, frightened him with legends of wolves and Pookas breathing blue flame and snorting thunder. His staff his only weapon, he hurried home each night, pushing the goats, holding one eye on the evening shadows and raven moon.

He dreaded the loneliness but as moons passed, he learned to be alone, to think, to imagine, and to dream. Faithfully, he studied his mother's lessons and practiced his father's weapon skills and as long seasons changed to earth's turns, he grew tall with shoulders square and voice low. This time of solitude seeded a quiet confidence as he learned his soul.

But today was his birthday and mom promised his favorite, potatoes and mutton. His mouth wetted in his sleep.

He pictured her proud smile as he bragged his learning the lessons. They would talk while she cooked, in Spanish, French, and Greek as she was taught as a child. He boasted his numbers from memory and could read the hardest book. Alone with the goats from gray dawn to dusk, he studied, determined hard, loving to please her.

Fitful, Jamey rolled and curled against the damp welcoming his mom's warm hug and soap scent. The thump of her heart against his ear made him feel loved, but embarrassed because of his age. He was too old for that now. He must stand tall like his father.

His dream brought forth Meg, his wee sister, just eleven, tall and delicate with eyes of heather blue. She would pester him till he yelled, causing big tears to roll from her hurt, making him feel rotten. She depended on him to defend her from their teasing brothers but he always lost the wrestles because they were older. They thought the two mere children and he didn't like them much.

The chilled night wore on and his family dream faded, flowing sour, and he felt alone and afraid. His body twitched and jerked as new morning visions tortured him. Dreams of blood devils in red chariots attacked his family and he slew them one by one, blessing his father for teaching him the way of weapons since he could lift them. Standing before the demons, he bellowed his war cry as his dream blades sung and arrows sank deep into the scarlet spirits, screaming and wailing their pain, falling in bits at his feet.

The black dawn shook the edge of his dreams as he woke slow, stiff and cold. Finally, a patch of sunlight poked at him and he stirred, at first not recalling what happened. Why was he sleeping here? His thoughts were jumbled as he pushed up and forced his eyes open to the mayhem spread around him. Numb and drained, he sat hunched, staring blank in a stupor. He wished he were dead. Why didn't he return sooner? He could have fought at his father's side.

He shivered with the dawn breeze as he sat dulled, without moving. But, as time slipped, the sun warmed and he realized the need to care for his family. As he stirred, anger and hate started flowing through his veins. It felt good. He forced his mind sharp, looking close over the killing ground, vowing to God and the devil the murderers would pay with their lives. Flushed with thoughts of blood revenge, a cold calm settled. He knew what he must do.

He looked close noting the entire area raked clear as far as he could see. There were no weapons or arrows. There were no footprints or hoof tracks. All the farm animals were scattered around, dead, with the cottage burned and still smoldering. The large barn, half-standing, somehow resisted some of the flames. There were no signs of a fight except for the dead. He searched the area again and found nothing. It was as if evil spirits caused the horror as a passing joke.

Discouraged, he returned to attend the dead. Moving numbly, he removed his mother and sister from their death crosses. Tenderly cradling their cold bodies, he choked with tears as he gently pulled the iron spikes from their wrists. As he lowered them to waiting blankets, he saw they were cruelly ravaged with cuts to cause pain. The slashes covered their bodies ending with slicing and ripping their breasts. Jamey gulped for breath, feeling a wave of sorrow as he imagined their pain and suffering. He prayed they swooned on the first cut.

Going to his father, he cut the bindings, noticing his father's death mask frozen in a snarl of hate. It was clear he was forced to watch the torture and death of his women. Carefully, Jamey uncurled the body and saw a sight so horrible his body started shaking. He couldn't stop. The killers cut out his heart, leaving a ragged crusted hole ripping the stomach open, split up the gullet. Jamey, swishing his tongue, tried to rid the tin taste of blood air as his belly roiled and wretched dry. His mind could not reason how one could commit such an atrocity.

Time passed.

Weak and shaking, his mind renewed his determined hate as he wrapped his father in a blanket and then checked his brothers a distance away from the torture site. It appeared they had been surprised and killed quickly. He wrapped their bodies taking note they had not been abused.

Still in a daze, he mechanically started digging a common grave in a shady grove where they often played and ate meals. The digging calmed his soul as sweat dripped freely. He shoveled hard, remembering past times when his father watched them scuffle and fight over strong complaints from his wife. Built thin, Jamey was rabbit quick learned from seasons dodging and chasing goats. His brothers were thick, heavy, and strong. His father, checking they didn't go too far, knew they must learn to survive in a hostile world. He began instructing his boys when they matched the height of his broadsword. Every day, without excuse, with bow, swords and dagger, he taught them everything he knew, drilling them tough, forcing the sweat, watching with pride.

Then, when alone with the herd, Jamey secretly practiced all those seasons until exhausted, mastering each weapon plus the sling and whip, all to surprise his father. Now his father would never know. He would never see his proud smile again.

Sunset shadows grew long on the heels of the night. Finally finished with sweat dripping, he stared at the empty hole, his mind returning to the forgotten present. Taking a deep breath of despair, he carefully carried his draped mother and sister to the gravesite and laid them gently against the damp earth. After pulling his brothers to the plot, he returned to his father.

As he pulled the body, the blanket fell to the side showing his father's pained expression. Reaching to replace it, Jamey noticed an unusual lump in his withered cheek. At first ignoring it, his curiosity caused him to touch the bulge with his finger. There was something hard in his mouth. Jamey was afraid to look, unwilling to face any more horror, but he did not want a foreign object to mar his father's final rest. Determined, he gently pried the mouth open and was shocked to spot a finger stuck between the gum and the cheek. He didn't remember fingers missing from his brothers and his father's were all there.

Puzzled, he hesitantly pulled out the sticky finger. It was ragged cut at the base with a gold ring attached. His mind tumbled as he realized it must be a finger from the enemy. He examined it close and noted the finger was thin and long, not callused, with the nail clean and trimmed. Guessing it to be the baby, he slid the ring from the bloody stump and examined it more carefully. It seemed real gold, cut and carved by a skilled artisan. An intricate design of some kind of beast clutched by a snake with small letters around the bottom he could not decipher.

Could it be *A family crest*? he wondered.

Excited with this evidence, he pocketed the ring and turned his attention back to his father, moving him to the grave. He placed him next to his mother with the brothers at his side and Meg next to his mother. Done, he stood back and sighed, resigned, as he looked down at the five members of his family, blocking out their wounds, imagining them whole.

Dusk breezes chilled him as he started to cover the bodies with gentle shovels of dirt. He worked determined, every movement steadfast as his thoughts remembered his mother instructing him to use reason and logic to solve problems. With that thought, he reviewed the events as the grave slowly filled.

He realized even under severe mental and physical torture, his father managed to hide evidence to identify their killers. Further, he knew the attack occurred shortly before he returned because the fire was still hot and the bodies warm. Nothing appeared stolen and since the farm was many leagues from traveled roads, the killers must have been mounted. His father's hog-tied kneeling position facing his mother and sister revealed he was forced to witness their torment. This meant they knew and hated his father and wanted him to suffer. Also, because such a large area was raked thoroughly, the murderers wanted to cover any trace leading to their identity. Searching for the ring, they cut his father open believing he swallowed it. Since his death was fresh, the cheek had not yet withered and the ring stayed hidden. Finally, Jamey knew the killers enjoyed their work.

His thoughts returned to the present as he realized the grave was finally filled. Exhausted and soaked with sweat, he straightened to face the brass sun hitting the earth. A dim moon waited patient as he felt the deathly silence and loneliness of the dying day. Shivering, he slumped to the cool ground and curled in a protective ball, weeping softly, before drifting into a deep slumber next to his loved ones for the last time.

Again, dreams haunted his weary body as he relived the horror. He pictured the killers scouting the area, charging in on horseback and quick killing his brothers. During the fight, his father managed to bite off one of the attacker's fingers and hid it in his cheek. He fought fiercely but was overwhelmed and hog-tied, propped on his knees, and forced to watch the torture of his wife and daughter.

Jamey moaned in his sleep, feeling his father's rage and horror. The night drew on and finally as dawn peeked, his father appeared in a vision, standing strong before him, imploring him to avenge their deaths.

His words sunk deep to his bones, "Jamey, my son, you must enforce God's justice."

The edge of the dream jerked him awake with his father's plea now his holy oath. Jamey stood slow and stretched, feeling a bit of peace, his torn heart starting to change to a desire for purpose and action. He took the ring from his pocket and examined it closely, burning the image in his memory. As he stared at the ring, his sad eyes turned determined and cold. After one last chore, he would leave this day to search for the owner.

Checking the charred barn, he found a smooth plank and spent a half morn carving a grave marker. Then, fashioning a cross, he nailed the marker to its center, pounding it firmly in the ground at the head of the gravesite. Satisfied, he stood back and silently read the chiseled words.

MY FAMILY

FATHER Thomas Michael Fallon

MOTHER Elizabeth

SISTER Megan

BROTHER Thomas

BROTHER Michael

NOW IN GOD's HANDS

He wondered why he put the last words. How could God allow this? For the first time he doubted God's being. But the words were there. His mother would want them. So be it.

With a sigh, he turned away. It was time. Gathering his gear, he suddenly remembered his father's weapons and took off running to the barn. He dug through the charred mess and found the practice arms destroyed. Anxious, he dug deeper with his hands, yanking away charred boards and mangled farm tools, hoping for the best. The last board pushed away brought a rare smile. The wrapped bundle yielded them all, dirty, but intact. With a relieved whistle, he hauled them to a shade tree and carefully cleaned and oiled them to working condition. Then, he went to the burned cottage and dug out the small amount of coin his father saved in a tin under the floor.

Salvaging enough clothes for most weather, including his father's favorite buff jerkin brought from Spain, he mounted the swords, crossed on his back, and lashed the daggers at waist and boot. He left the long but slung the short bow and quiver of arrows over his shoulder and tied the two whips on each hip with quick release knots. Last, to complete his gear, he plopped a floppy hat on his head and slung a shoulder sack with flint, food, and water over the other arm.

Ready, he returned once more to the family graves and bent on his knee. Taking his father's knife, he sliced his palm and dripped his blood over the marker, whispering hard, "I swear by your blade and my blood you will be avenged." Then, he gently petted the marker a final time as new tears welled and a choke caught his breath. Finally standing, he squared his shoulders with a final farewell, turned, and walked away, never to return.

I swear by your blade and my blood you will be avenged.

ChAPTER 2

J AMEY FIGURED TO search the outer edge of the raked area to find tracks or some sign showing the direction the killers went. Walking the area, he noticed they carefully raked an irregular circle around the cottage about a furlong wide. As he walked the outer border, he guessed there were many men to complete the task in such a short time. Moving slow, he soon spotted brushed hoof tracks moving east. Excited, he studied the deep prints in the spongy turf, seeing shod horses moving at a gallop toward the ending day.

Blood pumping, he imagined overtaking and killing them all. Then his shoulders slumped, remembering they had a two sun lead and he was afoot. Although he hated horses, he wished for one now.

Gritting his teeth, he sucked a breath and started jogging at an easy pace with an eye to the trail. He jogged hard, sweat wet, pushing, as the sun fell over the top of its arc. Leagues later, when the sun slipped low, an aching stitch hit his side with each stride and he gritted his teeth, running through the pain. His throat felt like dry sand and he gulped swallows from the goatskin on the run. His tall body, weight thin with muscles wiry tough, covered the ground fluid smooth. The weapons dangled and bounced, rubbing his skin blood raw as he sucked gulps of air past his thumping heart. His legs, like dead stumps, beat the ground in an unending rhythm as time turned slow against a downing sun.

A silver slice of moon started its glow when the tracks stopped in a cluster. Heaving for breath, he finger whipped the sweat from his brow as he studied the tromped grass and spotted another raked path leading to the side. He moved careful, following its trail, sword drawn, near twenty rods and discovered five fresh mound-raised graves. Roused at the chance of finding more clues, he dropped down and started digging feverishly with knife and hands. In no time, he found a man's body, naked. He unearthed the other shallow graves and found four more the same.

The damage was varied; one appeared strangled; two others, by the head angle, broken necks; another, a smashed throat; the last, no blood marks, no visible cause. None were missing a finger. Jamey figured his father, unarmed, had killed them with his bare hands and the killers were hiding the bodies, stripping them to conceal their identity.

With the moon full up, the night closed in under moon-cast shadows and he decided to camp for the night. Resting under a heavy oak, he gobbled two raw potatoes as the night quiet settled and lingered around him. Feeling alone in the dark, he curled in his cloak as tears again flowed for his lost family. Regrets flooded his thoughts. If he had just returned sooner, he could have fought by his father's side. He could have defended his mother and sister. He could have died with them. Finally, worn down, his eyes drooped in sleep with pleasant dreams of his loved ones.

The new dawn peeked pale red and he was on the move at an easy lope. He felt strong, determined, each stride sure. Late morn and a warming sun found him at a wide stream and the end of the tracks. Kneeling, he doused his head in the icy water and shivered alert. After crossing, he lost time searching for tracks up and down the bank. Frustrated, he cursed blue as he retraced his steps, scouring the ground. Finally, he spotted the trail leaving the creek many furlongs downstream. Pissed at the delay, he bettered his pace with a small smile, feeling clever. He was smarter than the killers covering their escape.

When the day faded, he stood wide-legged at the edge of a well traveled road near four horses wide. His prey's tracks disappeared, completely covered by other travelers. Jamey pondered which direction finally guessing to continue on the same bearing toward the growing night. Pushing on, he jogged late by moon glare until he chanced across a small roadhouse sitting between fat trees. Lantern light leaked out cracks and shuttered windows as his ear caught fiddle music mixed with laughs and curses. Wary, he approached careful and stopped at the door, listening, weighing the wisdom of going inside.

Worn and hungry, he dared the chance and entered, staying alert, taking stock. The small public room carried a few old tables and a short-standing rail against the back wall. Choking smoke from the scullery and pipes of the few patrons hung thick as fog below the short ceiling. Coughing, he worked his way, timid, across the room in sweat-stiff clothes to the bar. Checking over his shoulder, he leaned awkward on his elbows, dirt caked and smelling like a manure mound. The din turned quiet as he glanced around, feeling the stares sizing him as the landlord moved his way.

"Sir, are ya still servin?" he asked low.

The landlord squinched his nose, catching his eye.

"If ya got coin, boy."

Red faced, Jamey dug in his pouch and dropped a two-pence on the counter.

The landlord grunted, scooped it, and slid a plate of watery stew in front of him. As he wolfed it down, he saw a sign for a bed and bath and decided to stay the night.

"How much to stay?" he asked with a full mouth.

"Three-penny, but ya stink boy. A bath first and two-pence more."

Jamey blushed again but dug his coin.

The next morn, clean and rested, Jamey pulled a chair in the corner of the planked porch enjoying thick porridge and bacon under a sullen sun. After a few short questions, he learned from the serving lass the band of men he followed stopped the night, two suns back. They were foreign of some type speaking poor English with a tall one in command. Heartened, Jamey felt sure he was tracking true.

At the same time, he noticed five men tabled on the far side eating and drinking ale. They were loud and drunk this early, teasing and grabbing the young wench as she jerked away, slapping their groping hands. Her tears rolled as they laughed, shaming her with lewd words. As Jamey watched, he felt his anger rush, thinking of his mother and sister treated the same. The landlord came out to try and tame them but one pushed him flat. Another grabbed the lass, trying to kiss and fondle her as she squirmed and screamed. Jamey saw her fear and could be silent no more.

"A ther mate, leave er be," he said in a raised voice, standing to face them.

The five turned, noticing him for the first time.

Glancing at each other, one pointed at him and joked, "Aye, boy, who ya be? Ya be her man or savior?"

"Jus leave er be," he answered in a flat voice.

The bullies quick sized him, seeing a mere boy. With a sneer, their leader tossed the girl aside and moved toward Jamey, yanking his short sword. His mates followed, unsheathing their steel, moving to each side, blocking his escape.

"Yer goin to bleed a bit, lad," he muttered, hunching forward, planting his thick legs wide in a practiced fighting stance.

Jamey was scared, never fighting real with a sword. His legs felt like wet rope and his hands trembled as a spike of panic hit his belly. He wanted to bolt and quick glanced for an escape, feeling real fear for the first time.

"Aye, I wan no trouble," he said meekly.

Sensing him weak, the five moved toward his defeat. Fear sweat chilled him. He started to run and the leader faked a teasing lunge toward his gut. As the blade swished close, Jamey's mind suddenly clicked and in practiced move, he stepped to the side, sliding both broadswords from his back, taking position.

A calming spirit filled him as time slowed.

His move angered the attackers and they advanced in a half circle to cut him down.

Jamey's curbed anger, building since the deaths of his family, exploded in his father's war cry as his swords, whirling in a balanced dance, cut down two. Shocked, the remaining three wavered a moment but then charged as one. Jamey waited for their death.

It was done. He stood panting, dazed, glaring at the bloodied bodies as his mind clicked back and absorbed his deed. He heard the landlord's voice.

"God's cross, I never see the like!" he exclaimed. "Run boy, they frens be close. Weel cover fer ye. Take to the forest."

Jamey, speechless, grabbed his bow and sack, leaped the rail, and vanished in the thicket, leaving the landlord to tell a tale.

After many leagues running hot towards a late sun, he plopped weary to the forest floor, sucking deep breaths, feeling his heart pumping in his toes. Finally, after a time, he calmed and lay flat, gazing toward the treetops wondering what happened at the roadhouse. When the foreign sword near cut him, suddenly, he became someone else. Time and movement slowed and he keenly sensed every move. He remembered his father's stories about the gift but until now, did not understand. His father told him in every battle, his mind clicked to that of a pure warrior. His grandfather was the same.

Jamey knew this gift saved him as his eyes fluttered shut while a distant wolf bayed at the moon. The lonely cry made Jamey's heart heavy as he rolled in his wool cape against the night mist whispering thanks to his father for his warrior training. He drifted off with visions of his mother, beautiful even with the rough scar across her cheek, smiling her love.

After two more suns of hard travel running dawn to past dusk, Jamey stood on a low hill overlooking a large village. Inquiries from passing travelers and landlords along the road about the band he hunted kept him true. He could taste he was close. Never visiting a village this big made him nervous and uneasy, but with a huff and a shoulder shrug, he started down the hill wondering what waited. Around the next bend, he stopped short, blocked by a rag-tag gang of boys. On guard, he measured them quick. Some looked his age but most were older, like his brothers.

"Tis a toll road, mate. Ya must pay to pass," he hollered, huffing his chest, sizing Jamey with a snicker.

Wary, Jamey's muscles tensed on guard as his eyes narrowed suspicious.

"Whas yer cost?" he asked.

"Will take whas on yer back," the bully shot back with a mean smile.

Now knowing their intent, Jamey numbered them near ten, some small, most big. He wanted no more fights.

Thinking fast, he asked, "If I show ya some magic, will ya bless me wi a pass?"

The big bully, confused at his meaning, shot back, "Wa ya mean, magic?"

As they hesitated, Jamey slipped his whips free. The next sound in the fading light was the whistling crack of invisible lashes tearing their knives and clubs away. The gang froze, stunned at the feat, glancing at their leader for charge. Startled as they, but bent on upholding his station, he reached for his knife in the dirt. A crack and a yelp stepped him back holding a slashed hand.

"I wan no trouble lads, le me pass," he threatened low, walking cautious through their numbers.

The gang moved aside murmuring their respect as he stepped past and put some quick distance before they found their courage.

A sandglass later, tired and hungry, he entered the village at twilight and the start of evening festive. He had never seen so many people at the same time, some merrymaking, the rest cursing their bad fortune. Bawdy ladies of the night with tits half out called from windows bartering their best price. As people jostled about, he wound between them, watching close as street smells mixed with sticky whore's perfume stung his nose, forcing shallow breaths. It was much to figure.

His eye caught a dangling sign, "Mermaid Inn—Rooms to Let". Sucking a breath, he pushed through the doors and wiggled through to the crowded bar. Lessons learned from the road taught him to speak with bravado to avoid any test. His one advantage, besides the weapons strapped on, was he was taller than most. Skinny and looking a boy gave him a contrary appearance, but other than a few glances, they paid him no mind. After some bartering for a bed and food, he trudged to his room overhead balancing a bowl of mutton stew and buttered hunk of black bread. Soon after, with belly full, he plopped on his pallet fast asleep over the din of the great room.

The morning clamor caused a waking groan as he slowly opened one eye. Coming back from a peaceful dream, he wondered a moment where he was. Awareness fast sunk in, though, as squawking hawkers bellowed their wares outside his window. Horses clomping and dogs yelping made him give up and roll out of a surprising comfortable bed. After a fast toilet, he was down in the public room spooning up some steaming gruel and gingerbread. Finishing quick, he wiped his mouth on his cuff and headed for the street with a dagger and one whip at his waist. He left the rest of his gear locked in his room with an extra coin to the landlord for security.

The morning sun squinched his eyes as he wondered about his next step. He knew the killers came this way but no clue where to search so he retreated back inside the inn and struck up a conversation with his bribed host.

"The next town be seven, no, eight suns ta the north, nothing but a shack or two. This be the village Rye, perched on the sea, she is, with ships from the world." the landlord said, pointing to the hill. "Tha be Cambor castle lookin over river Roth, laddie. Count Radford be our lard and protector."

He paused with a side-glance at Jamey, sizing him.

"Ya come at a good time, laddie, tis carnival days with celebations and tornaments for a full moon," he stated with good humor and a toothless grin. "The men ya seek most likely be here. All come to the festival and only leave when tis done, not before, I lay my stick to it."

Jamey struck out the door deciding to explore around and figure his next move. The warm sun brightened the smells of the puddled manure and slop. Stepping careful, he ambled through the lanes marveling at the great numbers of people milling about, all shapes and sizes, young and old, finding their way till dark. Later, after a couple of corners, he stopped short, in awe, staring wide-eyed at the ocean. He remembered his father's tales but never imagined this.

The water went on forever blue stirred by huge foaming waves. Smells of black tar and fish filled the air as he gawked at ships large and small with sticks and ropes everywhere. Men were loading or unloading one thing or another in a busy rhythm of curses and orders. Wagon masters, wielding horsewhips, rolled their freight in numbers as far as he could holler. Bustling taverns with small huddles of stony men lingered about debating this and that. They all looked torn in some way. Patches on eyes, wood legs, bent backs, less than five or worse, a hook on an arm stump gave all a hard look. Their surly glance his way discarded him quick as a lubber.

Turning back to the sea, he gazed out beyond the end of things and closed his eyes, breathing deep, feeling a sudden sense of escape and freedom waiting for him to take. As the fresh salt air cleaned his lungs, he felt his heart quick beat thinking of unknown adventures waiting as he grasped how large the world must be. His thoughts floated not wanting to return but as the sun climbed, his dreams returned to the present and he continued to explore the town. Huffing up a hill, he decided to stop at an alehouse for a cool drink and ponder how best to find his family's killers.

After a few cool gulps, he noticed this section was better worn. The folks were more orderly and well costumed with fancy carriages with tasseled tops making easy way along crowded fares. Cobblestones covered most lanes with wood walks leaving clean air contrary to the mud and dust from the lower lanes. Delicious smells wafted over, matching the variety of fresh fruit and bright flowers. He liked it here.

chapter 3

S HE WAS SO excited it was impossible to sit still. She tried with all her might but her body wouldn't listen. It was going to be a wonderful morn. May Day was finally here with the festival and her birthday in just three more. She was to be thirteen, finally a woman and noticed with pleasure the young swains and older men looking at her differently.

Clarice, standing in front of her looking glass, spied uncertainly at her image. She had done it often but this morn was different. She must now evaluate her appearance as a lady. She was tall for her age and much too thin, she thought. She ate like a pig. Her hips were narrow and her breasts were taking their time. Turning sideways, she cocked her head noticing they only stuck out a finger knuckle fat, a small knuckle at best. She was pleased, though, they were firm and pointed and not saggy like some older matrons she saw. The only trouble was her nipples were sore all the time, but mother assured her it would end soon.

She turned face on, happy with the patch of soft down starting between her legs. One more step to being all grown up. Of course, the true measure was her menses that started several moons ago, scaring her witless until her mother patiently explained the woman's curse. She hated it, though, and dreaded that time.

Shaking the thought, she looked at her hair. She felt this was her best feature. Full gold with red shadows, it hung soft and natural in easy curls down the middle of her back. Everyone complimented her on its honey gold beauty. Sun, shadows, and candlelight affected its hue but always made her appear bonny fair. Matched with big tan eyes, a tiny nose, and full lips, she was destined to a classic loveliness worthy of her station.

She must hurry. Mother was taking her to the village to shop. She rarely left the castle grounds and this was to be a real treat. Her father, lord of the area, kept them locked like prisoners worried for their safety. This was just the fourth time in her entire life she was allowed outside the great walls. She was always busy with studies of music and such and it seemed everyone on the outside was having more fun. She knew it certainly must be more exciting than her life. She never had friends her age to play with and often felt lonely. Sighing, she smiled, satisfied, for now she was grown. She was a lady.

Hurrying to her mother's rooms, she greeted her father, chatting incessantly, tapping her slippered foot, signaling her mother to hurry. Her coltish manner strained against her lady's training, reining hard on her bottled energy.

Wearing her favorite pink dress, she thought it too young for her current age but that would be corrected shortly. She was going to buy the most expensive and beautiful dress she could find and then she would look like the woman she was. Of course, it must be imported. Watching her mother, she remembered her training. Hold your head high, chin up, and back straight.

"Mother, please hurry. The morn is late."

The canopied carriage passed through the gates and rumbled over the drawbridge. Two uniformed coachmen with two footmen behind kept a careful pace between their castle escort of six lancers close in front and six at the rear. As they rolled down the hill, villagers of every stripe stopped to stare with nodded bows. Clarice liked to show off and why not? Her father was a count, confidant to the king, and she was his daughter, a young woman of age. These peasants were her subjects and it was only fitting they should honor and pay homage. This was exciting. It was hard to sit still.

Clarice leaned out, spotting the cluster of buildings and shops up ahead. She hoped they stocked the latest fashions from France although she heard the newest designs were from Florence and Venice. She was anxious to see the modern lace from Spain but since King Henry was in tiff with King Phillip over religion, the shops may not have any. Perhaps something in the new silks.

It seemed we were always quarreling or fighting with some country or another, she thought. It did not make much sense to her, but, she shrugged, the world was what it was. In fact, she overheard her father last eventide cursing those rag-tags up north. Their nerve, the Irish papists couldn't even speak the proper King's English. He was forced to send money and arms to the king to keep them down.

Shaking those thoughts, she wiggled with excitement as their carriage pulled to a stop across the lane from the shops. She hoped they had the new silk velvets.

chapter 4

AS HE WATCHED around, Jamey noticed the high walled fortress at the top of the hill and while he admired its might, a tasseled coach clopped up with its small convoy. Noting its elegance, he watched its driver pull back the reins stopping close in front of him. At the same time, the footmen swung smoothly from their rear station trained to assist the finely dressed ladies from the divan. Curious and taking his last swallow, Jamey dropped a coin on the table and walked toward the road guessing they were mother and daughter of some high rank.

As he approached, they glanced his way before turning and crossing the lane. Jamey, catching their eye, smiled, amused as he watched the sway of their soft movements, thinking of his mother and sister.

Suddenly, a one horse sedan whipped around the corner full gallop, sure to strike them. They were looking away, unaware, when Jamey shouted a warning. The mother jumped forward as the daughter turned to see who yelled. Without thinking, he dove forward, knocking her nose first into a fat mud puddle. His momentum caused him to fall on top of her, sploshing her even deeper.

The surrey galloped by and Jamey cursed all horses as the sputtering daughter, staggering, climbed to her feet in a rage, arms out in shock with smelly slop dripping from slippers to hair. Onlookers smirked as the girl and Jamey stood staring at each other. By her look, he guessed she was not going to be grateful for saving her life.

"You mule, look what you did," Clarice cried.

Speechless, he looked at her muddy front with watery muck dripping from her nose. Because he fell on top of her, he escaped the mess. Seeing her embarrassment, he held back a smile as he tried to explain.

"Sorry miss, but the wag—," is all he could get out as he tried to hand her his kerchief.

"Sorry, sorry! Look at my dress! You, you, you," she sputtered.

Her mother, witnessing Jamey's actions, rushed to her side and guided her to the walkway helping her wipe her face. Jamey followed, wishing to apologize.

"Thank you sir, for this action," the mother said, trying to hand him a coin.

Jamey, shaking his head in refusal, looked at the girl.

"No mum, no need. Is she well?" he asked.

Her dark eyes, fuming, stared back through a muddy face.

"Well! Well! Look at me. I'm a mess, you fool!" she retorted with all the indignation she could muster.

With that, Jamey cracked his pent up smile, fervently apologizing, remembering how it worked with his mother and sister.

With her daughter still in a rage, the mother steered her toward a shop to get cleaned up. She looked over her shoulder and said, "Well, thank you again, sir . . . ?

"Jamey,.. Jamey Fallon," he answered as they both disappeared inside.

Looking after them a moment, he turned and started up the hill, forgetting the kerchief.

Inside the shop, Clarice complained to her mother for being nice to the lout causing this disaster. As the mother helped her into a new dress, she explained how Jamey's action saved her life and when she settled, she would realize a dirty dress was a small loss.

"Well, he should have been more gallant. Besides, he laughed at me. I should have wiped the smile from his face. I noticed he escaped the mud. This dress is ruined. He should have to pay. He laughed at me! Can you believe it? I hope we meet again. He will be sorry," she went on and on until her temper finally cooled.

After a short time, wearing a new dress, twirling in front of the looking glass, she asked in an uninterested voice. "What was his name, mother?"

"Jamey Fallon."

"Jamey, hmm," she mused. "He is Irish. I am not surprised."

Her mother just smiled, knowing her daughter, and tucked the muddy kerchief away for a later time.

As Jamey walked away, the curious crowd parted for him, making pleasing comments including an old man, "Good deed, ladie."

Jamey nodded and asked, "Do ya know em, then?"

"Aye, most do, ya must be recent here."

"Aye, just yestereve."

"Well, those be the grand Count Radford's wife and only daughter, Clarice," he said, pointing to the castle.

"Clarice . . . is not English."

"Nay, the wife was brought from France. Some high house or other," the old man put in, checking the fire in his pipe.

Jamey, warming to the codger, remembered his purpose.

"Mayhap ya can assist. I'm searchin fer a band of aboot ten men mounted, hangin tight, come this way most three morns past."

"Nay elp ya there laddie. This be carnival time. Folks from most afar with horsed men aplenty for the turnments."

He stuck the pipe between dirty teeth and sucked. "Do ya now their colors?"

The old man's question hit tough. The only thing known about the killers were they numbered ten or twelve, mounted shod horses, and one with a lost finger wearing a gold ring, which was now tied around his neck. Disheartened, he thanked the old man and started back down the hill to his inn.

The old man yelled after him, "Turnments on the morrow. Ya mayhap see em there."

Jamey waved, thinking the trail cold. He needed a lucky clover or an answered prayer.

chapter 5

J AMEY ROLLED FROM his bed at the first sound of morn with renewed purpose. His father appeared again in his dreams telling him not to falter. With breakfast done, he headed out the door with fresh bought clothes, whip and dagger. Bent on a closer look at Cambor castle, he climbed the hill whispering his prayer vow once again. Soon, beads of sweat proved a warm day as he joined the gathering crowd moving through the massive gates. Never seeing a castle, much less a visit, he was excited and hesitant at the same time, feeling odd mixing with so many people, unsure of the result.

Boots and hoofs echoed the wood as he glanced over the drawbridge at the putrid water. Scum slime covered the moat water warm as a blanket most thick enough to walk on and whiffs of rotten eggs squinched his nose. He spotted age old women at its edge stooping to scoop the green mold and carefully slide it into tiny potion bottles. Their skeleton hands moved deftly like an artist as they cackled about matters known only to them. Merlin's sisters sure, he thought.

As he gawked, one old hag turned, glaring straight into his eye not a horse length away. She looked a century with eyes bright as an infant. Her gummy smile chilled him as she waved her craggy finger, pointing at him, mumbling a chant. The rest, with their mocking snigger, made him hurry his pace through the castle gate ignoring any further curiosity.

The castle courtyard opened up before him with sights to behold. Music and tinkers of every type stirred the crowd as banners and swallow pennants of the rainbow waved with the breeze. Rat-tat-tatting drums from every direction proclaimed the starting celebration. Jamey, feeling the pulse, was soon lost in the crowd. The large grassy field surrounding the palace had some of every type while minstrels and buffoons vied for attention over troubadours and jugglers. He wandered past peddlers and hucksters, smelling delicious fruit and food and snagged a cool beer for twice its value from a boy yelling the bargain from the top of his lungs. Dancing bears and bouncing tumblers jumped to tunes from flutes and fiddlers trying to be drowned out by bagpipes and horns. The villagers laughed and giggled, ate and drank, pointing to the marvels surrounding them. It was a grand time.

He wandered by ornate jousting tents with squires and snorting battle horses. Knights with wispy plumes and weighted armor moved about as best they could with streamers and guidons held high by liveries proudly waving their standard. To his left, meadow green grounds marked the gaming arena with elevated seating on the shaded side. Various straw targets, kept clear by sweating warders, were cordoned, marking certain distances with two judging platforms high on the line to enforce fair matches.

Jamey, mingling with his now warm beer, felt the mood of the crowd when bunches of trumpets blaring the first contest caught his ear. Not knowing their meaning, he moved with the mob circling the target area and overheard a remark it was to be the archery contest. Looking around for a good place to watch, he spotted a cluster of oak trees next to the raised viewing area. Sitting high in a cool tree sounded like a good plan but he noticed warders and soldiers shooing folks away, keeping everyone from the same idea. Looking further back, he noticed a high wall behind several rows of the trees that brought a smile. He would simply climb the rear tree from the wall and move from tree to tree in the higher branches out of sight of the warders.

In short order, he straddled a branch nestled in thick green leaves with a perfect view of the whole target area. The viewing stand to his right was already crowded with spectators under elegant awnings set by bright flags. As he glanced curious, a single trumpet pronounced the arrival of Count Radford and his court. Jamey watched, fascinated, as they paraded forth in their finery to the top booth with tenting richer than the rest. The entourage of soldiers and servants were showing their best as commoners gave way. The count looked an old man as he was being helped by two attendants. Directly behind, he guessed, were his wife and daughter. Jamey smiled, recognizing them the same from yestermorn, thinking she looked much better without the mud.

She seemed some older than his sister, or acted older. He thought she looked full of herself but admitted she was pretty. Tall and slender, wearing a soft yellow gown finished in black trimming borders, her apple-blond hair swayed softly past her shoulders. As she moved to her seat at the left arm of her father, he heard someone from the crowd yell, "Clarice", causing her to turn with a warm smile and a knowing wave.

Well, maybe she wasn't a witch after all, he thought, remembering her angry face full of mud.

On command, the crowd noise settled as the bard called the contestants forward. Jamey, intent on the proceedings, heard a rustle in the tree to his far right. He glanced over, nothing, but more rustling caused a sharper look. Now, he spotted a man dressed in all green perched about the same distance from the ground and guessed he had the same idea for watching the contests. The man stared solid at what was before him, unaware of Jamey.

More trumpets blared and the archers stepped forward for their turn. Jamey glanced again at the other tree and noticed the man, ignoring the bowmen, close watching the center stand where the count and his family were seated. As Jamey started to turn back to the field, he saw the man heft a crossbow to his shoulder. Following his line of sight,

Jamey's mind quick deduced his intent. Alarmed, his mind clicked and in a snap, his whip wrapped a lower limb and he swung down with a howling roar, crashing into a soldier at the base of the tree. Before the soldier hit the ground, with one motion, Jamey tumbled, snatching the soldier's bow and arrow, twisting to the side as he slid across the grass on his back, letting the arrow fly.

His warning shout shook the assassin's aim as everyone in the gallery looked toward the wild man swinging from the tree. Time and silence seemed endless to Jamey lying on the cool grass looking up to the branches. Then, the crumpling and cracking of tree limbs announced the assassin's limp body hitting the ground flat on his back, an arrow neatly stuck through his lower jaw into the skull. The killer's bolt hit off the mark, slamming into the heavy wood throne, missing the count and Clarice by a finger.

Soldiers swarmed in and grabbed a winded Jamey while others circled the count with swords drawn. As they yanked him to his feet, Clarice and her mother gasped, recognizing the boy from the village. Captain Bullard of the castle guard, furious at the security breach, hauled Jamey away.

In the dungeon, the soldiers roughed him believing he was part of the attempt on the count's life. Angry and confused, Jamey stood shackled with a purple eye and sore ribs. The captain was particularly angry Jamey penetrated the protected area making him look foolish. Hourglasses turned with Jamey's repeated explanations, which finally were verified by many witnesses. Captain Bullard did not believe such a boy could do what was reported but the facts backed Jamey's claim. Angry, he grudgingly reported his findings to the count.

While he was being questioned, Clarice and her mother informed the count of Jamey's actions coming to their aide in the village. After the Captain's report, he ordered Jamey brought before him.

By this time, Jamey was in a sour mood, standing wide-legged and stubborn, resenting not being believed. Flanked by two guards, head down and sullen with wrists chained, he wondered what would happen to him now. Fate seemed bent on preventing him from finding his family's killers. Feeling very alone, he heard a tender voice ordering the removal of his bonds. Clothes torn, dirty and sweaty, he looked up with a black eye and bruises to a friendly smile at last.

A quarter-moon later, Jamey's life was changed. After learning of Jamey's actions saving his life, the count insisted he remain at the palace. Jamey, surprised, felt honored and privileged to sit above the salt and dared the chance to tell the count of his family's fate, hoping for his assistance. The count was moved to action but after a half moon, no clues were found. The hated ring, examined close, was thought a signet of some sort, possibly part of a coat of arms. It was unfamiliar to those at court and with so many different bands from other counties and distant lands attending the festival, the needle was lost. But later, alone with his thoughts, for some unknown reason, the count suspected the attempt on his life was somehow connected.

Jamey was stumped. He was at odd ends not knowing where to turn so decided to stay for a time until he figured his next step. As a welcome guest, he was given his own loft and shared meals with the court. Clarice decided to forgive him for pushing her in the mud and offered to give him a tour of the castle grounds.

Clarice reminded him of his sister and they became friends as suns passed. He thought she was quick-minded, but sheltered, asking unending bunches of questions. She casually mentioned, several times, she was now thirteen and probably would have to marry soon. She flirted, teased, and pouted, depending on her whim at the time. Jamey thought her actions a mystery, confusing him, thinking she acted silly like his sister.

This was a different world and he felt overwhelmed by his circumstances. He stayed alert, listened close, and made sure he observed events smartly around him. He concentrated on being courteous and respectful, reminding himself to speak proper as his mother taught.

One midday, Clarice was showing him the stables and her favorite horse, "Pearl". Even though he had no use for horses, he had to admit she was a beautiful animal. Solid white with a black diamond on her forehead, she pranced nervously, anxious to run.

"Let's go for a ride, Jamey."

He panicked. He had never learned to ride. The only horse he knew was the old mare on the farm. She was stupid, stubborn, and mean, plus she nipped him every chance. He disliked and feared them at the same time so he quick started thinking of a good excuse.

Clarice noticed his funny look.

"You do ride, do you not?"

"Of course."

Watching the stable hand saddle the horses, he figured it was probably not difficult. He could fake his way. Just stick your feet in the boots and pull on the reins one way or the other. Easy enough.

After Clarice mounted Pearl, he took a deep breath and swung to the top of his mount in a surprisingly practiced manner. Just as he was feeling full of himself, the horse bolted forward full gallop across the courtyard. Jamey hung on for his life, legs and arms flapping and swinging and in the next breath his horse skidded to a halt.

"YYYyyyiiiii," he yelped, flying headfirst, wide-eyed, flopping full belly into a waiting lily pond. He stumbled to his feet, soaked and sputtering with broken lily stems clinging to his head.

Clarice laughed so hard she nearly fell off Pearl. Jamey, embarrassed deep, seeing Clarice's giggling tears, also started laughing realizing how foolish he must look. He sheepishly glanced around hoping no one else was watching.

"Well, how did you like that trick?" he asked matter of fact, trying to make the best of it.

"Very skilled, sir," she said, wiping her tears. "Can you do it again?"

"Well, I could most likely."

Still giggling, Clarice graciously agreed to finish the time with a stroll. Wandering through the garden, his clothes dried quickly from the warm sun. Clarice casually took his hand as she jumped a puddle and didn't let go as they strolled the winding paths under the protection of the walls.

The next eventide in the garden, she contrived their first kiss by asking him to teach her how to use his whip. As he held her arm to show the movement, she turned her back and leaned against him. He felt the soft pressure of her body as she pretended innocence. Trying not to notice, he lifted her arm to demonstrate the motion when she suddenly turned to face him.

Her lips were rose soft as he tasted her sighing pleasure. Feeling his body stir, he pressed for more but her mother abruptly called and she pulled away. As she ran from the garden, she turned, catching his eye with a teasing giggle, leaving him standing in a daze.

Captain Bullard, buried in the shadows, watched with narrowed eyes. Make fools of us, will he, he thought. He's just a mere boy. It was pure luck. The assassin's bolt would have missed without his interference. His demotion of the soldier responsible for clearing the trees was sure and quick. He fumed. After listening to the gossip of the court, one would think he is a hero knight instead of a common boy, skinny at that, playing a man. Well, I will make him the fool. But first I will report today's mischief to Mistress Radford.

Jamey's weapons, delivered from his room at the inn caused wild gossip about the court. The captain, curious, inspected them carefully and hatched a plan. He would teach this speckled whelp.

When Jamey came to collect his property, the captain began a friendly conversation. As they talked, he discovered Jamey's father was

Captain of the Guard for their King Henry causing his jealously to flare hotter. Grudgingly, but with his best acting, he apologized for the rough handling by his men, begging him to understand their confusion believing he was the assassin. He personally gave him a tour of the castle defences, the guard's quarters, and with gritted teeth, asked him some advice on some invented matters. He expressed fake sorrow for the loss of his family and after several suns, gained Jamey's confidence and trust.

Shortly after, an opportunity bloomed. He discovered Jamey's weakness and his plan took form. One midday, sharing the noon meal, Jamey bragged in front of the ladies about his father's lessons and ways of weapons. Quickly, the captain acted impressed and suggested Jamey demonstrate his skills for his guards and the castle court. After watching Jamey's clumsy fall into the pond, he smiled to himself sure the young fool would make an ass of himself. He couldn't wait.

Jamey, realizing the mess he just stepped into, wanted no part of any demonstration and tried hard with excuses. But the captain was clever, making the suggestion in the presence of Clarice and her mother. Seeing their excitement, Jamey's male pride couldn't refuse, so he grudgingly agreed. Clarice clapped and giggled, thinking it a grand idea. Captain Bullard, slapping Jamey on the back, agreed.

Two suns later, eventide, the courtyard and balconies were crowded with castle guards, the whole castle court, the count, and of course, Clarice and her mother. Jamey, standing in the corner with Captain Bullard, was so nervous his hands shook and his stomach felt bottom up. The Captain was very helpful, too helpful, and Jamey suspected he wanted him to act a fool, which was sure to happen if he didn't settle. Silently cursing his pride, he took a deep breath, and held out his hands. They were still shaking. He was a fool.

The time had come. Jamey looked formidable slowly walking into the makeshift arena, broadswords crossed against his back, whip tied on each side, and daggers at hip and ankle. A quiver of arrows strapped down the center of his shoulders and a short bow in his left hand completed his armament. It looked too much on his thin frame as Captain Bullard smirked, relishing Jamey's fall from grace. But to make sure, he planned a surprise. He fidgeted, anxious, tired of the attention and admiration everyone was heaping on this skinny pup. He couldn't wait to gloat.

With the carpenter's help, Jamey arranged for two targets for arrows plus three stuffed straw men holding wood swords and knives and an apple atop each head. Also, they rigged a rope to pull a moving target rapidly across the yard on his nod.

Standing to the side, he took a last deep breath and looked to the count to start the affair. As the crowd hushed, he noticed Clarice's sure look. Swallowing hard, hands trembling, he walked to the front of the platform and gave a short bow. Clarice tossed him her scarf and the crowd cheered. His hands still trembled.

Jamey took his position. Two trumpets sounded. The crowd fell silent and the count motioned for Jamey to commence. Jamey turned, worried, and mumbled a quick prayer to his father. Reaching his mark, he felt the change flood over him and quick calmed, moving toward the center, low crouched. Then, in a blur of motion, he sunk four arrows dead center in the targets before the crowd's first breath. In one flowing motion, swinging the bow to his back, he swung his arms up with both whips singing. The cracking metal tips stripped the three swords from the straw men's hands as six more lightning cracks ripped the knives at their waists and splattered the apples off their heads. Everyone watched, open mouthed, as the moving target suddenly whisked across the field and he launched the two throwing daggers, striking dead center.

The whole affair finished in less than a double cockcrow. Jamey slowly straightened to the hush. Stunned, his audience stayed quiet, unbelieving. Incensed, the captain, watching Jamey drop his guard, gave his silent signal and four guards suddenly broke rank, attacking Jamey's back with a howl, swords high. Jamey spun, facing the charge as his mind clicked, stone cold. With one fluid move, his two broadswords flashed forward in a dancing rhythm, colliding with the lunging guardsmen. Two were disarmed straight with deep cut hands as he pressed the attack. The last two dropped their swords and ran. Jamey stopped, confused, while the crowd whooped their pleasure believing the incident staged.

Clarice was in love. Her mother's eyes narrowed in thought. The captain of the guard's hate boiled.

CHAPTER 6

I T WAS GRAND, huge. He watched in awe as it drew near. The elder standing next to him warned certain, it was a monster.

No, it was not that. He was sure. But maybe it was a sign from God.

It had three leafless trees on its back perfectly straight and evenly spaced. They were laced with many vines and covered with puffed white clouds. Colorful birds flapped at the top as it moved slowly toward them, leading with a large spear. It was wondrous thing.

Chang stood on the beach with his little sister, hands cupped, squinting against the white sun. The whole village chattered around him, pointing at the distant marvel. He had fished here since a child and knew the sea. His small village on this tiny island survived on the fruits from the water so this vision from God seemed only right it would appear from that which nourished them.

It was just a big boat. So big it had little boats. Chang was still excited but disappointed as it anchored and he watched smaller boats with odd looking men row towards them. Tall and strangely costumed, their hairy faces reminded him of the legends told by the ancient shamans.

The village elder stepped forward, smiling, to welcome the hairy ones. As the first stepped from his launch, with a dull smirk, he pulled his long knife and swung in a practiced move. The villagers came quiet in horror watching their patriarch's head fall from his body. Screaming and panic filled the air as the invaders pulled their swords and moved toward the others.

"Run Cho Ling, run, …hide." Chang screamed at his sister and charged forward.

Anger and revenge hit Chang's heart and the other young men as they attacked the invaders unarmed. Shock changed to fury as his black eyes turned cat wild. He lunged with the skill taught by the old masters, breaking the first enemy's arm with a single twist. The second fell with a broken neck. Chang's arm was bleeding from a saber slice as he flew through the air breaking the jaw of another. The fourth died with a crushed heart from his single blow. But in the end, they were too many and wrestled him down.

Dazed, he stood tied looking at the massacre. The blood stained sand swirled in wild mosaics, defying reason. All the babies, small children, and elders lay dead. He shook himself, clearing his head, listening to the moaning and wailing of his people. Huddling in fear, they were herded, chained, and dragged toward the small boats.

Panicked, Chang yelled for his sister, fearing the worst. She was his only family and still a child. Hearing his call, he would never forget his relief when her innocent face peeked from behind the others. He would also never forget the fear frozen on her face and his failure to protect her.

On board the great ship, they were stacked in the dark hold with ankle irons locked to beams. Chang did not understand why they were spared and not killed with the others. But as the wind filled the white sails, there was one thing he did know. The elder spoke true. It was a monster.

chapter 7

I t was pitch black and groaning rope Jamey first heard. The musty smell of dank air made him think of the cave near home he used to explore. Grogged dull with aching bones, he shook his head to clear his thoughts. As he sharpened, he shivered from the damp and sounds of creaking wood marking each rolling motion. A needle of fear hit as he lifted up, smacking his head on a heavy beam forcing him back to his knees. Now his head really hurt. Confused, he belly crawled in an unknown direction on moist planks until he bumped into a rough wood wall.

Jamey was scared. Was he dead? Was this hell? Not being able to see confused him as he sat hunched, listening close. He thought he heard far off voices. Why was the ground rolling? He forced himself to calm, staring into the black dark. More rumbling noise? Why was the ground pitching? His eyes strained, finally squinting at a far off pinhole of light. He scooted toward it, wincing at the splinters.

The light beam, silk thin, gave him hope as he yelled to anyone. He hollered louder. Suddenly, a blinding light smacked him in the face as two hands reached down and dragged him from his cave. Weak and stiff, he reached deep and leaped to his feet, crouched, ready to fight. Eyes stinging from the glare, he fought to focus on his captors and as they took shape, he found himself circled by hard men and mocking laughs.

"Settelee down lad, settelee down," a calm voice said.

Jamey turned to see an older man, smiling.

"Was this place?" he asked. "Where I be?"

"Yer on the good ship, *Grace,* matey."

He looked around wide-eyed with open mouth at wood decks and masts with ropes like thick spider webs. The warm sun felt good on his damp clothes while his mind wrestled with this puzzle. Blue sea stretched forever around him as he wondered how he ended here. His last remembering was the castle, enjoying the day with Clarice and a hearty meal rewarding him for his display of arms.

"This way, lad," the old man motioned.

Jamey dumbly followed as his mind tried to sort it out. How did he end up in the middle of the ocean? A shake later, he was standing in the captain's cabin looking at a stern face and hard eyes. He was so befuddled, his eyes watered in frustration, figuring he was kidnapped.

"Straighten up boy, look alive," the captain barked, sizing him up.

"My name be Captain Bowden, ship's master. This be Mister Dooley."

The captain pushed his face closer.

"You, boy, are a stowaway and will be treated as such."

He pushed nose to nose.

"Your laziness on this good earth will not be tolerated on my ship."

He turned and snapped, "Mister Dooley, he will be your charge to make or break, is that clear."

"Aye, capten . . . out wi ye, boy."

Jamey followed Dooley to the sun drenched deck not knowing what to expect. It was clear Dooley and the captain did not care how he happened aboard. His thoughts raced, deciding to mark time, keep his mouth locked, and do what's told until he could figure this mess. One thing certain, he sorely wanted to come face to face with Captain Bullard.

Two full seasons slipped by and Jamey discovered he loved the sea. He was awed by its fitful nature from hushed flows to wrathful roars of thundering waves. The unforgiving measure of its life challenged the soul of any man who dared to mate with it. But those that did, and survived, built a bond unmatched. Earth's massive force, dared by sailor and ship, filled one's heart with sweet victory after each passage.

Clean salt air and burning sun turned Jamey brown and hard. He thrived on all that was ordered, from scrubbing the bilge to tired watches on freezing topmasts. The pure adventure cheered him. Even dead tired, he hopped to on command, bearing his full share and more. He was young, strong, and could bury most. In the beginning, the crew ignored or scapegoated him but his readiness to learn and do some of their duty soon changed their look.

He enjoyed twilight as sea the most, resting with elbows on the rail, gazing at the dimming sun casting the world like a peaceful dream. This time was special as he looked back on his past imagining his family safe. He sighed, remembering his sister, skinny and sweet, eyes big with mischief, always wanting attention. She had a beautiful voice that could cheer or start a tear. He missed her. He even missed his brothers.

But he missed his father and mother the most. His father was his hero. Jamey practiced his weapon skills endless seasons over many earth's turns determined to make him proud. One noon, after watching the carriages pass by on the high road, an idea grew thinking whips would make herding easier. He recalled time stretching forever as he carefully cut, oiled, and weaved two whips three times his length. He loved the music they made, snapping like lightning. Like his father, Jamey used both hands the same, fast and sure. His brothers lacked the skill but were stronger, thick built, and stout on their feet. He remembered teasing, dodging and darting, taunting them to fury, making them look foolish trying to trap him. But if caught, they had twice the might and it hurt.

His mum was mum as his thoughts turned, watering his eyes. He couldn't stop. He missed her deep. His fantasy imagined he was on a trip and when he returned everything would be as it was. They would be a family again. But then the horror of that black day flashed back, flaring his anger.

Finally, the sun again melted leaving night at sea and like countless times past he fingered the hated ring on a leather lace around his neck, renewing his blood vow.

The Grace sailed with varied cargo to most ports of France, Germany, and Portugal, then, through the warm Mediterranean to Spain, Italy, and Greece, always hugging northern waters to avoid Barbary pirates. Between passages, Jamey thought about his mother's studies from her Greek teacher, Aglio, and how she passed her knowledge of the world to him, her son. At the time, he believed the lessons a waste, thinking he would never need them in his life. Now, here he was in a world where he could speak many languages plus remembering her rough drawn maps, he could picture more clearly the countries in relation to the sea.

During this time, he studied and learned every part and purpose of a sailing ship and could work all with the best. Careful to keep his own counsel, he always wore a friendly but serious smile staying dumb around his shipmates about his skills with weapons and other tongues. Even the captain, forever keeping a sharp eye, was dark. But Jamey, over time, staying alert, even managed to learn bits and pieces of navigation.

A night or two of liberty at each port refreshed the crew for the next leg of their voyage. Jamey was intrigued by all the different towns and villages they dropped their anchor and most times followed along watching his rowdy shipmates pester the local women and drink till sodden. After two earths turns plus a bit, sailing the sea, Jamey turned seventeen and his mates led him to the wharf to become a man.

At the local tavern crusty Samuel shouldered a doxy, both laughing drunk.

"Here ya be lad, ripe and ready. Les see ya give her a yard."

He laughed till he choked, smacking her on the arse. She giggled, squinting at Jamey with blurred eyes, sensing him young and shy.

"Come now boy, it wont hurt," she slurred. "I've trained the bloody navy."

With grog aplenty and eyes squeezed shut, Jamey became a man. He was jibbed proper till he turned beet red, but all in all, he agreed with a wide smile, it was a bonny good time and wanted another go at the first chance.

Each port was its own but the same. Jamey avoided the grog because it was bitter hard and hurt the next morn. Wenching was fine, though, and he pursued the activity with vigor. In between, he wandered the towns alone enjoying the foreign people and lands, practicing their speech and observing their ways. When speaking their tongue, he was amazed how friendly they were and often was invited to share a meal while being introduced to many shy and hopeful daughters.

On those times he forgot himself, his quest and vow pushed aside. With no clues except the gold ring, he questioned whether it would ever be. But, the guilt of failure always nagged, haunting him in his sleep as he relived the murders. Often, at midnight, hearing his fitful screams, a shipmate shook him awake. Every salt bedded down in the fo'c'sle wondered and whispered about the horror he met, but none dared ask.

Mister Dooley let him be. Jamey caused no trouble, moved smart, and learned clever. He was odd from the rest but carried his share without grumbles. Friendly and a loner plus quiet by nature, there was only one shipmate he was drawn to, a man named *Chang.* The first time Jamey saw him he stared in wonder, never knowing a man with his look. He was an oriental sort with a black leather piece over his right eye. All hands called him *Patch.* A head shorter than Jamey, he was twice wide and ox strong. He stood like a stone with bull legs planted apart solid to the deck, able to stop any wild boom. He spoke little and grunted often with mangled English. One look at his face and slivered eye told Jamey he had suffered life as he. As time and oceans passed, they became brother mates, neither fitting with the rest.

Jamey learned the fine art of sailing from Patch and the barnacle backs. He watched close, listened tight, and studied shrewd, but was still branded a green-hand boy, far from a blue-water man. The old salts before the mast had smelled hell in their wanderings and any equal must pay the same price.

Knowing him Irish, they teased till he was pissed. One morn, doing the day, the sea was flat with a foggy drizzle and with a snickered nod to another, they tried him again.

"God's tears boy, it be an Irish hurricane we be havin," the salt declared, grinning with a wink to another, the crew chuckling.

Jamey, catching the jibe, fake peered at the sky and laughed, advised by Patch.

"If ya get pissed," he said. "The'll never stop stingin ya. Drop yer pride, laugh wi em."

"Ya be right, ther mate," Jamey shot back. "Best bear a hand before she gets a bone in her teeth."

The crew laughed as one slapped his back and started a cherry ditty.

"A song is as good as ten men, ho-ho-ho-ho, hoist her long and stick her low, ho-ho-ho-ho, she be hot . . . ."

And so it went as all hauled the sheet to a together beat.

Jamey quickly learned, *A red sun in the morn had water in its eye"* meant it would rain on the day. An *"Irish man of war"* was a barge to be towed, An *"Irish fitout"* was to go naked, and an *"Irish pennant"* was a loose end of a rope blowing free in the wind acting like a flag.

Jamey laughed but he learned, sometimes hard, but he learned.

He also learned to read weather and taste the position of the ship. He was in awe when seeing his first waterspout and St Elmo's fire spark off the rigging. On special nights, he watched phosphorescence glow from the wake bright enough to read a book. Old sailors, after crossing themselves, swore it was the glow escaping from hell's fire. Of course, his learning was not done without fables of mermaids and merman and witches and sea serpents, every tale told straight faced, sworn by the teller's soul to be the honest truth.

Between watches, Patch taught him to body fight like his ancestors, naming it *karate.* Taking position, he stood fearsome with a belly grunt roar and raven hair swishing against skin burned rusty. His one sliced eye saw deep causing a fake man to shake and slink away. Any other daring to challenge would do well to first ponder long and hard.

Jamey was a good student, though, learning at the cost of yanked muscles and purple bruises.

As pay back, Jamey taught Patch to throw a knife and snap a whip, popping a rum cup from twenty paces.

One port, one night, knocking the neck over a shared bottle of grog, they learned the other's tale of misfortune. Jamey listened close to Patch's telling of the raid by the Moroccan slavers. With voice low and bitter, he told how his village was ravaged and the young stolen to sell on the slave blocks somewhere off the African coast. He was just past his sixteenth summer and his little sister, *Cho Ling,* seven summers less.

In the casbah, on the slave docket, he watched his sister sold to a wealthy Arab. Listening close, he caught his name, *Bahon Cadif,* and burned it in his memory as the gold ring was in Jamey's.

Patch's rough voice sunk deep to a whispered hate, telling how his sister was dragged away pleading for her brother and how his mind snapped allowing his body to do the impossible. In blind fury, he grabbed the chain at his wrist, popped the link with his bare hands and lunged the length of his leg irons, breaking the neck of the slave auctioneer with one blow. Roaring his rage, he dragged chained slaves behind him trying to reach his sister. Two slave guards jumped at him and fell dead with crushed hearts. Barked orders from the overseer and a half score more guards weighed on, pinning him to the ground. The slaver, not wanting to miss a profit, gouged his eye instead of killing or maiming him. He still remembered fresh, the slaver's sneer leaning over him as his thumb ripped the eye from its socket.

He was sold and condemned to a galley ship, but with luck, was freed after one earth's cycle by a British man-of-war. After a time serving, he was released in England where he shipped aboard the *Grace*. He never saw his sister since but was resolved to search like Jamey. A forever seven turns of the world had passed but he would never stop until he found her.

With the telling of his tale, Patch worked his grief into renewed anger. Then, after hearing Jamey's telling, they both vowed over the last slug of ale to serve as one in search of justice.

Way late, the landlord rang the closing bell and Jamey wandered outside, sucking in some fresh air to clear his head. As he waited for Patch to settle accounts, two rough sorts approached to enter the inn. As they stepped around, they pounced on his back, knocking him bent low, pummeling him with fists and belaying pins. The sobering peril caused his mind to click as he dove forward, tumbling in a summersault, landing in a fighting stance.

Just then, Patch stumbled out of the inn, three sheets minus one and muttered, ""Ho ther, was this?"

"Look alive, Patch, tis a press gang," Jamey yelled, crouched low with a puffed eye and a knot on his head.

"Ha, ha. Weel, seems we ga the double-dealers surrounded," Patch snickered, feeling the grog, happy to end the night with an honest fight.

The press gang felt strong with their advantage in numbers and separated in threes toward Jamey and Patch. Fast as hound's wag, it was over, the six defeated, moaning with broken arms, fingers, ribs, and a jaw. Slumped on the ground, they whimpered their grief as the biggest cried, "Enough, enough, we give."

"Me thinks their berth will need six more hands," Jamey said with hardly a huff.

With a laugh, Patch threw his arm over his friend's shoulder as they strolled back to the ship singing a ditty.

"Now here me boys, here me good. Her name . . . . ."

Sailing with the morning tide found them hard aboard after the rowdy night. Aches from the grog were shaken away as the hot sun brought shipboard routine as the two did their duty. It was sailor's time as a stiff wind slipped the ship on a steady course neatly through the azure sea.

Next port, Athens.

Two morns out dawned a smoky sky and a dying moon. The ocean lay flat as glass matching the ship's dead sails. Every small sound seemed to scream as the tense crew bided time. The starboard purple sky and mumbled thunder told a tale heard before by the old salts. The dog before the master caused deadpan stares warning the worst as Jamey fidgeted with his rigging blade. No humor this morn as whispers foretold the advancing tempest. Resigned to the worst, sail was ordered short reefed with bow pointed dead ahead.

The captain paced the stern deck cursing the luck, ordering all battened down with safety lines fore and aft. Each man wrapped his waist with a short line to tie down quick, every eye to the gale. Time turned with a forever wait, finally ending with a puff of air and a distant howl. The sky blackened as twisting water funnels danced in bleak harmony proclaiming nature's power. The first storm's blast beat the bow, raising the ship straight on its stern, barely holding in the wall of water. It shuddered, raging against the wave, finally victorious, settling down for the next onslaught.

The devil gale howled its intent, lifting the ship's bow straight while Jamey, wild-eyed, held on for his life amid distant screams and curses. Patch, grunting his worry, scrambled to stay aboard, fighting the crashing waves sweeping the deck. Lines snapped, whipping like sabers against sickened sounds of cracking masts and screaming pain.

"Cut away quick now, lads," the boson rang out.

All able hands jumped too, knowing the danger of a mast in the water forcing the ship broad of the sea. A broach, certain to roll the ship, would seal their death. Fevered hacking of axes and knives against tarred rigging echoed against the growling hurricane. Flying rain stung like hornets as a bow scream warned about the next wave. The ship's bow rose once more, this time to die.

The strain ripped the safety line flinging Jamey and Patch over the side, sinking in the wild sea. When Jamey broke the surface, he watched the ship flip over from the stern landing upside down. As the sea rolled in tune high as a mast, he heard the slow crack of the hull being torn in half among the screams of the condemned men. Jamey twisted around, searching for Patch, when suddenly, he surfaced, sputtering.

"You okay?" Jamey asked.

"I good, I good. Wher the ship?

"There, behind ya, downside up."

Helpless, they watched the boiling ocean slowly suck the dead ship to a watery grave. Numb, Jamey knew their mates lost were fated, locked in Davy Jones' locker. He prayed their souls be resting in Fiddler's Green.

Then, as quick, it was over. Ending thin rain peppered the cool water, calming it. Jamey and Patch hung onto bobbing debris, taking stock, figuring what to do. Except for a gash on Jamey's arm they were in pretty good shape. Patch wrapped the cut and both started collecting floating hunks, lashing them together as best they could. In a short time they had a credible raft, a piece of canvas, and a dead pig.

The calm waters showed no others alive so they worked as one preparing for survival. They bled and butchered the pig, stuck the hunks in a rigged canvass sack and hung it over the side depending on salt water to preserve it. Next, a make shift mast was chunked in a grove and a slip of cut canvas rigged for a sail. Planks of wood for an outrigger and rudder added a bit of security.

Finished, they both flopped down for a rest.

"Wul, we lookin pretty good, huh?"

Jamey nodded. "Tis a ways from land though."

"Which way, ya think?" Patch said, lifting up to scan the sea.

"The stars will tell."

As the sun dimmed and tipped low, they rigged a loose slung awning for shelter and rain catcher before collapsing in sleep.

Late moon, the wind shifted, creaking the mast, and shook Jamey awake. Lying in silence, he stared at the velvet night peppered with diamond stars. Lapping water at the raft's edge lulled him as the quiet dark brought memories of his mother and sister. He missed his mother's meals and Meg's silly chatter. Fingering the hated gold ring still at his neck, he knew that finding the killers seemed as likely as a mule dropping a foal. Recalling his life's turns since that black day, he felt hollow, low, a shedded shell beat by guilt.

He failed, it was simple as that. With a resigned sigh, he rolled over and dozed, his dreams conjuring his father angry at his self pity, scolding, *"My son does not weep in skirts. He fights brave as I."*

Jamey jerked awake and looked about, sensing his father's spirit. Then, with a jolt of resolve, he cursed his weakness, studied the stars, and adjusted the tiller. He was not dead yet.

The warming dawn renewed his spirits as he looked at a snoring Patch. Well, he thought, at least he had a good friend to suffer with as he nudged him awake.

"Keep the sun starbard, shake me when oerhead," Jamey mumbled as he curled, already asleep under the shade of the awning.

The ocean was flat and time dragged. Patch finally shook Jamey under a blistering sun and empty horizon. Thirst plagued them.

"Wha now?" Patch asked.

"We must rig a sea anchor to hold position till the sun falls."

Patch nodded and went to work cutting a circle of canvass. Taking a length of manila rope, he separated the strands and laced the canvas into the shape of a cone. Then, he tied three strands at holes poked at the outside edge and tied them together several arm lengths out ending up with a chute. Standing forward, he whirl tossed it near three rods front of the bow and tied off. They lowered sail and rested in the shade waiting for time to pass, both quiet, dreaming of cool water.

By late day, their lips were cracked with tongues like dry wood. Hoisting the sail, Jamey knew anywhere north in the Mediterranean would yield most friendly lands. Falling south meant Africa or Morocco chained to a galley.

Jamey studied what he could.

The water lapping along the raft seemed near two knots of current while the sea stayed flat with a hot breeze pushing East. Cupping his hands over his eyes, he surveyed the cloudless sky that yielded no rain.

The day seemed forever and the sun never blinked.

Finally, the sea cooled the falling sun and he welcomed the borning stars to better fix their position. He was grateful the captain of the Grace was careless about leaving his manuals on navigation for him to sneak a look. But knowing their position did not help their thirst and both knew luck was thin and without water, the devil was counting.

The next morn broke the same. Lips split and bled and talking hurt on glass throats. At sun's height, they dropped the sail and settled in with the sea anchor. Their bodies ached and movement was hard in salt stiff clothes. Raw sea water burned every scratch but halted any festering. The pork disappeared, chewed off most likely by a shark. Neither put it to words but both knew they could survive but two more suns under these conditions. So, with blurred eyes, shifts were manned to scan the end of the sea.

Time slugged as Patch stared north for a time. Sore, he shifted positions for his aching back and jerked alert. It was just a flick but he was sure it was a sail. Time never ended, staring with his good eye, afraid to blink. Finally, the next swell left no doubt, he spotted more sails bloomed, head on.

"Hey ha, Jamey, a ship, a ship."

Jamey jumped to his feet following Patch's point to the full white wings of a good size vessel closing fast on a collision course. In a half glass, their waves and yells brought the ship close alongside, heaving too and hoisting the pair on deck.

Luck smiled. The ship was British, a man-of-war, patrolling northern waters for Barbary pirates. After fresh water, they stood before the first mate explaining their fate. With a two meal ration and a gift of one sun, they were issued a half shirt, striped, and a black scarf. The next morn, they were ordered before the captain and after a question or two, were drafted into the English navy serving aboard the *HMS Vanguard*.

chapter 8

"AYE LAD, THER'S dirty weather." Mister Baines, the boson spat, glaring at the sky and turning to Jamey with a hard look. "Hank the top mast and keep a bright eye. Sing out if ya spy the winds of the dragon."

Jamey snapped too and scampered up the tarred ratlines to the heaven high of the ship. He still hated heights, most much as horses, but he held his eyes locked to the pennant till he stood on the top peak, holding tight, catching his breath.

The mast rolled and pitched announcing the coming weather. Each lurch below greatened his sway tenfold as he surveyed the darkened sky. Lightening cracks and cannon thunder gave fair warning to all in its path. Glancing down to the deck, he saw all hands as busy bugs, snugging, lashing, and priming for an ugly sea.

It'll hit hard on fore I can pray, he thought, remembering the last gale that sunk the Grace, tossing Patch and him overboard.

"Saints, tha be moren a full Christ day back," he said aloud against the wind.

He kept a weather eye as he let his thoughts drift. Much had passed since. He was now an able body seaman aboard a British warship patrolling the Mediterranean for Barbaries. After saved, he and Patch mended quickly and were pressed by the captain as he saw fit till docking in England.

Thinking it a fair bargain, they eagerly jumped to their orders. The ship flew thirteen sails, which some swore was unlucky, mounted on three masts. A full barque she was, mounting sixty-four cannon of different weight on two decks with a slim beam to cut sleek through the sea. The military trained crew moved with purpose backed by crisp officer orders. Mock battles with rendezvous patrols were ordered, keeping every mother's son up and ready and after one earth's turn plus four patrolling with daily training, they were cocky and ship sure.

Patch and Jamey looked forward most to gunnery training, studying every position and action with care. With each cannon manned by six, the gun captain snapped the nine orders while the lesser captain bed and coins, primed, pointed, and fired the hole. The shot gone, the barrel was quick swabbed wet and the loader rammed home powder and ball. All hauled up the iron through the gun port, a fuse was fast cut, fire wick touched, and the cannon boomed its blast, recoiling against block and tackle. The explosion deafened ears and started the repeat of the nine. Gun crews competed fierce for speed and praise and Jamey's team rated with the best. Proud, they slept on bare decks in most weather hugging their gun like kenneling dogs, always ready to wake her up.

Distant thunder snapped his thoughts back as the squall crept closer. No waterspouts yet, he noticed. Looks to be curving a length starbard, he reasoned, and if we tack larbard, we might miss the worst.

Taking the drop, he hit the deck and reported his sighting to the boson. Mister Baines grunted his suspicion but barked the order over the wind, swinging the bowsprit hard larboard. In a short space, the storm skidded past leaving a light rain cooling the deck.

"Ye got a good eye ther, lad. I reckon yer a seafarin man," the bosun muttered with a half smile. Jamey puffed up.

The next morn the bosun's pipe whistled all hands to the weather gun deck. Jamey and Patch stood curious with the others watching a sailor hauled from the hole in irons. An old salt to his side muttered low to no one. "Tha be big Biddle was caught sleepin his watch. T'will be the rope ends for him."

"It be Mose's law, sure," another said.

A man's height above, the captain stepped to the stern rail surrounding the quarterdeck, his officers a pace back watching the crew close.

"Seaman Biddle slept his watch," the captain said. "A clear breach endangering ship and crew. Forty less one to be witnessed for example."

Biddle looked sorry for himself as Mister Baines marched him to the bulwark.

"Thirty nine it be with the cat-o-nine," the old salt whispered.

"Aye, and a thieves' cat, no less," his friend added.

"Whas that?" Jamey asked low.

The old salt looked at him like he was dumb.

"Tis a whip, lad, with nine tails, each with a metal tip to steal the meat."

"Aye," another piped in, "They'll make him sure marry the gunner's daughter."

Biddle was halted before a cannon and ordered to mount its length with an embrace, belly down. Baines quick knotted his wrists to the pintles and ripped his shirt back.

"Do your duty, Mister Baines," the captain ordered.

A marine began a drum roll followed by the boson's swing of the first lash. The crack and yelp made all wince as Jamey watched the first grooves well with blood. The lashes, cracking like pistol shots, dug deep. Biddle cried like a newborn as the finished numbers were slow counted under the tense beat of the drum.

Finally, it was finished, the drum stopped to a hushed crew. The only sound was Biddle's whimpering as he squirmed, his back crossed with countless ribbons of blood. The cook stepped forward, checked his eyes and pulse, and nodded to the captain. Another threw a bucket from the sea across his bloody hide.

Ship's crew was dismissed.

Moons and seasons passed with no action. The daily training became tiresome and like the rest, Jamey felt it was enough and any more just a waste. All felt one good fight would go a long way. But as time passed slow and fast, Jamey learned more of the sea. He knew the stars and weather and understood the phases of the moon and its control over the ocean. The restless sea seemed to speak to him and no more honest voice ever crossed his ear. He listened close, trance-like, knowing its message, no matter how hard and cruel, would always be true. If one respected its power, a partnership could survive.

"Sail ho, sail ho, off starbard quarter. No colors."

Every eye turned to the sea as the captain snapped his telescope full out. Orders were barked as the ship came about, giving chase. Jamey and Patch flew up the ratlines with the rest to unfurl more canvas. Excitement pulsed through the ship as the word passed labeled her a Barbary pirate. The hunter finally found game.

Two turns of the glass put their ship abeam with cannons out and primed. Jamey, standing at his gun station, felt his head thrumming, taking note the pirate ship was just half their size but well armed. Every salt stood stiff and ready, awaiting orders, when the enemy suddenly raised their white to the regret of the crew. Stand down orders were barked and a boarding party launched as the rest relaxed at their post, disappointed.

Suddenly, in a flash, the pirate's gun ports flew open, firing at close range. Cannon thunder shook Jamey, catching all off guard. The

Vanguard rocked, trembling from the blast and the starboard bulwark blew apart sending cannon flying across the deck and splinters like arrows. The ship's launch hanging off the beam exploded, the twelve man boarding crew killed straight out. Ship's officers screamed orders. Jamey jumped too, feeling blood running down his face. Glancing behind, the gun crew was down. Torn bodies groaned and screamed, twitching, dying on the bloody deck.

He barely heard his orders, moving automatically as trained. Smoke and fire everywhere burned his lungs. He felt his gun shudder and blast. The gun captain screamed orders and they raced to reload not knowing what they hit. It seemed to take forever. More enemy shot raked the deck and more of his shipmates screamed. Again, they hauled their gun out and fired the hole. Another thunder and Jamey hauled to reload. Distant yells and screams in tongues he did not understand were mixed with curses and prayers. A wayward bucket for the flames splashed across his back and he jerked back, the heated steam burning his skin. The gun captain's holler brought him back to duty, cursing, as he hauled forward with the rest. The captain fired the hole. Again, they yanked as one to reload, panicked, not knowing their luck.

Jamey sensed a distant crack like thunder. Patch yelled and grabbed his arm, pulling him low. The main course yard fell like a mighty oak crashing into the bulwark, smashing their gun. Jamey, dazed, pushed himself up from the deck seeing the gun captain crushed against the heavy iron. Brains and blood stuff oozed from his skull as moans from the rest of their crew told the worst. Numb and dizzy, Patch yanked him to the closest cannon still in service. In a trance, Jamey moved without thinking, helping to load and fire.

Suddenly, a huge fireball exploded on the pirate ship to the hurrahs of the crew. Jamey peeked over the rail to see the Barbary ship in shambles, the stern settling heavy. All enemy fire ceased and white flag raised but the Vanguard kept a steady barrage until the ship went down. Survivors jumped ship floating on what they could, fear painted on their faces, begging for mercy.

From his hailer, the captain's cold orders sounded, "Hear me men. A bullet hole between the eyes for each coward for this craven act. Let their meat stuff the shark's belly."

Marines scurried up the rigging with muskets to snipe those in the water trying to save themselves. Cap and ball, carefully aimed, poked bloody holes in their heads. Jamey, without emotion, wiped the blood from his face, watching them scream and moan before sinking beneath the sea.

Finally, it was over. They had won but paid a heavy price. Thirty-two dead, ten dying, and the ship badly wounded. The captain was in a fit and all were ordered double duty to clean and repair. Both Patch and Jamey felt blessed they fared well. Patch not a scratch and Jamey just a cut across the forehead. The daily drills had turned the tide as every mother's son did their duty without a second thought. Jamey now understood the value of training. A lesson learned.

A moon passed and the Vanguard, although wounded, was again ship shape. The dead watch done, Jamey stretched, welcoming the streak of dawn and a routine morn. Looking aloft, he knew dead sails spelled the doldrums.

True enough, the morn, settling dull, was first smiled on by the salts because it gave them leisure. Two more suns slipped, spelling the same, and the devil's prayer book passed time with some. Soulful shanties, at first welcome, drifted over the deck but were soon damned and killed by lively ditties. With one eye for the boson, the click of devil's teeth on deck made some curse and others whoop. But as the white suns dragged on for a quarter moon more, even slackers got tight and the chief mate ordered all to whistle the wind and whistle hard.

Jamey turned twenty-two without notice.

*

"Orders are in mates, we're goin home."

Hurrahs and yelps of good cheer filled the ship. In two moons with a fair wind, they would see the English shore. Spirits soared with captain's orders of an extra ration of a drop of rum. Free time was spent by some carving gifts for their sweethearts as they dreamed of future plans. Jamey and Patch, remembering their vows, leaned the rail wondering their next move.

A quarter-moon later under fair weather and steady heel, the crew was holystoning the deck below a staring sun. As Jamey leaned forward with a scrub, the gold ring around his neck slipped from his shirt, dangling down.

"Hey mate, was at yer neck?" an old salt asked. "Tis catchin the sun right perty."

Jamey looked down at it swinging."Tis jus a ring."

"From a lass's heart?"

"No, an enemy."

The sailor leaned over for a closer look.

"God's pain! Tis so," he said. "I seen another the same."

Jamey stopped, quick alert. "Where mate? Ya know the owner?"

Jamey held patient, without a breath, as the sailor cradled the ring for a sharper study.

"Aye, tis the same. The owner took these three fingers."

He lifted his left hand, less three, to Jamey's eyes.

"I'd likely not ferget."

Jamey pushed for more. The sailor said the ring's image was burned in his soul. Years back, he and his mates were captured in a skirmish with the Spanish and sentenced to the galley.

"It was a single deck affair for a family of high rank. The owner and his sons drove us hard for sport and punished the rower missing a beat or failed the pace. I was one shamed and tortured one noon."

He paused with a stroke of the stone.

"They held me tight as he hisself cut these a knuckle at a time."

He looked down sad at his two-fingered hand.

"The dog and his litter laughed at my misery. I member like yester, lookin down, my eyes stuck on his ring as he nipped mine off."

The sailor sat back on his legs and took a breath. "Twas a long time ago."

Jamey fired questions but came away with few facts of benefit. It happened near twenty earth's turns past with the ring's owner most likely very old or dead. The old salt marked him medium height with dead white skin and black snake eyes. His face was thin with a long nose and seemed learned and sly. Among the galley, he hated the English more and relished their pain. The old sailor could recall no more and no name. Jamey asked till his head hurt.

That eve, as the moonlight glowed silver over the water, Jamey leaned on the rail gazing at the line between sea and sky, imagining them connected, sewn together, limiting the size of his world. Perhaps then he would have a chance of finding his family's killer. He sighed with the fantasy knowing the world was vast. So big, he could not imagine the end. Sighing again, he whispered to the breeze, "How do I find one man in all this?"

Friendly waters brought the channel storms, one chasing the other, forcing Jamey and Patch to hone their sailing skills to the point of exhaustion. A half moon from homeport, the ship was hit by a noreaster hard on the bow. Bare poles were ordered save for a reefed mizzen to hold the bow straight.

Jamey and Patch, aloft with another three, were wrapping the last canvas when a block snapped under Patch's weight. Falling, he let out a yell, cracking his head against the mast and ended hanging from a top spar, head down, a line twisted around his ankle. Dangling like a wild anchor in the galeing rain, he swung fierce with each role of the ship, each sway promising to smash his senseless body to a pulp.

Later, topmast men would say they never saw the like. Jamey jumped like a monkey out on the footrope, cut a line and tied off around his gut, sizing the angle, and with the next swell, dove into space. Timing and fortune were his swinging out in a wide pendulum arc and snatching his friend's limp body in midair. Those watching against cracking lightning and stinging rain, imagined him a flying ghost as back ground thunder shook the ship.

Jamey, swinging wild, clamped Patch tight with one and with the other, gathered the lose line slopping below and whip threw it to the gawking sailors to pull them in.

After lowering Patch to the deck, they dumped him in his bunk. The cook examined him and shrugged his shoulders with a shake of his head. Only time and fate would tell. Jamey sat by his side without moving.

The next morn, Patch groaned and opened his eyes. He would be well.

That eve, with Patch standing on his own twos with a wrapped head, his mates clapped him with a party and stolen rum. Stories of

Jamey's feat were told till they hurt each one better than the last. Patch quietly listened to all and as he looked up at his friend, their eyes met with a silent pact. Though hell knocked, they would give their life for the other.

*

"Land ho, . . . land! Off larbard bow."

All hands eagerly gazed at the shadowed hump of the English shore as spotted molly hawks circled above. Home at last.

After a few turns of the glass, sundowners secured the warship fore and aft with shore leave granted to all hands, save the unlucky bones crew.

As Patch and Jamey strolled along the wharf, they set a strange pair. Alike in the cut of their clothes with wide step and rolling gait, the similarity ended there. Jamey was tall and slim with broad shoulders and brown hair, sun bleached, hanging long on his neck contrasting hard with the bull-like stature of his friend. Patch's shorter muscled body belied his nimble speed. His black eye patch, matching his raven hair, detracted from his ever-watching good eye hidden in tapered lids. Their sea swaggered walk, topped off by rigging knives at the waist, warned all to avoid any test. Blood brothers true after a forever time before the mast for their trust was tested in many a tight quarter at sea and strange lands.

"Patch, ol man, this be tha port tha took me away. She be the village Rye."

"Weel, be dogged. Ya mean the same wher ya kilt the lord's assassin?"

"He be a count, Count Radford, . . . true it is." Jamey said pointing to the fortress. "There, his castle on the hill abeam of ya. We'll send a messenger askin to visit on the morrow to collect my da's weapons and, mayhap, get some questions answered I've stored awhile," he said, remembering his kidnapping and shanghai.

"But this eve we toast my home. We'll bloody well twist the cork, knocking a neck or two."

Jamey slapped his friend on the back and turned into the old Mermaid Inn where he first slept eight earth turns back.

The next light was gray and damp as they sat by an open window on the tavern floor. Cleaned, but still loggered from the night's drink, they scoffed the morning fair of the best sea pie they ever tasted. The fish and vegetables, between layers of bread washed down with ale, soon settled their gut and put them on the dusty lane in good spirits. Jamey noticed the village certainly had grown some as tinkers and travelers, mixing with carriages and wagons, bustled about dodging for position.

The messenger returned with a warm invitation so they hiked their breeches and started the hill. Jamey was anxious to see old friends, especially Clarice. On the way, they passed the place where they first met when he knocked her in the mud. Jamey told the story and Patch howled, picturing the sassy lass muddy from head to toe.

Both wore knee high Moroccan boots with fitted black trousers. Flounced open white cotton shirts cinched with wide leather belts, hanked with short swords, simpled their look. Sauntering by with bare heads and hair neatly tied back, passing wenches gave them a second glance and early doxies tried to fatten their purse.

At the gate, they were received by the castle guard and ushered toward the main hall. Following a step behind, Jamey remembered the tournament, the count, his weapon demonstration, and Clarice and her mother's kindness. He wondered how he would be received, thinking, after so long, they might hardly remember him. He prayed his father's weapons had been protected.

The guard led them to a large receiving room off the great hall. High ceilings filled with baroque paintings seemed to move as one walked about, admiring. A grand fireplace with an ornate mantel finished the far wall and its blaze, glistening from crystal chandeliers, cast the room a golden tint. The grand room was divided into three personal areas for private conversations by careful placing of soft leather and velvet couches. Oriental rugs with confusing designs and colors complimented large oils and wall hangings, creating a warm comfortable setting.

As Patch was squinting, looking at the art, Clarice and her mother entered.

"Jamey, Jamey, I cannot believe it!" Clarice blurted, rushing forward, all smiles, taking his hands. "Where have you been? Why did you disappear? We thought you dead."

One question after the other poured out, not waiting for answers. Her mother smiled politely, watching close, also wondering how he returned.

"I should be angry with you. You never said goodbye," she continued, faking a pout.

Clarice was beautiful, not the skinny little girl he remembered. And although she chattered excitedly, he saw her mature and poised. He admired her simple eggshell dress to the neck flowing modestly over her body. He noticed Patch's narrow eye open a little wider when she entered. He wondered if she remembered their first kiss and with her look, decided he would like another chance.

Jamey, all smiles, still had not been able to say a word until she finally took a breath and Patch was introduced. Clarice and her mother's flat expressions hid their alarm at his foreign look, but their gracious welcome slacked his unease some. Never before visiting a castle or in the presence of fine ladies, he felt awkward as his brown skin turned crimson. Jamey never saw him so strained and vowed to tease him later.

The morning drifted with stories and news of events since Jamey disappeared. Clarice was sorry her father could not receive them because he was ill but Jamey's weapons were safe and well cared for. Clarice was shocked and her mother feigned surprise when he related how he ended up on the merchant ship. The three pondered that time, but it was still a mystery after trying to match memories with questions and facts.

After tea, the two moved to take their leave when Clarice remembered her party two suns hence. She invited them both, insisting they come, no excuses. It was her nineteenth birthday. The gala event was to be on their yacht with a promise of music and good food. Hopefully, her father would be well enough to join them and Jamey could pay his respects. Clarice was so excited refusal would be cruel so promises were made.

chapter 9

"AH, VICTORY AT last, is mine," Damon whispered smugly. "After years of patience and planning, I will finally destroy these haughty English."

The voyage from *Espana* was particularly tiring. But after two storms and a wasted quarter moon, it still left ample time to complete his mission. Just then, his covered carriage hit a rut, jerking him from his seat while he cursed the poor English roads.

"Your excellency, thank you for this audience. My liege, King Phillip, sends his best wishes and looks forward to this treaty between our two lands."

The practiced words slid from his oily mouth as he paraded his arrogance. Damon bowed short but stood tall with a hard sinewy build. His conceited air fit his narrow face and patrician nose made longer by a violet-black van-dyke. His long sloping forehead highlighted thick meeting brows protecting hooded eyes and when he spoke, his thin lips drew back and his tongue seemed to flick. At first glance, one was reminded of a snake and those in his inner circle secretly referred to him as *El Serpiente*. This pleased him.

Queen Elizabeth pretended a warm reception. "Welcome, *Señor* DeSago, I trust all our wishes have been accepted."

He was pleased the royal chamber was well attended. The queen, her four ministers, along with the bishop and the castle guard, stood smug as he. He cherished the moment they would be brought low.

Damon took note of Sir Walshingham, one of the queen's favorites. Damon knew he was responsible for England's secret intelligence with spies plaguing the French and Spanish courts. He will be one of the first to die.

He, the Spanish Viceroy, *Señor* Damon Vasquez DeSago, was attended by two ministers and his personal guard. All were regally attired for their station for this special occasion. DeSago's preferred color was deep burgundy with splashes of gold for these formal affairs. Today he added a matching cape lined with gold satin. His dress sword, a gift from his king for this plot, hung low hiding his ever-present dagger strapped to his back. His soft burgundy cap, fitted with a short gold feather, matched knee-high boots and gloves. His confidence bordered on conceit as he watched these stupid English fall for the trap.

"*Sí*, your excellency, my liege, King Phillip, has agreed to the conditions and signed his acceptance. He eagerly awaits your majesty's signature to perfect the alliance."

Damon had labored for this moment since his father's death. His obsession burned his heart and consumed his life. With his father avenged, he relished the fulfillment of his final vow, the destruction of the English dogs.

Glancing around the room, the chamber reminded him of a time long ago when he served his father as a young Spanish envoy. He shivered cold remembering his pain staring at his father's lifeless body propped against the stone wall, fear frozen on his drained face, eyes dull dry, with his severed arms floating in clotting blood. Then, the torture of hiding his grief in the face of these Protestant dogs was the final insult. It still seared his memory, a raw scar burned forever in his heart. His father died serving his country and now the English would pay. Taking a quick breath, he cautioned himself, hiding his hate as he smiled slick, savoring the day of retribution.

The English minister interrupted his thoughts with a polished flair. "We will review the final document and celebrate our acceptance at the signing on the morrow. Your forbearance and diligence in this matter is commendable. We will relate our pleasure to your king."

"*Gracias, Señor* Walshingham," Damon returned, bowing with a hidden smirk. He turned proud and marched from the chamber, his entourage matching his step, each click of his heel meant to draw the eyes of the English lackeys.

He was anxious to return to his homeland but first he must arrange a clandestine meeting with the Jusuit Priest, John Ballero. Their planned uprising of loyal Catholics had to be timed perfectly with the invasion. Also, he personally delivered the coded message from King Phillip to Mary, Queen of Scotland, to stand ready. He could tell she was anxious and impatient. That was good. Keep them hungry for the greater glory of Spain.

Six full moons had passed before this day with another two probably to complete his grand betrayal. He must be patient. The last dispatch held good news. His much younger brother, Carlos, his only remaining family, received an appointment to minister in King Phillip's court and Damon wanted to use his influence to assist his advance. Since their father's murder, Damon shouldered the family's duties and mentored his brother as his father would.

But one vow he swore, staring at his unarmed father floating in his blood, was never, never, allow himself or his brother to be defenseless. So, Damon trained with deep passion in the fine art of the sword. He practiced ruthlessly with the best fencing instructors in Germany, England, and Spain, and ordered Carlos to do the same. He was now expert with the blade in any form.

After the morrow, he thought, I will relay the signal to the fleet. Then I will have most seven suns to travel to the coast and visit my friend, Count Radford. The thought made Damon's blood run remembering his stupid assassin's failure to kill the old count those years back because some peasant spoiled his aim. How long ago had it been? He reflected. Must be eight summers past. Well, perhaps this was best, he could now celebrate his current victory and pursue Radford's daughter before joining the armada. What was her name again? ....Ahh, yes, Clarice. What a ripe plum. I believe I will prepare a special surprise for her birthday.

Damon's tongue flicked with pleasure.

CHAPTER 10

BEAUTIFUL SUN welcomed Clarice's day as Jamey and Patch strolled to the wharf and spotted Count Radford's sailing yacht docked tight. Both thought the same, *bonny handsome.* Small, but ornate in every quarter with heavy gold leaf layered over carved scrolls from mermaids to Zeus, she shone in the morning sun. The bright vessel had a stocky beam for comfort and two masts hanging eight sails. Her elfin figurehead, also leafed in gold, matched her title, *Fantasy.*

Shimmering pennants and family flags set the mood as they were received by a soldier at the gangplank and led aboard to the Captain of the Guard. Jamey's eyes narrowed seeing the same Captain Bullard that swayed Jamey into the weapons demonstration the day he was shanghaied. The captain welcomed them with a flat expression and Jamey promised himself a private chat before this sun was done.

Jamey and Patch were dressed close with high boots polished special. Black trousers and silver silk shirts cut and sewn in Greece carried long bloused sleeves and high collars. They finished with colorful sailor scarves and soft leather belts hanging gemstone dress daggers neat at the hip.

Confident, but ill at ease in the presence of nobility, they were escorted to the quarterdeck. As they approached, it was a sight they had never seen. A huge white awning held in the center by block and tackle shaded the aft deck. The fringe was scalloped and trimmed in black with pink gaused curtains, lightly draped back, wafting in the day's breeze. Neither had seen anything on a ship so fine. The decks were cluttered with easy benches and fat colored cushions threatening to trip the crew with every step. Ladies and gentlemen, most a hundredfold, milled around the decks further hampering the sailor's hop.

Clarice caught their eye and excitedly welcomed them. She took Jamey's hand, dragging him toward the small group circling her father. Patch followed, uneasy, a step behind.

Jealous suitors noticed Clarice's attention toward Jamey not knowing they both decided, without words, to be just good friends, like brother and sister. Clarice had considered Jamey as a possible suitor, but her mother reminded her he was without rank, money, and sadly, he was Irish. The final reason, of course, he was Catholic. Clarice thought it a shame because she was attracted to him. She still remembered their first kiss and she liked his company. He made her laugh, with his rascal eyes, and she thought she would like to kiss him again to see what would happen. Perhaps she would take him as a lover after she married.

"I am so happy you are here," she said, stepping between Patch and Jamey as they approached her father. "I feared perhaps you would not."

Her familiarity annoyed her mother as they paid their respects to the count. The unusual fanfare also attracted the attention of another, standing at the rail, circled by his entourage. A strange pair, he thought. A rather rough lot, looking young and old at the same time, they look a lower station but are welcomed as equals. Staring at Jamey, he felt an inner warning.

Jamey felt the eyes and turned to see the figure glaring back, greeting him with a nod and a sneering grin. Jamey thought him familiar, something about his cut, knowing they never met. He shrugged and turned his attention back to the group.

Damon also thought this was a special day. It fit his plan perfectly. Celebrating Clarice's birthday on the water gave him an excellent opportunity to escape to his galley before the surprise attack by the Spanish fleet. But, he could not resist some flair and final insult as he thought of his surprise, smiling clever. A flawless plan.

Finally, docking lines were tossed and two longboats with a score of oarsmen put their backs to the towing lines, pulling the yacht away and into the wind. The crew moved with practiced duties, setting sail not enough to slip the deck. This was to be an easy day ensuring the comfort of the guests with a probable limit of thirty leagues from shore, and no more, with a flat return before dark.

Jamey and Patch, watching the sailors, envied their duty, easy work for old salts that swallowed the anchor but now recruited for the count's crew. Looking aloft to the blooming sails, they agreed she was a fine wee ship.

As the sails grabbed the wind, Jamey and Patch took a break from the festivities. With elbows on the rail, they gazed at the rippling sea feeling the pleasant sun, enjoying the day, letting their thoughts drift.

"Sir, I beg an introduction."

Jamey turned to face the eyes that watched him earlier.

"I am Damon Vasques DeSago, Viceroy of Spain, friend of the count and admirer of Clarice, . . . and you sir?"

Damon was tall as Jamey with a skeletal build. Regally dressed, but without pomp, he wore short boots with bloused leggings in rich burgundy, his favorite. All matched his leather vest over a full white shirt collared high. His slick reptilian appearance braced the wearing of a full rapier, unusual on such a day, along with a single glove on his left hand. Three personal guards stood a pace back, watched tight, armed the same.

Jamey stood straight, bowed slightly and returned, "Jamey Fallon, at your service."

Damon paled and trembled at the name. His black eyes narrowed as he quickly gathered himself. Jamey tensed, sensing danger, and Damon's guards stiffened, causing Patch to set his stance.

"Did you say Jamey Fallon?" he asked in disbelief.

"I did sir, have we met?" Jamey said, searching his memory.

"No, no." Damon said, quickly recovering. "But I might know your father. Was he not the Captain of the Guard many years back for your King Henry?"

"Yes, he was, sir, Thomas Michael Fallon was in the king's service."

Damon's hate welled full, taking every bit of his practiced control to resist stabbing Jamey where he stood. But that would not do. His mind raced. He must be patient. But how, he thought? I killed them all. I took his father's heart.

"*Si, si*, I remember him well. I was a young Spanish envoy at the time. I remember there was some nasty business of an attempt on the king's life by a member of his court. I recall your father saved the day."

"Aye, he told me the story as a young boy," Jamey answered.

"And how does he fair?" Damon inquired through narrow eyes.

"Murdered." Jamey's voice turned bitter.

"My whole family, by lowly cowards. You see the only one left."

Damon's inner smile could hardly be contained.

"My sympathies, good sir. I regret my inquiries brought forth unpleasant memories. I pray today's celebration will return your good cheer."

The tension cooled, relaxing the group a bit. Patch stayed tight, feeling the danger, not knowing why. Damon's group excused themselves to mingle with the others as Jamey and Patch turned back to the rail.

"Well, wa was that about?" Patch asked.

"Did you feel it too?"

"Feel it! Fer a wink, I thought it be a battle to the death."

"Something strange fer sure, ther's somethin . . . but?"

Jamey's memory was blank.

Damon and his guards slipped casual to a private corner at the bow. His mind quickly melded these new events into his plan. It could not be more perfect with the final killing of the Fallon clan and the defeat of England at the same time. This would almost best the pure pleasure he felt slaughtering Jamey's family. He savored the moment he would tell Jamey that fact before slitting his throat. Damon's body trembled in anticipation while he instructed his guards, adjusting his plan. Pleased with his cleverness, his tongue gave the smallest flick.

Pleasant time passed as the sun warmed. Clarice was happy, flitting from guest to guest, pleased to be the center of attention. Jamey and Patch watched in amusement as prospective suitors tried to position themselves attempting to gain her favor. Clarice pretended not to notice, thoroughly enjoying keeping them guessing.

In the distance a cannon boomed and everyone on the yacht turned to the sound. Another blast, followed by trumpets and drums, announced the arrival of Damon's galley. As planned, it was gaily decorated with banners and pennants of every type and color. One sail was raised flat with the salutation, "*Feliz Copiano* Clarice", painted full across in vivid red and yellow. From the foredeck, uniformed Spanish sailors played a cheerful chantey with all visible crew outfitted in their best.

Patch and Jamey sized her up as she drew near, ready to lay too. It was a command galley with sixty-four oars and two masts carrying large lanteen sails. The armament was light, with sixteen cannon, floating close to the water. Designed for the flat seas of the Mediterranean, Jamey questioned her seaworthiness in the English Channel. She was an old ship with old ways but shipshape none the less, ready for any test.

As the galley pulled alongside the *Fantasy*, Damon stepped to the bulwark and boomed over the chatter of the guests. "A little surprise, Clarice…. Happy birthday!"

All on board were impressed, hooting their approval, and Clarice reeled with delight.

Jamey and Patch watched with the rest as the galley shipped oars and tied off abeam of the yacht. Because of the fanfare, they did not notice Damon's guards move silently behind them. Damon was anxious to see everyone's face when he sprung his trap. He climbed atop the rail with a smirk, looked over the party, and announced with a flourish he could not resist. "Ladies and gentlemen, your attention *per favor*." All turned toward his voice. "As of this moment, you are my captives and prisoners of Spain."

He sneered, watching their silent disbelief turn to screams of panic as hidden Spanish marines stormed the yacht with pikes and swords. At the same time, Damon's guards jumped Jamey and Patch from behind, slugging them with belaying pins, and quick lashed their hands behind their backs.

In a heartbeat, it was all over. Protests and outrage from the captives reigned as all males were tied and separated from the women. Damon, standing cocky on the quarterdeck with the galley captain, watched Jamey and Patch dragged forward and thrown on their knees at his feet.

Clarice, in silent shock, watched her father, angry and red-faced, waddling, huffing, to stand before Damon. "Sir, are you mad? Our countries are at peace. Is this some jest? I demand . . ."

Damon, turning slow, crooked his smile and in a practiced dagger move, sliced the count's throat. The count, eyes bulged, fell to the deck writhing in pain, grasping his neck as blood pumped his death. Clarice's mother swooned and Clarice screamed, falling to his side. Even the Spanish sailors winced at *El Serpiente's* cruel action as they watched his tongue flick, tasting the blood in the air.

Jamey and Patch, kneeling, still dazed from the rap on their heads, glanced at each other knowing they were next and needed a plan fast.

Damon, bored with the blood, looked up and peered over his shoulder at Jamey and Patch with eyes of death. Jamey's mind raced as Damon moved toward him with raised blade, hate burning in his black eyes. Jamey's anger pulsed and in a surprise effort, lunged forward full bore, butting into DeSago's gut, hoping for the best. With teeth his only weapon, he glomped onto what was close, Damon's gloved hand. Both tumbled to the deck as Jamey wiggled to stay on top, trying to butt DeSago with his head.

Damon's guards jumped in and yanked him away, holding him on his knees, head bent back, with the glove still in his mouth. Damon, cursing, climbed to his feet in a full rage. Jamey twisted and jerked against his captors refusing to surrender. As he stared back at DeSago, his anger changed to numb shock. Damon's hand was missing a finger. His mind raced, noticing the other fingers were thin and soft like the one in his father's mouth.

"Yer the one! Yer the murdin snake tha killed my family."

Damon, humiliated by Jamey's surprise attack, blanched white with hate. His fury exploded, ignoring those around him.

"Yes, yes, you young whelp, I am the one and you will know why before you die," he ranted, wild-eyed. "Your father killed mine at the king's court when I was a young envoy. I was there to see him shamed and swore on his death he would be avenged."

Damon moved toward Jamey with his dagger, tongue flicking. "Now your death will satisfy my vow."

"*Señor, señor,* a word before you strike," the Spanish captain interrupted.

Damon turned, angry. "What is it, *capitán?*"

"A word in private would be to your advantage."

The deck fell quiet as they stepped to the side. The captain informed Damon there had been a fever on the galley killing over half the men at oars. They needed every able prisoner to man the stations to ensure their escape and rendezvous with the armada. Damon told him to take the rest but he was going to slit the throats of these two, pointing to Jamey and Patch.

Patch was thinking fast.

The captain, thinking only of the success of their mission, added. "Your hate is understandable but a quick death is less satisfying. Would not your vengeance be better served watching him die slow, starving in his own filth as a galley slave?"

Patch listened sharp, saw Damon's hesitation and blurted, "M-lord, m-lord, please ha mercy, no put me wi him." He nodded at Jamey, talking fast. "He no fren o mine. I show ya. I cut his throat fer ya. Gimmee yer blade. I cut him good. He die fast." Patch rattled on, "I kill em quick. He weel never feel it, m-lord."

"Quiet, you dog," Damon snapped. "The whelp will die slow along with you."

It worked, Patch thought as Damon turned and kicked Jamey in the gut. Jamey doubled over, crumpling to the deck.

"So be it *capitán*, take them," Damon snapped.

The order was given. Jamey, half-conscious, and Patch were dragged to the galley, stripped naked, and chained to the oars. Jamey was barely aware of the leather lace ripped from his neck with Damon's ring and pocketed by his captor. Clarice's suitors and all other able men were shackled the same. Their privileged lives, marked by their pasty white bodies and sniveling whimpers, were over forever.

Patch, chained behind Jamey, whispered at the first chance. "Jamey, Jamey, can ya hear?"

Jamey, slumped over in a stupor, slowly nodded.

"Ya mus play their game. Make em think yer beat. Play the brokin man, ya hear, bide yer time mate, ya hear?"

Jamey nodded, half in a trance.

CHAPTER 11

SHE WAS TINY, fragile as a summer sparrow. She tried desperately to make herself even smaller, praying to be invisible.

She seemed always afraid since stolen from her island home. The others taken from the village were scattered and now she was alone in this strange land. She often wondered and worried about her brother. She remembered him trying to come to her aid at the slave market and they beat him. She remembered his scream of pain and the blood in his eye as they dragged her away crying. She prayed to Buddha he still lived.

She cried often, alone.

Cho Ling was now sixteen and a woman, although a small one. A Malay beauty perfectly proportioned in every way. With slick raven hair falling below her waist, her smooth dusty skin highlighted large teardrop eyes of deep emerald sure to melt any heart. Her every movement was inborn with a sensual gentle grace that was difficult to disguise.

Moving through her daily chores, she carefully masked her beauty, keeping her head bowed and eyes lowered. She concealed her femininity by binding her breasts with hair tucked up short and wore dull clothing. With always a deep salaam, she perfected her slave manner to appear uninteresting. She slept in a small unused closet, her sanctuary, her little nest, and tried to be nothing, a shadow in the corner.

Her mistress thought her a thing, a furnishing. Seven birthdays a slave, never leaving her mistress' rooms, she performed household duties and ate very little. Her only words, "Yes mistress," as she made herself even lower than the other slaves. She was treated as nothing and she felt the same.

Her only pleasures were stolen moments with the small squirrels and dainty birds in the walled garden. Alone in their company she would allow herself a rare smile for she felt one with them.

Although her misery seemed eternal, deep inside at the center of her soul, her spirit lingered with an ember of hope. Cho Ling was born with the patience of her people and her heart, though small, fluttered not as a small bird, but with the strength of an eagle.

Someday she would soar.

chapter 12

SOME TIME PASSED before Jamey gained his senses. Stripped naked, he was chained to a tier in the bowels of the Spanish galley. As his mind cleared, he first became aware of the stench, making him retch. Breathing through his mouth, he looked around the gloom at ten score or more of men, naked like him, slumped at the oars. A narrow ramp down the center of the keel separated the larboard and starboard ranks of slaves. The two souls chained to his station seemed barely alive. Skin over bones, sweat dirt covered, accented festered scars and blood scabs on their backs. Pained moans and death coughs matched the stink and body filth on the deck plate ensuring a slow death for all. As Jamey's plight sunk in, his mind flashed back to the count's yacht and DeSago's face.

He cursed himself. The sailor spotting the ring dangling that day scrubbing the deck described its owner perfectly. It was DeSago, or perhaps his son.

"I'm behind ya, Jamey."

Jamey turned, seeing Patch naked, chained like him with his eye patch gone, showing a gaping eyehole to further shame and strip him of all dignity.

"Member wha I tol ya. Play their game. Act a brokin man, bide yer time."

Jamey didn't have to pretend. He was broken with despair.

"My God, Patch, wha kinda hell is this?"

"I been here before mate. I know we look lost, but have faith fer a bit. Jus listen close."

"Wha about the others?"

Patch leaned forward, dropping his head, and told Jamey about the rape and murder of the women. Clarice and her mother were carried below decks, fate unknown, but he suspected the worst. All those able were chained to the oars and the rest received slit throats. The yacht was scuttled, no trace left.

Suddenly, a lash cracked across Patch's back and he jerked straight with a low curse, bending back in pain.

"*Silencio gordo*," the oarmaster barked.

Jamey looked up at the ugliest man he had ever seen. Short and stubby legged with a thick meaty body, naked as them but for a dirty loin cloth. His baldhead, with wrinkled meat, sprouted from his shoulders with no neck holding black beady eyes, stuck close to a bent pig nose. Just below, sticky toothless gums dripped slobber from fat lips like split fillets. His smell made Jamey's stomach turn. It was clear his brain was as dull as the flat look in his eyes.

The whip snapped and Jamey felt the lash cut across his back. He felt his muscles spasmed in pain, arching him back. The cutting leather barbs stripped chunks of meat leaving blood trickling cool down his back. His muscles knotted as old Biddle's fate under the thieves' cat flashed in his mind.

"Don neber look ta me, ya bug. Keep yer head down."

The pain renewed Jamey's anger. It felt good. He embraced it. He felt his blood pump in rage, craving revenge. It made him feel alive. But then, as soon, the anger and hate tortured him to despair knowing his family's killer was above deck on this hell ship and he was helpless. His family and now the murder of Clarice and the others caused tears to well in anguish and defeat. This was the final insult, the final disgrace. A just God cannot let this stand.

A clatter on the upper deck broke his thoughts.

"Set sail fore and aft," a voice ordered in Spanish.

Then, marines, muttering curses, came down to the oar deck with buckets of seawater, dousing the oarsmen and planks to wash the body filth through the scuppers. The salt water hit Jamey's open cuts, smarting the pain, and he gritted his teeth refusing to give them the satisfaction of enjoying his misery.

"Ready oars," the oarmaster bellowed.

The two next to him slowly came to life.

"Follow their moves," Patch whispered.

Jamey grabbed the oar handle, matching their positions.

"On da beat," the order sounded and a pounding mallet banged against the thump stone. He felt the vibration through the ship's timbers with every swing.

BOOM—BOOM—BOOM—BOOM.

Jamey tried to keep pace with the two men, bracing his right foot against the logger beam to stay steady, taking some strain from his back.

BOOM—BOOM—BOOM—BOOM.

The pulsating beat never ceased as his muscles fast dulled with ache. The stench was forgotten as he gulped air, his brain tuned to expect the next blow of the drum. Time was forever and his muscles screamed. His eyes watered. The beat forever beat. His muscles cramped. The pounding hammer never, never, stopped.

BOOM—BOOM—BOOM—BOOM.

If it would just stop a moment, just a moment.

BOOM—BOOM—BOOM—BOOM.

Jamey's mind and body were numb. His throat burned. His mind drifted. His body yanked and pulled the oar on its own. He was dimly aware of his heart pumping in rhythm to the drumming blows.

This was hell.

Jamey turned, glancing at the hulk beating the thump-stone with two huge mallets. He sat straddled and chained to a stump with eyes sewn shut. His slack dulled face showed insanity. The pounding sledges long ago deafened his ears needing certain jabs by the oarmaster for his orders.

BOOM—BOOM—BOOM—BOOM.

The rhythmic beat stroked a perfect unending cadence until the soul wanted to scream. Madness would be a blessed relief.

Finally, the sun hit the sea and the order came. "Ship oars."

The long sticks stopped, cradled in the rowers' laps, as they slumped, exhausted.

"Ya do fine, Jamey. It be better next morn," Patch whispered.

Jamey thanked God he had a friend and was not alone.

The oarmaster, named the Pig by those chained, stopped at the rank in front and pulled a slave's head back showing eyes flat white. With a curse, the Pig pulled an axe from the rope at his waist and with a quick blow, chopped off the slave's foot below the shackle. In a practiced move, he lifted the footless leg with the withered body hanging like gutted game and kicked stuffed it overboard through a scupper. Then, he lumbered forward to the holding cage and yanked a replacement to the empty position, locked him to the post and kicked the bloody foot stump aside.

Jamey stared in numb disbelief. His mind could not fathom the savagery until he remembered this was Damon's ship, the sadistic killer of his family.

After beans, water, and a weevil filled biscuit, he fell into a fitful sleep dreaming of escape and the many deaths of Damon DeSago.

The lash slashed across his back and jumped him awake. He jerked around to see the sneering face of his tormentor.

"*Hola, Señor* Jamey Fallon, I pray you slept well," Damon said, catching Jamey's eye with a smirk. "Are the lodgings satisfactory?"

He laughed mean with pure pleasure seeing Jamey's humiliation.

Jamey looked up like a cowered dog, sputtering crazy sounds, letting spittle dribble from the corner of his mouth. For good measure, he wilted, scooting away in feigned fear. He wanted to rage against Damon, swear his death, but remembered Patch's advice. *Just play their game. Let them know you're broken.*

"Ah, you do well to fear me. But this is just the beginning. Before I am done, you will beg for my dagger across your throat."

Smiling with pleasure, he ordered the oarmaster to cut his rations by half.

"Whip him to a slow death," Damon said, sniffing his perfumed kerchief. "I want him to know what I have done to him."

The oarmaster grunted with a shrug as Damon stepped away, anxious to leave the stench.

The suns turned with daily visits by Damon. Patch's whispered words of hope were all that kept him from giving up and wishing for death. Each morn Damon reminded him of his failure as his body and soul weakened ever more. Damon reveled in his misery and thanked the captain for his recommendation.

On the sixth dawn they sighted the armada and by the noon sun, the admirals and squadron captains assembled in the main cabin. After pleasantries, the officers warily reported bad news. Fully a fourth of the fleet was missing, lost or sunk from channel storms. Coastal actions by English privateers nipping at their flanks further checked their readiness. Some captains complained their ships did not measure to the faster maneuvering English. In addition, mercenary troops promised from France did not march, lacking the tribute promised by Spain.

DeSago was in a fury. His invasion was falling apart. His snake eyes hooded against lips stretched, blanching white in a snarl of disgust. He ranted and screamed crazy at the officers until he was hoarse. Although alone they feared him, together they stood firm in their advice to turn the fleet to prevent a complete disaster. Their recommendation was to retreat with lessons learned and plan a future campaign. England was ignorant of their design and with the treaty in effect, they sat lulled into thinking all was well.

Damon stormed across the cabin, hunched, glaring at the officers, his tongue flicking his rage. Then, he stopped and faced them, the cabin stood dead quiet but for the ships creak. As the officers returned his look, he seemed to grow before their eyes, looming, evil, eyes hooded, mesmerizing, ready to snake strike, wanting to kill. They shrunk, suddenly afraid.

Then as fast, he calmed, his mind always in control, deciding the advice was sound. A clever man would plan for the future rather than risk defeat, and he was clever. But, as his mind plotted, he knew he must return immediately to Spain before the fleet. He must placate his king and paint a positive picture of events. After all, he reasoned, much was accomplished and with the treaty, they were still in a perfect position to strike the English when better prepared.

The next morn, Damon transferred to a fast sloop. He planned to kill Jamey before leaving but many more at the oars had died. The Captain assured him Jamey would be dead when the galley reached Spain. He would see to it personally.

Another full moon passed with the galley sailing into the Mediterranean on the final leg to Spanish soil. All fat had melted from Jamey and Patch. Their muscles were stone hard from constant rowing on a diet of beans and hard biscuits. Patch knew they would have to figure an escape soon or they would waste, leaving them too weak to break free. Patch looked at his friend's scarred back, every sinew highlighted by a sweaty sheen. He knew the muscles would soon thin to mere strings, leaving skin covered bones and ribs.

Each night they whispered different plans of escape. Whatever the decision, both knew they needed the Pig's axe to chop free. Once loose, though, they muddled, trying to figure how to take the ship or slip away. There had to be some way and it had to be soon. Spain was not far off.

Two morns later, breaking light brought panic on deck. Two Barbary pirate ships slipped close in the night and were attacking on both beams. The Spanish captain cursed himself for advancing ahead of the main fleet and ordered the men to prepare for boarding. Jamey and Patch listened to the uproar as swords crossed and arrows flew. Then, a cannon blast hit just aft of their oars killing two rows of slaves. Choking smoke filled the tier with body parts and blood all around as others, wounded by flying slivers, screamed and bled.

"This be our chance, Jamey, stand ready."

Jamey nodded, reaching deep for strength as the Pig hustled toward them fixed on the mayhem from the blast. At the last instant, Jamey shoved the end of his oar between his stumpy legs causing him to pitch forward in front of Patch. In one slick move, Patch yanked the axe free and chopped into his melon head before he hit the deck. His body still death twitched as Patch started hacking at the ship's timber around the spike trying to free his ankle.

The spike held deep and sweat poured from his frantic chopping for what seemed an eternity. Finally, he pried the iron eye loose, tossed Jamey the axe and moved down the gangway searching for any weapon. Fighting overhead was fierce and it was difficult to tell who would fall. Freeing the rest of the slaves was useless. All were half dead, unaware of the battle on deck.

With a whoop, Jamey was free and joined Patch watching the fighting through the grating above. A glance to the other told them to wait, knowing there would be fewer to fight on either side.

A half glass later, it was done. Jamey recognized Moroccan voices and figured the pirates won the day. Just then, the hatch to the slave deck was hauled back and he told Patch to follow his lead as they scrambled on deck, trying to look strong. Both praised the corsairs on their cleverness, honored their bravery and thanked them for their rescue.

The two were circled swift by the pirates still worked to a blood pitch. Both sensed their mood and kept talking, knowing they would kill them just for pleasure. Naked and dirty, they looked a sight with a smell a hog would love.

The pirate captain stepped up. "Kill em."

As swords and knives lifted, Jamey yelled, "Hold now, if treasure you want."

The crew halted at the magic word.

"What treasure?" the captain asked, eyes narrow. He was no fool.

Jamey saw him as jumbled blood standing short but hog bone hard with high boots and rusty chest armor. His uniform was decorated with a tricorn hat of purple stuck with a yellow plume. A striped sash and fat leather belt with hanging daggers, balanced against a boarding sword, completed his look. Not liking these two, his snarl showed metal mean through black-gapped teeth.

"The tale quick or die."

Jamey was thinking fast.

"Don tell em Jamey," Patch murmured, guessing his tack.

"Well cap'n, tis a tale to tell," he said, pausing for effect, glancing around. "Tis worth sparin our skins a spell to prove we speak right. A half curse more an we'll offer proof."

The captain straddled, thinking they were lying. But if not, he would have a happy crew. As he mulled, Jamey pushed.

"Let me an me mate get civil so we can talk like men. You'll not regret it."

A half sandglass later, washed, with clothes from the Spanish dead, they stood confident before the captain and crew looking more human and equal to the rest. All the spoils had been transferred to the raider's ship and the galley was sunk with the living slaves. Their panicked screams of despair rang in Jamey's ears as he pretended no concern. It was hard to see but merciful by some mark.

Jamey stuck his thumbs in his belt planning to act slow in the head.

"Weel cap'n, a smart man ya be."

"Speak plain mate, bout the treasure." the captain barked impatient. He sensed at the edge that no good would come from these two.

"Aye capn, but first ya mus know we be brethren too. Just yanked a moon back and shackled below to the oars. Our secret kept dark till now," he said, trying to stall, thinking his story as he went. "Again, our thanks fer savin us from sure death."

"The treasure mate, or die," the captain said, low and hard.

Jamey feigned fear. "Weel, it be off the Africa coast not moren thirty leagues plus ten, best guess. We canna tell ya. We hafta lead ya." His mind was working, talking loud for the benefit of the crew.

"Safe passage and tis yours," Patch added.

The captain smirked with a grunt. He liked the looks of Patch even less.

"We don need the two to show. Kill the one eye," he snapped to his guards.

Before his fellows could move, Jamey jumped in, "Nay, tha be no good capn. Thers the hitch. We each jus know a part. The two joined will point the way," he said, close watching the captain's face, giving him his most honest look. "No lie, 'twas done to keep us true."

The captain leaned forward, mulling with a sharp stare at Jamey as the crew murmured on the puzzle.

Jamey kept talking, "Tis God's truth, cap'n. I swear by whas holy. Ya nothin to lose. If we play false, ya can murder us hard. Seven suns, at most, fer a grave full o-gold."

The captain glanced around, shifty, seeing support for Jamey's tale. His gut was suspicious but guessed it worth the gamble. He would play the hand, but if false, they would die by his blade.

The two pirate ships set a course south by west toward Morocco. Jamey and Patch jumped too, working with the men and set to making friends. By the falling sun, they learned the captain was hated but protected by his four officers. Their loyalty bought with full captain shares of booty, same as him, at the expense of the crew. They all grumbled but none had the brains to mount an organized mutiny.

On free time, Jamey and Patch plotted their next move keeping an eye on one pesky fellow hanging close that skulked and slipped every nook. They watched him sharp seeing he was an ugly creature most likely friends with the devil.

A fellow mate close by, when asked, told his story low and careful, eyes worried, "Best keep a dagger's distance ther, mate. Fer sure ther be devil spirits guiden his bones."

It seems that in a past battle, he took a saber slash down the middle, clear to the skull, splitting his face in two. Bandaged fast, off center, the mismatched parts healed right side up and left side down, leaving a purple knobbed scar dead center from brow to chin. A first look watered every eye, not from pity, but by pain. It was a sight that caused one to sign the cross as the breath was sucked in shock. Plus, he was swarthy as a moor and stature small with the rest of his face craggy as a walnut. And if God was not cruel enough, he had a ragged ear, chewed, supposed by a rat. Michelangelo could not have picked a better model for Christ's traitor.

But God, they guessed, realized he'd been unmerciful so graced him with a snap quick mind and the balance of a cat so they nicknamed him *El Gato*, real name, *Botac*. El Gato, *the cat*, could scurry any rigging and tight rope the topmasts of any pitching ship. Sinewed with wire strand muscles and nimble quick as his namesake, he was a clever rogue that seemed everywhere, knowing all in his world. Outwardly, he enjoyed his repugnance with a traitor's sneer but his mind cursed the heavens for his fate and his heart hated the world.

The crew watched him with a wary eye and some would slit his throat just for comfort if they could catch him. A few attempts at midnight were met by his glaring eyes, for he slept the same each night, upright, his back against a bulkhead, snoring with eyes wide open.

With this warning, Jamey and Patch leaned on the rail, one eye over the shoulder, marking him close as they planned their next move. Morocco was just two suns out.

"The plan's too wild. The galley sucked your strength," Patch warned, shaking his head.

"I'll not miss. My da taught me well."

Never seeing Jamey wield his swords, Patch pushed. "Better me then, with my weight." Patch looked in Jamey's eyes and saw the stubborn blue. "Awright, he's yours, I pray yer right."

Jamey slapped him on the back. "The morrow will tell."

El Gato studied the two unable to hear their whispers. He lived this long not being the fool. His bones told him the two were not their claim and at the right time, he might profit. He knew the devil knew him and accepted his lot. A master spy and a student of human evil, he expected no favor. His constant smirk knew men's treachery being hired often as an expert with the necklace. With every step silent as a cat's paw, he was a phantom stalker with the garrote. His victims never knew they died.

The next noon at eight bells they played their plan. Jamey, faking work, blocked Blacky's path, the biggest of the captain's guards. Blacky, grunting his impatience, kicked him aside.

"Ya big whale, watch yerself," Jamey insulted.

Blacky, a head taller and twice the weight, snickered, and backhanded him across the face.

Jamey purposely took the blow, falling hard to the deck. The crew stopped at the ruckus as he stumbled to his feet. "Ya cannot fight fair, mate?" Jamey shot back, facing him square, feet planted hard. "I challenge ya. What ya say men, can I have a fair fight?" He purposely kept repeating the word fair.

From the rear, Patch's whispers urged the brethren as they cheered, calling for a fair contest. Blacky, first taken aback by Jamey's nerve, growled his anger, declaring him shark bait.

The captain looked on, sensing the crew's mood. He had to let the fight go knowing his four guards could not hold back a together crew. He should have slit their troublemaking throats when he first found them. Treasure be damned.

Stepping front, he ordered, "Clear the deck."

He was sure Blacky, most twice Jamey's weight, would kill him in a flick, sealing his position and power.

Blacky was hard heavy but light on his legs. Bare bald and so black he seemed purple, he flashed white eyes under a heavy skulled brow. He squared, facing Jamey bare-chested with Turkish trousers held by wide leather belts double crossed over both shoulders. He liked to kill. He enjoyed the sound of the gurgle or the hack of flesh. Simple and dull-witted, it made him feel powerful and feared. With sneering contempt, he glared at Jamey with smiling blubbered lips, feeling sick pleasure. He would enjoy this.

Blacky and Jamey were fast enclosed in a wide circle on midship deck. Some climbed the rigging for a better look while others started the wagers. Secretly, the group favored Jamey but knew Blacky would take the day knowing his strength and cruelty in past fights. All, rightly, gave him a wide berth.

With a deep breath, Jamey stepped to the weapons rack at the main mast and drew two boarding swords. Feeling their heft, he noted the poor condition and balance. The heavy blades made him wonder if he was up to the match. A full moon in the galley with little food took its toll. He was twenty or better under and although his upper body was powerful from rowing, his legs were stiff and shaky. He looked weak with ribs like barrel staves and a belly sunk to his spine. Hollow cheeks and bright eyes made him look half dead already as a sliver of fear niggled, thinking he should have picked on the smaller officer.

Blacky's neck sucked in as he stepped to the mast and huffed his chest full, grabbing two of the same from the rack.

Patch slipped silent in back of the Captain's remaining three guards.

El Gato watched.

The crew started shouting their favorite as the gladiators slow circled the other in the kindled air. Both looked calm, watching the other for the first move. Jamey knew his swords, when sung, could easily kill the big black but he knew he had to put on a good show to sway the crew to back him for command of the ship. He glanced at Patch to make sure he was ready.

He was.

Jamey stopped, cocky, lowering his sword points to the deck and barked with a snickered smile, "Well, ya sack o blubber, ya gonna fight or dance?"

The crew went silent with the insult, some snickered.

Blacky's nostrils flared and jaw muscles bulged. He would kill this white puppy with a thousand cuts. With a gutter growl, he charged across the deck towards Jamey as the brethren cheered the start. Jamey feinted to the left but jumped right, leaving Blacky empty air. Chasing goats as a boy taught him well. As Blacky rushed by, Jamey slapped him on his arse with the flat of his blade. A whoop of surprise from the crew added to Blacky's rage at the demeaning blow. Crazed, he spun around, crouched low and stalked wide-legged towards Jamey's death.

Jamey quick glanced, catching the nod from Patch. It was time. Ready, he moved in a circle left and started his singing swords. At the same time, his mind clicked as the brethren watched, eyes round as pieces of eight at the blurring blades. Blacky's next charge would be his last.

In three hardly seen slashes, Blacky's swords hit the deck, hands still attached just before his head tumbled from its shoulders. The headless body still stood, confused, as his neck stump pumped, spraying blood trying to figure out what happened. The ship fell silent as the body finally crumpled looking for its missing parts. The stunned crew froze as Jamey quick moved on with the plot.

Patch, also amazed, whacked the remaining three guards across the back of the head with a belaying pin, felling them to the deck. Jamey jumped over the headless hulk to the captain and pricked his blade under his chin, pinning him to the mast. The captain, owl-eyed, froze on tiptoes. Jamey turned to the crew.

"Now lads, ya got wha asked, be it me and the treasure for command or the good cap'n here?"

Patch moved to protect Jamey's back as the men murmured for and against. Then, a loyal crewman, hidden behind the mast, lunged at Jamey, his knife held low meant for the belly. As quick, a thrown dagger hit the assassin solid in the heart, dropping him like an anchor.

The tense moment broke when Gato swung from the rigging, pulled his knife free, and stood next to Jamey.

"I'm with ya mate."

It was over. They won. The ship was theirs. Jamey's next thought was how to solve the problem of the phantom treasure.

Over the next two morns, they cemented their control. The other pirate ship was boarded and the captain relieved with Patch in command. Both pirate captains, in irons, were locked in a low hold with contact ordered only by Gato. Jamey and Patch moved to the master's cabins and dressed to fit their new station. New loyal ship's officers, with Gato's advice, were chosen with final approval by the crew. New ship's articles, drawn and sworn over a boarding ax, marked proper shares for all.

After witnessing Jamey's skill with the cutlass, no man dared question the changing orders. Tales in the fo'c'sle of his daring feat grew and when told to the men that did not see, it created even more respect for the new captains.

Alone that eventide in Jamey's cabin, Patch raised his tankard high for a toast, his smile wide. "We did it mate, we did it!"

Jamey's mug, tipping his friends, smiled. "We'r a good team awright."

Feeling their luck, they gulped the sweet rum.

"Was next? How bout the treasure?" Patch asked.

"Been thinkin on that. We be close to where you and yer sis was sold, true?"

Patch's eye brightened. "Yer right ther. The slave market be south and east a bit, a stick close to Algiers."

"Well, what say you we check to see if we can find her?"

"It be hard. Fate mus bless us," Patch murmured, suddenly hopeful.

"We got luck this far. Les give it a go. Were close an I been thinkin a plan… Look here," Jamey said, pointing to the chart table.

chapter 13

"STICK IT SLOW," he ordered. "Twist it."

The rusty sliver pushed against the old man's skin until it could yield no more. The iron poked through with a spurt of blood over the screaming pleas of the dying man.

"God *Diablo*, I love this," he reveled, trembling with delight, licking his lips, savoring the metal blood taste in the air. "I love their torment."

His thoughts centered, instructing his attendant to shove in another shard. The old man's eye bulged with pain as he pleaded for mercy.

"*Por favor, por favor señor*, in God's name, kill me quickly, have pity."

"Do you confess to God you fathered the witch you call a daughter?"

He hoped for more denials so the torture could continue. He loved the suffering. The pain was beautiful.

The old man hung limp from the shackles, barely conscious with one eye gouged, leaving a blood-dripping hole. His front teeth were broken, fingers cut off, and his soft belly skinned. The raw smell of black-red blood filled the room with the sweet stench he loved. He enjoyed watching the air turn it from shiny red to black syrup thick. He hoped the old man would last a little longer. It was so enjoyable.

The attendant pulled the prisoner's head back at the question and his one eye focused slowly on the face of his inquisitor.

What he saw was the devil himself. Covered in a black hooded robe hiding his baldhead, he stood stumped fat. The glare from the fire pit off his bright beady eyes made him look like a rat peering from his hole. The old man swore they glowed from the fires of hell, one eye black as death and the other cold white.

Father Tomás laughed, watching the old man's fear. He loved the terror they felt. He truly believed he was gifted the devil's eyes.

Tomás was always short with jutting features set with round rodent eyes. He remembered his grandparents crossing themselves when his one eye turned. He was eight when he woke one morn with a headache and one eye turned ghost white with a thin black ring. In sunlight, his head hurt terribly, like stabbing needles. The *medico* just shook his head and crossed himself with his keepers, agreeing Tomás was possessed with *diablo vista*, the evil eye.

Other children in the village taunted and poked him with sticks calling him a "*blanco carne* bastard". With a body soft and pudgy, his sneak walk marked him a coward as he retreated in hate, mumbling threats of revenge. His grandparents tried to beat the evil from his body with thick sticks. He was not their blood and they only took him in for the bribe. Afraid to murder, they let him live but resolved to do their Catholic duty and exorcise *El Diablo* from his evil body. They chained him in the root cellar where he cowered, snarling, trying to escape their blows.

Tomás learned to hate deep over that time, his only fear, fire. Like any animal, it intrigued and frightened him and when his family keepers discovered his fear, they controlled him by poking torches in his face. The orange fingers mesmerized him, believing it to be the devil's beast, even more vile than him. Tomás knew *Diablo's bestia* devoured all in its path, its appetite voracious, all consuming in its evil.

Tomás learned to love all pain except pain from fire. Even the rain drop flicker from a candle chilled him to the bone. He feared and coveted it for fire was the ultimate torture. He wished he was fire for it was truly the prince's beast. Any other pain was wonderful. It made him feel alive. He especially enjoyed slicing his own skin and tasting the blood.

Over many earth's turns, Tomás developed an animal's cunning for survival. His black and opaque eye, under heavy brows, furtively watched for any opportunity to escape. Crouching in the damp hole, he worked his chains against a granite stone every night, grinding until his hands were raw. Finally, at fourteen and a full moon, fate broke a rusted link and he escaped. Roaming the village, he discovered his true calling, hunting others and the ecstasy of torture.

She was a young girl, named Maria, leaving the field in a rising moon. God, it was good, so good, he loved hurting her. Gouging her with sticks and tearing her flesh made him feel faint with rapture. The pure joy of seeing her fear and pain watching her bleed to death pumped his blood to final ejaculation. He sliced his arm completing his pleasure.

"Thank you God for making me the devil's consort," he whispered, relishing his kill.

The first is always the sweetest, he thought. Of course, there were many others. He lost count. Before moving on, he ravaged the whole village with his final revenge, his keepers. His hatred boiled as they goaded, telling him his mother and father had thrown him away because he had *Diablo's* soul. He deep hated his unknown mother and the man that sired him.

With rage only assuaged by blood revenge, he smiled, remembering his grandparent's pitiful faces, clutching their puny crucifixes. He cut their arteries, taunting them as they slowly died and then, with a flint touched to oil, he loosed the beast to devour them. He thought it funny their names were Jesus and Maria. They died too quick.

He remembered the exact moment his epiphany dawned. It was at his lowest despair, lying alone in the black of the cellar, shivering from the cold, wishing for death. It was simple if one just thought about it. People hurt and tortured him. They were Christians and followers of God. So God is responsible. Since God hated him, he hated God. *El Diablo* is God's archenemy so he would join forces with Satan to torture and kill Christians in his name. Really, it was so simple if one just thought about it. He smiled, with rapture, recalling his deep dream about Satan, circled by his flaming beast, anointing him, filling his soul with black grace.

But now, at last, he was a priest, *Monsignoire* Tomás Miguel Costa, God's *generale* in the holy order of the inquisition. It had taken many earth's turns of deception but Satan gave him the strength. His badge of authority from Rome covered the entire Christian world. He, the grand inquisitor, enforced the twenty-eight articles of the inquisition against accused Jews, Protestants, infidels, and heretics. His personal guard, holy *Familiares*, rooted the devil from men's souls wherever it might be.

"What a comedy," he giggled. He was really *El Diablo's* general and foremost advocate. He killed Christians for pleasure and, of course, to please his prince.

"The old man is dying you fool. Quick, burn his hand, that will wake him."

The sweating soldier put flame to the old man's hand causing him to jerk and scream, his only eye bulging in pain. Father Tomás reached and twisted a shard sticking in the dying body and asked again. "Do you confess old man? Do you admit you fathered the witch named Maria?"

The old man's mouth parted, blood spittle dripping, staring back, his eye glassed, unseeing.

"Damn, damn, he is dead, you idiot."

The soldier withered in fear.

Tomás suddenly calmed.

"No matter, pig hook him to the wall for example. The day is late. We will save the witch for tomorrow."

Tomás wanted to retire to his quarters to cut himself and fantasize about the old man's agony. That was the best part. He enjoyed prolonging his pain until the ecstasy could be borne no more. His ultimate release allowed a rare deep sleep, dreaming of tomorrow's torture.

He was one with *El Diablo.*

chapter 14

THE TWO MERCHANT ships sailed past the garrisoned fort into the port of Algiers and tied up smartly to the pier. Two suns labor with council from their Moroccan mates readied the pirate ships for this ruse. Their look was now ordinary merchant ships with proper flags displayed and crew cleaned.

Jamey, posing as a French trader, debarked his vessel with a retinue of six Moroccan mates and assistant, Patch. With a cocky flair, they roamed the town, keeping a sharp eye, talking to shop owners and street vendors, spreading the lie. This was their first of many voyages for goods to ship to France. Jamey flashed gold and word spread fire fast creating local dreams of a quick profit.

One pesky fellow hung close begging to be their guide claiming no one knew Algiers better. His whining chatter never ceased while Jamey pretended no interest. Finally, sensing Patch was going to hurt him if he did not quiet, he pretended to give in and put him on pay.

"A guide may be useful, as you say. I want to know the city and purchase the best goods at fair value."

"*Oui, Monsieur*, I am your man. Razza is my name. No one knows better than I," he quipped in a singsong voice, bowing continually.

"Also, I want contact with those of influence to secure my welcome for future voyages. Can you do this?" Jamey asked, thinking he enjoyed acting the wealthy man.

"*Oui, oui, Monsieur*, I know all who hold power in Algiers."

They spent the sun's light pretending to shop, asking one question after the other. Who ran the city? Who was the wealthiest? Who had the most influence? Who sells slaves? Are they good quality? Patch and Jamey listened sharp, hoping to hear the name of the man who bought Patch's sister, *Bahon Cadif.* Razza rattled on, naming all that was asked, like old friends, except the one they wanted to hear.

"Who has the best ivory? The best silk? The best pottery? The best jewels?"

Razza ticked the names off one finger at a time ending with, "Ah, Bahon Cadif, the jeweler," he ended with pride to prove he knew all.

Suddenly alert, they continued to ask other questions mixed with general inquiries of the jeweler, pretending no special interest. As night lanterns lit, they finished by asking about prices and locations, paying close attention to Cadif's residence. Back at the ship, they paid Razza well and instructed him to return in two morns as the morrow was to be spent seeing repairs to their ships.

Razza backed away, bowing with hands at prayer, blessing Jamey's generosity, assuring him he would be prompt.

Jamey and Patch dismissed the crew and returned to scout the city alone in the fading light. They lingered around Cadif's house with an eye for the best trick to accomplish their mission. Both, without words, thought the same, the task will be tough. The house, a small fortress, was large with two levels surrounded by a stone wall three men high. The only entry was a heavy double door planked with iron in front and a small arched gate securely barred in the rear.

While they skulked in the shadows, a small wagon rolled up to the front gate. The driver lazily dismounted and slammed the large knocker three bangs followed by two more. Four counts later, he repeated the bangs in the same order. Jamey and Patch exchanged glances with a grin as the gates swung open and the guard waved the wagon through.

Strolling back to the ship, they mentally mapped the route through the narrow lanes. Later, after a quick meal, they hunkered over the candled chart table to fashion a plan.

The next morrow, the full light was spent briefing the crew, assuring them the treasure was in Cadif's house. Jamey hoped the lie would not get their throats cut knowing the crew had one God, his name was gold.

Assignments were made and instructions repeated ten again. Gato was left to command the ships with orders for their part. Timing was critical. Lives depended on it.

The search and rescue of Patch's sister was kept secret.

Later, as the moon rose, Patch leaned on the ship's rail alone, silent with his thoughts, daring to hope Cho Ling was there, safe. He had dreamed this time since that black day on the docks. His eyes lifted staring at the peppered stars, entreating the heavens to help him save her.

The split moon rose bright. It was time. Jamey and Patch huddled with six more hiding under a sail cloth in the wagon bed. A last decision caused them to mount a long brass nine pointing out the rear loaded with scrap shot. It was a tight fit and after a bumpy ride and grumbles, the wagon finally pulled up outside the double doors of Cadif's residence. The Moroccan pirate driver hopped down and swung the iron knocker, using the signal. Time stood quiet but finally the doors dragged open and the pirate jumped aboard, driving the wagon through.

The gate guard's arm hailed a stop.

"Who are you? Where is Azul?"

"Azul is sick. I bring the load," the pirate lazily replied. He liked this trick.

"What do you carry?" The guard asked, moving toward the back of the wagon. Patch tensed, his blade ready to strike.

"Goods for your bakers," the pirate braced as the guard reached for the sailcloth.

"Do not delay me, the meat will spoil," he added. "You and I will feel your master's anger."

The guard stopped, remembering he was also due to be relieved and was looking forward to some wine and a promise made by his woman. With a glance, he waved him through.

"Hurry then, around the side to the first door."

The pirate flicked the reins, smiling, thinking he was very clever.

Out of sight in the rear, all jumped from the wagon. Jamey knocked his long bow and shot a whisper arrow a full distance through the mouth of the guard in the watchtower. His men gaped, amazed, all thinking the same but moved quickly as planned to the scullery, tying and gagging the frightened slaves and securing the house.

Cho Ling popped awake in fright. The screaming, mixed with bangs and slams, caused her to curl tight, tucking her head and clutching her knees. If she could just fly away, she prayed. Her dark tiny closet was her only safe haven. She hugged herself, still as a nesting quail, listening to her mistress babbling between clunks and thumps. She heard them enter the room outside her thin closet door. Then, everything was quiet as she strained to hear.

Moments, like ages, passed with muffled orders and curses when footsteps, hard and heavy, moved close past her cave. She trembled, afraid of monsters of every type. Maybe they might not find her. *If she could only fly away.*

Her sanctuary door banged open. She jerked jumped and flattened against the back wall, shrinking even more, her heart thrumming, eyes squinched shut.

"Cho Ling, is it you?" the rough voice sounded in her native tongue.

She peeked. The light stung her eyes as the shadowed monster with one eye loomed over her looking like a black ghost. It was like one of her night shivers. Maybe she would wake up.

"Cho Ling, is it you?" The voice, softer as his meaty hand took her arm and gently raised her.

Confused and frightened, she stood tiny and cowering. Patch looked close but it had been so long. She was the only one of his kind in the household but this girl was the same size as his sister on their island long ago. Cho Ling saw the huge man's disappointed look.

A tall white man came over. "Tis her?"

"Nay, she's tittered and can't talk, it looks."

"We have to go. Our time is up."

"Give a shake." Patch said, turning to the girl, calming his voice.

"Look here, I'm looking for my sister, Cho Ling. Do you know her?"

Cho Ling tucked herself lower, terrified until she heard the word sister and looked up at the stern face, seeing the good eye the same as hers.

"It is you, brother?" she asked timidly.

He quieted, looking closer at the small girl. "Yes sister, it is me."

The white man hollered, "Grab her an les go."

With a quick hug, he carefully lifted and slung her around to his back, slipping her into a sling rigged like babes carried by mothers from his village. Wide-eyed, she hardly breathed watching the white man barking orders at the men ransacking the rooms.

"Patch, thers no value here. Does she know wher the master hides his gems?"

Patch asked in their tongue where Cadif hid his wealth and where he was. He had an old score to settle. Cho Ling pointed to a hidden room with a vault. In no time, a hole was busted in the wall displaying a king's ransom. Jamey gave a sigh of relief, their shipmates would cheer.

When the men started hauling the treasure, a fat pudgy man hiding behind a chest, squealed, hopped up, and tried to run. A mate snagged him by the collar and chuckled. "Hola, Patch, this be wha yer lookin fer?"

Patch stared at Cadif as memories of the slave quarters shook his mind. He looked the same, except fatter and oilier. Patch stalked toward him, sister hanging on, to finish what he dreamed a thousand nights.

Cadif, seeing murder in Patch's eye, squirmed and wiggled against the pirate's hold. Panicked, he hard twisted loose and waddle-ran toward the stairs. Patch, hot behind, reached for his neck just as Cadif glanced over his shoulder and tripped over a treasure chest, crashing through the hand railing head first. His pitiful scream stopped with the melon splat of his head hitting the stone floorbelow. Patch, with Cho Ling peeking over his shoulder, looked down, quiet, feeling the silent relief of justice served. They heard Cadif's last moan as his blood oozed over the white marble making its own art.

Patch returned back to the task. Cho Ling hung onto her brother's thick neck, perched in the sling, eyes bright and round, heart drumming like a wren. This high, she had a great view.

Then, she heard the alarm bells ring as lanterns and voices came alive from outside. The white man gave a curse, shouted orders, and they were out of the house, jumping in the wagon and racing through the open gate. Their team of two galloped hard, wagon bouncing, through the narrow alleys toward the wharf. Glancing back, she saw eight guards, mounted hot and gaining. At the next turn, the team scrambled to a stop with a sliding jerk, the white man shouting, "Give em splinters from the nine, Patch."

In one motion, her brother yanked the jacket and fired the hole. The peppered blast dropped half the eight. Her saviors whooped and the wagon took off, pressing the horses to the limit.

After passing the next corner, she watched a wagon pulled across the lane by two and flipped on its side, blocking their pursuers. Racing by the next alley, another wagon was pulled across the lane and flipped over, jamming the way. Suddenly, an explosion shook the air and she looked forward at the glow of a huge fire. She held on to her brother tighter.

"Ho, ho, right on time, Gato did well," the white man hollered.

"It'll keep em busy, fer sure,"

Two more sharp turns, close to capsizing, and the wagon slowed quick, acting normal as any other. The team, blowing hard, trotted to the dock and halted at the ship's gangplank.

A huge warehouse was aflame at the far end, some distance, drawing the whole town's attention. The orange fire glow cast deviled shadows as the band hustled aboard their ship with the treasure and chopped the docking lines. The last four salts blocking the lanes raced from the dark and jumped aboard, huffing deep.

After casting off, the ship slipped on the tide and started a gentle roll. Cho Ling, still on her brother's back, was taken below. Squeezing down the narrow passageway, she heard the white man snapping orders. In the cabin, Patch swung her down, hugged her and instructed her to stay put before disappearing back on deck.

One glass later, they watched the dock fire fade as they floated past the harbor fort. Outside the channel, the sails took hold and the ship bent to the wind. The sudden heeling knocked Cho Ling off her feet, banging into the bulkhead. Rubbing the bump, she laughed in relief. Her brother saved her as she dreamed forever. Now she would be happy. Exhausted by the excitement, she fell asleep on Jamey's bunk.

Eight bells clanged her awake. Lifting up on her elbows, she wondered a moment where she was. Then, a rare smile covered her face as happiness filled her heart. She was finally free.

She tried to wash and straighten herself as best she could. It took some doing balancing against the roll of the ship and pouring into the bowl. Pulling her hair loose, she let it fall raven slick to her waist.

Standing on tiptoes didn't help much trying to see herself in the looking glass and balancing on a stool on a rolling cabin sole was dangerous. She straightened her simple mint green shift, pressing her hand against the wrinkles, wishing she had proper clothes. It was a little cold.

A light knock at the door brought her eyes around to see her brother standing with a big grin. They stood a moment, looking at each other, seeing the changes time had made. Suddenly they laughed and hugged, talking at the same time. Her heart flowed with happiness.

It was a long sun. The treasure was divided according to ship's articles and Jamey announced he was returning to England. Patch also introduced him to Cho Ling.

A rap on the cabin door and there he was, tall and slim with smiling eyes and cocky grin. She had only seen two other white men in her life and they were not like this.

"So this is who we risked our life for?" he teased.

"Aye, Jamey, this be my wee sister, Cho Ling."

She stood, head down, eyes lowered, hands folded together, stilled quiet. Sensing her embarrassment, Jamey calmed his voice, thinking of his sister.

"I am pleased to meet my friend's sister, Cho Ling."

She nodded and bowed, whispering in her limited English, "Than you."

Both knew she endured much over the years. Then, finding her brother, the rescue, the ship and the open sea was a lot to fathom. Jamey excused himself. He still had not seen her face.

That eventide, Patch escorted her on deck. She felt wonderful with her brother at her side. They had spent most of the day exchanging stories of their separate fates and she cried for both of them.

The slow setting sun felt good against the tickling breeze. Cho Ling's raven hair flowed soft like a flag as they joined Jamey at the rail. Her brother gifted her some silks and according to her culture, she fashioned a clever wrapped sarong flowing to the deck. She seemed to float as she moved with feminine grace.

She watched him standing straight with a strange instrument in his hands, intent on the sun as it kissed the sea. Hearing their approach, he turned and watched her graceful moves. She flushed, feeling his eyes touching her. Eternally self-conscious, she kept her head bowed as trained.

After a short briefing with Patch, he looked at her, somewhat puzzled.

"I hope you are comfortable, Cho Ling," she heard him say.

"Yes, very much, than you," she whispered, head down.

"Look up and see the ocean," Patch said.

Shy and unsure, she held her gaze low by habit of slavery. Jamey, a little impatient, stepped in front of her.

"Come now, let us see who you are," he said softly, putting his finger under her chin, gently lifting her face to his.

As she came into view, his grin turned serious. He was expecting the face of a child but saw the beauty of a young woman. Perfect pearl skin against the blackest hair he had ever seen. His heart quickened as she lifted her eyes to his. They took his breath. High cheekbones cradled opal soft eyes so deep Jamey thought he might fall in. Her exotic essence stirred his blood.

"By the saints, Patch, she's a beauty. How can this jewel be your sister, you ugly sot?" he said, smiling with mischief as their eyes held.

Hypnotized, Jamey added, "You have eyes green as gems and as beautiful."

Drowning in her innocent gaze, he remembered his delicate sister, recalling her pet nickname and on impulse, said, "I will call you Jade from this day to always remind you of your beauty."

Jade lowered her eyes, feeling the thrill of his touch. Her heart fluttered full brimmed as her face reddened. She felt faint.

"Patch is my brother, which means you are my sister," he added, breaking her spell.

Jade did not want to be his sister.

*

So, Jade it was. Even her brother called her the same. She loved it. It made her feel special and pretty but mostly because it was Jamey's name for her. She would pray to Buddha for his love.

As moons filled and passed, the ships routine ruled. They were hit dumb when she prepared a mat for sleeping in a tiny hanging locker and furious, learning of the life and conditions she endured. She was promptly settled in her brother's cabin and he bunked with Jamey. Thrilled with her own space, she took charge of their cabins, keeping them spotless and in order at all times. From that day, their clothes were clean, neat, and in good repair plus she prepared special meals against the eye of the grouchy ship's cook. It was wonderful taking care of them.

Topside, she was restricted to the quarterdeck away from the curious crew and at day's end, they insisted she join them for the evening meals. Over laughs and giggles, her eyes bright against gimbaled candles, she quickly learned Jamey's tongue. Afterward, the three strolled the officer's deck and for the first time since stolen, she felt loved and important protected between the two men. With balmy twilights and changing colors of sea and sky, she wished time would stop as the salt air cleansed her soul and blazing sunsets promised a good morrow.

In Jamey's company, Jade could not help gazing at her feet, head bowed because of her slave training, plus, she was afraid he might see the growing love in her eyes. Jamey, busy with ship's duties, thought she was just shy and was determined to tease her out of it.

"Come now, Jade, let me see those beautiful eyes."

Blushing, she would slowly lift them to his and he would sigh.

"Ah, what beauty, my day is made," he said, teasing with the truth.

The voyage chucked well with fair weather and a together crew. When the two oceans met an all hands parlay was held. In short order, the one ship, under a newly elected captain, went their way, wanting the same life, afraid of England and past sins.

Gato cursed his folly and decided to tag along with the two adventurers.

Jamey's mission, not yet shared, was to inform Queen Elizabeth of Spain's designs and seek a letter of margue for legal right to raid Spanish vessels. He hoped a suitable gift of Cadif's jewels and his father's reputation as captain of the guard would sway any decision in his favor.

Later, standing alone on the quarterdeck, gazing at the hued sky, Jamey thought once more of his lost family and his vow. Finally knowing his family's killer, he pledged himself again, swearing he would avenge them.

"You will die by my hand, Damon DeSago."

chapter 15

THE SUN BURNED and the earth was kettle hot. Waves of heat rippled, blurring her view as salty sweat stung her eyes straining to see the field's end. Frustrated, her finger swept the wet from her forehead as she blinked under cupped hands. It seemed forever long.

Gazing over the stunted corn, the steamy mist wafted skyward like spirit waves. Fat beads rolled between her breasts as she straightened and arched back, hands on hips, stretching sore muscles. The sun was just middle high and she was already tired. She felt the cracking heat burn through her cotton shift as she wiped more drips from her brow. She would not work at the inn this night.

Again, her golden eyes surveyed the field with a shading hand, wishing it smaller. Then, with a hard sigh, she sucked a mouthful of stale water from the goatskin letting it dribble down her chin and chest. Sloppy soaking her scarf, she slapped it around her neck, welcoming the trickle down the curve of her back.

With a resigned breath, she bent again, attacking the devil weeds with hacking swings, beating its own rhythm, allowing her thoughts to wander, wishing for happier times. There weren't many.

"It is not fair," she muttered to herself, eyes watering in anger. "Why does it fall to me?" she asked, stopping to stomp a fist-sized spider before stooping again, swinging the machete.

The incessant sun never blinked.

She hated being the oldest left with ten brothers and sisters. With her drunken father and mother broken by life, their care fell on her. It wasn't fair.

"When my sixteenth comes, I'm leavin, no matter what," she whispered to the air as the machete killed another immortal weed. "I'll run to the biggest town in Jamaica. Santiago, thas were I'll go."

Maria was different. Born Maria Aurora Aragon sixteen turns past this November, her father was a distant relative of Catherine of Aragon, Princess of Spain and divorced wife of Britain's King Henry the eighth. Before Maria was born, her father was banished to Jamaica by his relatives for reasons he kept secret, even when drunk. He married her mother and worked a small patch to stay alive with their children, hoe in hand, sweating at age five. Being the first, she knew no other life except what she heard at the inn.

Inheriting her mother's French blood, Maria was fair compared to her brothers and sisters. Her midnight hair and gold-cast eyes, big and round and rimmed in hazel, seemed to verify that claim and set her apart from the rest making her ripe for teasing.

"Maria, you got goat eyes." A younger brother declared one day. The others laughed, even her father, and she was called goat eyes from that time. Hurt, she felt alone and different but as the seasons passed, her heart turned tough, angering her manner. When pushed too far, her amber eyes flashed, warning her Castilian blood ran hot. Then the caution was, "Best not mess with Maria."

The village inn was her only relief that allowed a smile. She loved to sing and had a natural voice, ripe and strong, and the landlord let her perform some nights for any coin tossed. Those few times she was happy except for the lewd words and hands of old men slapped away. Even her brothers tried to touch so she kept her guard.

With a sigh, she bent again to clear the corn, dreaming of something better, someday, someday.

"These damn devil weeds."

Her machete chop killed another.

CHAPTER 16

FATHER TOMÁS WAS elated. *El Diablo* again smiled on him. He snickered, reading the thick parchment again as his thumb brushed lazily over the thick ink, tracing the curly signature. His dark prince filled his soul with black grace. He was the anointed one.

Tomás giggled. His holiness, the pope, granted his seal of approval to extend the holy inquisition to rout the devil in their western lands; the Indies, Jamaica, Hispianola, and the Americas. And all was to be under his Catholic power. Every Christian and heathen soul would be judged by him and in this effort, of course, he would gain worldly riches.

He was surprised he actually salivated when he contemplated this new power. Now his unfettered torture would expand, using different methods he developed by trial and error. Of course, he reminded himself, the true test of perfect torture was a fine balance of ultimate pain without death. Tomás smiled, knowing he was the master, his name was feared throughout Christian Europe. Now his power would reach to the end of the world. The thought brought forth a soft giggle.

He looked around with satisfaction, standing still, tasting the fear in the air. The chamber of the inquisition, *Casa Santa*, was his improved design. It was a stark narrow room without windows and sparsely furnished with a long table sitting five chairs on one side and just one on the other. At the far end was an altar covered in black velvet with a lone crucifix and six candles cupping a bible. The last piece, a pulpit, stood to the side with a single candle eye high. He followed the basic design from his hero, Father *Tomás Torquemada*, who forged the current grand movement.

Tomás thought it no mistake he was named the same so he made a special pilgrimage to the monastery, *Saint Tomás of Avila,* in Father Torquemada's honor. He remembered standing in the sacristy, completely silent, feeling his body soak in Torquemada's evil, Satan's angel on earth. His ecstasy filled his member full.

Finally, he shook himself from his trance. He had much to do. Father Tomás Miguel Costa, protector of the faith. He giggled again.

That very night, Lucifer visited him, his revelation unveiled.

Tomás twisted in his sleep, sweat bathed his spongy body, his heart pulsed and pounded as he gurgled in a fit, his blasphemy pure, the command sure.

Satan called forth his Incubus to lay with his mother and Tomás was conceived from his foul seed. Now Tomás, son of Satan, the anointed one, was chosen to go forth and prepare the way. He, Satan's prince, was chosen to rid the earth of God's favorites. The time was at hand. Satan, King of Gehenna, ruler of the netherworld, will rise, conquer and smother the earth, his final dominion complete.

Tomás squirmed and jerked, chewing his tongue, arching, spine bowed, his grand mal gorged. Moments later, he lay, spent, at peace, his tongue blood soaking his robe.

"Your wish is my command, almighty one."

*

As he shuffled about, hidden in his black hooded robe, one was reminded of a rodent scurrying around preparing for this newest venture. With careful whispers, those under his charge called him the *Diablo's Rata* and knew he was without mercy. His beady eyes, one black, one white, flitted nervously as he wrote orders to his guard, the holy *familiares*.

Two ships would serve him flying the papal flag of Rome on God's mission. His ship was christened the *Santa Cruz*, the other, *Santa Bella*. Both galley ships, seating one hundred and sixty men at oars, were more suitable for flat waters. Knowing their command limitations, the two ship captains, already upset with their orders, were introduced to Monsignor Tomás Costa and silently prayed God was not angry with them.

The small convoy finally cast off and Tomás frowned, remembering the hardest part would be the three-moon voyage. No one to torture for three long moons. It would be difficult but he would manage. He would just have to suffer.

He couldn't stop giggling.

BOOK THREE

CHAPTER 1

ENGLAND AT LAST. Finishing the birthing of the ship in Rye, Clarice's village, they hustled to the Mermaid Inn where Jamey left his father's weapons. True to his word, the innkeeper kept them safe and for an extra coin for storage they were again in Jamey's hands. They felt good, like old friends.

With the heft of his father's gear strapped on, Jamey had purpose again knowing his family's murderer. He was one step closer to finding justice and revenge. Patch, never seeing him so armed, was amazed by his warrior look. He now understood Jamey's talent with the sword.

In the dying day, they decided to scout the village. Jamey stripped his gear, but for a whip and dagger, before heading out the door with Patch at his side, rigging knife on his belt.

"Everthin looks the same," Patch commented.

"Aye . . . I wonder the fate of Clarice and her mother?"

Before dusk, they climbed the hill to Cambor castle and asked the answer from the major-domo. At first suspicious of their cut, Jamey's gold piece wiggled his tongue as he pocketed the coin, lowering to a whisper, glancing over his shoulder. The tale was, he said, that after the attack on the count's yacht, Clarice was held for ransom and the mother released to collect the tribute. All others were murdered except those sentenced to the galley. The mother, after witnessing her husband's throat cut, was frantic to save her daughter and raised the ransom demands through friends, pledging their wealth and properties. The gold was paid and Clarice was released, sadly, in poor condition.

The blood money created a huge debt bringing the family to ruin but because of their title, they were treated well, protected by relatives. They moved from the village to London, he thought, and shortly thereafter Clarice married some Duke. There was no more news since that. The servant fingered the coin in his pocket, guessing its heft, and said he knew no more, closing the door in their face with nary a good day. Jamey and Patch glanced at each other, thinking quiet on the news as they wandered back to the inn.

"They lived then," Patch muttered half to himself.

"Aye, but the cost. The privileged know not the pain of the world."

Later, at dusk, they sat in the public room against a quiet corner, backs to the wall. A hearty land meal of venison stew over thick bread matched Patch's tongue pie under heavy cut bacon. A shared jug of purple wine with pears and cheese made them both feel like new men.

Next morn found the two on deck with last orders for outfitting the ship before Jamey left on his mission to seek an audience with the queen. A messenger was dispatched ahead while Jamey traveled in a well appointed carriage with horsed guards front and rear. The tribute from Morocco he carried for the queen gave him an excuse for not riding a stupid horse. Horses still made him sneeze, plus, he wanted to look smart with his entourage to sway any decision in his favor.

He hoped the rumors were true that vast wealth on the Spanish Main waited there for a brave crew. He would gain those riches to ensure a successful hunt for his family's killer. The thought made his blood warm as he pictured Damon's hated face.

Patch stayed behind with funds to outfit the ship and provisions stocked for a voyage of four full moons. Additional gun ports were cut to mount six more cannon allowing her to bark thirty-six at once. Crew, shipwrights, and merchants of every stripe pressed from morn till rising moon. New paint from stem to stern, bolts of new canvass cut and sewn by callused hands were hanked on with new cordage spliced and reeved through fresh greased blocks. Then, heavier planks steamed and bent to the bulwarks changed her to a formidable fighting ship. For good measure, they bedded two Long Toms on the bow and levered the standing rigging taught and sealed with fresh pitch. Patch added an extra spritsail to the bowsprit and stuns'ls to every spar on both masts giving the ship faster way by half more through the water. Of course, the bowels required a bit more ballast and the masts extra standing rigging, but the debt was worth the prize.

While Patch was busy on deck, Jade commandeered the aft cabins and recruited the ship's carpenter to modify their two by building a small cabin between. Before Jamey left, they wrestled with the problem of what to do with her. The ship was embarking on a dangerous venture, fate unknown, and a female on board, no matter how small, was foolish and believed unlucky by the crew.

When informing Jade she would have to stay behind, she dropped her head a moment in trained submission. But then, she straightened up with wet eyes as tall as she could declaring in no uncertain terms her intention to sail with them. She would not stay behind and that was final.

So it was her tiny cabin was created between them. She loved it. She had her own space with a bunk and chest topped by a coveted looking glass. Womanly touches with silks and brocades plus balls of sweet soap from a tinker on the wharf made it feel like home. She also had one wide hatched window looking aft to the sea so she could lie in her bunk and daydream.

For the first time she felt safe and secure in her comfortable nest. She slept at peace hearing her brother and Jamey's snoring through the bulkheads. One night, grinning, she discovered if she imagined just right, their tenor and rhythm matched melodies of music from her childhood. She felt alive and worthy with her own place between the two she cared about more than anyone else in the whole world. With pure pleasure, she assumed her duty in the sterncastle, keeping everything shipshape, including the forward cabins of the four lesser officers.

Between labors, brother and sister visited the village. All was new and wonderful to Jade, visiting shops and dining at better inns dressed in her new finery bought by her brother. Patch escorted her proud, acting the worldly man as they toured here and there. Jade asked unending questions forcing him to fib a bit to save face. It was a special time.

The crew felt right. Some older hands elected to swallow the anchor landlubbered with something soft. With Cadif's portion of jewels heavy in their pocket, their ending days would be pleasant. The others, a mixed bag of Turks, Africans, Moroccans, a couple of French convicts, and a spattering of Irish worked and fought together now for a time. Their faith in Jamey and Patch had won a large treasure rescuing the sister so they willingly signed on with dreams of a hundred-weight or more on this new adventure. Lined up straight and sober, they placed their mark on the ship's log and swore, hailing with a slug of rum, "A gold chain or a wooden leg, we'll fight beside ya."

Expected grumbling about Jade aboard, sure a bad luck omen, were soon put to rest. The crew figured although she was kittle cargo, she'd been lucky so far. Plus, she was too small to be a full woman so she must still be a child, which although unusual, would not upset the Gods. Also, she was Patch's sister and Jamey's favorite and none wanted to press the issue in those quarters. But the chickens jumped when she found out they thought her more child than woman. She stomped around for a time in a full fit until Jamey told her he thought she was a beautiful lady.

"Bonny fair, you are. Any man who says different will feel my blade."

Suddenly, her day brightened.

Workers jumped too as suns passed and the next full moon found the ship turned right. With a step back and a proud look, a true sailing man knew his ship was as a wench, handsome as a woman from stem to stern, anxious to serve her men. Treat her right and she'd stay true. The bond of trust between ship and sailor could only be felt by those who been there for they knew she was a living spirit.

On schedule, Jamey returned with smiles and a letter of marque in hand. Queen Elizabeth remembered his mother with fondness and was distressed to learn her fate. During his short stay, Sir Wallshingham, the court's intelligence minister, carefully briefed him. He was informed of Admiral Drake and Raleigh's expeditions and the tensions with Spain. When finished, Jamey left the queen's court with knowledge of a bigger world.

Jamey inquired of action against DeSago for crimes reported by Clarice and her mother and was told that charges were made to Spanish authorities. They investigated and their report declared DeSago acted on his own, a pirate, which we should be familiar with, and a warrant posted. King Phillip demanded the same warrants be issued against

English pirates to demonstrate good faith and action taken, forthwith. The message was clear. Spain would turn a blind eye and do nothing.

Jamey's inspection of the Raptor brought high praise to Patch and crew. Jade was excited to show him her efforts, but Jamey, noticing, lingered on deck. Jade, sensing his tease, gave him a dirty look, making him take pity as he flashed his rascal smile and followed her below. Again happy, with a wide grin, she showed off their spotless cabins and with some blushing, hers.

Back on deck, hands on hips and a final look around, Jamey declared the ship shaped for sea, only lacking her christened name. Informing all he had a surprise or two, he excused himself to the dock and returned with a huge eagle, screeching. His head and eyes were covered in a soft leather hood meant to calm but the jostling carriage ride made him furious. Patch and crew looked narrow as it shrieked and flapped its man size wings, digging talons hard into Jamey's leathered arm.

"Was this?" Patch asked.

"Tis a sea eagle. I found him in the queen's court, trained personal by a Turkish clan high in the mountains of Mongolia. It was presented to the queen but ignored under the care of the royal falconer. Biggest I ever seen."

"Was he fer?"

"Yull see in time. He is the reason for our ship's new name. We will christen her the *Raptor*.

"Raptor?"

"Means 'bird of prey'. Tis what we will do, prey on the Spanish."

Jamey turned and gave an order to two standing close. Jumping to the dock, they hauled aboard a huge thick-skinned drum most round as Patch's height. They grunted it in position, midship, mounted on its side in a cradle and lashed it tough to the mainmast.

Patch watched with many questions he decided not to ask.

Hearing the eagle scream, Jade peeked, poking her head through a hatch. She loved animals of all kinds, especially birds. She thought they were much better than humans. Climbing on deck for a closer look, eyes round with excitement, she thought the bird handsome and regal.

"She butiful," she whispered, approaching softly.

"Tis a male," Jamey said. "Better away Jade, he'll bite. He's still worked hot."

"I know," she said somewhat perturbed. "I not afraid. I no wan to scare him."

Murmuring softly, Jade moved to the side of the huge bird and he calmed immediately. Jamey and Patch looked at the other amazed at her affect. Jade was born a soul mate with animals and since a small child was aware of this special bond that welcomed her to their world. She crooned, petting its head and neck as the hooded bird bent low seemingly wanting to nuzzle.

"God's breath," Jamey said, feeling the depth of her spirit as her jade eyes, soft as northern moss, rose to meet his.

"His name will be *Gara*," she announced.

"Wha tha mean," Patch asked.

"The Claw." Jamey said.

Then, they overheard her whisper to the great eagle as she stroked the soft feathers.

"I will soar one day with you."

The last to complete was mounting a new figurehead chiseled from an oak beam. A large eagle ten hands high with wings spread wide and swept back, looked ready to attack with its neck stretched forward, open beaked and reaching talons. The whole affair was double gilded in gold except for the red glass eyes. When complete, a small celebration was held at the bow and the ship was christened *El Raptor*.

On the tide of early morn, the Raptor set sail for the Indies in search of Spanish gold.

chapter 2

AS THE SHIP drew near, he watched the purpled land rise ever larger. The clouded mist seemed dreamy as the gray mass lifted slowly from the sea with every passing turn of the glass. Home, he missed it. Carlos, he missed him as much. Damon hoped his dispatch to France was timely. A full earth's turn and four had passed since seeing him last. Damon lazily watched the crew skipping aloft to dump canvas as the ship eased sure and smooth into the harbor of Malaga, Spain's beautiful city. His thoughts were broken by barked orders and the hustle of the crew as the ship was smartly brought against the pier and cleated down. A hurrah from all set the mood. It was good to be back to his beloved land.

Because of his title, he was the first to step the gangplank. When his foot touched the ground, he realized he never allowed himself to feel affection except for his country and his brother. Now with their father avenged, his sole purpose was fealty to his king and the return of his family to power. It was his father's passion, costing his life, and now, Damon Vasques DeSago, his son, would complete the task in his name.

"*Hola, hola*! Damon, over here."

DeSago turned to see his one love.

"Carlos, my boy, you received my dispatch."

They embraced quickly but warmly.

"*Si*, I just arrived yestereve."

DeSago stood back and studied his brother. Tall as him but handsome, he was only twenty-five but a full man, a true *caballero*. He thought of him more as a son than a brother for he was now forty-two. Carlos was but a year when their father was murdered. He would be proud of Damon's' tutorage.

"How was France?" Damon asked.

"*Magnifico*, especially the *señoritas*," Carlos said, returning a smile.

"Your studies?"

"Done, *fini*."

"And their tongue?"

"*Oui, monsieur*. I can pass for any Frenchman.

"*Bueno*, and the sword?"

"I attended Saint Marcus as you instructed. You were correct. The Germans are masters of the saber, but I still prefer the rapier."

"Good, we will practice together on the morrow. But now, let us eat. Ship's fare is poor and I want to hear all the news."

Damon was pleased with Carlos's confident manner. He now had the skills and polish to assume his place. Damon would promote him at court if his meeting with *King Phillip* went well. Carlos was ready to play his part. Their father would be proud.

"A toast," Damon hailed, holding his glass high, matched by Carlos. "Our father has been avenged, completing the first of my vows. Our family name has been cleansed and is now ready for greatness."

"Hear, hear," Carlos braced.

*

Damon's audience with King Phillip was the next noon. Rumors said he was not happy. Fortunately, the fleet was still a quarter-moon out and Damon's scheme was already forming. But first, he would test his brother's art with the sword.

"*En guarde.*"

Carlos, cocky, assumed his stance boldly.

The poniard would not play a part this day and Damon thought to catch him napping with a flick of his blade in quarte. Carlos parried smoothly with a sure smile, fighting back a riposte. Damon, pleasantly surprised, parried in return.

"*Hola, Bueno!*" Damon said, quickly returning the attack, switching from thrust to cut.

Carlos leaped clear just in time. "Remember brother, this is just practice."

Carlos advanced with a feint and a clever moulinet, wheeled, coming back slash to point.

Damon parried all with effort, feeling the jarring clash to his shoulder. Embarrassed, his blood turned hot. Determined to teach his brother a lesson, he leaped forward, hammering Carlos's blade with cuts and thrusts, quarte, septime, prime. His speed slammed into Carlos as he tried to parry in vain. Sensing victory, Damon's tempo quickened, attacking, snarled lips showing his lost temper.

Carlos, sensing life or death, could not stand the pace and retreated from the field.

"*Por dios,* brother, *Alto! Alto!*

Carlos' alarm snapped Damon back to the present with apologies.

"*Lo siento mucho,* my son, are you hurt?"

His rage turned immediately to concern.

"*Pedir, perdón,* I lost my head.

Carlos looked at his brother with concern. Damon was always in complete command, master of his emotions. It shook him to see him this way.

"Recent pressures have been difficult." Damon said, brushing the incident aside, throwing his arm over his brother's shoulder.

"You have learned well but you must practice more."

Carlos gritted his teeth. His brother was never satisfied.

"I am good enough. In fact, I was challenged and fought a duel," he announced with some bravado.

Damon was shocked. "What! What for?"

"A *señorita* honor, in France."

Damon was furious, taking foolish chances over a woman, risking his plans.

"Do not look so alarmed. I won."

"I can see that. I forbid this recklessness for no purpose."

"You are my brother, not my father," Carlos snapped back, determined to stand up for himself. He was his own man.

Damon, sensing the challenge, calmed.

"I know, but you seem like a son and I am old enough to be your father," he said, his manner turning solemn.

"I made holy vows on the grave of our father. One..., was to raise you strong to carry our name. Second, was to avenge his death and the last, to finish his work to defeat Protestant England."

Carlos, seeing the passion in his eyes, relented.

"I apologize, brother. I know you want the best for me. We will work as one."

*

The rumors were as Damon heard. King Phillip was in a fit. That bitch, Elizabeth, refused a liaison marriage, again. Her and her puny island had the audacity to abandon the true faith declaring their land Protestant while Mary was cooling in Scotland. And now his invasion failed. His royal navy, the largest the earth had ever seen, fought not one battle. Changes would be made.

His ministers scurried around trying to soften the bad news as various ambassadors huddled with some amusement in the corner. The Flemish courtier watched close, as always, along with Sir Standon, the Florentine ambassador, waiting for this moment. Damon DeSago's fall from grace.

The heavy chamber door swung wide and the court crier announced, "Your Excellency, Don Damon Vasgues DeSago."

Damon marched forward in a liquid motion, head held high with complete confidence, daring anyone to challenge him in any arena. Except for his liege, the king he served, they were all lackeys in his eyes.

Damon halted in front of the throne, snapping his heels.

"Your report *Señor* DeSago. I pray your news does not match the rumors."

"Your highness, I bear good tidings."

Exactly one sandglass later, Damon stepped into the antechamber with a satisfied smirk. Although difficult in some quarter, his presentation was a complete success. The King was pleased with the new treaty designed to hide their intentions. He was pleased, also, with Damon's plans in place with Mary's good followers and the upstart Jesuit, John Ballard. He was excited to hear of their full support to rally the Catholic dissidents on Phillip's order and satisfied that Mary stood true, waiting patiently.

But most of all, because of his crooked truth, DeSago was pleased Phillip understood he made the correct decision to cancel the invasion. He persuaded Phillip that intelligence showed England was not as weak as first thought. Also, he made sure he planted a few comments about the inadequacies of some of the fleet commanders, touching on the admiral just a bit.

The *victoria grande*, though, as his heels clicked along the marble hall like castanets, was his new appointment to Viceroy of the Indies, Spain's new world. He convinced Phillip he was the one to ensure the gathering of riches to finance the largest invasion force in the history of the world to defeat England. Damon's chest puffed to its limit. His wealth and power now assured. He felt omnipotent, ordained by God.

With a smirk, Damon spoke to the empty hall, "Machiavelli would be proud. Borgia, I could teach you a trick or two."

Finally, he would be rewarded for his suffering and his father's murder. Soon England would fall and the good name of DeSago would be remembered forever in history.

*

"*En guarde,*" Damon said, taking his position.

He would teach his young brother some tricks today. He pushed Carlos hard.

Afterward, they sat in the tavern *Bali* overlooking the frantic harbor with ships from around the world doing merchant trade, including England. Damon thought it a mockery Spain would trade with the enemy as he looked further along the pier to his ship finishing the last loading.

Damon sipped his wine.

"I leave within the hour."

"I still do not understand why I cannot join you."

"It is dangerous. Francisco will aid me and our cause. His training better serves our purpose."

"Sometimes, I believe you prefer him over me."

DeSago looked hard at his brother-son.

"Do not ever say that again. You are my only blood."

Carlos shrunk back. "I know, I know, I just want my chance."

"You have your duty here."

"And what is that?"

"You must marry and have a son to carry on the DeSago name."

"Me? Why not you?"

"My duty is to secure our wealth and position for the future."

Carlos turned and looked out to sea. He had many women and would better try his hand on this adventure.

"The decision is final?"

"*Si*, it is."

Damon stood to leave with a final word. "Make sure she is beautiful and has a brain."

Carlos watched with envy as Damon's fleet sailed west under escort by his best friend, *Capitán* Francisco Luis Vargas.

chapter 3

"WE SAIL WITH the discipline of a ship of the line," Jamey ordered.

"Salts won't smile," Patch said.

"If it pays gold, they will."

A half-moon past found the Raptor sailing south-southwest with fair wind and bright weather allowing fine-tuning of ship and crew. With the piping whistle hot, drills and training were ordered and every task sand-glass timed. Sailing maneuvers from tacking, coming about, and wearing ship were repeated till muscles cramped. Jamey knew this skill meant survival over the accuracy and speed of the guns. In short order, despite low curses, the men were getting to with a pipe and a tune making the Raptor one with the sea.

Patch was right. The crew grumbled with looks dirty but gunnery training soon livened their spirits and would mark their fate in the end. Squads were detailed and practiced speed of loading and firing accuracy. Patch spurred all with jibes and curses, plus wagers and rivalry mixed with earned praise, honing the crew quick as one.

One early routine wondered the men and Jade. Every breaking sun, Jamey lifted Gara from his perch, removed the leather hood, and sent him aloft. All watched him climb ever higher in lazy circles, finally sailing on the wind like a ship at sea.

Later, with shrill whistle blasts, Jamey whirled a leather leash with a chunk of fresh fish tied to the end. The great eagle stopped in the sky, tucked his wings, and dove as an arrow, fanning its wings a snap before the deck, wrapping finger long talons wicked as lion claws around Jamey's leathered arm and calmly accepted his fish treat. His piercing eyes, tiger gold, accented a massive hooked beak as he perched quiet, returning the stares of the men, his power never in doubt. Some crossed themselves unsure of his true spirit.

The great bird entranced Jade as she watched every graceful move. She dreamed deep she could soar the same. *Some day, Dear Buddha, someday.*

"So Jamey, how ya know bout these birds?" Patch asked one eventide while Jade was feeding Gara.

""Well, ya know "Fallon" from ancient Gaelic means *little hawk* or *falcon* so it be in my blood. I trained peregrines since waist high tending the goats. They be smaller but the same. Trained four over the seasons. Resting in the grass, I would watch them soar and hunt till dark. If ya know their moves, ya can see wha they see."

He paused, watching Jade's caring attention. "Gara will be our topmast man hailing "Sail Ho" by the tilt of his wings. We will know any ship before they know us."

"Ah, will it work?"

"I venture it will. Ya know, I been thinkin long. The same when I was all seasons with the goats. I got a pot of ideas, maybe some foolish, some not."

"Do it ha somthin bout the carpenter's work?"

"Aye, yull see at trainin on the morrow."

Jamey remembered his father's stories of battles past as he sat cross-legged at the hearth . After the meal, bunched around the evening fire, he would scratch in the soot explaining different tactics and ploys to frighten an enemy before a battle. He taught sure, as one who lived it, that a man with too much fear proved a poor warrior. Now Jamey, his son, would test his father's teaching.

The next morn, he addressed the crew on the weather deck explaining Gara's purpose and his plans for attacking enemy ships. They listened close, in some wonder, never hearing such ways, but after some questions, thought them worthy. It was worth a go.

Late noon, thirty men picked based on long slim arms were issued a leather pouch fastened with a wax linen cord and a sack of shot, each a fat knuckle round, about a quarter weight. Wood targets shaped like men were propped at the fore end of the midship deck most thirty paces distant. With a sling in each hand, Jamey stepped forward to demonstrate. With a quick move, both slings whizzed and whipped naked to the eye and cut loose the shot, smashing and splintering the two target heads. The crew was amazed at the damage from just a piece of cord and pouch. Murmurs and comments from some remembered stories of such feats from past days, but this was something. One old salt muttered, "Member the good book, lads, . . . David and the Goliath?"

Some nodded but all agreed that ten from a sling for the time of one powder shot was good odds. They never witnessed such a feat. Jamey didn't mention practicing his old skill when visiting the queen.

"A sling against a musket?" Patch asked.

"Aye, da told us hard the old was better than new until the new was old," Jamey answered.

"Humph, weel know soon enuff."

Serious lessons and a quarter- moon bore fruit. A gold doubloon nailed to the mast for the man with the best eye spurred the practice. But it was a dangerous time topside with wild shot flying everywhere. No one dared be forward of the targets as lead balls bounced and ricocheted off rigging and spars leaving a few knots on heads and not a few holes in the sails. But practice paid the piper with a squad being counted on to pluck an enemy from the rigging and clear any deck.

El Gato watched sly and learned.

After a half moon, fate passed the ship some luck. Gara was released for his early flight and Jamey soon noticed the change. The eagle's graceful circles became elongated and his soaring speed slowed just a breath, but Jamey knew the voice. Many earths' turns observing peregrines told the same. He ordered course change and full canvas. The crew hopped too and topmast orders to look alive boomed aloft. Jamey figured their invisible quarry was still a full sun out based on his best-guessed distance of the eagle from the sea. They should overtake their prey near dusk.

Ship's officers were summoned and briefed. If a Spanish ship and all went well, the attack would be ordered first dawn. All hands to be reminded of orders and duty.

"Keep them settled," Jamey said, catching every eye. "We have a sun and a moon to wait."

Talk turned low and sober all around. Wonder and excitement mixed with fear spelled grave business. The training sessions were never more true, but when the sun dragged down and gray with no sail sighted, the crew's tension ebbed.

"What? Was this?" Jamey asked, surprised.

Patch mounted the deck with head slick shaved but for a shock of hair sprouting from the crown of his head. A fat thumb round, tied tight with a topknot, it flowed like a horses mane a pinch past his shoulders. He looked a different man.

"This the way of my people tha go to war. I been meanin to do it fer a time."

"Tis a strange look. Ya might scare em to death."

Patch stood stout legged and bare-chested except for the heavy crossed shoulder leather belts holding his weapons. A long hilted sword hung curved in a black ornate scabbard with another, but smaller, on the opposite hip.

"Whas yer weapon?"

"When ya tol me what yer da said about old bein better than new, I dug it outa me sea locker." Patch said, sliding the slick blade from its sheath. "This be the sword of the samurai used by our warriors of old. It be a *Katana* and this, its wee mate, a *Tanto*."

Then, Patch took a fighting stance holding the steel slice high and the sun licked along the blade glowing waves of tempered blue. Any enemy foolish to challenge would sure say an extra prayer.

"Tis a pretty piece, fer sure." Jamey said.

Gara's flight at dusk told Jamey the same. They were headed dead on. Suddenly, the peak boomed, "Sail ho! Sail ho!"

"Where away?"

In a quick slip, the topmast man swung to the deck. "Cap'n, tis west by so-wes, two points oer starbard bow. Must be six, seven leagues, two ships, one heavy in the water."

The crew's excitement pumped full again.

"Run in topsl's," Jamey ordered.

"Why that? Wer gainin."

"I don want them to see our whites jus yet. The suns dead. We know her course. We'll lay back till morn."

A dull sun rose on calm seas and dewed decks. It was time. The Raptor made its move. First, Gara was released to soar and Jade ordered below. Then, the Raptor's colors, a huge flag four times bigger than most, was run out from the topmast. Cut from the finest white silk for best flow, it was bordered red with blood dripping across the top. In the center was a huge raptor, with wings wide, swooping with gold eyes peering down at a human skull in its talons. Sewn special at the queen's palace, this was the first time seen by the crew.

A whoop of surprise and excitement erupted along the deck.

"The pipes," he barked.

With orders, an Irish lad pumped the bag full, scorned the usual battle march, and piped an Irish burial tune named "Song of the Banshee". Its wailing cries of doom, like the scream of a fiend, wafted over the quiet sea.

On the chased ship, the Spanish crew watched the Raptor's actions and their hearts filled with mounting dread.

"The drums," Jamey ordered.

A burly Moroccan stepped to the man round drum with two leather balled clubs, held high, and started a battle beat. Its thunder, shaking the air, vibrated the bones of every man, striking courage in the Raptor's crew and wild fear in the enemy.

The quarry ships ran.

"As we planned, Patch," Jamey said, grabbing his double bow fashioned like his father's. Patch stood by with a balance ball as Jamey sat and rolled back, both feet braced against the staves with a man's length arrow knocked and ready to fly.

"Ready, Jamey. She bout right."

As the Raptor started its slow ocean roll back to center, Jamey nodded and the torch was touched to the arrow shaft sleeved in an oil soaked cloth peppered with gun powder.

"Fire!" Patch yelled.

The arrow sailed lazy across the dawn line like a fire dragon's spit and sizzled the sea just forward of the fleeing ships. The second fire bolt, sparking from the powder, dropped aft of the stern of the military escort.

"Ya got the range."

Jamey nodded, let the third fire bolt fly, hitting the center of the escort ship with a hurrah from the crew.

The Spanish ships hove to and waited, never seeing spitting fire bolts soar so far, knowing they must surely be carried by deviled angels. Officers screamed orders and crews scurried too, dousing the fire, as confusion and fear spread over the deck. First, a great white headed eagle circles their ships, sure a bad omen. Then, a blood flag with hawk and skull swayed in the wind to the tune of the pipes, matched by bone drums and bolts of fire. It was too much.

Dropping their sails, the Spanish sat becalmed on a flat sea and second primed their cannon waiting for the swoop of the Raptor. With prayers and promises quiet and loud, they waited for the sea hawk like cornered rabbits sure of its fate.

"Ya gonna give em more fire?"

"Nay," Jamey answered. "I don want them to strike their colors. Our lads need the fight for their spirit an the trainin tested."

He turned to Gato.

"Man the starbard guns an slingers aloft."

The Raptor tightened. Gun ports slammed open and cannon crews ran them out. Aloft, slingers took positions in the rigging and crosstrees. Grappling hooks and boarding swords were stacked at the ready next to fire buckets and decks wetted down.

Spanish crews waited, every drum boom matching the beat of their heart. Suddenly, the drum doubled, hammering its rhythm, and the Raptor quick came about abeam the wind. The blood flag whipped its conflict across the air in a final threat as the sails filled full. Now knowing Raptor's intent, the Spanish swung their cannon to bear starboard, waiting for the range.

Suddenly, in a whip, the Raptor tacked like a simple turn of a carriage.

The Spanish officers stared in open mouth shock as the Raptor, magically, was now on their larboard beam, banking down against closed gun ports. In the next breath, the Raptor's broadside, a shout away, raked and splintered the escort ship full across the beam. Devils, saints, and gods were cursed and beseeched as panic spread through the Spanish ranks like a deadly fever. The merchant ship, observing the carnage, struck its flag, praying for mercy.

It was done. The tales would be tall. Gato's eyes narrowed in wonder.

The Spanish officers surrendered their swords to Jamey in open awe.

"*Como se ama ustead?*" the Spanish captain asked.

"I am El Raptor. Enemy of Spain and friend to England," Jamey answered in their tongue with a thin smile.

The Spanish officer's blanched stern, realizing they could expect little mercy. Jamey and Patch read their minds.

"Have no fear *capitán*. You and your men will be spared so you may return with my message and warning."

Prisoner work crews soon transferred all the Raptor asked. The military warship was stripped of all fighting gear and cannons hurled overboard. When finished, all enemy crew were transferred to the damaged ship and the merchant prize manned by Raptor's crew. With minimum food and water and a single mast left for slim canvas to barely make way, the Spanish ship was left to limp back to Jamaica with a sealed message from the Raptor.

Standing at the rail, the Spanish captain watched the Raptor sail over the horizon feeling fortunate to be alive. The limited sail would delay their return for many moons but allow ample time to get his account of the action in order. But would anyone believe him? He hardly believed himself. The Spanish command and the Viceroy's plot to disguise the treasure ship as a simple salt vessel sailing outside normal sea-lanes turned out to be foolish.

Fingering the sealed message from the Raptor, the captain silently cursed Damon DeSago's stupid plan.

chapter 4

THE RAZOR-SHARP BLADE slid smoothly over his arm. He was always intrigued as the blood welled up thick, like quicksilver, behind the slicing steel. He thought it funny there was never pain, just pure pleasure, showing itself by the filling of his pulsating cock. He licked the flowing blood, completing his hardness.

Father Tomás lay naked on his bunk. Three full moons at sea with no relief. He was seasick for a quarter and the rest of the trip was as miserable. He hated the sea. He hated the ship. And mostly, he hated sailors. They were a surly ignorant bunch, including the captain.

But fortunately, *El Diablo* took pity on him. This morn, a sailor hanking canvas aloft, fell with a wailing scream, bouncing off spars and rigging before hitting the deck. Tomás saw it all. While others were in horror, he could hardly contain his pleasure. His body trembled and his small cock started to swell watching the sailor's blood leak over the deck. He needed to retire to his cabin immediately to satisfy himself. Three moons without torturing a soul was far too long.

He almost ran to his cabin, locked the door and yanked his robe over his head. Standing naked with his soft bloated body, his hairless skin, like watered milk, looked sticky slick as his eyes drifted to the small black patch between his legs. He climbed in the bunk and lay still. His spongy skin bloodless as his jowls sagged, muttering the devil's tongue, fantasizing about the sailor's fall. Before closing his eyes, he looked at his growing cock with loathing. Its tininess reminded him of his first time.

He was thirteen and her name was Maria. They were alone in a barn when she teased him, urging him past his shyness until he took off his clothes and stood naked before her. She stared at his runted member, poked it with her finger, and laughed.

She died slow. He smiled, remembering her shocked eyes when he removed her breasts. His cock got harder as he stroked. From that time, he loathed his pasty body, only able to feel pleasure by another's torture or cutting himself. His legs and arms were covered with white ribbley scars. He thought it funny how he got excited by debasing his body as he licked his blood, his mind drifting, his member throbbing.

The woman Tomás called grandmother was also named Maria. She beat him, starved him, chained him, as she crossed herself, calling him *El Diablo*. He enjoyed killing her also. He knew without knowing the mother who abandoned him was named Maria. He knew it had to be. All women that hurt him were named Maria. It was very logical. Maria was the mother of God. God was the enemy of Satan. Tomás was Satan's consort, his favored minion. God's mother, Maria, hated Satan and therefore, Tomás also. So all women named Maria were to be despised because they were sent by God to hurt and destroy him. But, he uncovered their secret plot and would strike first by destroying all women named the same. His master, El Diablo, would assist.

These memories, mixed with fantasies of the sailor's pain, brought his stroked cock to final release. He whimpered, lapping his sticky blood while his sallow body spasmed.

chapter 5

MANY FULL MOONS rose and fell reaping scores of victories and work aplenty. With this last battle won, the Raptor sailed lazily north licking her wounds with everyone battle weary. The hot season slipped in and it was time for a well-earned rest. All hands looked forward to Barbados and its offerings.

Standing on the quarterdeck watching the rolling sea, Jamey suddenly felt stoked hot. The sun broke beads of sweat, soaking his clothes as his body shivered with a chill. I must be tired, he thought, just before collapsing to the deck.

Patch grabbed him, hoisted him over his shoulder and carried him to his cabin, dumping him on the bunk. Jade, knowing the signs, moved to action.

"Fever! You go, you go," she said, pushing Patch to the passageway.

"Way—jus a shake," he said, resisting.

"You go. I do, I do. Keep fever in cabin," she ended by closing the door in his face.

"Bring lots water," she hollered through the panel.

In short order, Jade had him stripped under warm blankets, cooling his forehead with a damp cloth. He was already unconscious. She knew the fever from the slave houses and even in her village. It struck her when a child and she knew only time and fate could break the spell. She also knew only the strong survived.

"But you strong," she whispered sure.

Four suns fell into the sea with no change. As sweat and convulsions mixed with delirium strained his body, Jade learned about his sad past by his fevered ranting. His nightmares and rambling anguish over his family's deaths brought her to tears. She was forced to hold him down as he jerked and tossed in violent throes screaming DeSago's name. She also wondered who was this, *Clarice*?

Patch stayed close. He informed the uneasy crew who gave the area a wide berth. He slipped water, food, and linens through the cabin door quickly closed. Patch had no God but he offered a prayer to Jade's Buddha.

As Jamey's body continued burning in shock, she tried to balance his temperature in vain. Desperate, she made her decision. That eventide, under a half moon, she undressed and slipped in the bunk, hugging her naked body against his. Although aware of appearances, she was determined to do whatever was needed to make him well.

The next moon the fever broke. Jade, exhausted from no sleep and worry, lay naked against him breathing a sigh of relief as his body relaxed in sleep.

After cooling him with a damp cloth, she curled again to him allowing herself to rest. The curve of her body fit perfect against his as her eyes drifted over his nakedness. Her mound, gently pressing against his hip, gave soft pleasure as she absently brushed her hand over his chest, slowly drifting down his flat belly. Her gaze, moving shyly, lowered to his furred patch and curiously centered on his manhood. She peeked at her brother as a child and heard many stories as a slave but this was the first time she had seen a man.

On some impulse, she touched it with her finger and thought it a little spongy. Suddenly it moved, startling her. Watching with interest, it turned up somewhat, growing a little. Like a cat with a string, she couldn't resist and timidly touched it again, this time holding it between her thumb and finger. As she more carefully examined it, it actually started growing larger and harder before her eyes. Jamey's soft moan as he wiggled his hips upward a bit caused her to quickly let go. Worried, she started petting it softly, hoping it would calm down before he woke up.

Everything got worse. It was now rock hard and every time she stopped petting it, he would moan in obvious pain. Perhaps she needed to be sterner. Jade circled the shaft with her tiny hand, slowly pumping it down, whispering softly, "Rest now, go down, go down."

Jamey squirmed with unconscious excitement as his fevered brain dreamed of Clarice and women in different ports. He groaned, seeking relief.

Jade panicked. Look what she started. No matter what she did, it just got harder. Jamey's breath was raspy. Maybe he will die. Jade pumped even harder.

The explosion amazed her. His shaft swelled and jerked in her hand. Pearl thick juice squirted, making her jump as it splashed across her breasts and neck. Holding on in fascination, it continued its ebbing throb, finally shrinking back to its original size. She took a deep breath of relief, thank you Buddha.

It was only then she was aware of her own unconscious wiggle against his hip. Her flush built quickly as she rubbed to her explosion of waves of pleasure. Her breath settled slowly to a soft sigh as she curled, exhausted, against his chest. As she drifted off, she glanced at his face noting his contented look. *Was that a smile?*

Jamey, waking the next morn, felt like a new man. Properly clean and covered, he rolled over to spot Jade puttering around the cabin. Watching her female moves, he smiled, remembering a certain dream about her.

Jade, turning at his sound, met his gaze with turquoise eyes and blushed bright red. She would die if he remembered. She didn't mean it. It acted on its own. It wasn't her fault. She tried to calm it.

"Good morn."

"How you feel?" she asked, holding her breath.

"Good. If yull turn around, I'll get up."

Thank Buddha. He does not remember. She would sure try not to provoke it next time. She frowned wondering why she thought there would be a next time. She wondered why she looked forward to it.

Just then the topmast hailed, "Land ho, Barbados!"

chapter 6

H E WATCHED HER
tight with a gleam in his
eye, enjoying the way
she moved. He knew natural female magic was inborn, not learned.
Her earthy movements would bewitch men like a moth to flame. He
wondered if she knew she had this power, probably not.

Pedro had stopped for the night making his way for a coin or
two, stealing what he could. He paid her father a peseta for a straw
bed with a plate of lamb stew and water for the mules. A Spanish
gypsy he was and proud of it. He lived all over, always by his wits,
with some good times and some bad. This was a bad time and he
needed a new trick.

"Do ya dance girl?" he hollered as she continued her chores.

"I can sing a bit," she shot back, a little cocky.

"Weel then, give me a tune now," he said, pulling his old gittern from the wagon.

"Not now, I'm hot and tired," she said, grumpy from the sun's labor. But as she walked away, she glanced over her shoulder with flashing eyes. "Maybe later".

"Your name then, *señorita?*"

"Maria," she shyly answered.

The moon rose soft and at his urging, Maria sang a light-hearted ditty against his gittern. Her sultry voice stirred him and her eyes, he knew, would sure melt any man's soul. She had the magic. She was his new trick.

*

Maria Aurora Aragon was free at last. Her father forbade her leaving, but determined, she wrapped her meager belongings in a scarf and left without a tear. It was four seasons passed now, including a Christ day, with Pedro, visiting most every village in Jamaica, always avoiding Santiago. She hoped for a visit, but Pedro shooed the idea, claiming it was too big with many like them, but she supposed it a lie. Some enemy most likely waited for him.

Maria loved the singing and the attention and Pedro was nice like a proper father. He treated her like his own, talking and teaching her gypsy ways on the long hauls between villages. He was called "Pedro the Gypsy", always welcome but never trusted. His visits always brought a piece of pleasure to dreary lives, especially with Maria.

Pedro's wife and children perished a time back in a fire. Although on trips between villages, they shared stories of their lives, Pedro never spoke of his loss. Since the tragedy, he roamed the land and now started the circuit once again with Maria to Spanish Town, Negril, Falmouth, Ocho Rios, Port Antonio, and her favorite, Port Maria because it was named after her.

The worst stop, though, was Montego Bay. Located on the opposite end of Jamaica, it was a sweltering hellhole with adventureres of every stripe. The small hamlet was surrounded by jungle with constant calls of wild animals making sleep hard. But, Maria was a good trooper and after her last performance, settled in her curtained booth to tell fortunes. Pedro taught her the act and she discovered she had some talent. She always foretold a little bad news and finished with some good. But there were few women at this end of the world and those here looked ill-used. Few men sought her second sight, afraid of being witched in some way.

As Maria started to close, a young girl about her age stuck her head through the drape to ask her future. Built big, but pretty, she seemed not to belong in this place. Maria asked her to sit on the opposite side of the small table and gaze into the glass ball. Maria was tired after the day's travel, the show, and now telling fortunes. As she studied the young woman, she knew what her question would be before she asked.

After a few general questions, she had enough information to create a believable prediction.

"Will I find a man to love me and take me away?" she asked, shyly.

Maria, feeling her sadness and longing, remembered her own plight just four seasons past. Well, she thought, at least she would help her feel happy for awhile.

Maria stared at the glass ball, trancelike, looking heavenward and closed her eyes, palms turned up, faking a spell as she hummed low. Then, with stern brows, she studied the palms of the young girl, clucking, before raising her eyes to meet hers.

"Things will be the same for a time but then there will be a big change in the village. You will meet a man you will learn to love but you must be strong and ready to leave all behind."

Maria finished with a fake sigh wondering why she said it that way. It just seemed to flash in her mind. Pocketing the coin, she watched the girl come alive with a dream smile and wished her well.

As she finished closing, she thought, some soothsayer she was, she never even learned the girl's name.

*

Maria loved to talk as they traveled from village to village. She talked about this and that, flitting from one subject to the other. She liked to talk about her Castilian relatives, stretching the truth a bit with each telling.

"You know, Pedro, Catherine of Aragon is my great Aunt. She wrote to me a few times. You know, she was married to King Henry but he turned Protestant. My Aunt was furious so he divorced her. She is still considered a queen in Spain, though."

Pedro always listened patiently, making her eyes sparkle when he told her he heard the very same from a visitor just last year.

Her eyes flashed wide, pressing him for details and he had to tell a few more innocent fibs.

He found her energy limitless. On a first meeting, one was drawn to her eyes, speckled gold that cast a spell on every man. They were the window to her soul, tough and tender, but innocent. They would dart about, excited and curious, missing nothing. Her magic eyes, always a mystery, and tempting figure mixed with girlish tease, entranced both men and boys. If there was any escape, her sweet voice and sultry dance doomed them.

Pedro watched over her like any proud father. He taught her about life, how to dress, how to flirt, how to manage men. He finished by teaching her sleight of hand, how to pick a purse and lock, and how to use her ever hidden dagger. She learned to act and think rabbit fast and Pedro was proud.

He also observed her wariness and distrust of men and worried about her future happiness. But with a shrug, he guessed time and the right man would change her heart.

Pedro never stole from the poor or folks treating him friendly. He did enjoy thieving from mean people or those that owned locks. He figured anyone who owned a padlock could afford to live without what was behind it. He could pick and slip any hasp in a blink and Maria was a worthy student.

After each visit to the villages, Maria's popularity grew and money was thick. Pedro purchased a better team and wagon, fresh greased and painted. The team of heavy hoofed grays, standing high at the shoulder, could top any hill. The wagon, near new, was covered with fresh canvas and included a small draped partition to allow Maria some private space. On the road, passing travelers alerted the villages ahead and when their wagon rolled in, a happy crowd waited.

Maria's popularity soared. Her lively voice and gay spirit gathered crowds and left them cheering. With Maria's eyes wide, he purchased several new dresses causing her tears to roll. Never had anyone given her a present. She was so grateful and happy, Pedro felt awkward and then angry no one before him had treated her with any kindness. Well, he thought, it would never happen again.

Maria was a good companion. She made him laugh. She would say things at times that made no sense and then would share her thoughts showing great wisdom and sensitivity. She was a mystery and good company for an old man and he was happy once again. Pedro knew life was what it was, no more, no less. Make the best of it and survive as you could. These times were good and Maria's world was exciting.

*

"Pedro, Pedro, *parar*, wait, it's me, Conchita."

Pedro pulled back the reins and twisted around.

"Oh no," he said, rolling his eyes.

Maria turned, spotting the woman running toward them, skirts flying.

"Who is she?" Maria asked.

Conchita stopped and leaned against the wagon, huffing, while Maria and Pedro climbed down.

"This is Conchita. She used to work for me."

Conchita pushed herself straight, hands on hips.

"I ben looken fer you. I am ready to come back."

"*Lo siento* Conchita, but Maria here works with me now."

Conchita slowly looked Maria over from head to toe, smirked, and ignored her.

"Humph, come now Pedro, you need a full woman to catch the men, not this stick."

Maria blushed with anger, smelling the rum on her breath.

"You're too late. What happened to your man?"

"He was a pig. He keep selling me to men too cheap."

"Well, I have nothing for you, sorry."

"But I am better than her. I have more tits and my skirts fly higher. You know that."

Maria stared at her wide-eyed.

"But I have Maria now. It is my decision."

"Humph," she said, thinking fast. "Take us both."

"Ho, ho, two cats in the same cage. I'm no fool."

"*Por favor* Pedro. I need something."

"I have nothing Conchita, sorry."

With that, Pedro and Maria climbed back aboard and shook the team down the lane. Maria glanced over her shoulder at the angry woman standing wide-legged, hands on hips, in the middle of the road.

Conchita yelled after them, shaking her fist. "You and your *punta* will be sorry."

Maria sat quiet. She had never met such a woman.

"Pay her no mind, the rum talks," Pedro said.

"What happened?"

"She ran off with some *cabrone*. He must have abused her."

Pedro quieted a long moment before saying, "She stole from me and I cannot forgive her."

Maria sat very still as Pedro fell quiet.

Never more serious, Pedro finally turned, catching her eye.

"Never cheat friend or family, Maria, Never. Remember that," he said and turned forward, silent with his sadness.

Camping on the outskirts of the next village, they put on their usual show. It was a good crowd, better than most. Maria was in high spirits spurred on by dreaming men yelling their favor. Her swirling skirts matched the tambourine beat against yips and yahoos of men with heated blood. The bonfire's snapping glow gave tempting glimpses of her charms as the seducing rhythm of drumbeats drove the men to a hot pitch. Maria's tempo whirled ever faster spreading the wild fever, threatening a riot, when suddenly, she stopped, crouched low in her skirts. The male crowd hushed, then, erupted with hoots and howls of praise.

Pedro, setting his gittern aside, always watched close, keeping a protective eye. Maria was still innocent, not quite understanding her affect on men. She sang and danced for the pure joy unaware she stirred deep male desires.

From the shadows, Conchita watched Maria dance and her blood flushed with jealous hate, cursing her, blaming her for her plight.

*

Pedro and Maria continued their travels. Pedro thought she was a perfect partner. Her confidence and poise grew each day. He taught her gypsy ways and gypsy life. Maria was never happier.

She hated Jamaica stuck on the farm but now found it beautiful. The lush jungle was thick with life, each with a strange sound and full of cascading waterfalls, big and small, rushing and roaring to their destination. Sprays of light poked through thick lanky palms seducing bright colored flowers shameless with their blooms. Wild macaws, painted as bright, announced their arrival with squawks as their wagon rumbled through. Monkeys, swinging through the jungle, screeched their anger at the intrusion as great hawks watched, circling silent above.

Maria especially enjoyed the sea cliffs and listening to the crashing sounds of the surf. Time forgotten, she gazed at the endless sea watching the marching ranks of waves as soft sea breezes rested her heart. Then, with a dreamy sigh, feeling the vastness of the world, she wondered her fate.

Thinking about it later, it was strange how it happened. Her faith in God was renewed on one such eve when Pedro stopped by a large lake. She gaped wide in wonder at stick legged birds with rope necks as far as she could see, leagues and leagues. Pedro named them flamingoes. As she stared, a sudden noise caused them to rise as one and she marveled at the sea of white, rising blanket thick. The multitudes seemed to lift forever, wings thundering the air, sparkling gold against the twilight sky. Then, her breath stopped as she felt a sudden peace, sensing the majesty of their spirit while they circled ever upward, unending, completely shadowing the land. The natural majesty filled her spirit heart, renewing the marvel of God's creations.

*

The black day happened in Port Morant. One sliver moon, after a street performance, some men drunk on rum pushed for Maria's attentions. When Pedro stepped between, the sodden gang hit him across the head with a handy cudgel, knocking him flat. The next morn he took a fever and that eve, called her close, whispering his last, "There be an iron box in a false floor below the bench in the wagon. It is for you. You are my only kin." His voice drifted lower and Maria bent to his ear. "Remember child, not all men are the same. God's made one for you."

Pedro died that night.

Maria thought her world ended. She couldn't stop crying as she visited the small church every morn, praying for Pedro and asking God what she should do. On the eighth sun, she bucked up and dried her tears, angry at her self pity, remembering Pedro's words. *Maria, God always provides a path from the dark.*

As she walked to the stables, she remembered the hidden strong box. Making sure she was alone, she dug it out and when she snapped the lid, her eyes grew big as eggs finding a small fortune in gold. She cried again knowing he was her only friend who truly cared for her.

The next morn, she sold the rig, sold everything, and struck out on her new life.

"Santiago, here I come."

chapter 7

H E HAD THE pirate dog.
The reward would be his.
"More sail, lieutenant."

"Aye, *Capitán*."

The topmast crew scrambled to the rigging, spreading more canvas to catch every wary breeze.

"*Capitán*, they are all in the wind."

"*Mui bien*"

They were closing fast. *Capitán* Francisco Louis Vargas smiled.

*

"Run out the stunsels, Patch. Clap on more cloth."

Patch shot back, "Capn, she got a full blanket now. The bow's dug deep, digging her grave."

Jamey turned, silently looking at his first mate, realizing there was no more speed in her belly and looked aloft, knowing the canvas already breathed deep.

*

Francisco commanded Spain's newest warship, smaller than a first rate but two times the speed. With twice the cannon, She proved faster through the water than the Raptor. Francisco, although young, was given this command because of his passion for excellence. Strict discipline ensured a tight ship, a blood ship, and he was without humor. His ambition allowed no quarter, his loyalty to his patron, Damon DeSago, without question.

A sandglass later the two ships met with thundering broadsides. Francisco raised his brass-leathered scope to survey the damage and smiled. One more salvo would end it. The Raptor would be his. The glory, reward, and DeSago's gratitude would ensure his wealth and power.

"Ready to come about, lieutenant."

"Aye *capitán*. Helmsman, ready to come about."

"Ready the port guns, lieutenant."

Aye, *capitán*."

Francisco watched the gun crews snap to the orders with practiced speed and smiled again.

*

Jamey misjudged. Everyone did, but he was the captain. He was responsible. No one guessed a Spanish man-of-war could crease the sea so swift. The Raptor's starboard rail was in shambles with a full rank of cannon dead. Pricking smoke folded over the deck like graveyard fog stinging the eyes as men scrambled against the fire manning a bucket brigade. Cracked spars and ragged rigging stumbled every step as torn bodies floated in blood. Jamey knew another barrage would be their end. Raising his glass, he watched the enemy prepare to come about.

Snapping his scope shut, he thought of a gamble.

"Ther be one chance, Patch. We mus wear ship for advantage."

Patch stared back, numb to the plan, knowing the two would collide.

"It mus be perfect timed on my order. Stoke the larbard cannon."

Patch nodded, without understanding, shouting orders to ship's officers.

"Add a half more charge of powder," Jamey ordered.

Patch hesitated with a questioning look.

"Now Patch! No questions," Jamey ordered, eyes hard.

Patch turned too.

*

"Come about, Lieutenant. All starboard guns stand by."

Francisco listened to his lieutenant repeat his order, feeling the smooth heeling of the ship's deck. He smiled, savoring the finishing broadside.

*

"Wear ship, NOW!" Jamey ordered.

*

Francisco could not believe his eyes. The Raptor's sails suddenly cranked in the opposite direction. The fool plans to board us. Francisco, turning to order for this new event, watched, with alarm, the Raptor's foremast quickly twist, taking the sails aback. The tactic dawned on him too late. The Raptor slow stopped, twisting to his stern.

Francisco realized he was trapped.

"Hard over, hard over!" he screamed. "Hard over, I say!"

He ran to the stern rail watching silent smoke ballooning from the Raptor's larboard guns. Then, their cannon thunder rang in his ears as he ducked for cover. He cursed God, feeling his ship shudder, as eighteen guns from the Raptor blew away his stern castle and rudder. They were crippled, without steerage, allowing the Raptor to take its time with a fate of sure death.

Francisco stood resigned on the splintered deck. He could not bring his cannons to bear while the Raptor hung astern. One more broadside at this range would finish them. Belly rage consumed him, cursing his fate as the despair of defeat sunk to his marrow. He was forced to strike his colors.

*

Jamey's crew hurrahed. They turned the tide. Certain defeat twisted to victory. Jamey breathed a sigh of relief. Patch, smiling, ordered the cannons stoked.

"Capn, three ships closen quick four points off starbard," a sailor yelled, pointing to the sea.

Jamey swung his glass around to see three ships flying Spanish colors closing full and bye.

"Blast the fates, Patch. Tis too full a pot," he said, lowering his telescope. "Set to the wind, full canvas to the night."

The moon-slivered night would swallow them invisible before another bell.

As the Raptor caught the wind, Jamey turned with a smirk, waving to Francisco's raised telescope.

*

Francisco blessed the heavens for this reprieve, his mind already working to fashion his account to save face. Desago would be hard to fool. He paced the deck piecing false facts.

He was sure he saw the pirate, Raptor, through his glass, get hit and fall to the deck. Yes, that was it. He saw him get hit. He must have been severely wounded, their broadside so complete. It was the devil's luck he escaped. Even the three Spanish ships assisting could not coral him. The devil's luck of the rising night saved him.

As the raptor vanished into the black void, Francisco's eyes hooded, his anger flaring deep, vowing to meet the Raptor another time.

chapter 8

"THIS WILL BE our home," Jamey said, clapping Patch on the back as they surveyed the reaches from the hill.

The island was small, allowing total visibility of all shores from the bluff. While a cool sea breeze brushed them, Jamey pointed out the best location for the harbor with a narrow promontory, just past, to serve as the watchtower. To the North, the island's main point of defense from blue water attack was a natural bouldered seawall perfect for mounting cannon. The other three sides were protected from weather and hard sea by a ring of islands with water too shallow for any serious invasion. The concave center, formed eons ago by a volcano, sheltered a wide meadow and a small lake for growing food and tending stock. All this

was surrounded by jungle green palms of every stripe making it all deep
and lush.

"White Bay Cay will be her name to match the beaches of white
sand…. She be bonny fair, eh Patch?"

"This be a good spot awright," Patch added as his eyes scanned the
land.

"Our house will be on this highland overlooking all."

Jamey's thoughts excited him more. "And tis but a few suns to
friendly ports. Tis well hidden among the other spits and close to
Spanish waters." He paused, pointing southeast. "I'll wager tis but a
quarter moon away, straight there. We can hit and run without much
fear."

Patch nodded but felt uneasy down deep, not knowing why.

The work started. Supplies and materials of every type were bought
or commandeered throughout the area. With the exception of the
Raptor's crew, all workers brought to the island were ordered hooded to
ensure location secrecy sailing to and from the island. Jamey recruited
with generous coin experts in all fields from farriers, carpenters, and
farmers, to cooks and artisans in rock and iron. All bustled about,
tripping over the fine furniture, cloths, and china from captured spoils
that complimented collected native craft.

Jamey felt fortunate to recruit Sir Raymond Wallace, recently from
Liverpool. Originally traveling to the new world to seek his fortune,
he relented to Jamey's sway, especially when reminded of his duty to

England and raids against the Spanish. His eyes widened best, though, when he knew his work on the island would earn most of his fortune.

Sir Wallace, a man before his time, was schooled in architecture, shipbuilding, surveying, and charting the seas. A creative gentleman with a spirit of adventure, he worked closely with Jamey and Patch identifying their needs and problems before designing innovative ways and procedures to solve them.

One such problem was island defense so a watchtower was built on the East point at the end of a thin peninsula next to the only deep-water approach. Reaching mainmast high, it held quarters for sentries and reflective oil lamps for silent signaling across the island. To protect the channel, a bronze bell in the tower was knotted to a manila rope reeved down through rolling blocks and strung alongside thick black anchor chain. Both lay on the sandy bottom but could be raised with levers just below the water's surface to halt any ship. Any vessel striking the chain also caused the bell to toll. This same security system was repeated at the harbor entrance around the bend supported by a small fort mounting six eighteen-pounders ready to answer any test.

A small stream fed the natural lake formed in the center of the island. Sir Wallace, with some labor, created a waterfall, which allowed the waters flow to turn a pulley system of buckets hoisted to a barreled reservoir tank at the top of the hill. From there, bamboo troughs, from here to there stretched over the island, providing fresh water to the most needed places.

In between construction, Jamey and Patch sailed, irritating the Spanish on short raids with every foray reaping useful items for their new home. The last sortie yielded a ship of animals of every type, which thrilled Jade. Horses, mules, goats, ducks, chickens, cows, and a funny looking animal called a llama filled the farm area. But the most important prize was a crate of homing pigeons given to Jade for her personal attention to train a covey for future message flights. Jade, wide eyed, sensed the importance of the task and felt proud to be depended on. She promised the best and fastest carriers.

At dusk, Patch and Jamey relaxed after the meal in their unfinished hacienda as Jade hustled about seeing to their comfort. They always brought her some surprise from the raids and she excitedly wondered if they had one this time.

"Jade, can we talk to ya?" Patch asked.

Turning, she looked at both, each with a silly grin, standing there with hands behind their backs.

They did this every time. They loved to make fun.

"Les see those pretty eyes first," Jamey teased.

Jade shyly raised her gem green eyes, holding his gaze with her heart.

"Ah, beautiful as always, I could look at you forever."

Jade flushed hot. He always made her blush and he enjoyed doing it. She could kick him.

"Guess wha we got ya?" her brother said, breaking the spell.

With that, they both brought their arms around holding two black fluffy kittens. Jade's almond eyes opened wide with delight. She loved cats and had one as a child. These were beautiful. Coal black with fluffy fur set around amber eyes. Speechless, she carefully took and hugged them close.

"They call them Pan-thers," Patch pronounced as best he could. Jade cuddled them as she found her voice. "Oh, than you, than you! Pan-Thers, Pan-Thers." She was off to give them some milk.

Patch and Jamey, glancing at each other, enjoyed making her happy.

Several suns later Patch asked if she named them yet. She looked at him a little puzzled.

"They are Pan, Thers," she said.

"But what are their names?"

"Pan and Thers, as you say," she repeated with conviction.

And so it was.

Two seasons passed. Pan and Thers grew fast with some alarm to Jamey and Patch. It was plain they were not ordinary cats but Jade had them well in hand. They followed her everywhere accepting her position and domination. She mothered and trained them carefully, her loving eyes peering into theirs creating a close spiritual bond with unspoken words. Her graceful movements convinced them she too was a cat, one without fur, but still a cat.

Jade taught them to leap, to hunt and stalk, and tolerate Jamey and her brother. Their size and weight soon grew the same as hers and their wrestling matches left her huffing and puffing. She had special collars made of hammered silver trimmed in gold over leather. They growled their dislike but it made them look rich and regal.

She loved to watch them move. By sun, their slick ebony coats shimmered with fluid motion changing to flat black sentries at night, roaming without a whisper like spirit shadows. There was not a mouse in the house. Patch and Jamey watched in wonder as the three moved around as one and pitied those who tried to molest her.

Island work continued. An orchard with oranges, lemons, and grapefruit were planted, surrounded by a fence of breadfruit trees. Also, a few almond and walnut were mixed in with berry bushes and an olive tree. To the left, the farrier, who doubled as a horse trainer, tended to the stables with workhorses and wagons. A small farm area was planted with beets, beans, and parsnips with a smaller patch for cabbage and from the new world, corn. The completed corral butted against the lake allowing easy water access for animals and crops.

Granite trails, a narrow wagon wide and lined with whitewashed rocks, circled the island with feathered pepper trees, bowered low, creating shaded tunnels here and there.

At South Point, the lane opened to the small wharf and harbor area where ship stores were saved along with tools and equipment of every type. Behind the harbor buildings, a circled camp of tidy white cottages with red tile roofs made a pleasant community. At dockside, the Raptor was berthed and received close attention by the crew under the second mate, Gato. Charged with her care, he kept her shipshape and ready for sea.

*

They saved his life on their last raid.

While searching a Spanish prize, Gato found him angry, sullen, and terrible seasick, chained in a dark hold in the bowls of the ship meant as a gift for King Phillip for his pleasure. One look and Gato quick named him *Montaña* for he stood battle horse high with branded tattoo scars covering his chest and arms. Brought before Jamey and Patch, his fierce wild look was mulish, declaring in sloppy Spanish with chest puffed full, he would rather die than stay on this pitching craft. Proud and unbent, he declared he was a prince in his Maya village revered by his people because of his sky height and he expected to be treated with respect. Watching him standing lordly and defiant, Jamey and Patch looked at him with some amusement but understood his anger.

"You are now free," Jamey said. "You can join us or go your way."

Montaña's eyes narrowed, suspicious of these white men. His village was burned flat three seasons past and everyone, including women and children, were murdered by men looking the same. He wanted nothing more than to be back among his own.

During the trip back to the White Bay, he was surprised the Raptor's crew treated him equal, in awe of his stature and body carvings. Jamey and Patch respected his pride and showed they trusted his worth as a man. Over sun's turns and lazy sea days, Montana heard their stories when slaves of the Spanish.

On one sun, second watch, Jamey called him forward and returned a Maya dagger found in the Spanish plunder. Excited, with eyes wide, he explained as best he could it was a ceremonial dagger of the Mayan deity, *Chac*, God of rain and lightning. Hugging the knife to his chest, he bowed low, grateful to these white men.

By the time the Raptor tied up at the dock, Montaña began to trust these strange men and was beholden for his rescue.

By the time the next moon slivered, Jamey and Patch, in a quick huddle, made their decision and offered Montana the post of overseer. Huge, friendly, and loyal, he spoke English worse than Patch, but made his point. Presented with the task, he blushed with their trust, grateful for the offering. Standing puffed proud, he accepted, sealing his loyalty till death. This island was now his home since all in his village were slaughtered.

When the next morn upped, he was introduced to Jade. Both stared open mouthed at one another. She was amazed at his height and the carvings on his body, and him, because of her delicate size and beauty. But even with the physical look completely at odds, an instant bond was birthed and they became fast friends.

But a truth kept to his chest, Montana was most happy he would sail no more and be seasick.

Responsibilities were clearly defined. Jade maintained the great house and compound and he supervised the rest of the island. Meeting daily, they enjoyed each other's company discussing island problems, big and little, laughing at each other's English. It was a good time.

On one return trip, they gifted him two huge mastiff hounds, the largest he ever saw. Full grown with white short hair and black muzzles, their long legs and bull jaws could challenge any enemy. Standing on their hinds, they were as tall as Jamey and on their fours, were near high as Jade.

"A giant needs a giant dog," Patch told him.

Montaña named them, *Perro*, the same for both because they were inseparable, like Jade's cats. Also like her, he took them everywhere except the compound. Jade's big cats certainly would not allow that intrusion and it was a battle neither wanted to see.

Montaña, with war hammer cradled across his arm, patrolled the island making sure everything was correct. With Perros at his left and right, they presented a fearsome sight and no one, even drunk, dared challenge them.

The great house rose majestic from the cliff in the glowing sun. Its near completion spurred a decision to host a party to celebrate and reward all that labored. Most had only viewed the fortress hacienda from a distance and now, inside, "ooohed" and "aaahed", admiring its grandeur. On the terrace, flickering candles of every size lit the grounds in a gold glow among garish banners and pennants. Long tables of food and roaming music makers created a festive mood as workers and ship's crew mingled about. Barbecued scents drifting on tropical breezes tempted appetites quenched with flowing rum. Veranda dancing, with squealing children underfoot, added to the din of a good time.

The great room presented a huge hall with levels double plus a half high. The ceiling, covered with adze-hewn beams with stirrup stringers perfectly slotted, copied a church. The balconies, lined on three sides by arched promenades, jutted curved alcoves giving an expansive view of the large leaded windows overlooking the sea. Curved wrought railings, shiny black, contrasted stark against white walls and gold sconces. At one corner near the leaded windows, a large open atrium with tropical plants was a sanctuary to pairs of macaws and parrots of every color. The grandeur of the Indian design, mixed with sturdy Spanish and French ideas, created a heavy airy mood loved by all.

The evening scene was complete with a rising moon reflecting its arrow light across the sea, creating soft hues and romantic shadows. Party guests laughed and danced in good cheer, proud of their island.

Jade, moving with female grace, welcomed guests, answered questions, and gave quick tours. Always quiet and shy, this was her time. After this eve's party under the full moon, the high walled compound would be off limits except for these special celebrations. The compound was the private world for Jamey, Patch, and Jade.

The home, regal and rich because of Jade's ministrations, shone with furnishings, brightly colored, against cool hand-ground terra-cotta flooring warmed with oriental rugs and heavy wrought candelabras.

Pleasant oil paintings, brightened by tapers, seemed alive hanging on high walls highlighting a massive fireplace. The heavy stone hearth underscored a carved beamed mantle, a parting gift from Sir Wallace. Finishing touches of scattered deer and bear pelts, warmed under several swaged chandeliers holding scores of candles, completed the stately mood. But in the end, it was the bouquets of island flowers and gracious hosts that made the hall welcome and friendly.

With a firm command from Jade, Pan and Thers retired to their favorite beam high in the vaulted ceiling. There, they crouched, religiously watching their mistress.

A short time later, a sotted sailor grabbed Jade in a happy belly hug. The panther's roar echoed through the hall as they leaped to kill. Everyone froze as Jade quick twisted away facing their charge with a wave of her hand, halting their attack. The cats belly crouched, snapped low by her silent command, giving a last warning growl toward the drunk before leaping back to their perch. The room, death quiet, slowly stirred with the guests murmuring their wonder, keeping one eye on the cats. The drunk never knew how close he came to his end.

Jamey's reaction to the event was slower but just as tense. In the opposite corner, watching with a protective eye, he jumped forward, drawing his sword. After Jade stilled her cats, her eyes found Jamey's with grateful wonder, filling her heart with hope.

The music rose again and the moment was over. As the party cheer continued, Jamey settled back, sheathing his sword, and surveyed the guests thinking of all they had accomplished since chained to the oars.

It was much, but his vow of revenge, unfulfilled, still nagged his soul. He quickly shook himself, chasing the thought, refusing to be glum this night.

Jade's attention returned to the guests. Her perfect figure filled a modest sarong in whimsy damask of pale green that matched her eyes. Her ebony hair, swaged up, then fell, flowing down the length of her back. A jeweled Persian dagger, in matching case sparkling with diamond and emerald stones, hung low on her hip from a gold braided belt. Its gold wire hilt swirled to a jeweled pommel able to open by a hidden latch exposing a hollow handle for poison or perfume. Created special for a Persian princess, Patch, with a blush, presented it to her mumbling she was prettier than any princess. Jamey agreed.

Her costume, complete with a slave bracelet designed special by her, graced her arm so she would never forget. The filigree gold and silver bangle, filled with amber gems, circled her small wrist and clasped with a thin gold chain leading and fastened to a single gold band on her center finger. The unusual adornment was admired by all.

Jamey enjoyed observing her from a distance. Beautiful and delicate as a flower, bossy and sassy as chili, exotic and desirable as a woman and . . . . . . suddenly, Jade's eyes lifted, finding his. It was as if she sensed his thoughts, her mossy gaze meeting his in a knowing moment of desire.

Then, as quickly, the press of the guests broke the spell as she was asked another question.

As Jade turned away, he realized he was trembling.

"Watch yerself, Jamey boy," he whispered low.

*

The rest of the moons cycle brought hard work with routine island matters. Treasure shares were divided before the mast according to agreements. A full inspection of the island, led by Montaña, took several suns. Although tiring, even with generous siestas, it was the chance to praise him and the others for a job well done. Those that slacked, the right question got their point across. Jamey and Patch were never concerned with poor workers or bad attitudes because Montaña solved those problems before coming to their attention and they were content not wanting to know how.

"The island be shipshape." Patch declared.

"Aye, the Raptor's crew could take a lesson," Jamey finished.

Montana's chest swelled with a smile spreading across his beefy face. His hounds, sensing his happiness, wagged wild.

"Job done, I'd say," Patch said with a wink to Jamey as they started up the hill and home.

Both looked forward to eventide. Jade always set a delicious meal and later the three would lounge by the pond at the edge of the cliff watching the sea slowly swallow the sun. Both gained some pounds during this time though they worked several hours each night to finish their hidden treasure cave.

Jade discovered the small cavern through a narrow hole during construction but stayed silent until alone with her brother and Jamey. That same eventide, with pitch torches, they explored together discovering it half the size of the Raptor and surprisingly cool and dry. After a quick conference, the decision made, they stacked their treasure here, the secret held by just the three. Cave echoes gave Jade the shivers but it was her idea to use a false panel in the pantry for the secret entry. She also suggested a surprise in the entrance for intruders. A heavy grate was fashioned that would suddenly drop if a lever was not cocked, trapping any thief. Finally finished, the three stood back with hands on hips admiring their work. Jamey's praise on Jade's cleverness blushed her parrot red.

They also regularly trained with hand weapons and practicing Patch's martial arts. Jade, joining in, enjoyed the karate and usually had the two men huffing for breath in short order. She loved it especially when Jamey grabbed her. Patch thought she waited a little long to break free. But if she thought they were holding back because she was female, much less small, they received a swift kick.

Every morn, the day's routine ruled. Plus once a moon, Jamey and Patch held court at the harbor docks with spokesman for different groups on a wide variety of issues. Acting as judges, they listened to stories and facts sworn over the cross of one kind or the other, and then, with a short whispered conference, a decision was rendered. Disagreements between neighbors, who owned what, who owed who,

who worked hard, who didn't, who did right, who did wrong, were all mulled and decided. There was a stockade of sorts and public blocks, but mostly punishment was extra work or a fine. Jamey's temper, quick to flare on some issues, was balanced by Patch's settling force, insuring fair verdicts. Their island justice, enforced by Montaña and sometimes swallowed hard, worked, and there were no appeals.

Before the Raptor sailed on another hunt, hard decisions were made about who wanted to leave to rejoin the outer world. In addition to the right replacement to do the work, released workers talking too much from drink or coin always threatened island security. Although all living souls coming and going were blindfolded heavy, talking about minor details, collected and matched, could point an enemy close. Extra effort was taken to prevent loose talk from threats of death to emphasizing loyalty to the crown. They tried to make every break on good terms but they knew it was the one chink in their armor.

Happy the sun was done, Jamey and Patch huffed up the hill to their home looking forward to the day's end and relaxing with Jade in quiet companionship. Later, with the bottle of wine dry and the full moon settled, they retired for the night. Sleep was impossible for Jamey as he leaned alone on the rail of his veranda, restless, staring at the quiet ocean. Looking forward to the morrow's sail, thoughts of his murdered family tormented him often like a green wound. He started thinking seriously about returning to England and somehow figure a way to find DeSago and kill him.

Deep with that thought, the side of his eye caught a quick shadow down on the beach. Alert, he peered close knowing Jade and Patch were asleep. This was their private beach, forbidden to others on the island. Just then, his eye caught another ghostly movement and he grabbed his telescope.

Balanced against the rail, he scanned the area as the moon bathed the beach in a pearl glow. Suddenly, he froze as the scope focused on Jade standing at the water's edge with her cats lounging nearby. His breath stopped as her thin cotton shift slipped from her shoulders and dropped to her feet. Stepping from the curl of cloth, her tanned body, silhouetted against the pale sand, outlined her exotic beauty. Nature's nymph, sure, his mind figured. It was impossible to turn his eyes away.

Spellbound, he watched the gentle arch of her back lower to slim curves of feminine hips. Her midnight mane, moon glistened, swayed slick black, brushing against a perfectly rounded rear. Breathless, he was afraid to move as she lazily stretched, raising her arms to gather her tresses high. Her feline moves shook Jamey's body as she turned slightly, outlining her perfect profile. His breath quickened, silently cursing his trance.

Jade finished her slow turn and faced his scope. Teasing moonlight glowed over her dusty skin as his eyes drifted slowly from the beauty of her face down past slim shoulders to dark nipples hard from the warm air. His lens drifted ever lower past her flat belly to her narrowing midriff and stopping at her shadowed mound. She stood relaxed, legs slightly parted, looking toward her cats. As Jamey's fantasy imagined the taste of her, she suddenly lifted her eyes and looked straight into his telescope. Chills hit his bones knowing her emerald eyes sensed his desire.

Guilty, he backed away knowing he was too far away for her to see him. He felt like a small boy getting caught peeking. But still willing to risk all, he raised the scope again in time to watch her smooth dive knifing into the dark surf.

Flushed hot, his heart kettle-drummed as his body trembled with desire. Retreating to his room, he took a deep breath, fighting for control.

Thank God they were sailing on the morrow, he thought.

CHAPTER 9

"HARD OVER, BLAST ya, hard over!" Jamey yelled.

Sulfured smoke was everywhere. The topmast spar splattered across the deck fouled the larboard guns. Loose rigging jammed clue lines on the mainmast, locking the sails, and the helm was unable to respond.

Jamey realized they were losing the battle. The Spanish captain was clever. He did the unexpected and Jamey, too late, realized they had been lax and cocksure. After exchanging several broadsides, the Spaniard knew Jamey was unable to maneuver and turned his ship bow on, bent on ramming the Raptor midship.

"Fire as you bear, rake their masts!" Jamey shouted. "Clear those guns Gato. Patch, hear me, get a gang and clear the rigging." Jamey grabbed a spoke on the ship's wheel to help force the rudder. No luck.

They were trapped. Jamey stared, hands gripping the rail, watching the enemy's bowsprit move true on a collision course. Raising his glass, he spotted the Spanish captain with a smirk standing on the aft deck. Jamey knew he was already counting his victory and fame at defeating the Raptor. His scope switched to the bow and the heavy reinforced timbers and extra braces mounted on the bowsprit. He realized the Spaniard devised this very action, savoring the ten stones of gold for the Raptor, dead or alive. Jamey knew they would be boarded in a half glass outnumbered three to one.

"Prepare to repel boarders!" he ordered as his heart sank.

Suddenly, cannon blasts broadside from his bow tore into the Spanish ship. Jamey spun around to see a small galleon with a colorful high stern coming to his defense. Flying the brethren colors, the blood flag, flapping mean, announced the pirate vessel as another round shot raked the Spanish ship, blowing the bowsprit to splinters and cracking the mainmast.

Trapped between the two, it was too much. The Spaniard struck his colors, praying for mercy.

Jamey and his boarding party climbed larboard on the prize at the same time their savior and crew topped the starboard rail. Meeting mid-deck, both pirate captains held a wary eye.

Jamey looked at a titan, least twice his weight and a head taller with long blond-white hair. His beefy face surrounded beady blue eyes, even smaller because of his squint, around a squishy nose red from drink. Barrel chested and heavy-armed, he saddled a fistful of weapons of every type. His look was done with short boots and baggy britches covering mast thick legs.

Jamey kept his guard not knowing what to expect. He smiled a greeting thinking this brethren could be more of a threat than the Spanish. Patch followed a step behind with the same thought.

"Lo mate. We showed in the nick, huh," the giant grunted low, breaking into a wide smile of dirty teeth.

"Me Johan. We are new to these waters, huh, We are Dutch, fresh from Africa."

Jamey relaxed a bit and returned the greeting, clasping the giant's hammed mitt. Orders were given and the ship secured. At Johan's bidding, the three retired to the Spanish master's cabin for a parlay. After a nod to Gato, Jamey and Patch followed with a wary look to the other as they watched Johan stoop low, turning sideways to fit.

Once below, he plopped down hard behind the ship's desk, grabbed a bottle, broke the neck and poured sloppy, topping the pewter mugs.

"El Raptor, huh. So you the one the Spanish fear, huh. You no look so tough this day, huh."

The giant belly laughed.

"I have me name too. The Spanish call me *Toro Loco*."

He roared again, swigging the grape spirit from the jagged bottle neck.

Johan was terrible loud but seemed good-natured. His voice boomed as he watched keen eyed, wondering if Jamey knew of the Spanish reward of ten stones of gold. With that big a pot, his ship could return home with enough to build their new life. Although pirating was good sport, he reminded himself they were here to steal enough to start their own colony. But he liked the cut of the lad and the way he fought. But ten stones of gold, it would be hard to pass. He would decide later.

"Bring more wine!" he bellowed at his mate.

Jamey and Patch just wanted to strip the ship and go their separate paths, but they also did not want to insult this hulk, figuring his name, "Crazy Bull", was earned for a reason. With a glance to the other, they decided to stay a bit and humor him.

A full sandglass later and two bottles dry, they watched Toro's eyes turn brighter and manner surly.

"I must give orders to unload the cargo." Jamey said, pushing up from his chair.

"Ho, ho, friend Raptor, you mean to load my ship, huh?" Johan said, leaning forward, his smirk challenging.

"She be our prize, captain," Jamey returned, serious, sensing a clash.

"But I save your arse, huh?" Johan said hard, sitting straight, losing his smile.

"So it be mine now, huh."

Jamey stiffened, determined not to let this bag of wind bully him.

Patch tipped to the brewing trouble and piped in, "Now mates, each has a claim. Les settle this sensible."

The bull remained seated, swiping the wine from his chin with his cuff, not smiling, staring tight at Jamey, who returned the same.

Patch quick added, "Methinks we should cut equal, or better, wager the whole on lady luck, cards or dice."

The two captains glared hard at the other. Jamey, hearing Patch's words, realized his tact.

Jamey fake smiled and raised his tankard.

"Aye, Captain Toro, les not a few goods spoil a fine time."

"Sounds God's fair way, huh," the bull grunted, lung low, pretending calm.

El Toro decided as the wine hit his head he would kill the puppy, take the cargo, and collect the reward of ten stones of gold.

Patch and Jamey held their gulps, exchanging jibes, watching Toro get sotted. Unsure of the next move, they wagered this giant would handle softer if he was three sheets. They soon cursed their reasoning as his manner sunk darker. Both watched careful as he sat sullen at the table, head down with eyes turned up and hooded, blood red, eyeing them through thick brows. His kill glare dared with lips flared back like a lone wolf guarding its bone. Jamey and Patch sensed the coming storm.

All of a sudden, Toro, with a grunt, stood and staggered wide-legged, squeezing through the passageway to the upper deck. Jamey and Patch followed, alert for anything.

"Did ya ever see one so big?" Patch whispered.

"He could anchor a first rate, sure," Jamey returned, stepping to the deck and moving to the side.

Toro clambered across the deck toward the Spanish captain and without warning, smashed his fist against his jaw. The crack sounded like an ax against oak and the crews fell silent. With a growl, Toro yanked his sword, lifted the limp body by the scruff and chopped, lopping its head off. Eyes wild, he dropped the body in the blood and stood thick to the deck, glaring at all, relishing every man's fear.

Toro, planted hog bone hard, looked toward Jamey, sneering, with a trickle of froth at the corner of his curling mouth. Mean drunk crazy, he barked orders to set the circle.

"To blades with dice or cards me pretty Raptor. Our steel will decide, huh," he challenged, his cutlass whipping the air.

Jamey, pissed and ready, moved to the opposite side of the circle while Patch tried to cool the bull's blood.

"Here now, Toro, drop yer blade. We be all the sa . . . . ."

"Stand aside, ya one eye stump," Toro growled, pointing his sword at Patch.

"Or yull be the first ta stare at yer belly bowels, huh."

The insult turned Patch to face Toro, his one eye narrowing to a lizard slit. His patience gone, his anger rose to answer the scorn. He turned calmly toward Jamey with a cocked grin.

"This one be mine," he said solid.

Jamey nodded, hollering to both crews, "The victor decides the spoils."

Taunts and yells rounded in the air as Toro and Patch, eyes bored, squared off.

Wagers, quickly hawked, favored Toro as one circled the other slow and mean. Patch, drawing his Katana, shrunk dog high, feet wide, legs coiled. Toro, sobered, hunched, lowering his head, shrinking it back into his shoulders like a turtle.

Suddenly, Toro charged straight with a bull snort matching his namesake. Nimble for a giant, his cutlass slashed and whipped at Patch who dodged to the side in the last nick, planting his leg in the way. Toro tripped forward, full speed, grinding his nose into the splintered deck, slamming into the bulkhead hard as a cannon ball. His crashing bulk trembled the ship as his roar of pain and anger hushed the crowd cat quiet.

In a flash, Toro jumped to his feet, twisting to face Patch, jowls cramped in hate. His eyes bore at Patch as he swore scurvy low, blood bubbling from his snorting nose.

"Whoreson, your belly bag will be a purse for my bitch."

Patch slouched in a fighting stance so deep his hair rope swept the deck. His one eye glistened, watching the giant with amusement. Then, with a howl, blowing blood, Toro charged again, legs wide, careful this time, hacking at Patch who suddenly vanished. His speed, so fast, it even surprised Jamey as he flipped, twisting in a flash, landing behind the giant and slashed kicked him behind the knees. Toro tottered, falling slow back like a chopped tree. Jamey thought to yell timber as Toro's wind-milling arms lost and he crashed flat, shaking the deck. Patch, already high in the air, came down with heels pointed full weight into Toro's gut. The whoosh of pain could be heard deep in the bilge as Toro rolled, curled and squirming like a newborn, gasping and sucking for air like a sick bagpipe. Toro would not collect his ten stones of gold this day.

Two sandglasses later, the ship's parted with no hard feelings. Both crews respecting the fight, satisfied with a story to tell at many a port.

As Jamey and Patch, elbows on the rail, watched the pirate ship sink over the horizon, Jamey asked, "Why'd ya let him live?"

"He saved us. We owe him one time."

Jamey nodded and gazed quiet at the rolling sea, thinking the same, but knew deep that Toro was an enemy best buried.

Time to refit in Barbados.

chapter 10

THE RAPTOR DROPPED its kedge in the sea sand an arrow shot from shore. All hands were in good spirits anxious to feel solid ground, spirits, and female company. The fire watch cursed their luck, standing sour at the rail, watching their mates scramble to the longboats dreaming of women and grog.

Barbados, a frontier port, was a waypoint for those willing to risk for more. The village bustled, crowded as a slaver, through sun and moon with those seeking a second breath before charging ahead. Men and women, some cautious, most wild, busied themselves pursuing their fate.

After a meal, Jamey and Patch leaned against a post at cornering lanes watching the crowds. Wagons clanked and rattled stirring sticky dust while drivers cursed and cracked their whips. The rest on foot elbowed and swerved for position with women avoiding eye contact and men staring hungry.

Lazy, with bellies full, they had time to spend before night moon and tavern time to wet their throats.

Watching the shadows grow, Jamey casually noticed two women pass by, chatting, as they stepped in the road. Just then, a crash from tipped crates spooked a horse and wagon. The animal, wild-eyed, lurched toward the women sure to trample them.

Jamey jumped forward, grabbing the one in danger by the shoulders and pulled her back. Losing her balance, she fell against his chest as the wagon whisked by. Startled, she turned to thank the stranger and stared in disbelief. A man now, a little taller, but still him with that silly grin.

"Jamey, Jamey Fallon? Tis you?"

He looked back, confused, not recognizing her. She was smartly dressed with a wide brimmed hat and very attractive.

"Tis me, Clarice!"

His smile widened, realizing it was. Clarice, not dead, the first girl to catch his eye what seemed a century past.

"Clarice, by the saints! what are you doing here?"

"I might ask you the same," she countered. "You just saved my life, again."

"Well, at least I didn't push you in the mud," he said with a grin.

"I remember that morn, it wasn't funny." she said, turning mock serious and swatting him playfully on the arm.

"And I didn't get my kerchief back."

Both laughed and quickly introduced their companions. She remembered Patch after he pointed out he shaved his head.

Clarice and Jamey stood smiling at each other not knowing where to begin. There was so much to talk about…. He noticed her wedding ring.

"Dear Jamey, we must visit. You must come to supper this eventide. Bring your friend Patch. Here is the address," she said, handing him her card.

As she strolled away, she peeked over her shoulder with a coy smile, "Eight O'clock, don't be late."

Jamey sensed some urgency in her voice but didn't understand.

"There be trouble there, mate," Patch murmured.

"What do ya mean?"

Patch just rolled his eye.

*

At eight straight, a maid welcomed him into a small receiving room in a very large house. Patch begged off with an excuse neither bought. Clarice's calling card listed her husband's name as, "Sir Walter Gingham—Solicitor General". Jamey didn't know the title but by the looks of the house, he knew it involved money and status.

He was wearing more traditional clothing. A simple white bloused shirt with open collar and doublet. It was tucked loose into plain dark breeches with calf high boots quickly purchased. They hurt. His hair, shoulder length, was slicked back and he wore a broad leather belt holding a short sword with a sheath knife hidden at his back. He fidgeted while he lingered, remembering she also kept him waiting when fourteen.

Wondering why he was so nervous, he looked up to see her floating down the stairs in what he suspected was a planned entrance. She was all smiles, excited to see him as he felt his blood quicken.

"You're just in time, welcome," she said warmly, taking his hand. She was happy he was alone.

Clarice was all grown up. Her gold-red hair with a lemon tint hung free at the shoulders over a fashionable clover green dress. Open at the neck, the gown hung free to her ankles, which he wagered, had no petticoats. She was stunning. He stared and she noticed.

"You looked a buccaneer earlier with your high boots and sword. I think I like you as a pirate."

"Well, I'm not a pirate," he responded seriously, concerned she guessed his trade.

"Oh, I know, but a lady can dream, can't she," she said, flashing a coy smile.

"Walter, my dear husband, has been delayed," she added. "But this will give us time to share our news."

Taking his arm, she led him to a rear garden patio filled with plants and varied colored flowers stuffed in all four corners. Caged white doves, nestled in scarlet bougainvillea, cooed at one end under a full latticed covering. Fitted with rattan chairs and a cushioned day couch, it was small but cozy.

Before finishing their first cool tea, Clarice learned everything that happened to him since the terrible day at her birthday party, except his Spanish raids. In turn, she avoided conversation about her capture by DeSago. She trembled slightly and stilled for a moment, finally telling him it was too painful to speak of. Then, she perked up saying that after she married, her husband was transferred here, to Barbados. England was desperate to colonize the New World as soon as possible and he assisted the travelers with a variety of tasks.

"Enough of my boring life, I want to hear more of your adventures."

Just then, a door closed and Jamey saw her stiffen.

"Oh Walter, there you are," she said, standing, giving him a peck on the cheek.

"Come meet an old friend."

Her husband was handsome and every bit the practiced English gentleman. Older, a soft life left a paunch that complimented a full head of silver hair. Jamey smiled, shook hands, and the three visited over tea before being called to dinner.

Later, after a pleasant evening, Jamey took his leave and as they escorted him to the porch, a messenger arrived. Walter made his apologies and turned to attend his business. When alone, she took his arm and said, "I want us to go on a picnic tomorrow."

Jamey, caught off guard, looked at her, wondering, and started thinking of an excuse.

Seeing his expression, she said, "Tomorrow for sure. Please do not refuse me. We have not seen each other in so long. Walter needs a respite. Everything will be ready. Meet me here at noon," she ordered.

"I have some business tomor—"

"Ooh, just make it a little later. I already made all the plans. We will not be gone long," she said, catching his eye with a hopeful look.

Not wanting to disappoint, Jamey agreed thinking she was right, they hadn't seen each other in a time. He did enjoy her company and anyway, they had to wait for the ship to be loaded plus Walter wasn't a bad sort.

When he said good night, she handed him a small wrapped package.

"Here is a present for you."

Surprised, he opened it and found his old kerchief he gave her to wipe her muddy face so long ago.

"God's breath, you saved it all this time?"

Her mischievous smile and teasing eyes scrambled his thoughts.

Walking back to the house, she smiled, remembering his amazed look and thought how clever she was. She was friendly and warm, the proper lady, welcoming him. She didn't mention she spent hours rooting through her mother's old trunks in the steaming attic throwing stuff all over looking for the stupid kerchief. Thank goodness her mother never threw anything away.

Next noon, Jamey arrived dressed similar to the previous day with thigh high black boots, tucked pants, bloused shirt, and a bright bandana. Instead of a sword, he carried his father's quillon dagger at the hip and the rondel dagger hidden in the top of his boot. Last, a matching bright sash held one of his whips under the shadow of a wide brimmed gaucho hat.

"Well Sir," she said, "You look very dashing. "You're not going to carry me off, are you?" she teased.

Clarice wore a thin linen dress, milk white with a wide brim hat the same. Again, he noticed she was not wearing many petticoats and figured it was because of the warm day. It lay open, modern at the neck with a rather low bodice and a bright sash at the waist, matching her hatband.

"I have our mounts around back."

Jamey panicked, forgetting this possibility. He assumed they would take the carriage.

Seeing his grief, she asked, smiling, "You do know how to ride now, do you not?"

He blushed. "Of course," he said with bravado, dreading this moment.

Clarice couldn't resist teasing him as they walked around the side of the house to the waiting carriage. They looked at each other and started laughing.

"Thank you for taking pity on me," he said.

As the carriage rolled down the lane heading for the coast, both were in a fine mood as they chatted in the warming sun. Clarice mentioned Walter had to work but insisted they go without him and enjoy the day.

Her hair, the color of wet ginger, rich and lush, was curled to her shoulders and tamed back with a soft green ribbon. Her manner was warm and attentive and after hitting the first rut, she casually slipped her arm through his. He glanced at her with some amusement. She was only twenty-two but acted more. She was lovely with classic features and well aware of her beauty. Cultured, mannered, and strong willed, she was a woman who knew what she wanted, which was unusual in this time. But there was something else, he thought, some pretence?

At the end of a full hourglass, Clarice directed him around the bend to the edge of a low bluff, green and plush. The cool breeze, clear as a spring rain, swayed the rye grass like ocean waves. Pulling the team to a stop, Jamey looked out at the endless ocean, calm and serene, while a few sparrows zipped around complaining of their intrusion.

Clarice, in charge, grabbed the blanket, handed the basket to Jamey, and led him over the bluff to a secluded grassy knoll. After spreading the blanket under a big shady oak, she turned and faced the cliff, gazing out to the endless sea. Jamie watched her standing, shoulders back and arms out, facing the water, taking a deep breath. She was beautiful, bonny fair, as he felt her female essence float and surround him. There was no controlling the sudden flush sparking through his body.

"I love it here," she announced. "Tis my favorite place."

They plopped down on the grassed cushion, kicked off their shoes and tossed their hats. With a sigh, they lounged casual in silence, letting time drift, watching the roaming clouds. She asked about his years in between, wondering about his past loves carefully avoiding any mention about that terrible day on her father's yacht.

She rose up on her hands and knees and asked, "Are you hungry yet."

Her smile was full of mischief. Jamey stared up at her and wondered. "Aye, I missed the morning fare."

Clarice was always thorough in her planning as she set the food out, anxious to please. As she leaned over, serving the different dishes, she was aware of Jamey's eyes on her bosom. Lunch was perfect.

Full and relaxed, he pulled his shirt loose, set his knife and whip aside, and laid back, chewing on a green stem. Clarice shed her hose and rubbed her bare feet in the cool grass. When Jamey looked away, she unfastened the top button of her dress.

He laid there, hands behind his head, watching the puffy clouds saunter past when Clarice slowly moved over him and kissed him softly. Jamey, surprised, held still not knowing what to do. As her kiss lingered, he tasted her growing desire and dared to respond, gently placing his hand lightly across her back, pulling her into his body.

Moments later, Clarice slowly broke away, holding his gaze, her tawny eyes darkened in need. In a practiced move, teasing, she slowly pulled the top of her dress to her waist. His eyes drifted to her full white breasts, watching the nipples grow pink hard from the cool breeze. His mind raced. His blood flushed hot. He couldn't believe what she was doing.

Lifting her leg, she straddled his hips and slid her skirt to her waist. "Love me Jamey."

Their eyes held, locked in lust as she unbuttoned his trousers, circled his growing member and slipped it into her wet sex. Her eyes glazed feeling her belly filled with him.

"Pump me hard," she ordered.

It was a wild afternoon.

Jamey stayed quiet on the ride back not knowing what to say. He was fuddled at her boldness but admitted he enjoyed it very much. This was the wildest lovemaking ever and he wondered how she was so experienced. As she chatted, he was amazed at her demeanor as if nothing happened.

Stopping the carriage at her home, Jamey helped her down and she purposely brushed her body against his.

"I reserved a table for us at the Cranberry Inn for dinner later. Pick me up at seven-thirty," she stated.

Jamey was dumbfounded, "This night?"

"Yes, silly, do not look so surprised." She smiled, reading his mind. "There will be others there and Walter, we will have fun."

"I lack the proper clothing," he said, searching for an excuse.

"Well, get some. Tis still early. Seven-thirty." With an innocent smile, she turned and walked inside the house.

Dinner was enjoyable. The inn was the best establishment in Barbados and well attended. Clarice was the perfect lady greeting those she knew. They were alone. Walter was delayed with a problem at work, which surprised him as well as her complete lack of concern about appearances.

Clarice wore a pastel yellow dress in glistening satin with at least one petticoat on a narrow farthingale of starched linen, the latest from Spain. Her collar went to the neck and looked proper like the rest of her. He wondered how different she acted, the perfect lady. It was as if she were two different women.

Afterwards, he admitted it was a pleasant evening and he enjoyed himself as he pulled the buggy around the side to the carriage house. As he started to step down, he heard her whisper, "Jamey."

Turning, he looked into her smoky eyes. Her wicked smile held him as she casually leaned back against the corner of the cushioned seat and slowly lifted her skirts, spreading her legs.

"Put it in me Jamey."

Jamey honored her request.

The next noon, the carriage headed to the beach on the south road with a team of two setting a fancy trot. He dressed much the same as before, loose open shirt with high collar and sweat scarf. His dark pants, tucked in high boots, held a dagger with the other hooked to his waist opposite the whip. She dressed in an easy manner in pale lavender, full skirted with no petticoats that freshened her look under a large brimmed hat colored the same. Both were anxious to get where they were going.

Turning the curve, Jamey pulled up short. Five toughs on foot, brandishing swords and knives, blocked the road helped by a log. Jamey quick realized their intent. It was to be robbery, maybe rape and murder by their looks. One grabbed the horse's bridle and another ordered them down. Clarice grabbed his arm, clearly frightened.

Jamey's mind clicked and slowed. As he gently took her arm away, her eyes met his, blue iced, and seemed to belong to another man as his lip curled, sure and final. Then, he turned back, facing his foe, and started to dismount. When his foot hit the ground, he jump rolled in a forward tumble, popped to his feet, and with a snap of his wrists, whip threw both daggers at the same time. Both hit their mark, sunk to the hilt, square in the throats of the robber holding the horse and the leader barking the orders.

In a flash, Jamey's whip was singing, slashing the remaining three across the face, arms, and body. The snapping cracks cut so fast they dropped to their knees begging for mercy. The whip's metal tips kept ripping bits of meat from their hide like a hungry vulture. Falling to the ground, they wailed, crying for their lives. Holding back his hissing whip, he swore their death if he saw their faces again. As they scrambled through the brush, Jamey rolled the log back, pulled his daggers from the throats, and swiped them clean across their clothes.

Clarice, trembling with fear and excitement, watched his flint-cold eyes as he climbed aboard and whipped the team down the lane. Her blood was so hot from her fear she told Jamey to hurry to their secret place on the beach. Once there, she quickly unrolled the blanket and tore her clothes off. She was wild, in heat, stirred to a fever pitch by the danger and threat of death. Jamey responded to her demands as best he could until finally her multiple pleasures satiated her and she fell into a deep sleep. A time later, she woke but seemed in another world as she sat, staring at the empty sea.

"Are you well?"

She stared quiet, not answering.

"Clarice?" he said, softly touching her shoulder.

She turned to him from another time and whispered, "DeSago . . ."

Her voice drifted silent in pain as a tear rolled down her cheek.

The name made his blood flush.

Then, of a sudden, her face brightened with a smile, returning to the present. "Tis so wonderful here with you," she said, resting back, curling against him and falling back to sleep.

He lay still, holding her hand, his mind spinning. Hearing DeSago's name brought a thousand questions. He wondered about her wild behavior so foreign to her sex. He somehow thought it related to the time she was held captive by DeSago. He wondered, watching her peaceful sleep, what scars that monster burned on her soul.

The following turning suns were crazy. Jamey never experienced such wild love. Clarice's heated desires drove him mad with wanting her. Her imagination and daring at times worried him thinking they would be discovered. They made love every place possible. If he told someone he would not be believed. So reserved and proper in public, she gave no hint of her drives. Decently modest one moment and a rutting libertine the next, he thought he was the luckiest man in the world.

But the suns passed and it was time to sail. He went to Clarice's home to bid good-bye and was invited in as usual by the servant. She excused herself after directing him to knock on the closed door as Mistress Clarice was in the parlor. Surprised because it was out of the ordinary, he went to the door and knocked lightly.

"Come in, Jamey."

When he opened the door to the shaded room, hazed rays of light with dancing dust squirted through the drawn drapes, leaving the room a dreamy hue. Stepping inside, he stopped, suddenly frozen by the erotic scene before him. Clarice was lying back propped on the day couch, her thin linen dress curled to her waist with one leg resting over the back of the couch and the other, open wide, to the floor. One bare breast hung out of her dress, nipple hard, as his eyes traveled to her smoky lidded eyes. She was spread naked, moaning softly, fingering herself slowly with one hand and rubbing a banana between her legs.

Jamey felt himself getting hard as she smiled, asking him to come to her. Moving closer, he could taste her sex as he watched her hips move slowly in concert with the thrusting fruit. She whimpered as she reached for him, pulling at his buttons while her writhing motions pumped it deep. Freeing himself, she hungrily took him in her mouth, moaning her self-pleasure as Jamey watched, hypnotized, trembling at her wild abandon. Then, with a soft cry, her hips reached for more, exploding in continuous jerking spasms, sucking the yellow phallus as her mouth begged for his drink.

Both throbbed to a slow rest, completely spent, quietly holding each other until their strength returned.

"Did you enjoy that?" she whispered.

"Hmmm, hmmm."

"While I was waiting for you, I started thinking of the danger on the road and became so excited I couldn't wait," she giggled.

"Thank goodness you arrived on time."

As Jamey returned to town, he thought of his good fortune and looked forward to a return trip. He smiled, easily admitting it was the most insane and best time he ever had. He marveled at her simple goodbye. With quiet reserve, she merely asked when he would return, showing no emotion or tears. No wonder her husband's hair is all white, he thought, as he gingerly walked toward the inn to meet Patch. After four suns, he was exhausted and a little sore.

Patch, spooning some fish soup, spotted Jamey walking toward him.

"Jamey lad, you been riden a horse?" he asked loudly.

Jamey flushed red and Patch howled, laughing, choking on his food, eyes watering, slapping his leg.

"Tis not that funny," Jamey said, sitting down.

"It looks ta me ya might a fell off a time or two," and he roared even harder, head back, pushing away from the table, attracting stares from people across the lane.

Jamey looked away trying to ignore him.

"Okay, okay, jeesh Patch." Jamey mumbled, waiting for him to quiet down.

"Sorry mate," Patch chuckled. "Could not resist."

On early tide, the Raptor sailed with a belly load against the rising sun toward White Bay Cay. Jamey, elbows on the rail, recalled the wild week and for some reason, suddenly felt saddened for Clarice. He realized she showed no feelings other than her need for sex and to be in complete control. He did not know what happened but she was not the same bubbly person he knew before DeSago. God knows what horrors she endured. *One more reason to rid him from the world.*

Gazing out at the forever sea and sky, he silently wished her well, sensing they would never meet again.

*

Look at them, Jade mused, every time they return from a friendly port they have those silly grins. Knowing what they'd been up to, her anger flared, upset with her brother and furious at Jamey.

They noticed she never hugged or greeted them as usual when returning from Barbados and their surprise of two lovebirds in a gilded cage made this time even worse. Both shrugged at the other as she grumped around all evening.

Later, after dinner around the water, she looked at Jamey and her irritation turned to sadness wondering why he did not want her. Jamey sensed her gaze and glanced over to her questioning eyes in time to see tears rolling down her cheeks. Unable to hold them back, she quickly stood and rushed into the house.

Jamey felt a stab of pain knowing he had hurt her. Patch felt rotten too as they sat silent with their guilt.

chapter 11

THE DIM HALL was empty but for them. Flickering candle glow bounced off stone-gray walls as they spoke low to dampen their echoing voices.

"News from the Indies, Sir Walshingham?"

"Yes, your grace, good news."

"Our treasury must be filling then?"

"Thanks to our sea dogs our navy is growing daily. We soon will equal Spain's might."

"I'm curious for specifics, sir," Elizabeth asked, leaning forward to hear her master spy's latest intelligence.

Sir Walshingham stood tall with hunched shoulders. Built slim, uniformed in black, he seemed always to be looking at the ground.

But if one watched close, you would see his eyes forever scanning his surroundings through thick furrowed brows. A skilled artist in intelligence and human treachery, he missed nothing.

"Madam, Francis Drake is now called *El Dragón* on the Spanish Main. He and Walter Raleigh have taken many prizes and continue pushing their efforts towards our first colony in the new world."

The queen sighed, "The Spanish ambassador again has pressed King Philip's demand to recall our privateers. The last was frosted with a warning."

"There is reason to fear Spain yet, my queen. My agent in their court reports they are still busy with the Turks. We have time."

"What else then, sir?"

"Remember the young captain, Jamey Fallon?"

"Yes, yes. His mother was at court and well known to me. What of him?"

"He is feared as much as Drake. The Spanish call him *El Raptor*. He plagues the Spanish waters and your grace's portion doubled more than Drake's and Raleigh's combined."

"Hmm, if memory serves, tis not Viceroy Damon DeSago serving Spain there?"

"Yes madam, he is, the same that kidnapped and murdered those at Cambor castle."

"And the man Captain Fallon believes murdered his family, true?"

"The very same, madam."

"Well, we must reward him for his service and inform him of the viceroy's presence," she stated.

Walshingham stilled for a moment, his mind working.

"A thought madam," he said, careful. "If we inform the good captain of DeSago, he will abandon his privateering to pursue his enemy. This would reduce the flow of Spanish gold into your treasury."

He paused for effect, watching close.

"Also, I regret to remind your grace the captain is Irish and Catholic. Tis a pity," he said, shaking his head in faked regret. "But such is life. Captain Fallon must be content with his share of treasure."

Elizabeth sighed again. But trouble with Mary in Scotland and the Jesuit rebel, favoring a Catholic would not do. Politics can be cruel.

"Well then, see that he is assisted in all other matters. Powder, supplies, anything he needs. See that you relay my gratitude."

"Yes, my queen."

Queen Elizabeth walked slowly away with a frown, skirts swishing across the slate floor.

"Tis a dangerous game we play, Sir Walshingham. The world is changing quickly. God help us."

Walshingham stood and bowed, watching with deep admiration as his queen took her leave. His fierce loyalty to her had thwarted two assassination attempts and many lesser treasons. His eyes narrowed considering more plots. Unfortunately, he pondered, Captain Fallon may have to be sacrificed to Spain, a token to buy more time. Catholic Spain's hand seemed everywhere.

Well, so was his.

*

They met on the Golden Hind. Jamey and Patch were formally piped aboard by the boson's whistle and were greeted by ship's officers in full uniform. Jamey, hiding a smile, knew they were trying to impress and intimidate them. He also knew they failed.

Both privateers wore full shirts and trousers stuffed in high boots shined bright for this occasion. Weapons were tucked tight in wide leather around waist and shoulders. The two presented a contrary look. Jamey was tall with bleached brown hair to his shoulders and his mate, built stout and skinny-eyed, was baldheaded but for a hair rope growing from the top.

"Welcome aboard, Captain Fallon."

Jamey's eyes followed the voice to a short man in full dress uniform sporting a neatly trimmed van-dyke. As his hand rested lazily on the hilt of his sword, his chest puffed as he gave a short bow and clicked his heels. Jamey returned the same and looked up to see the no nonsense eyes of the ship's captain, always in complete control.

"Thank you Captain Drake," Jamey formally returned. "This be my first mate, Chang Ling."

Ushered to the aft deck under a sail awning, their eyes scanned the ship. The Golden Hind was smaller than the Raptor but well armed. The high stern castle, brightly painted, at first glance made the vessel look unstable but a quick survey of the rigging showed a sail plan low and fast. That explained how the ship closed the gap to the Raptor so quickly that morn.

The three settled in under the shade at a small conference table placed for just this occasion as a crewmember served a goblet of wine. Without fanfare, Drake, clearing his throat, read communiqués from Queen Elizabeth.

Intelligence stated Catholic Spain was even more determined to force its faith on England. The Jesuits, in league with Mary, Queen of Scotland, threatened revolt. Spies and intrigue smothered the court with several assassination plots unmasked. The queen was desperately trying to launch more ships for an inevitable war.

He and Sir Walter Raleigh, along with Captain Fallon and the rest of the privateers, were indispensable for supplying Spain's treasure to that end. The queen extended her warmest gratitude to her Sea Dogs. Further Intelligence proved King Philip planned to invade England as soon as possible. A revolt from within, led by the Jesuit rebel, along with an invasion from Scotland and Spain from the sea would crush the monarchy. And now, Catholic France signed an alliance with Spain leaving England to stand alone. The climate looked gloomy.

As they talked, Drake sized Jamey as he relayed new orders revoking all letters of marque held by British vessels. Pressure and threats from Spain made this action necessary allowing the queen to disavow any official support for the privateers. This move was meant to stall Spain's excuse for war before England was ready.

"Captain Drake, may I see the written order? Jamey asked.

"Of course," Drake said as he handed it over, surprised he could read.

Jamey quickly scanned the order and was not pleased. This put everyone on their own. Without the backing of the crown, they were freebooters, pirates with no country, and the queen still expected her share.

"Tis the same for you, Captain Drake?"

"Yes, officers and all," Drake said, locking eyes with Jamey. "From this day, we will not wear our naval uniforms until further notice. Our queen regrets this order and asks that we continue our action against the Spanish until our navy is ready."

Drake caught the suspicion in Jamey's eyes and wondered about this El Raptor and his exploits. He was sure most was rumor and exaggeration but even if half were true, this young captain was his peer, deserving respect. He wondered, too, why he was specifically ordered not to inform him of Viceroy DeSago's location.

Weighing Jamey, he also wondered about his motivation. Lacking title and family of influence, maybe it was just his desire for treasure, nothing more. It was clear he was an intense and serious young man.

Jamey sensed Drake's study and glanced at Patch, deciding to end the visit and take their leave. He was not as patriotic and loyal as Drake. He was an outsider who would never be accepted and only sent treasure to the queen to maintain his letter of marque. The rest was to amass a fortune to seek out and kill DeSago. It was his only mission, no other.

*

"This not right," Patch said.

"Leave it be."

"But we be the first. They take the bows."

"Leave it." Jamey repeated.

"Who are these Raleigh and Drake?"

Jamey sighed and pushed away from the rail, looking aloft to the Raptor's sails.

"Why they get the bows?" Patch pushed.

"Drake and Raleigh are titled and British officers."

"Why not you?"

"They are English and Protestant. I am Irish and Catholic. I am two strikes back."

"But we have sent the queen more gold, no?"

"Aye, fer sure," Jamey added.

"The Spaniards fear the Raptor more. Am I right?"

"Aye, but they fear *El Dragon* as much."

They both leaned the rail again, eyes to the sea.

"'Tis not right, I say."

"Leave it be."

Jamey quieted, finally saying, "Mayhap tis as it should be. They raid for the queen. We raid for revenge."

"Humph, the works the same."

*

Two suns later at six bells, Gara was aloft soaring in wide circles. In a short time, Jamey spotted the sea eagle's change in flight.

"Twist her north by north-east."

"Aye capn, nor by nor-east." the helm repeated.

Patch looked to the sky trying to learn Gara's signals.

The sighting spread through the ship. All were weary. Four moons of hunting left the Raptor's hold stuffed with the bow digging deep.

"Les pass this one, Jamey."

Jamey turned to Patch with a questioning look.

"The crew is worn and our ship heavy," Patch said, steady, holding Jamey's eyes.

Jamey turned and scanned the deck. Patch was right. He too was tired. Time to return home.

ChAPTER 12

THIS WAS HER turf, her little world to share only with Jamey and her brother. A squab flew in yesterday with a message they would arrive the next sun at dusk and she worked hard to make sure all was ready. She wondered what surprise they would bring this time. All the other gifts were wonderful except the last one, a cute monkey named *Sucio*. She soon learned why. The pesky animal messed everything and was filthy. She also thought it not funny, like her brother and Jamey, when he kept touching himself. She quickly banished him to the outside collared to a long chain.

But Jade loved the parrots and macaws plus the beautiful clothes and jewelry from their conquests. Their island hideaway was another world she loved and cherished, shutting out the memory and misery of her slave life.

One of her favorites was a lotus pond stocked with two prized peacocks strutting proud in a quiet garden area just outside her room. It was her dream wish since a child to have such a place of serenity. Mounted in one corner, an intricate golden altar supported a small statue she carved herself of the sea god, *Tien Mu Hos*. It sat cradled in a cupped alcove between joss sticks faithfully fired every day.

Never missing a new sun, she would stand, head bowed before her alter, hands at prayer, beseeching the sea god to protect the two men she loved.

As the sun settled lazy in the balmy air, she pulled herself from the warm pool. The tepid water was refreshing as her mind wandered with slow thoughts.

Everything was in order, everything organized. Complete care of the great house, the atrium, her pets, food preparation, and the care of her two men when present. It was difficult work demanding careful planning but she loved the responsibility because it made her feel useful and worthy. Suggestions were made to hire someone to help but she sternly refused with the exception of a tall hand or a strong arm from Montaña, her friendly giant. She smiled to herself picturing him as big as she was small.

She was excited about the morrow, four full moons had passed since they sailed. She whispered an extra prayer to *Tien Mu Hos* for friendly seas and their safe return. She missed them terribly but also cherished the solitude and quiet time with her animal friends.

The drying drops beaded, trickling down her naked body as she lowered herself at the water's edge between Pan and Thers. As the still air warmed her, the shadowing dusk with lazy clouds lulled her thoughts dreamy.

Jade turned, feeling Pan's tail sweep slowly up between her thighs. Without thinking, her legs opened as the soft fur caressed, tingling, like a teasing feather. Her breath caught at the pleasure from the big cat's tail as it continued the innocent stroking. She moaned, her body flushing with building pleasure.

Soothed, she found Ther's tail and lightly brushed it against her flat stomach, tickling, moving slowly to her breasts. She watched her nipples grow pebble hard as Pan's tail continued teasing inside her legs. Her breath quickened as a hot pulse filled against her beating heart and her hips began moving slowly, in tempo, rising to meet the tip of the torturing tail. Each furred touch at her center trembled her in ecstasy, quivering in desire.

Her whispered groans announced every tease, driving her wild. A sweaty sheen glistened off her bronzed body as her hips pumped, wanton, hungry, to the rhythm of animal heat. Her big cats, with golden eyes watching, sensed her need and purred their comfort.

Tears welled over glassy eyes as her body begged for release. She felt her wetness as she strained against the endless gentle torture of the petting tails, shaking her soul. She spread herself further and arched higher, begging, begging. Please, she murmured and then, suddenly, her writhing body exploded in waves of shuddering rapture. She thought she might die as fluttering surges of bliss with each tail's touch a sweet torment. Her fantasy real, she pumped wild in complete abandon with mewling sounds of love.

"Jamey, Jamey."

Then, with a settling shiver, she fell back, sated. Moments later, with a deep sigh, she turned and curled around in the hugs of her great cats and drifted asleep.

*

The bell in the watchtower bonged and the signal cannon boomed. They were here. Jade rushed to the veranda and watched the Raptor making way slowly through the narrow channel into the harbor. Even from this distance, she could see excited people running to the docks to welcome home the privateers. Each voyage seemed longer than the last, she thought, but they were finally home and festivities would start on the morrow. But this night, they were hers to enjoy alone in their hacienda. She knew they enjoyed this time also for they were able to rest their bodies with no demands.

The sun was tired, three bells before night. She had a special meal planned. All their favorites from kidney pie to cocoa pudding. Her table, decorated with fruit and fresh flowers, set a welcome mood as she anxiously watched under cupped hands.

Impatient, she climbed, jumping two steps at once to the parapet with telescope in hand. Huffing, she braced between a crenel on tiptoes and snapped the scope open, settling the lens on the Raptor floating against the wharf. She watched dock hands with moves sure cleat her snug with spring lines fore and aft. Focusing tighter, she spotted Jamey and her brother jumping to the pier, sail bags slung over their shoulder. Dirty clothes to take care of later, she thought.

"Can't they go any faster?" she said to her cats.

"They are like turtles."

She watched them stop to chat and greet their fellows wasting more time. Her foot tapped impatiently.

"Don't they know I am waiting? They are slower than turtles, even snails."

Pan and Thers cocked their heads toward her not understanding what the fuss was all about as they boringly watched her pacing around.

A quarter-glass later, Montaña delivered them to the compound gate. Swinging the heavy doors wide, her reserved manner could not hide her excitement as she first hugged her brother with one just a dash longer for Jamey. They were all smiles, talking at the same time, strolling arm and arm to the house. Pan and Thers gave the men a sniff and turned away, unimpressed. They didn't see the fuss.

Dinner was perfect and Jamey and Patch stuffed themselves. Later, scrubbed with fresh clothes and a full belly, they retired to the veranda holding sweet rum drinks. Jade followed with sugar treats as they lounged lazy, gazing at the oranging sun melting slowly into the sea.

"This the life, hey Patch."

"Betterin fighten," he answered, resting his feet on the table.

Jade was thrilled with their gift of a boudoir set cased in silver and precious gems. Lifting the lid, all accessories were fitted and displayed in purple velvet. It was relieved from a Spanish count who had stolen it from the Turks. Her heart, full and happy, matched her wide eyes as her hand petted and closed the lid, anxious to play with it later.

"A fine meal, sister,"

"Aye, as always" Jamey added.

"Did ya miss us sister?"

"No, I fine alone," she teased.

"Well, maybe we should take our leave, Patch." Jamey said, making a mock attempt to rise.

"Okay, maybe I like you little bit, you stay little while," she said, flushing, her eyes down-turned.

Jamey, watching her, settled back with a broad smile.

"Let me see those magic eyes, then," he teased.

Jade as usual, blushed, slowly raising her deep emerald eyes, bravely, to his, while her unsure soul prayed for his love.

"Ah, they're so lovely," he whispered, holding her gaze with a small smile, denying a deeper stirring.

"Be ther more coconut, sister?' Patch asked, breaking the spell.

Jade passed the bowl with a twinge of sadness.

"Wha a nice evenin," he sighed.

"Aye," Jamey added.

"Sister, I guess this be yer best spot when alone with yer cats?"

Jade, remembering last evening, turned with alarm and guilty green eyes. Then, sensing just an innocent remark, she blushed deep crimson and quickly padded toward the house.

"Wha did I say?"

Jamey shrugged at the mystery, but then remembered a similar blush when he had the fever.

CHAPTER 13

ANOTHER SEASON TURNED and it was time to go home. It was a good hunt. The Raptor came about smartly full to the wind bound for White Bay Cay.

At the end of the day's run, Jamey and Patch took a rest, elbows leaning on the bulwark of the aft deck. The crescent moon hung like a tipped cup against a sable night of velvet, telling the tale. A sailor's faith knew she was pouring water.

"She be full, thas sure," Patch observed. "Weel have wet decks on the morrow."

True to legend, the iron gray morn rose still in a dreary mist. The naked sun hid behind the sea as a curtain of silver rain fell in the distance. Shaggy head clouds told the timeless tale of the tempest storm.

"The cup tol true. We're in fer a blow," Patch declared.

"Stay the course. It might pass," Jamey said.

"Huh, yer wishin. They be dolphins on our bow."

Jamey surveyed the sky once more. "Les batten down then."

"Sam'l seen a rat on deck."

"Humph, Sam'l sees the virgin riden the devil too."

Distant back lit lightning, dimmed through racing clouds, announced its closing march as quakes of thunder vibrated the ship's shrouds.

Faster than a whistle, the gale hit, trumpeted by cannon thunder. Bright blades of morning sun vanished behind the drizzled dawn as chilled wind whipped across the decks. Shrill gusts and sheeting rain hit like musket shots as the Raptor dug deep in the black sea. Spears of lightning, cracking like Jamey's whips, blinded the eyes before chased by Thor's thunder while bare masts, stark lit like winter trees, reached for the heavens, beseeching.

"Dump all canvas, save the mizzen on short reef," Jamey ordered. "Helm, keep her steady to the wind. Look lively."

"Dolphins be gone, Jamey."

Words were not necessary as both stared at the sky remembering the torrent storm that doomed their ship long ago.

The sea, rolling high as castle walls, smacked the bow, crashing over the decks with smothering avalanches of water. War hammer waves in perfect rhythm swept the deck, straining the rigging beyond limit.

"It don look good," Patch yelled over the sea howl.

"Check life lines fore and aft, every man a harness," Jamey shouted.

Jamey, looking bow on, spotted the deadly gray curl creeping toward them. It sprouted from the sea with a dragon roar twisting like a thick wild snake to the heavens. The funnel, gulping like a swallowing throat, seduced the excited sea racing toward it, pulling the ship, seeking the sucking whirlpool.

The Raptor bobbed helpless, moaning its displeasure. All knew it was a single plank between them and eternity as they waited for nature's decision. Wind-singing shrouds strained tight as a viol and furled sails hanked tight, twice, tore loose, warning the worst. Standing rigging, ripped from deadeyes, snapped lines that waved like Irish pennants pointing to naked spars with flapping canvass.

Suddenly, the deck lit bright as day as the sky shot scores of jagged roots of lightning toward the sea. The bolts seemed everywhere, the air shuddering with roars of thunder, bellowing its rage.

The Raptor groaned its pain as the crew hung tight for their lives. Sheeting rain stung like hornets, sucking their breath as they watched, helpless. Below, the ship's guts crashed and banged from loose gear, threatening to crack its oak ribs.

The Raptor's bow dipped, spinning in the whirlpool, destined to follow the funnel sucking up the sea. The crew held tight, each with a final prayer as the ship slow lifted ever higher. Screams of fear, deaf against the roar of the storm were heard only by the devil as a final white bone of lightning, chorused by explosions of thunder, snapped and glowed the heavens, rattling their teeth.

Then, suddenly, it was over. The Raptor settled, floating natural in a calm sea. Warm sun splashed over the decks as the hurricane slithered away without another word, seemingly considering them unworthy to eat.

Jamey and Patch looked to the other and started laughing, relieved, wondering how they were still alive. Not a man lost but some banged hard. The Gods that argued their fate must have been fierce, Jamey thought, grateful to him that won their reprieve.

"God's angel, sure, was braced on our bowsprit," Jamey declared.

El Gato, standing near, silently agreed.

The Raptor limped along licking her wounds while the crew mended what they could. No other ship, said they, could live through such dirty weather in that devil sea of darkness. Every sailor gained a new respect and loved her even more.

The next orange morn, the Raptor, rounding close on to a headland, surprised a Spanish man-of-war less than a league off their bow still trying to recover from the storm. Both ships were taken aback as crews turned alert with captains barking orders to come about.

"He gonna run to starbard, capn," the helm hollared.

"Ha, bear him straight, Jack," Jamey ordered. "Get the starbard guns hot, Gato."

The crew jumped too wondering if this was smart. They looked worse storm-battered than the Spanish.

"Four slingers to the rigging," Patch ordered.

Scope out, watching the enemy's course, Jamey jumped to an idea. "Patch, we're going bow on before they figure us. Man the boarding party."

Long months at sea trained the crew to act as one. Grapplers quick took the rail, ready, as the long toms on the bow were primed and run out.

"Hard over, Jack. Take her midship . . . . Fire as you wish, Patch."

Bow on, the Raptor was a narrow target and their cannon, with one load hot with ball and chain, felled the Spaniard's masts with one shot. Slingers took down the helmsman and officers on deck as the boarding party jumped and swung aboard. A quarter-glass later, it was over.

The next two suns were spent stripping material and supplies to make the Raptor whole again. The Spanish prisoners turned out hard with a promise to keep their lives.

The day fell, surrendering to the moon and the Raptor set full sail toward home. Jamey, tired, stood quiet at the rail gazing at the golden sun blazing at the edge of the sea. Its fiery light, glowing off smoky clouds, gave way like stage curtains announcing the speckled night. He fancied twilight at sea more than any other. A pale copper sky matched against a slurping hull brought him some peace as he imagined his ship whispering to him.

He listened as the wood blocks squeaked, "You can pull tighter." The lines twanged back, "Give me some slack," and the sails sighed their pleasure, "I love the wind." The ship's timbers groaned and creaked, "Lend a hand," while the standing rigging stood stubborn, "we can take it and more." Finally, bright pennants and flags snapped, "Look here at me, how grand I am," and when her temper flared, her iron cannon argued her rage.

Jamey, scanning the decks, looked aloft knowing a master's rule and ship's faith determined life and death. He petted the rail, feeling part of her and finished the conversation. "Together, my Raptor, we will challenge the sea and battle any enemy."

Then, his mind drifted back to his lost family and thoughts of failure sunk in. Nine winters had passed and still their killer was free. He wondered if God would allow him his revenge. Staring out to the dimming sun, he whispered his vow once more.

"Every breath DeSago takes is a breath of unfinished justice. I must end this."

Two more seasons passed.

chapter 14

"**A**RE YOU CERTAIN?"

"I hear em say the name," Patch answered.

"Bring him here," Jamey ordered, thinking fate was surely fickle if Patch heard true.

In short order, the Spanish captain, wary, stood facing El Raptor, scourge of the Spanish Main. After this day's battle, he now understood why.

"*Capitán*, my mate here tells me you sail under orders from *Señor* Damon DeSago. Is this true?" Jamey asked, his eyes like spikes, forcing his voice calm.

"*Si Capitán* Raptor," the Spanish captain answered with narrowed eyes.

"Where is his *domicillo*?"

The Spaniard was no fool and hesitated, realizing he had information to bargain with.

"I have your assurance my men and I will be well treated."

Jamey half smiled. "You have my word *Capitán*."

The captain hesitated a moment, standing stiff, weighing the importance of this information and decided their lives were more valuable.

"*Señor* DeSago is stationed in *Santiago*. He is the viceroy of Spain reporting directly to our King Philip." the captain answered, remembering he did not like the pompous viceroy.

"And his mission?"

"He is charged with safe transfer of cargo and the elimination of *piratas*."

Jamey almost laughed. He could barely contain his excitement. Patch, watching, thought he would bust. Jamey's thoughts raced. Damon DeSago here, in the Indies, seven suns away. *He will not escape my sword this time.*

"*Gracias, Capitán*. Your ship will be released after relieving you of cargo and weapons," he said, smiling to himself, adding, "Also, *capitán*, you will carry a message from me for *Señor* DeSago."

Jamey did not disable the ship as usual. Minus arms and cannon, he left it full for the sea with all sails and masts. He wanted the Spanish captain to return with all speed to Jamaica with his message.

Jamey was all energy, wanting to sail at once. He wanted to sail directly to Santiago, find DeSago, and end his life.

Patch listened patiently and after awhile, Jamey finally settled quiet, his mind centered, thinking and calculating different ways to reach DeSago. Patch stayed close, listening to plan after plan to this end. Finally, the candles burned low with no decision made.

The next morn, Jamey sent for Patch. With a mug of hot coffee, they huddled over the chart table. Jamey's mind was calm. During the night, staring at the bulkhead, he decided that a quick death for DeSago was too easy. Besides, intelligence must be gathered to allow any possibility of getting close enough for his blade. DeSago was a viceroy in a Spanish port with Spanish warships and protected by Spanish militia.

Thinking out loud, he said, "I want him to suffer. I want to destroy his standing and shame him. I will bring him low, then, I will watch him die."

"Thas a tall order," Patch said, taking a swallow.

"Here's what I propose."

Jamey spent the next sandglass laying out his strategy. Arguments and questions by Patch could not sway him.

"The games not worth a fig," Patch said. "The only prize, your grave."

"Do you have a better plan?"

"I don like it. It wont work. Yer lettin hate blind ya," Patch said. "And yull be alone."

"It will work," Jamey said with conviction. "I speak Spanish as good with these years practice. No one knows me there and DeSago has not seen me since the galley, most ten winters. I will change my look. I'm doen it."

"But who will watch yer back. I wont be ther."

"Gato will go. His ear knows their talk. He will act the mute."

"Humph, take a devil to catch a devil." Patch scowled.

He tried more reason but saw Jamey's look, seeing it before, and knew the decision was done.

Before the next changing moon, they were in position.

BOOK FOUR

chapter 1

THE OLD WAREHOUSE was perfect, merely a rock's throw from the wharf in the center of the hubbub. Lingering smells of tobacco and vinegar hung in the stale air as she strolled through the high-ceilinged chamber while nervous birds, high in the rafters, fluttered about. Her eyes followed them flitting through dusty blades of light piercing the high slatted vents as the bare floors echoed her steps. It seemed like she had company as the hollow sounds tapped a pleasant beat while her fancied dreams of a new playhouse bloomed.

Maria spent the full summer getting settled and learning the spirit of the town. Santiago, a Spanish frontier village, near circled a beautiful purple-blue bay. The sloping valley to the sea was hedged by jungled mountains alive with wild things proclaimed by squawking macaws and screeching monkeys.

The main street was earth hard three wagons wide with wood walkways lining every shop. Bright colored awnings added life as the low and the high moved about tending their affairs. Ragtag houses and shacks built in clumps behind the main street gave way to finer homes on the out-skirted hills. The two highest hilltops, opposite and facing the other, displayed the governor's mansion and the new Catholic church, each seemingly daring the other. Spanish soldiers patrolled lazy as sorts of every type mixed freely, hustling their daily fare as all towns do.

*

The first thing Maria did was change her name to *Señorita* Aurora Maria Aragon because it sounded more alluring. On further thinking, she shortened it to just *Señorita* Aurora Aragon. It had a nice sound.

Next, she carefully picked a banker unable to keep a secret and rented a respectable house acceptable to the wealthy but resisted jealousy from those with less. After furnishing it in good taste, she hired a gossipy housekeeper. She finished the façade with the purchase of a smart carriage and a large white horse, not forgetting the uniformed groom.

She fashioned her history in a practical way with just a bit of mystery. Her mother, a French aristocrat, was recently deceased. Her Spanish father, related to Catherine of Aragon, was a retired *generale* who traveled with his daughter to this new world in search of land and fortune. Sadly, the fever claimed him not five seasons past in *Hispianola* and she, his sole heir, immigrated to Santiago, a more civilized town with opportunities to pursue her passion in the theater. Her protector and godfather, *Generale Alonzo Mendoza*, would soon be joining her from Spain and would be grateful to those who welcomed her with kindness.

Maria spent a full moon carefully spreading bits of the story here and there knowing they would be collected, matched by gossip, and related to those that mattered.

Through her banker, she managed invitations to several teas hosted by nosy *señoras* and parlayed those into formal invitations for dinners, making sure one led to another.

*

"*Señor*, allow me to present *Señorita* Aurora Aragon. Aurora, this is *Capitán Francisco Luis Vargas* of our Spanish navy."

Maria thought he was quite handsome. He stood, shoulders back, smartly dressed in his naval uniform with jet black hair and gray ghost eyes. She guessed him to be about twenty-five, not very tall but she could tell he had a perfect build.

"It is my honor, *señorita*," he said firmly, bowing slightly, raising his eyes to catch hers with a confident smile.

"You two visit while I see to dinner," the hostess said, excusing herself, seeing the way they looked at each other. She would hope for the best.

Maria smiled, catching the gleam in his eye.

"*Gracias señor.* Are you just arriving in Santiago?"

"No, *señorita*, unfortunately, I have been to sea searching for the *pirata*, El Raptor."

He thought this would impress her. She was absolutely beautiful. Annette, their nosy hostess, informed him she was from a fine family with a sizable dowry. Francisco was a man used to making quick decisions and as his eyes coasted over her body, he decided he wanted her. Annette had whispered there were no other suitors of concern and he added under his breath, *or to eliminate.*

"El Raptor! Everyone is talking about that robber," Maria said. "I hope you catch him soon. He is affecting all our lives."

Maria, never more serious, believed the pirate would hurt her planned business venture.

She was dressed cool in a soft lavender day dress, high collared and half-sleeved with a darker sash. Her modest jewelry consisted of a single necklace with tear-dropped earrings and a double stoned ring, all mounted with the same amethyst gem. Her hair, lush and thick black with a tint of red, was accented by a purple orchid over one ear. But, it was her big eyes of amber-gold that captured him, lured him, and he suspected it was the same for other men.

"Do not fear, *señorita*, each day we get closer. I have sworn to deliver him to death or the hangman."

Sensing she was impressed, he decided on his next move.

"Please, call me Francisco, *señorita*."

Maria smiled. "And you must call me Aurora," she said, feeling her body flush. It was the first time she blushed since she was a child. Although he was a boaster and arrogant, she thought as he offered her his arm, he was handsome and very charming. He made her feel desirable.

As he escorted her to the dining table, he decided she would be his and spent the rest of the evening plotting his campaign.

*

Everything was proceeding as planned as she traveled about in her fringed surrey driven by her Arawak driver. She wore the finest clothes, was friendly and interesting, and soon became the talk of the inner circle. She played the part so well she knew Pedro would be proud. Maria also enlisted her maid's grandson of eight, named *Pepe*, a cute pale mulatto that adored her and followed her everywhere like a puppy.

So, to complete her trick, she dressed him in a smart-looking costume, hat to match, to be her attendant. With a gap-toothed smile, Pepe strutted important, one pace back, taking his position very seriously. Maria had to smother a laugh, watching his strut, but he was good company and made her travels as an unmarried woman more acceptable.

Her old housekeeper clucked, giving loads of advice, but kept Maria tuned with the gossip from other households. Pedro taught her that sharp knowledge of your opponent would win the day. Maria missed him.

She loved this ruse, almost believing it herself. Pedro taught her well. The few French phrases she knew along with her fair complexion and golden-hazel eyes convinced everyone of her origin. Her banker, with a whisper and acting the keeper of a secret, let everyone know of her inheritance.

Because of her experience entertaining with Pedro, she was exciting to be with. At teas and dinner parties, she invented interesting adventures to tell about music and acting, plus, with some ardent coaching, she would submit and sing a tune or two.

The young daughters of age admired and tried to be her friend. The married women worried about her beauty and strove to get her betrothed. The bachelors tripped over each other trying to be the first in line while married men watched and dreamed.

To impress her new friends of her piety, Maria began attending, every morn, the new church on the hill recently completed by the new *monsignoire* from Spain. Although she believed in God, she had never been inside a full church before Pedro's death, especially one this grand. But as her trips numbered, she began looking forward to visiting God and the Virgin Mary to thank them for her good fortune. It was time well spent as it lifted her spirits making her confidant about the day.

Kneeling alone in the chapel, head bowed, she never noticed the hooded padre with an odd *blanco* eye, lurking with growing hate, hiding in the shadows.

*

She was ready. It was time to go to work. The warehouse was purchased and converted in less than a full moon to Aurora's *Teatro Juego*, featuring a bar, full length along one side backed by bottled shelves and paintings. A barn door entry kept a draft of cool air flowing past a divided *restaurante* next to a planked floor for dancing. In the corner was a small raised stage backed by green velvet draping and ringed by oil lamps for the *musicos*. In the center, a full yellow wood wall divided the warehouse with gaudy signs announcing the *teatro*.

Entering the theater, one viewed seating for tenfold facing a large stage a man high. It was also ringed with oil lamps but bigger and brighter than the others outfitted with polished metal reflectors that illuminated the whole stage and draped backdrops. The louvered slats at the high roofline provided a chimney effect ensuring a cooling draft.

Standing alone in the empty hall, Maria twirled slowly, arms wide with a smiling sigh, feeling wonderful. Her theater, almost complete, was just as she envisioned. Her patrons would dine and dance with a finale of a theatrical performance. How she wished Pedro was here to see.

But there were problems. Maria would lie in bed staring at the ceiling, anxious. Expenses were much higher than planned and she was concerned with the number of workers she had to retain. She sighed, realizing that was part of the problem for she was too soft for those in need.

Exhausted, she whispered a prayer for strength before rolling over and drifting asleep.

*

It was a magic morn. Finally, her *teatro* was finished. Maria stood happy, hands on hips, appraising the finished building. Blazed across the whitewashed front, bright red and yellow lettering advertised her theater. The grand opening was the talk of Santiago and Maria's popularity soared. Handbills announcing the date were distributed by eager boys, for coin, that tacked one on every bare wall.

GRAND OPENING
COME ONE—COME ALL
Aurora's *Teatro Funcion*
Friday, November Ten.

Just a half moon away and the day before her eighteenth birthday, perfect timing, she thought.

During this time, Maria was trying to practice for the performance. Busy to distraction, she worried about the time left to prepare. She, of course, would be the featured performer, but she was besieged by requests to be included from the young bored women wanting to be noticed. It was difficult conducting fair auditions, considering the politics, but she realized some concessions must be made to retain favor.

Except for that pirate, El Raptor, everyone that mattered told her this was the most exciting event to ever visit Santiago. Maria hoped Francisco would capture him soon.

*

Everything went as planned, so far. In the last two moons, they purchased a small ranch and started a false mining operation four leagues from Montego Bay. Sitting far north and west of the Spanish sea lanes, these waters were rarely visited. The location was perfect, providing easy access to a small bay for anchoring the Raptor. The entire area was untamed jungle with clammy air, big bugs, wild animals, and rain, endless rain. Jamey was confident unwelcome visitors would not drop by.

Patch was not happy.

It was however, a short two suns sail south and east around the bottom coast to Santiago. They purchased two small sloops from a local coastal trader so they could come and go without comment.

To those curious, Jamey was a landsman, an adventurer with some wealth willing to take risks to advance his position. He learned to speak French on his last military campaign, which added culture to his manner. Although he had wealth, *Señor Jesus Christabel Ayala* did not flaunt. He was a caballero, loyal to his liege, King Philip of Spain.

Now ready, Jamey was poised to set his trap.

The other, wiry and short with a bony head, looked the perfect Judas. His beady eyes, always shifty, sat socket deep close around a fish-finned nose pointing to yellow teeth flashing a devil's grin. Shiver ugly with a slippery manner, Jamey and Patch often pondered why they trusted him. With a split face, his look menaced all, but so far, he proved steadfast. By deed, he had earned their friendship and was now the second mate just back of Patch. Although soundly protesting any value in his bones, his actions proved faithful. But something, both agreed, nagged them, causing a wary faith.

Patient as death, he squirreled around and knew every secret. Evildoers, seduced to trust by his crooked look, died, never knowing the knife was in.

Gato was the perfect spy.

CHAPTER 2

WHEN THEY FINALLY met, the air crackled with wickedness. Both sensed the depth of each other's depravity as if born from the same foul seed. They understood and honored, without words, each other's evil. When Tomás pulled back his hood, DeSago reared back with drawn lips like a snake, recoiling with a warning hiss. Although kindred spirits, Damon shivered, sensing the priest was mad and demented. He knew certain, seeing Satan's eye, Tomás would destroy him with pure pleasure to remain *El Diablo's* favorite.

"*Señor* DeSago, at last we meet. May God bless you and your mission in this pagan land," Tomás said, knowing how to flatter, standing stumpy in his modest church garb. He almost giggled at DeSago's reaction.

Damon quickly recovered, his eyes wary.

"*Gracias, Monsignoire* Tomás, but I know it is you that will tame this godless territory for the greater glory of Spain and the Holy Sea. I merely collect tribute to ensure the growth of our empire."

His flatter was equally slick.

"We each do our part with God's will," Tomás added. "I pray you were pleased with your inspection of our new church and the holy inquisition chamber below?"

"*Si, si*, quite impressive and effective at saving the souls of sinners, I'm sure. My aide, *Capitán* Francisco Vargas was equally impressed."

Damon knew the cave was for the priest's pleasure. Tomás' reputation for cruelty was well known and with the protection of Rome and his Eminence, the Pope, no one dare question his methods, even one in Damon's position. His interest was merely to plot how he could benefit.

The rest of the meeting was spent sparing, testing each other's strengths like a ferret and a snake circling before the battle of death. In the end, each decided to follow their own path, a virtuoso of his own wicked skill, knowing by instinct they would join together if necessary for mutual benefit.

The mongoose and cobra would meet again.

chapter 3

THE INVITATION ARRIVED by special messenger.

YOU ARE CORDIALLY INVITED TO THE

RECEPCION

SATURDAY-NOVEMBER 3, SUNSET

GOVERNOR'S HOUSE

Especial persona

Señor **Damon Vasquez DeSago, Viceroy of Spain**

Señor **Alberto Ciro Marcos**

Governor of Jamaica

Maria's day brightened. What good fortune, she thought, just seven suns before her grand opening. A perfect opportunity to promote her theater to the important people she would meet. My gown must be perfect.

*

It was a damp evening that Saturday. A misty drizzle coated the air as she stepped from her coach, holding her skirts, tiptoeing around the puddles. Stopping on the veranda, she took a deep breath to calm herself before walking into the foyer in the mix of the already large crowd, the rich and powerful of Jamaica. Suddenly nervous, she took another deep breath, glancing around hoping to see someone she knew. She felt her hands tremble a little.

By choice, she had no escort although several enthusiastic offers were made. Francisco was at sea checking a recent sighting of the Raptor, which gave her a free hand. It was somewhat scandalous and would raise a snobby nose or two, but, she reasoned, a little gossip and mystery would create more interest.

She chose a magnolia-white gown with the slimmest farthingale from Spain. Modestly cut to her neck, it was highlighted by cocoa lace, which swirled down between her breasts and met with another circling her slim waist. Her thick sable hair, with tints of red, hung to her shoulders in the newest style with a small pearl tiara. The same pearls at her neck companioned her teardrop earrings and ring. This, plus gloves and necessary lace fan of cocoa, presented her beautiful and regal.

She seemed taller with her slim figure because of a trick taught by Pedro. She took blocks of wood a finger high and nailed them to the heels of her slippers, which were hidden by her long gown. She thought it very clever even though it took some practice.

Jittery, she stepped forward to the receiving line suddenly wishing she had an escort. It was too late now, she scolded as she handed her invitation to the waiting hand of the uniformed attendant.

His voice boomed across the room, "*Señorita* Aurora Aragon."

Maria stuffed down a blush as every guest turned to see her descend the stairs, alone. With visions of tripping, she stepped to the welcoming line of the governor, his wife, and other notables. Remembering to smile, she moved numbly forward with a twinge of panic. Her stomach turned, suddenly afraid she would be found out, a poor peasant girl from the hills.

From the corner of her eye, she noticed several would be suitors move toward her when suddenly, her arm was taken. She turned to see Francisco's serious smile.

Maria smiled back, relieved.

"Francisco, what a pleasant surprise, I thought you at sea?"

"I returned late this noon. I wanted to surprise you."

"Well, I am happily so," she said as he stood puffed up and cocky.

The main hall was large and grand. The vaulted ceiling stood two floors tall with the perimeter circled on three sides by a wide balcony overlooking the main floor. Wall-hung tapestries, evenly spaced, flattered thick velvet drapes surrounding arched windows. The last wall had a protruding orchestra loggia next to a wide sweeping staircase leading to rooms upstairs. Velvet maroons swaged here and there made the room feel rich against Moroccan rugs and oriental vases.

Heavy tree-trunk beams, stained dark, spanned from wall to wall resting on corbels of gilded cherubs. On their center, eight down the row, hung wagon-wheel chandeliers of hammered iron balancing scores of tallow candles. Their golden hue made the men look dashing and the women lovely.

But Maria stood radiant among them all, charging the air with magic as the flickering light against her dark hair and flashing eyes drew instant attention. Beautiful and elegant at the same time mysterious and sultry, she was the envy among women and admiration of men.

Francisco, sensing the male interest, became more possessive. Maria, taking no notice, mingled in and out of the circles of guests absorbed in the festivities, seeking any opportunity to promote her pageant.

"What is the title of the play? Who were the actors? Was it too late to be included? What about costumes? Is it true women will be allowed to perform? I can sing and dance, please let me try?"

The questions and comments kept her busy. Thoroughly enjoying herself, she was the center of attention while Francisco, bored, became jealous of her favor.

Then, an attendant, drawing near, whispered something in his ear and he turned to Maria.

"*Perdón* Aurora, I must leave you for a short time. Duty demands," he said with regret, smiling slick. After a short bow, he turned and climbed the wide staircase. Maria watched him walk away and felt somewhat relieved for some reason.

Turning back to her group, she noticed an alcove off to the side with five church soldiers, huddled. Large white crosses stood stark on their black capes, front and back, as they listened close to a short robed friar. His hood covered his face in the shadows. Curious, she judged he was giving orders by his hand gestures. Suddenly, she felt an unknown chill.

Again, her attention was diverted by a new group of young ladies surrounding her with questions about her play. The crowded hall was full as servants strolled with silver trays of refreshments, while above, the musicians played easy tunes in the background.

The attendant's voice boomed, "*Señor* Jesus Christabel Ayala."

Maria turned with the others to a sudden hush. He stood tall, dressed in black with a white high collared shirt, open at the neck, tucked into fitted trousers. His knee-high boots with silver studs companioned his short scabbard sword. A long black cape, lined in scarlet satin, matched the wide sash at his waist. His bolero jacket, also silver studded, complimented a wide brimmed vaquero hat that he casually swept from his head with a practiced flair.

A quiet buzz filled the room as Maria stared with the rest. He was masked in an unusual way. Parchment thin silver sheeting, rimmed in fine gold, was pressed perfectly to fit the form of one side of his face. Everyone gaped as he descended the stairs into the crowd. Maria lost sight of him as the women around her whispered excitedly with giggles, imagining all sorts of romantic fancy. Maria noticed him as he moved through the crowded hall making introductions and charming the ladies. She kept glancing his way trying not to be too obvious as she absently chatted with her group. She scolded herself wondering about her interest in this stranger.

As he drew closer, she noticed the mask covered most of his forehead dropping between his eyebrows and turning to the side exposing his nose. It continued downward in a soft curve covering his left cheek, then down past the mouth to the jaw. It finished, following the jaw line back, disappearing in his hair hanging long to his shoulders. He looked dashing and mysterious.

Well, he is something, she thought.

Whispers and gossip spread quickly. *Señor* Ayala recently arrived from Spain and then from *Hispianola*. A wealthy caballero, he recently purchased a hacienda outside Montego Bay and was prospecting for silver. He received a serious facial wound in a skirmish with the French leaving him with a terrible scar. He wore the mask at all times which prompted female fantasies of his masked face above them, in their bed.

Suddenly, he was standing before her, his blue eyes holding hers.

"Ah *señorita*, we meet again."

He grinned with mischief, kissing her hand.

"Have we met before, *señor*?"

"A thousand times in my dreams," he said, eyes smiling.

Maria laughed lightly while the other women looked on in wonder.

"*Señorita*, I am Jesus Ayala," he said, turning serious. "I am at your service, now and forever."

"But you do not know me *señor*."

She liked this game.

"No matter, I know your beauty and it charges me to be your champion."

I cannot believe this *hombre*, she thought, as they seemed alone in the room.

"Well, my champion, you will be defending *Señorita* Aurora Aragon."

"Ah, the goddess of the dawn. *Si, mi belleza*, in all things."

Maria's hazel eyes twinkled with delight. He was teasing her but she was enjoying every moment. Men are a strange breed, she thought.

The other young maids in the group grew jealous

Just then a small bell jingled and the crowd hushed. The *musicoes*, raising their tempo, began playing the Spanish anthem and everyone turned to the flag displayed at the top of the wide staircase. Just to the side stood a tall lean man who turned, displaying his profile. A step to the rear, three uniformed officers stood at attention. One was Francisco standing straight and proud.

The tall one was dressed in a floor-long gown in maroon velvet with a gold braided belt with an ornate short sword, plain, but rich, at the waist. Maria thought his profile hard and sharp with a long forehead and patrician nose set between sunken cheeks, ending in a pointed beard.

The music stopped and he turned, facing his audience.

Maria took a breath, her first thought was that of a seraph serpent. An eerie chill started up her back when she heard Jamey, standing next to her, murmur something under his breath. She glanced over, seeing hate in his eyes.

The ballroom hushed silent, waiting.

The attendant boomed, "Ladies and gentlemen, I present *Señor* Damon Vasquez DeSago—Grand Viceroy of Spain."

With the smallest smirk, Damon started his descent and the crowd began applauding as the *musicoes*, playing a slow march, matched the rhythm of his step. Maria thought he seemed to float as his head turned slowly from side to side, lips pulled thin in a tight smile against his teeth. She imagined she saw his tongue flick between them, tasting the air.

Jamey interrupted her thoughts.

"A thousand pardons, *señorita*, but I must take my leave."

Maria turned, noticing his flushed face as he bent to kiss her hand, raising his eyes to meet hers.

"We will meet again, *buenos noches*," he said, turning and disappearing in the crowd.

Maria wondered about his sudden action when the women around her started chatting all at once about this mysterious adventurer. Maria's thoughts were spinning.

Moments later, escorted by Francisco, *Señor* Damon DeSago stood before her.

"*Señor* DeSago, may I present *Señorita* Aurora Aragon," Francisco announced, puffing proud.

"*Señorita*," Damon bowed, keeping his eyes locked on hers.

"My friend Francisco described you poorly . . . Your beauty is beyond words."

"*Gracias, señor*," she returned, blushing slightly.

Damon's black eyes bore into hers.

"He informs me you are bringing some culture to our new world."

"*Si señor*, a *teatro*, you must attend our grand opening."

Taking her hand, she felt his cold skin soak through her gloves. As his head lowered, she noticed his sloped forehead over bony brows. His snake eyes, sunk deep and slanted, looked black cruel. Below his sharp cheekbones, she saw his thin tongue flick just before his stiff lips touched the back of her hand. It took all her will to keep from jerking away.

"I will certainly try, *señorita*, but affairs of state may interfere. You must forgive me. *Capitán* Vargas will be your protector . . . But we will meet again," he said as he straightened with a final smirk and moved on.

Well, that was something, she thought, feeling the chill again.

Francisco hung back a moment, quickly making his apologies. He hoped she understood his duty to stay with *Señor* DeSago. To that end, he had assigned his lieutenant to chaperon and see her home safely. Before she could protest, he was off, leaving a very stiff uniformed officer standing by her side.

Maria tried to continue socializing but the close presence of the officer stifled the mood. She decided she wanted to go home but certainly did not want the company of this soldier.

"Lieutenant, would you be so kind to bring me some punch?"

Nodding stiffly, he left on his errand. As soon as the crowd swallowed him, she hurried for the door.

From the veranda, she noticed the mist still hung thick. Pulling her cloak snug, she scanned the dark, looking for her carriage.

"A moment, *señorita*."

Maria jumped, heart thumping, turning to face the stumpy friar she had seen earlier.

"*Por dios*, padre, you startled me."

"My deep apologies," he said with eyes narrowing, hearing her so easily beseeching her God.

"I am *Monsignoire* Tomás Miguel Costa, protector of the Catholic Church of Spain and *generale* of the Holy Inquisition."

Maria calmed, nodding warily as he bragged.

"There was no opportunity, before now, to introduce myself because of your popularity."

"*Loa Seito, Monsignoire* . . . . I am *Señorita* Aurora Aragon."

"I have noticed you almost daily at our new church."

"*Si*, I try to speak with Jesus and the Blessed Virgin every morn."

Tomás, flinching with sudden hate, said, "It is very faithful of you."

He hesitated, wondering, pondering from the shadow of his cowl.

"I find it unusual someone with your devotion and beauty is not named after your God's mother?"

"Oh, but I am padre," she said, hoping to please. "My middle name is Maria."

Tomás was suddenly elated. He knew it. She could not hide from him, another Maria, handmaiden to God. At that moment, he decided she would die slow and it would be special. His member twitched with excitement.

"Ah, I knew it must be, one with beauty such as yours must have a special place with your lord."

"Well, I pray every day," she said, wondering why he referred to her God rather than their God.

As Tomás pressed forward, the wall torches reflected on his eyes behind the cowl.

Maria flinched back in shock at one black and the other, dead white, staring back at her. Her body shivered with an unknown fear.

Tomás, with a sick smile, sneered at her reaction, hating her even more.

Pushing his face closer, he whispered a warning. "Remember, my child, your pain for your Jesus will test your faith."

Maria, frozen, stood wide-eyed, suddenly afraid as his mottled hand crept from his sleeve, touching hers. She wanted to pull away as he whispered, "We will meet again."

Then, with a sneer, he backed slowly away to the shadows, fading like an evil spirit.

Maria stood, silent, unable to move, finally whispering. "Well, that was something."

She hardly remembered the carriage ride home. Unsettled, preparing for bed, her mind reviewed the evening. Nagging dread hung thick. She felt frightened and flustered. It was some evening, she admitted. She was successful with promoting her theater. That was good. But the men she met.

One was a mysterious stranger with a mask no less, and the other, the most powerful man in the islands who reminded her of a snake. And the last, the church's general of the holy inquisition, sure an evil man. A small shiver settled low remembering each told her that they would meet again.

She sensed the three were not what they appeared, that was certain. But then, neither was she.

*

As Jamey's carriage sloshed toward home, he reflected on the evening. He planned his grand appearance to establish his prominence and accessibility to those in power. He also wanted to observe DeSago to study and learn his movements and habits. He further toyed with the idea to perhaps kill him if the opportunity presented itself and be done with his plan to first destroy his reputation.

But he did not expect to meet Maria.

When DeSago appeared on the balcony, he felt hate overwhelm him, trembling his body, and when Damon started descending the staircase, he realized he could not contain his anger. If he did not leave immediately, he would do something foolish. He must not let that happen, deciding a quick death would not serve justice. Then, his carriage bounced from a rock and he shook himself, his thoughts bringing forth Maria.

He loved her twinkling eyes, full of mischief. Gazing at her, they cast a spell, drawing him, big and round, compelling his attention and melting his blood. The amber centers, sealed in a chocolate border, showed every emotion. They actually changed star bright before his eyes with her child-like excitement and wonder as they talked. Then, in a flash, their hazel ring turned curious when he tried to impress her. Then again, they changed to translucent yellow with brown speckles as she turned clever and sure.

Did he really see all that in just a few moments? Yes, he was certain. She bared her soul through those eyes. But what did her eyes say when he took his leave? Did their goldish hue look disappointed?

Suddenly, he was uneasy, anxious, wondering if she was safe. As he stepped from the carriage, he made a silent promise to protect her.

chapter 4

D AMON ENTERED THE room with his practiced flourish.

The governor introduced, "Don Damon Desago, may I present *Señor* Jesus Ayala of Montego Bay,"

Jamey snapped his heels, bowing slightly to hide the rush of hate he was sure showed on his face. With a deep breath, he raised his head with a flat expression.

"*Señor* DeSago, my pleasure, I have looked forward to our meeting since my arrival and now with the information I bear, I believe you will be pleased," he said, forcing his voice calm while taking a quick breath of relief. Damon did not recognize him, yet.

Damon looked hard at Jamey, intrigued. He at first delayed this visit even though that stupid Marcos kept whining about financial benefits. He decided to turn on his charm for a moment to see if there would be any profit.

"*Señor* Ayala, welcome, the governor informs me of your work to date. So you found silver. Congratulations are in order."

His oily mouth hissed in feigned interest.

"Just a small vein to date, *Señor*, not much in terms of others. I have given the governor a chest of plate, however, to help you and Spain rid our waters of these *piratas*."

"*Si, Si,* come, let us retire to the veranda."

The governor's mansion, commandeered by DeSago, was the grandest building in the Indies. Spanish designed with arched porticoes and balconies, the red tile roof could be seen wherever one stood in Santiago and thirty leagues at sea. Besides the main hall that hosted last eve's reception, the second floor grand balcony surrounding the chamber contained dozens of rooms for offices and bedrooms.

Jamey, following DeSago, observed carefully wondering which bedroom belonged to the snake. He allowed a quick fantasy of slipping into DeSago's room in the dead of night, waking him to see his face, telling him he was the son of Thomas Fallon, and then, slice his throat. No, no, …patience, he thought. Take your time. First bring him down from his lofty perch.

Settling in rattan chairs on the shaded veranda, cool coffee was served as they chatted about the expected war with England, Spain's new world, pirates, and of course, treasure. Jamey, glancing at the view, absently noticed the new church sitting stark white alone on the opposite hilltop.

"Tell me, *Señor* Ayala, might I visit your hacienda in Montego Bay?" Damon asked, wondering just how much silver he was mining.

"Alas, *Señor* DeSago, my house is incomplete and the area is still very primitive and uncomfortable. What with the jungle and insects, the peasants are even now plagued with the fever."

"Well, perhaps in the future."

"Certainly *señor*, facilities should be complete by Christmas. It would be my pleasure to host your visit to ensure your expected comfort."

"*Señor* Ayala, I must ask, is the injury to your face so severe?"

Jamey's hand moved to the mask. The soft kid leather was formed to the contours of the left side of his face. Cleverly cut to cover most of his forehead turning down the side of his nose and covering all of the cheek and jaw, it continued back over the left ear disappearing under the hairline. A proper hole, cut for his eye, was the only visible part of that side of his face. It was bordered with fine leather lacing of a darker hue making it quite handsome, if not mysterious.

His intent was to draw attention to the mask and not his face.

"An unfortunate injury *señor*, received in a battle with France. I wear the mask so I do not offend."

"You are not bitter?"

"No, not now, but I was for a time. I am ashamed to admit I was angry with God but I have confessed. Now I just want to live my life. My only regret is no *señorita* will have me, not even an ugly one."

Jamey laughed, breaking the serious tone.

"I notice you have an accent?"

Jamey tightened, on guard, but smiled.

"*Si*, my tongue was also injured."

Damon felt no sympathy. The questions were asked merely for information to appraise this masked stranger.

"Well, *Señor* Ayala, what is your business with me?"

He was bored and saw no advantage from this meeting.

"Ah, *si señor*, I have information on the *pirata*, El Raptor."

Damon lurched forward in his seat, instinctively flicking his tongue, eyes hooded.

"What do you know?" he pressed with a hard whisper.

Jamey watched him close.

"A quarter-moon past, three English sailors floated ashore in Montego, shipwrecked. Two died within one sun but the other lingered with a fatal fever. He rambled crazy, making no sense, beseeching his God to forgive his sins. He ranted about Spanish evil destroying innocent souls." Jamey paused, deliberately, to sip his coffee. He sensed Damon's reaction and smiled inside, DeSago believed him. *This is the beginning of his death.*

"Continue *señor*, continue. What of the Raptor?"

"It seems the Raptor has been recalled by Queen Elizabeth with all the other pirates and will leave these waters immediately. Some rumor of a war with Spain."

Damon frowned, his mind working. If true, it would be a perfect time to safely move his personal riches to Spain without interference. But what war? Spain will not be ready to strike for at least two winters. All dispatches hinted nothing. Perhaps England has designs. No matter. He would simply pass this intelligence to King Philip and reap the credit. At the same time, he will secretly move his treasure.

"Are you certain of this information?"

"*Si señor.* Because of his fevered state, I told him I was his confessor and he would be forgiven only if he was truthful with his God. I remember his exact words, 'I swear to God and all that is holy, what I say is true.' He then rambled for a time about the evil inquisition and the true church of England . . . and something about killing Catholic devils."

Jamey took a swallow of coffee.

"He then lapsed unconscious. I thought pretending to be his confessor was a clever ploy to convince me he was speaking true," Jamey finished, alert, observing Damon.

Damon's mind was planning. Fate smiled. He would send his two treasure ships this moon under his personal supervision. The intelligence information about a possible attack by England would secure favor with King Philip if delivered personally. The timing of these events pleased him.

"*Señor* Ayala, Spain thanks you. Your information will be relayed to our king."

Damon stood, anxious to end the visit.

As Jamey was escorted to the foyer, Damon added, "*Señor* Ayala, it would serve you well to visit *Monsignoire* Tomás Costa while you are in Santiago. I would have him hear the blasphemy of this Englishman regarding his holy inquisition. But remember, just the information concerning our holy church, no more… You understand?"

The warning was clear in *El Serpiente's* voice.

Jamey bowed, pleased with himself, and took his leave.

After Damon watched the carriage trot away, he sent for one of his agents for a special mission.

*

As his team of two climbed the hill, Jamey regretted adding the extra about the inquisition and the church. He just wanted to muddy the waters and make his story more believable. Now he had to waste time talking to a priest. Oh well, he thought, at least Damon swallowed the hook and in less than the next moon, he and Patch would be waiting with the Raptor to relieve him of his treasure and his life. He was certain DeSago would accompany his ships to ensure its protection and also take credit for the information regarding the faked invasion by England. He must tell Gato to watch the loading of any secret cargo.

Pulling the reins, he stopped in front of the church with a grin, imagining DeSago's surprise when he discovered he was duped.

"*Buenos Noches, Monsignoire* Costa. I am *Señor* Jesus Ayala. I come on short notice at the direction of *Señor* Damon DeSago, Viceroy of Spain."

Jamey stood in front of the hooded friar anxious to pass the information and be gone.

"Ah, yes, *Señor* Ayala. *Señor* DeSago has mentioned you to me. You visit from Montego Bay, yes?"

"*Si*, padre," Jamey answered, a little surprised this priest knew of him.

"I have a small offering for the church."

Jamey, faking reverence, handed over a heavy chest of raw silver to the friar. He swore he heard Tomás' blubbered lips smack as he took it, testing its heft before setting it aside.

"Your God thanks you my son . . . . The purpose of your visit?"

Jamey repeated the tale again with just enough information regarding the evil of the Catholic Church and the inquisition. He added a little more detail enjoying making the slimy little priest squirm.

As his tale unfolded, Jamey's stomach rolled watching this creature of God before him. Hiding in the cowl of his robe, his odd colored eyes under shaved brows glistened cold. His white skin looked sticky soft and dead. Suddenly uneasy, Jamey spoke faster, anxious to leave.

Monsignoire Tomás did squirm but not for the reasons Jamey thought. He was alarmed about suspicions of Lucifer controlling the church. If believed, it would ruin his mission for his Lord, Satan. If a lowly English sailor rambled these thoughts, how many Spanish subjects thought the same? He must push harder to instill the fear of his office so no one dare question his motives.

Tomás thanked Jamey for the information and was suddenly curious about this man with a mask. Jamey's confident manner irritated him. His name, Jesus Christabel, the name of his Lord, connected him directly to God. Perhaps, in time, he could put him to the question. Judging from his injury, he would be able to stand much pain before breaking. Tomás hoped so, it would be more enjoyable. Perhaps some time, soon.

Jamey took his leave, impatient to be away. Snapping the reins, his carriage rolled past the side of the church and he noticed a lingering stench of death plus the din of complaining crows. Looking toward the sound, he spotted a large oak laden full of the raven fruit with numbers enough to sag the branches. Just then, the carriage noise startled them, sending them aloft like scores of black angels, cawing their hate.

A slight shiver passed through him thinking they were not burying the bodies deep enough in the church's graveyard.

*

As Jamey headed toward the wharf for his usual meeting with Gato, he turned to the sound of the bell bonging from the church high on the hill. As it tolled, the town folk poured into the lanes heading for execution dock. Excitement spread like a fever as the mob jockeyed for position wanting the best view. He heard one in the crowd say with excitement that five captured pirates would meet death today to entertain Santiago's good citizens.

Curious, Jamey followed and as he drew near, spotted the stocks and muttered, "Well, I'll be dogged."

Five were chained, lined up on display, dirty with mud and sweat, standing slumped with heads dropped low, resigned to their fate, except the one.

Johan, *El Toro*, stood wide legged, defiant and mean. Froth coated the corner of his mouth as he stared back at the mob, murder in his eye.

The afternoon drizzle had waned leaving the hot sun steaming the cobblestones. The humid heat,

mixed with the town slop, left the lanes smelling like rotten soup. But none seemed to notice,

crowding around the condemned, worried they might miss a good show.

A rank of drums from a squad of militia rolled a steady cadence and the crowd went quiet. The town crier stepped forward with chest puffed, holding the scroll high, shouting the fate of each.

"Two of the scurvy dogs to grace the gibbet, two more to rot in iron cages mounted at the harbor entrance. Hanged up drying till ravens strip their bones white," he boomed with enthusiasm. "A warning to all challenging Spain's supremacy in the New World."

Pointing at Johan, he yelled, "This last scurvy dog to be drawn and quartered, his pieces tossed to the sharks."

Jamey, shouldering to the rear of the crowd, climbed atop a wood crate, eyes fixed on Toro as the giant bellowed curses, frothing in defeat. The mob's taunts baited him and his beady eyes glared back, daring with contempt, his head sunk between his shoulders, snorting his rage like his namesake. Toro's chains rattled, straining from his might, and Jamey thought he might have the muscle to snap them. A part of him wished he would. That would be a sight.

This was the first public execution Jamey ever witnessed and was taken aback by the festive mood. He overheard a woman, just below, tell another this was as fine a time as Father Tomás' witch burnings. It seemed the whole town gathered with children darting in and out among hawkers trying to make a profit. The execution platform built a shoulder above the crowd was fitted with hangman knots lashed to a higher beam. The green water harbor made a pleasant backdrop with anchored ships and molly hawks yelping and swooping, searching for any leavings.

When the drums stopped, an officer barked an order, snapping four Spanish guards to attention. Hip drums, from the side, rolled a tattooed beat as the two to hang were marched forward to face the jeering crowd. A *policia*, scroll in hand, stepped forward, reading the charges once more as the noose was tugged snug around their necks.

The mob hushed, the trap doors sprung, and Jamey heard the snap thunk as the two dropped, stretching the knot, twitching, mocking the Saint Vitus dance. A tad tick later, it was done. He noticed they wet the front of their trousers as the still bodies, heads drooped crooked, turned slow in the breeze. Finally, hanging still like dead game, the mob hustled to the square wanting more blood.

At the same time, across the wharf from Jamey, Gato balanced careful on top of a two-wheel cart. People kept bumping it, threatening his balance and he slapped them with curses. When they turned to return the same, one look at his face made them scurry away. His sneer mocked them as he watched the gallows with some interest, wondering about human folly.

"The mob enjoys them dancin to the hempin jig," he mumbled with distaste.

He knew there would be no friend to pull their legs and a powder necklace would not be wasted. With a shrug, he hopped from the cart and disappeared in the shadows, deciding to give the two sentenced to the cage some poison after dark.

Jamey moved with the crowd to the square not knowing what to expect. Climbing some steps for vantage, he watched the mob set a large circle around Toro lying spread on his back, his arms and legs tied with long ropes hooked to four horses. Calling for silence, the crier boomed the sentence to the cheers of the crowd. With the rattle of drums, the horses were spurred and bolted away pulling in the direction of the four points of the compass. The horses strained, goaded by their rider's spurs against Toro's bellowing roar. Cursing, Toro fought back, curling his bulging muscles, and for a moment Jamey thought he might win the tug of war. Then, suddenly, his four limbs ripped from the sockets of his body. Toro's scream of pain echoed through the still air as his torso flipped and flopped like a landed fish until his heart pumped it dry.

Jamey turned away and left with a shudder realizing he would suffer the same fate if discovered. He pushed through the door of the first inn for a pint.

CHAPTER 5

ARIA WAS BUSY moving from patient to patient keeping everything orderly and efficient. She started the small clinic moons ago to impress those with influence but now she loved it. It made her heart feel good.

The doctor thought he never worked so hard as he sighed, resigned to his task. He detested being here but between his wife and Maria, he had no choice. He had to admit she was paying him well. If only they were not so dirty and pitiful. Thankfully, the midwives tended the pregnant. He could not bear that.

Finally, at sun's end, the long line grew small. Maria, hurrying around, again noticed the same woman leaning against the back wall, staring, measuring her every move. Wearing a filthy dress with sticky hair, she stood somewhat bent, holding her side, sure in pain. She looked young but old, watching with dark hollow eyes.

Maria walked over. "Can we help?"

"I got a pain in me belly."

"Come over here to the doctor."

She followed slowly, bent, gritting her teeth.

"Yer name Maria?"

Maria turned, knowing no one here knew her first name.

"Do I know you?"

"Aye, we met once…. Where's Pedro?"

Maria looked closer.

"Conchita? *Por Dios* . . . . Sit over here," she said, leading her to a chair.

"Pedro is dead. He was killed soon after we left you . . . Wait here."

Maria left to find the doctor.

Conchita wondered if it was the *cabrones* she paid with her body. Watching Maria in her finery, her long-ago jealous hate brought some life back to her dying body. It was her fault, she thought, she stole my job. She stole my chance. Now I can't get a peseta for my favor. And look at you now miss high and mighty.

Maria was busy with others but before she left she slipped Conchita a gold coin, wishing her well.

Without a thank you, Conchita snatched the coin like a hungry dog. Then, with brooding eyes, she watched from the window as a dashing

Spanish officer assisted Maria into the modern carriage. She noticed how he looked at her.

Well now, she thought. She's come high from a low place it seems.

"Pity me, does she, with her leavins. We'll see, me pretty. You with your false name."

She bit the coin, pure gold, metal honey, a taste like no other.

Conchita stopped a nurse.

"Who be the fine caballero?"

"That is *Capitán* Vargas. Is he not *magnifico.*"

As she headed for the wharf with the doubloon heavy in her pocket, her step was a little lighter with a full moon's coin for her demon rum and keeper of a secret.

*

It was three long suns. The most he had ever been away before was two. The fishing was poor but finally his little boat was full. They would be worried but he would have a little extra with this catch to buy a small gift on his way home. He missed them. He thanked God his wife had chosen him. His daughter, now a young woman, was as beautiful as her mother. His heart felt full. Juan was a lucky man.

He sold his catch, beached the boat, locked it tight, and patted it like an old friend. It was his one proud possession. He cleaned and repaired it with care and talked to it when alone in the open sea. They were a team that would always provide for his loved ones.

He trudged the hill with a fist of flowers and a small package of sweet dates, his daughter's favorite.

They were not home. Their small house was empty. A little annoyed at the same time anxious, he walked around the small plot, through the tiny garden and goat shed. They were gone. He called their name feeling silly. Nothing. Perhaps they went to the market or . . . ah, he knew, they must have worried about him being away so long and went to the wharf asking for him. It was odd they did not meet on the path. It was a small wharf. A worry lump grew in his throat. He would check with his neighbor. Juan's legs felt like wet straw.

"The *familiares* of the inquisition took them away last sun," the *señora* whispered from the cracked door, fear trembling her voice. "Six, with big white crosses on their chest. Jorge said they are accused of witchcraft."

Juan stared numb in disbelief. His wife and daughter witches! There obviously was some mistake. His women were like saints, always in church, every day, always nagging him to honor God. This was a big mistake. He must see the authorities and set them straight.

Juan ran up the hill to the church remembering some of the other women arrested and put to the test. All were accused witches, all confessed, and all were burned at the stake. Dread spilled into his heart remembering the people being forced to witness the horror and their screams as the fire consumed them.

Juan ran faster.

He must correct this wrong immediately. Witches! It was insane! He wondered who was their accuser. Whoever heard of a witch named Maria anyway, *muy dios*, it was the name of the mother of God. His wife and daughter were named Maria to honor Jesus. They would soon see their mistake. He would demand an apology.

Huffing, he reached the rectory door, clunking the knocker hard. Sweat, plastering his hair rolled down his face, dripping on his soaked shirt. Squaring himself, he wiped his brow and banged the metal ring again. He heard footsteps. With a deep breath, Juan stood stiff straight with fake courage as the heavy planked door opened.

A stern uniformed soldier with a bold white cross on his chest asked his business.

"*Buenos tardes señor,*" he started, hugging his hat. "I am Juan Rodriguez asking about my wife and daughter."

His hands shook.

The soldier, without expression, looked him up and down with contempt.

"They have been arrested for witchcraft," he reported with no emotion.

"But there must be some mistake," Juan blurted. "You have the wrong ones."

"They are being questioned now. You will be notified. Go away!" the soldier ordered, closing the door.

Juan stood paralyzed. His stunned mind raced. He must speak to *el jefe.*

He banged the door again, hard, feeling his anger build.

A small viewing panel slid open. The same cold eyes glared back.

"*Perdón señor*. I have information for your superior. *Por favor*, it is a mistake. I can explain," he pleaded.

The guard snickered.

"There is nothing you can do. Leave now or you will be arrested," he barked, slamming the slat shut.

Juan stood there a long time, confused, worried, and afraid. There was a sharp pain in his belly. He must find the magistrate. He will see the governor or even the new viceroy. He will talk to *Señor* Baca, the solicitor; Juan always gave him the best of his fish. They would help him. He was sure.

Four suns later, Juan stood numb in front of the waiting crowd. The small town square, filled with people of all kinds, mingled silent but for whispers here and there. Hawkers squeezed among the mob and brazenly flashed their wares, hoping for the best price. *Policia* barked orders, pushing and jabbing clubs into anyone close, trying to maintain order. All eyes, including Juan's, were fixed on the raised stone platform, a half man high, covered in black soot. On top were thick wood poles buried in brambled faggots stinking of rancid fat.

Tears ran down Juan's cheeks. No one had helped him. No one believed him. Doom twisted his guts. He failed his wife and daughter. They would die because he could not protect them. Why God, do you do this? He silently implored. Take me. I am the sinner. I will do anything, anything. Please do not let them die.

Standing glassy-eyed, near insanity, he heard the static roll of drums and slowly turned to see his loved ones for the first time since arrested. Sobs of despair choked him as he watched their withered bodies dragged forward wearing the Garment of Shame. The yellow sack cloths hung like shrouds displaying two blood red crosses painted across each breast. Painted front and back were grotesque figures squirming in the fires of hell. Mother and daughter were led, disgraced, shuffling forward in pain, their hair matted around their crazed faces and bright unseeing eyes.

The crucifix stakes, stark black against the azure sky, waited.

Juan's body started jerk shaking, his heart thundering in his ears. With eyes blurred, he watched a shawled woman quickly step from the crowd and press a rosary in each condemned woman's hands. He watched with gratitude, her sorrow, as she melted back into the crowd, eyes filled with tears.

He watched his family being bound to the stakes by the white crossed soldiers while another recited their sins loudly from a scroll. He could take no more. His mind snapped. "Lies, lies, lies!" he screamed, eyes wild, flailing. He bolted toward his loved ones, screaming gibberish, babbling with frothing mouth as he strained to break free from the soldiers holding him back. He twisted and jerked, trying to break loose as he watched the first trail of smoke lead the orange flames to his women. Hysterical cries rose from his throat as the flames flared, his singing screams matching theirs in a duet of death. Then, he collapsed with the smell of their burning flesh forever searing his soul.

Juan's world went black.

This is much better than the last, he thought. They displayed their pain well. Father Tomás, standing to the side, hid in his cowl, drinking in the horror. Standing downwind was the best, he knew, to enjoy the sweet aroma of the burning meat. Watching the crowd close for any trouble, he noted with interest the woman covering her face with a shawl brave enough to give the witches those stupid beads. He ordered a *familiare* to search her out.

Ah well, he thought, two more named Maria were dead, their souls sent to his prince. He smiled to himself savoring the sudden wiggle pleasure in his cock, relishing his fantasies in his bedchamber under a full moon.

Gato, the cat, watching all from the shadows, admired Maria's kind heart.

*

He was drunk, near death, for a full moon. He felt he would finally die and relished the thought as he laid in a guttered drain alongside a stable, curled in a ball, clothed in his own filth. He was no longer human. His friends, at first sympathetic, abandoned him, accepting his desire to die. With a last effort, he rolled on his back in the dung muck as his mind flashed with perfect clarity.

Visions of his wife and daughter, beautiful as ever, smiled from above, calling to him with welcome arms. He smiled back, serene, his body feeling no pain as the heavenly light surrounding his loved ones became brighter. Juan sensed his body slowly rising without effort, floating, as God's psalms filled his heart, his arms reaching to embrace heaven's peace.

But then, his vision twisted and filled with a blood-red stream of fire. Satan's face of Father Tomás loomed before him, laughing, mocking, stealing away his two loves. All was lost when, suddenly, a hand from heaven's white reached out holding the sword of Michael, the Archangel, vanquisher of the legions of Satan, his command certain.

Juan woke the next morn laying in smelly slop of manure mud. Lying on his back, he stared silently at the soft blue sky, in complete peace, his mission clear.

He aged twenty winters in one moon. His hair turned white overnight and his skin curled in deep wrinkles across his face. Old friends did not recognize him and he changed his name to keep it that way. He practiced a slouched shuffle reinforcing his pathetic station.

He obediently called his employer, "master", going about his menial chores cleaning the new church and grounds. When his master kicked and cursed him, he would meekly cower, begging forgiveness.

Juan thanked God every night for choosing him for this mission. In less than four full moons, he learned every nook and passageway, every door and closet of the church. He knew every *familiare* by name and face. He found the hidden passageway to the torture chamber of the inquisition beneath the church, guarded morn to morn. He discovered the secret escape tunnel leading to the death pit. He understood the use of all the machines of torment. But most of all, he learned the mind and habits of Father Tomás. Juan studied hard.

It was now time to act.

CHAPTER 6

H E HATED THIS place. The wet air hung like a slack sail, sucking a man's strength. He would gladly pay gold for a breeze. The crew was surly from the draining heat but it was all that prevented a mutiny.

A carrier pigeon just arrived. It was the only event to look forward to. Scanning the message, his spirits lifted a notch reading orders from Jamey to meet in Santiago this Saturday, November ten.

Patch and crew had anchored the Raptor safely in a hidden bay off a narrow inlet to a sharp dogleg larboard. A full sun's work building floating screens of jungle foliage to block the entrance made the ship invisible.

When Jamey and Patch purchased the jungle hacienda, they walked the property devising details of their plan. As they strolled, colorful screeching birds and howling monkeys filled the air, never ending. This, combined with poison snakes and bugs as big as one's fist, made Patch further doubt the cleverness of Jamey's plot.

"A man can chew the air," he grumbled. "Mark this Jamey, the men wont stand much past three moons, if that."

He knew the heat would bubble the pitch and tunneling worms would feast on the ship's hide. Most here was marsh swamp with blood sucking insects and the creeping vapor was a heavy stench of rotting muck sure to bring fever and spots. He didn't like it one bit, but the decision was made.

Patch first placed a manned roadblock in the only narrow lane to the hacienda preventing curious folks access by land. A half glass wagon ride put you in Montego Bay for food and supplies. But after a half moon of bucket sweat, the crew mumbled hard as one, "A hell hole sure, with nary a woman not claimed."

Earlier, Patch and Jamey established their ruse by telling the town folks they were prospecting for Spain and if successful, their small village would prosper. Gossip spread quick and the villagers, rumors fresh, started dreaming high.

Patch arranged for deliveries by only one person every quarter moon at a scheduled time. To prevent any unwelcome surprises, he always waited on the lane when the wagon rolled to the gate. On his orders, to fool the wagon driver, the crew acted the part of miners doing prospecting by walking around with picks and shovels. But, as soon as the wagon left, the crew did their usual, which meant lying around avoiding movement and the wet heat. The only real duty was tapping the Raptor, rotating three work crews, keeping her ready for the sea. But mostly, it was just sweating and waiting.

Patch was bored. He missed his sister. He missed white Bay Cay, but, most of all he missed the brothels he visited in the foreign ports.

It started with the third delivery. The old man driving the wagon arrived with the supplies as scheduled but this time he brought his daughter for company. All the men stared with the same thoughts.

"*Hola, amigo,*" Patch greeted, careful to act the friendly neighbor.

"*Hola, Señor* Patch, may I present my daughter, *Señorita* Roseta Leon."

Roseta looked Patch in the eye without the usual blushing young women displayed.

"It is my honor, *señorita. Mi casa su casa,*" Patch responded with respect.

"*Gracias señor,*" she answered with quiet confidence.

Roseta was nineteen and pretty. She was tall as Patch, well shaped, with ample bosom. She was old not to be married but available men in their small village were few. Her father brought her with him hoping for the best. He liked Patch from their first meeting even with his strange appearance. He loved his daughter but knew she must be married and *Señor* Patch was a man of means. It would be a good match.

Roseta guessed her father's plot and although marriage and children interested her, she was not going to be forced to marry a man she did not like. So far, all the men she knew were old, ugly, and poor. With those choices, she would rather die alone.

Patch frightened her and she didn't much like him. He looked fierce with just the one eye, slanted at that. She had never seen this type of man before with a rope of hair sticking out of his baldhead with a chest big as a barrel and muscles all over. However, she did notice he had a nice big smile and a pleasant manner.

By the sixth delivery, she fancied the way he conducted himself and looked forward to the visits. She decided to prod her father to invite him to dinner.

Patch arrived on time cleaned and polished with his tuft braided neat. After endless teasing from the Raptor's crew, he decided to bring gifts hoping for a good impression. Tobacco for the father, flowers for the women, and wine for the table.

The meal finished with good conversation with Patch remembering to praise the *señora* on her wonderful cooking. Then, after an acceptable pause, according to his strategy, he asked the father for permission to take Roseta for a short walk. The father quietly thought hard on the matter. According to custom, a proper chaperone would be required, but since his daughter was already nineteen and he approved of Patch, he relented, not wanting to put any obstacle in the way.

"Of course, *Señor* Patch, but just for one turn of the glass," he answered sternly.

Moon sparkles glittered on the shimmering bay under a star-peppered sky. The lukewarm night was perfect as they strolled in silence, both barefoot in the soft pearl sand. Roseta hummed a light tune as the hushed surf swished cool on their feet.

Patch's belly felt like a bottled beetle agonizing over his next move and what to say. Nervous as a tyke, his only experience was wharf-side doxies. As his mind wrestled, Roseta, after giving him a warm smile, stopped and sat on a big rock and stared quietly toward the sea. Patch, taking a seat next to her, figured the time was right.

Suddenly, he grabbed and kissed her.

He figured wrong, dead wrong as she stiffened and pushed away, whacking him hard across the cheek. Shocked and seeing a few stars, he immediately changed his tack.

"A thousand pardons *señorita*. Your beauty made me crazy. *Per favor*, forgive me."

Jamey taught him the smooth turn and he used it now, very sincerely, hoping for the best.

Her anger melted.

"Please respect me, *señor*."

At that moment, Patch saw her differently. He knew only the port bordellos that simply exchanged value for sex. This was very different. He saw Roseta now as a person with feelings and her own mind, a woman to be loved and protected as his sister. Befuddled with these new emotions, he stayed quiet as they walked slowly back to the house. He felt dumb.

Patch bid her mother and father good night, thanking them again for their hospitality. Roseta walked with him to the gate and Patch's tongue was still stuck. She most likely hated him, he thought. All the advice from his men suddenly disappeared, he felt awkward. At the gate, he turned to say goodnight when suddenly she leaned forward and kissed him on the cheek. Catching his eye with a coy blush, she turned and ran back to the house.

Patch was stunned. He rode back to the ranch feeling ten horses tall. His body tingled with a warmth he never felt before and he sensed his life would never be the same.

The next morn, the men, anxious for details, circled him with ready teasing. But all fell silent seeing the same look many times on other lost shipmates. They trudged away, lamenting his condition, agreeing no good could come of it.

Patch visited the Leons often and after a half moon admitted he was in love. He started having thoughts of dropping anchor, which shook him scared. To keep from thinking, he worked hot and hard but the same thoughts kept creeping back. He wanted Roseta to be his.

A half moon later, under a soft tide with their usual walk on the beach, he held Roseta in his arms and feeling his love, she surrendered.

chapter 7

"*Espana* will die in the Indies—El Raptor."

S CREAMING HIS RAGE, DeSago crumpled the message, tossing and tumbling everything in his path. He paced hot, stomping, yelling at everyone near. The ship's captain delivering Jamey's message stood quiet, squirming, knowing his career was ruined. But, he thought, at least he and his men were alive. There would be no reward for navigating the safe return of his men in a wounded ship, barely seaworthy. No, . . no reward. He would be blamed for the foolhardy plan to disguise the ships as salt vessels hoping to slip the gold through. It was clear by the viceroy's rant he chose to forget it was his idea.

"This . . . this mongrel . . . this yellow dog, Raptor," Damon hissed.

No one dared speak.

"This *pirata* dares threaten me and Spain."

Yellow spittle formed at the corners of his mouth as his brow skulled back, blanched white in fury.

"This pirate will die a thousand deaths. This I vow."

With that declaration, DeSago suddenly calmed, his slithering nature returned, chilling those in the room. All knew *El Serpiente's* fangs sank very deep.

*

The loss of another treasure ship further spread El Raptor's fame throughout Jamaica. Myths and legends told by returning sailors, to save their pride, were heralded over the Spanish Main. The one believed most true was sworn by the cross by a sotted tar that sailed honest before the mast until bought by the devil. Standing humped, red-eyed, with tankard foamed, he crossed himself again to prove his honor, telling the tale, daring any challenge.

After an eternity of disputes, it seems, the sea and heaven Gods formed a holy pact to reign as one, their pledge to be tied by a golden chain. To seal the bond, Neptune rose from the depths, his arm breaking the surface of the sea to offer the loose link to Thor descending from the heavens. As Thor reached to grasp his end, joining Neptune in dominion over nature's forces, the sea eagle, El Raptor, with devil sails flying and scuppers awash, swooped between and snatched the chain.

With the Raptor's fist now clasping the golden links, the Gods of the sea and heavens roared for Thor and Neptune were now enslaved. For as long as Raptor owned the chain, the Gods were bound to his will and bidding. Now any fool would know with El Raptor commanding weather and sea, none could expect a mere human to prevail, no one.

But one tale never wavered, told and whispered true. If you dared battle with El Raptor, you died. If the ship accepted its fate, officers and crew were spared, left afloat, less cargo and arms.

Spanish shipping was in turmoil. The interruption of transport incensed King Philip causing dispatches to DeSago with veiled threats demanding how one *pirata* could destroy Spain's commerce under the nose of a grandee that boasted he could defeat England. The King ordered DeSago to rid the world of this pirate and send him his gold, forthwith.

Damon was continually in a foul mood. His fencing lessons the first of every morn went badly for the instructors. Fighting viciously with his Toledo steel, he pretended they were El Raptor and left them with bandaged cuts all over.

DeSago, an expert swordsman adept with any steel, trained under the finest Spanish Dons. Those years ago as a young envoy, standing next to his father's cold body, he vowed never to depend on another for protection. His tall slim frame with long arms made him a target hard to reach and with reflexes fast as his kin, he struck swift as a cobra.

He was equally deadly with foil or rapier plus cutlass and claymore. Although he trained with the best Italian and French instructors, he polished his art with the German guilds with letters of patent from the Emperor, Frederick III. When his father called him to England, he finished training under the modern masters that preferred the slicing and hacking art of the cutlass. The famous swords of Herr Richter and Lord Chambers made him a master in all blades.

Damon enjoyed demonstrating his prowess with four opponents at once chosen from the officer ranks. He reveled in his riposte after feigning a defense and a successful parry. His physical build allowed him to marry the sweep of the cutting edge and lunge to perfection. He relished his victories and the resulting reputation. The King's court had no finer blade.

*

Reports of El Raptor's exploits continued.

Damon increased sea patrols, activating every military ship in the area and ordering more cannon mounted on merchant ships.

For a secret mission, he dispatched one of his smaller vessels, a two masted brig built for speed and maneuverability, mounting thirty-six cannon with handpicked marines and crew.

He promoted Francisco for command.

Francisco was Carlos's best friend and Damon had carefully observed him grow since a boy. Damon, assuming the role of father and teacher, guided both as they grew to manhood. He was impressed with the young captain's escort command from Spain and kept him by his side knowing he was hungry to advance, driven to gain fame and fortune. His was the only ship that wounded the Raptor, who, according to Francisco's official report, ran like a coward. Yes, *Capitán* Francisco Luis Vargas was his man. Damon was certain of his loyalty.

Damon was Francisco's hero in all things and loyal to the death. His mother and father died when he was young, leaving a small estate. Away at school, he was fortunate to befriend Carlos, Damon's brother and last living relative. Damon became Francisco's mentor and he affectionately called him uncle.

He admired Damon's skill with the sword and his ability to command. He watched and studied methods he used to manipulate those around him, thereby, increasing his power and wealth. He studied carefully, knowing some day he would do the same.

Francisco felt honored to be given this commission. He knew his success would ensure Spain's stature throughout the Indies and send a clear message to those who might follow El Raptor. It would also solidify his uncle's power and influence, and as a result, Damon's gratitude would make him wealthy and powerful.

Since his first encounter against El Raptor, he ensured his crew's silence with threats of death. Now, with this mission, El Raptor's end would balance the scales and he would be redeemed. When he returned triumphant, the final plum would be taking Aurora for his wife.

Francisco would not fail. He would find and destroy the pirate den.

That very noon after Francisco was assigned his secret mission, a messenger delivered a sealed letter to the governor's house addressed to the viceroy. Damon floated into the room still cool from a pleasant fencing lesson. He finally perfected a move he had practiced for four seasons.

With a flourish, pleased with the mission Francisco was pursuing, he dismissed the courier and opened the letter, spreading the paper open while sipping the cool tea.

His scream of rage echoed through every corridor. Guards jumped and servants shrunk from the sound. Damon's hand trembled, reading the message again.

"Your murdered dead will be avenged.—El Raptor."

Damon's usual calculated calm was lost. Throwing the note in the air, he sliced it cleanly with his rapier, screaming for his aides.

"Bring that messenger back here, now!" he yelled.

His usual floating movements reverted again to stomping and pacing, fantasizing about the many ways he would kill that pirate, the cur, the coward who would not face him.

The messenger was dragged back, fearing death. Damon forced himself to calm after learning the messenger was sent by the ship's captain just returning after attacked by El Raptor.

"Guard, arrest the captain and bring him before me immediately."

DeSago's black eyes hooded, his tongue flitting through bared teeth. That Spanish captain would now fear death.

*

She fidgeted, wringing her hands, never before in such a fine room, afraid to sit on the burgundy velvet. She spent some time trying to make herself presentable but this place reminded her she was from the gutter.

Finally, a foppish attendant walked through the heavy door. She had begged to see Captain Vargas.

"Ah *señora*, my apologies. *Capitán* Vargas is busy with affairs of state. I have been charged to relay your message."

"An me pay?"

"I am authorized to pay for the information if it is worthy," he said, trying not to show his disgust with this wretched woman.

An hourglass later, Conchita headed back to the wharf, mouth wetted, dreaming of rum. She staggered ever forward with her belly pain toward her favorite tavern, the heavy jingle of thirty pieces of eight resting in her pocket.

Later, in her cups, she would wonder, just for a moment, if this was how Judas felt.

CHAPTER 8

THE NEXT LATE noon after the governor's *reception,* Jamey accidentally bumped into Maria in the town square walking from her theater. It was just past siesta and the sun was still warm. Villagers started stirring with shops and vendors opening doors and dropping awnings looking forward to a cool evening. The market came to life with rich aromas of flowers and ripe fruit blended with caramel coffee and braised pork.

He was dressed cool with a baggy cotton shirt and knee high boots over loose trousers. His silver sword hung comfortable as he swept off his wide brimmed hat.

"Ah *señorita,* fortune smiles on me," he said, bowing with a cocky grin.

Surprised, Maria recovered with a warm smile.

"Hola, *señor* stranger, you appear again," she teased.

"Again, my apologies for last eventide. You must forgive me."

His blue eyes twinkled with fake sorrow.

The sunlight lit her eyes like daystars, full of life, happy and carefree, and with meeting Jamey, full of mischief.

"We shall see. I believe I will make you earn your forgiveness," she returned, blushing, snapping open her lace fan.

"Any penance to prove myself and regain your favor."

As her eyes held him, he felt bewitched and welcomed it.

"A cool treat in the shady patio across the lane would be a start."

She smiled, blushing deeper, surprised at her brazen behavior.

Returning her smile, he stepped beside her, offering his arm.

Her plain white cotton dress with few petticoats caught male stares. The soft fabric fit perfectly against her body under a brimmed linen hat and matching parasol.

Jamey's kid-leather day mask was again perfectly formed against his face. Its skin-toned tan gave him a rakish look making one almost forget he was wearing it.

The next hourglass was spent laughing and teasing in a hundred ways. A wizard would say it was his mix between pestle and mortar. The astronomer would declare it was the time of the stars. A cleric would proclaim its God's design. The fool, a fortunate wager. One thing certain, some magic fired the air only nature understood.

"My friends call me Jesse and . . . I count you my friend," Jamey said, his mood turning serious.

Maria paused, looked into his eyes and her heart warmed.

"Thank you . . . Jesse," she softly answered. "Please, call me Aurora."

"Aurora, a *beautiful dawn*. . . . but I find it unusual you have no other?"

"But I do, it is *Señorita* Aurora Maria Aragon," she returned, teasing.

"Ah, well then, you will be Maria to me, from this moment."

"But all my friends call me Aurora."

"You will discover, Maria, I am not like the rest."

When they parted, each knew without words they would be good friends.

The next afternoon they *accidentally* crossed paths again.

He waited in the shade of a palmetto as she turned the corner, greeting all passer-byes, her skirts swirling in a sassy saunter.

With perfect timing, Jamey stepped around the corner.

"Maria, what a surprise," he said as truthfully as he could.

"Hello Jesse," she returned, smiling with suspicion.

"The goddess of the dawn smiles on me this day," he declared, with some poor acting, looking piously heavenward, hand against his heart.

Maria laughed at his blatant fake innocence.

He was even more dashing today, she thought. A chamois mask, again formed to fit, highlighted piercing blue eyes.

"It is amazing, no? How frequent these chance encounters," she commented, her eyes sparkling their amusement.

Both laughed as he escorted her to the same patio for refreshment. She was happy to have a friend. Like Pedro, he was easy to talk to as she excitedly chatted about the problems and planning of her theater.

Between sips, she casually mentioned she was a little nervous because there was still so much to do and expenses were much more than expected. But, she sighed, she was confidant all would go well because an old sage, just this morn, predicted so. Also, with eyes twinkling, her birthday was the very next sun, which was sure a good omen. But, then, she frowned. That robber, *Enrigue*, the local supplier, was charging higher prices knowing she had no choice. Also, if there were not enough difficulties, a rabble gang loitered, pressing for coin to ensure her customers were not harassed. These, plus the many other problems, like hiring the best workers, auditioning, and finding time to rehearse, seemed never ending.

Sighing seriously, she took another sip, realizing she was going on and on but it was nice to talk to someone. She could tell he was interested, paying attention by asking good questions and offering sound advice. He wanted to know more about the gang of toughs, their numbers, and if there was some way to identify them. Maria could remember the leader missing an ear but that was all she knew. She reported them to the *policia* but they just shrugged. Jesse made her promise to be careful.

Jamey asked, "I believe I know your supplier, this *Enrigue* fellow, his last name is Sanchez, no?"

"No, that is not the one, his name is *Enrigue Ortiz*. He is not very honest."

"Well, I am sure we have the same banker, the one on Bantor Street?"

"Bantor Street? No, my bank is on Paz Lane."

Jamey, without expression, took careful note.

"Speaking of problems brings to mind another matter that you might guide me," she said. "A strange fellow seems to have adopted the position of my protector. I was alarmed at first but he seems to have my best interests . . ."

Jamey tensed thinking the worst as she continued. "Poor soul, he is ugly and mute but when a hombre made a vulgar remark and another hinted at a liberty, one glare from him and they shrunk away. They call him Gato. I believe he has a good heart but his actions seem strange. What do you think?"

Jamey almost laughed in relief. He would have to tell Gato not to be so obvious.

"Hmm, I would guess he is harmless. He has acted proper toward you?"

"*Si*, I feel sorry for him, even though he is lazy."

"I will have a word with him when next at the theater and give you my opinion."

With the many *accidental* encounters, their friendship quickly deepened. He loved her flashing eyes and feisty manner. Maria never had a true friend similar in age, especially a male friend. Except for Pedro, she was suspicious of most people, especially men. But, Jamey was different, she could relax with him and be herself.

She made him promise to attend her grand opening, reserving him special seats. She coyly added he may bring a friend but silently hoped, for some reason she did not understand, it would not be a female. He promised to be there.

As they stood to part, Jamey asked if he could escort her to the fighting of the bulls on Sunday.

"Oh, I am sorry Jesse, but I promised *Capitán* Vargas I would accompany him."

"*Capitán* Vargas?" Jamey flushed. "I have heard of him. Is he not Viceroy Damon DeSago's attaché?"

"*Si*, he was at the *recepcion*. You left so quickly you did not meet."

"Ah, perhaps we will, . . by chance of course," he said.

Jamey, disappointed, forced a smile, feeling a twinge of hurt he did not understand. Then, turning serious, he looked into her eyes, "Maria, always remember me if you need a friend."

Then, with a touch tip to his sombrero, he nodded and walked away.

*

On Sunday, late noon, the bloody sun retreated low in the musty air as trumpets summoned the people to witness the ageless battle of the bulls. Villagers, rich and poor, milled about gathering to the makeshift seating around the bull ring. Jamey eagerly waited out of sight for Maria to arrive. He wanted to meet this Vargas fellow for a couple of reasons. He heard Damon was his mentor and a family friend, therefore an enemy. But most of all, he admitted, he wanted to know if Maria was attracted to him. Was he jealous? No, he just wanted to make sure she was not being taken advantage of. She was his friend and he owed her his protection. He couldn't be jealous. Maria had shown no interest other than friendship. What did he expect? What did he wish for?

They were from two different worlds and he was not what he pretended. He was the enemy of Spain and must leave the island soon. They could never be more than friends. What did he expect? What did he wish for?

His mask this day was of wood, carved skin thin and trimmed in dark laced leather. His wide brimmed gaucho, shading his face dark, cast shadows over his white open collared shirt colored by a red sweat scarf at the neck. His boots went to the thigh, cuffed at the top with silver trim, matching the silver scabbard of his short sword hanging low on a silver studded belt. One ox-hide whip, slung casually over his shoulder, made him look more cowboy than pirate.

From the shadows he watched her step gracefully from the carriage. She was beautiful. Her sultry look, somehow innocent, was shaded by a full rimmed hat as she took her escort's hand and smiled at him. Jamey felt the same twinge in his gut as an uncontrollable flush of hurt and anger hit his heart. His mind panicked and stomach turned as the thought of losing her became real.

He knew then with sudden clarity he would fight any battle to possess her.

Jamey's eyes narrowed as they approached. Francisco, fully preened, was in dress uniform, arrogant and cock sure. Glancing around, he wanted to make sure others noticed him escorting this beautiful woman, *his woman.*

Jamey thought he was short.

As they approached, Jamey casually stepped from behind the shaded column in front of their path.

"By the saints, Maria! What fortune to see you here," he said, tying to act surprised.

"Jesse, I did not think you were attending," she said as she felt Francisco's arm stiffen, sensing the instant tension between the two.

"Jesse, may I introduce *Capitán* Francisco Vargas…. Francisco, this is *Señor* Jesus Ayala."

She took a deep breath hoping there would not be a scene.

"*Capitán* Vargas, my pleasure," Jamey said, bowing slightly, his eyes locked on the other.

Francisco nodded stiffly, noticing the unusual mask Jamey wore. This must be the hombre that provided the intelligence about El Raptor to Damon, he thought. But how does he know Aurora?

"Ah, *Señor* Ayala, my uncle, Don DeSago has mentioned you. Your information about the *pirata* Raptor should be useful. I am certain he will be my prisoner or dead very soon."

Francisco could not help boasting a little.

"*Si*, I have no doubt. Tales told say he is like a phantom in our midst. Who can say, perhaps he is even at the fights today cheering with us," Jamey said, smiling mockingly, then, added in a serious tone. "A foolish stunt sure, with you and your soldiers so close at hand."

Watching him smile at Maria, Francisco's eyes blackened at Jamey's impudent comment.

"And how do you know each other?" he asked, suspicious, his anger and jealousy flaring.

"*Señor* Vargas, it seems I have known Maria since the time when a young man dreams," Jamey said, smiling with mischief as he held Maria's eyes, pure gold and angry.

Maria felt like kicking him. The scoundrel, she just knew he was going to cause trouble.

"We met at the governor's *recepcion*," she added, somewhat coldly.

"At the reception? How strange I missed you sir, since I only left the *señorita's* side once all evening."

At that moment, Francisco decided he disliked this *cabrone* and would destroy him. His brazen manner and familiarity towards Aurora was not acceptable. He dared to address her as Maria. He is a dead man.

Maria, feeling the hate boiling between the two, looked at Jamey and his snickered smile, not knowing what to do. Just then, the arena trumpets blared and Maria broke the tension by leading Francisco away toward the bullring.

"We must hurry to see the first. It was nice seeing you, Jesse. Enjoy the fights."

As she absently listened to the crowd cheer, "*ola, ola*", she wondered what really happened back there. Jamey was acting like a jealous suitor and Francisco acted like he owned her.

Well, she had news for both of them.

*

Francisco set sail the next morn on his secret mission. Early noon, a messenger delivered a note to Maria saying he looked forward to his return as he had something important to ask her.

It gave her wary feeling.

*

With her opening in just seven suns, Maria noticed some strange occurrences she could not explain. First, an agent deposited a sizable amount with her banker to invest in the theater. The agent offered no explanation and refused to disclose the benefactor's name.

Next, that very evening, her night watchman reported spotting the gang of six, led by one-ear, approach the theater at middle moon. Since Maria refused to pay their demands, he worried they intended to cause trouble. The lighting from street lanterns was poor but he kept a close eye.

Suddenly, from nowhere, a tall figure, like a shadow spirit, appeared, blocking their path. In moments, hearing curses and rough voices, the gang fanned out, surrounding the caped figure. The next instant, he heard swords whipping through the air, glinting in the pale light. Then, the shadow vanished leaving the six sprawled over the ground. Although frightened, he cautiously approached for a closer look and found the whole gang slain. Wide-eyed, he crossed himself twice sure it was the spirit of death.

The next evening, Maria left the theater late after rehearsing with another woman performer. When they were steps from the carriage, three sots full of rum blocked their way demanding money. They pushed vulgar and Maria, angry, ordered them to let her pass. As she tried to step by, one grabbed her arm and at that instant, he crumpled, unconscious, blood dripping from his forehead, a lead ball rolling nearby. Shocked, Maria turned as the other two ran away. She heard a sound like buzzing bees plus two more whacks and the other two drunks collapsed, knocked senseless. Yanking her petrified companion, she ran to the carriage and climbed in pulling the woman behind her ordering her frightened driver to get away. Racing down the lane, she glanced back and spotted a figure deep in the shadows.

Gato melted in the dark, stuffing the sling in his back pocket.

*

When they again met *accidentally*, Maria related the events to Jamey over a cool refreshment. After finishing, her eyes round with excitement, she noticed his bandaged arm.

"Goodness, what happened?"

"This? Nothing of consequence," he said with small laugh. "Just a small cut from the carriage doing repairs. Merely a scratch."

The rest of their visit was spent discussing the pageant. Again, she mentioned in passing her difficulty with the local supplier taking advantage of her. The thief was asking ten times the value knowing her pickle. As they parted for the evening, Maria wondered why he never mentioned Francisco or asked about their friendship.

The next morn, *Enrique*, the supplier, personally visited her at the theater and informed her, hat in hand, all her needs would be filled at a discount. He would of course, deliver without additional charge. Surprised, she was grateful for his change of heart but wondered why his hands trembled.

The next late noon, relaxing on the shaded patio with Jamey, who just happened to be passing by, she excitedly announced everything was falling into place.

"The sage spoke true. All of my problems seemed to magically disappear. I believe, truly, an angel is watching over me," she said, wide-eyed.

"Strange events happen in life," he said. "Much like our chance encounters . . . . Who would question God's design?"

Maria looked at his innocent expression with curious suspicion.

*

Between visits with Maria, Jamey was busy meeting with Gato plotting the downfall of DeSago. Gato's intelligence was invaluable. He knew every movement of every ship, commanders, crew and military strength. He identified DeSago's ships, heavily guarded, loading cargo only under the moon and rumors collected from wayward salts confirmed it was treasure.

The largest ship, *Angelica*, the smaller, *Cortina*, were both merchant chined and would be escorted by two first-rate military vessels. Although rooting every gutter swab with coin and rum, one hole was still empty. Gato had failed to learn which ship DeSago would board. But, all else was proven when balanced against Jamey's intelligence.

As planned, Jamey loosed carrier pigeons every quarter moon to Montego Bay and White Bay Cay to keep Patch and Jade informed. Jade and Montaña were in charge of finishing and protecting their island home while Patch kept the Raptor hidden at Montego Bay primed to sail on Jamey's order.

The last message to Patch instructed him to sail to Santiago in the small sloop the morn of Maria's pageant. Jamey wanted to discuss the final plans and show Patch DeSago's treasure ships so he would know them on the open sea. Also, with two moons turned, he missed his friend and his counsel.

*

This night, under a rope thin moon, Jamey skulked in a dark alley, hunched, whispering, eyes shifting, realizing it felt good to have a friend nearby. The docks, wet from night dew, were bare. Any fool wandering alone would surely lose his coin or more. Lantern lit Inns, squeezed between dark warehouses, filled the air with sotted music and laughter from lost souls trying to forget their lot. Gato's territory, sure, he thought.

From the shadows, standing slouched, Jamey and Gato looked like scruffed dock monkeys as they watched the lanes close. Both idled around the different taverns acting sotted, catching any gossip before wandering the docks.

Weaving toward the ships, Jamey noticed the wharf area next to the treasure galleons was guarded heavy. Faking drunk, singing a ditty, arm thrown over Gato's shoulder, they stumbled toward the gangplank.

When near, Jamey's eyes quick measured the sinking water line before a marine, rifle at port arms, ordered them away. Gato's intelligence was firm, the loading was near complete.

"Yes sir . . . Offfficer. Ther be no sport here," Gato slurred.

As they weaved away, Jamey's mind was working. He knew high tide was due just two suns past Maria's pageant... Not much time.

Remembering Maria, he turned his thoughts to her as he realized the coming end of his plan. His heart turned heavy knowing he would be leaving her behind. Maybe he could come back. He conjured plans of taking her away with him, stealing her if necessary. She would learn to love him.

Gato's elbow nudged him from his fantasy, pointing to his ear. Jamey turned alert, paying attention to the minstrel's ballad drifting from a pub. As he listened, he grinned.

"Hey ho, hey ho.
Ya son of a gun, ya sailorman, pray listen now to me.
This be a tale of a devil ship, born of the serpent sea.

It be a clawed horror ship scratchin at your door.
A ship of sure death called El Raptor.
The capn's a wizard, the crew all ghouls.
Their evil laugh on the wind is for us fools.

Hey ho, hey ho.
Ya sun of a gun, ya sailorman, pray listen now to me.
This be a tale of a devil ship born of the serpent sea.

She comes fer us a ghostly ship, manned by a ghostly crew.
Her cannons hot as burning hell, stirring Satan's brew.
Pray with me, good mates, fer ya know this is the time.
To tally up yer last sweet prayer, ready for the final chime.

Ya son of a gun, ya sailorman, pray listen now to me.
This be a tale of a devil ship, born of the serpent sea.

With a smirk to the other, they melted in the shadows for the next step of the plan. Moments later, as his mute friend stood sentry, Jamey slipped without a sound into the warm tropic bay stripped to his trousers with knife strapped tight to his leg. He frog-legged silent beyond the reach of the lantern glow and dove to the hull of the treasure ships. Black night and black water made him invisible as he measured the draft of each ship. As he suspected, they hung deep limiting them to a certain time they could depart because of tides and the shallow sand bar outside the channel entrance.

Surfacing for air, he paddled without a ripple toward the stern, clamping his knife between his teeth, bent on leaving a little surprise. Holding onto the rudder with one hand, he quickly worked a sweat even in the cool water as he sawed his blade against the thick hawse leaving just one strand together. Finished, he treaded water as he studied the two war ships anchored in the bay. Gato said they were the escort vessels for DeSago's fleet.

Still treading, he surveyed their size and armament, which provided information on their speed and ability to maneuver. The gun ships were rigged for speed but the treasure ships were wide-bellied and full. The convoy of four would be slow but formidable, *a floating fortress*. He wondered a moment with sudden doubt if his plan could succeed. It was sure a thin trick needing fate's luck. With a curse, he shook away the gloomy thoughts, telling himself it must work.

"Ho ther, swab. You in the water."

Jamey twisted around with a low curse seeing a Spanish guard at the ship's rail holding a lantern high. Others joined him, straining to see as Jamey sunk below the surface and swam underwater out in the bay figuring they would soon search the shore. Lungs burning, he surfaced, sucking air. A fast glance around showed a long boat hitting the water manned full with marines and crew, their oars cutting deep, rushing toward him, lanterns held high. He heard one shout, spotting him, and dove again.

Gato, hearing the commotion, shrunk into the shadows, hoping for the best. He cursed low, knowing if Jamey was captured or killed, his chance for gold, either way, was lost.

Jamey broke the surface again, heaving for air, seeing his pursuers near a rock's throw back. At the same time, torches from search parties moved along the shore while other longboats were launched to join the pursuit.

Suddenly, hissing bolts punctured the water around him. He felt a sharp pain high in his shoulder and dove again. He was bleeding and tiring fast, the ache stabbing his body. He needed a diversion.

This time, instead of swimming away, he frog-legged underwater toward the first launch, kicking hard, breast stroking. He kept glancing up, searching for lantern glow reflecting through the water. His wind near gone, he spotted a light and kicked double hard, surfaced fast under the launch and grabbed the transom, pushing up with all his strength. The overloaded boat tipped scary hard, causing the panicked crew to shift their weight to the high end for balance. Then, Jamey reversed and pulled down with his full weight, rocking the boat over and pitching all in the water.

Screaming and splashing filled the air as soldiers with armor soon sank. Crewman grasped what they could to stay afloat while the other longboats raced to assist. Jamey, forgotten for now, melted away toward shore, drained and weak, listening to the screams of drowning men. He always thought it strange most men of the sea could not swim.

Timing, luckily, was perfect. With the guard's attention toward the water, Gato grabbed a lantern and smashed it against a pile of cotton bales near the ship. With a yell, dock hands and crew turned to the fire.

Jamey stumbled ashore bleeding and shaky. Exhausted, he started to slump when a cape was wrapped around him and a friendly arm slipped under his shoulder guiding him into the disappearing shadows.

A half sandglass later, Jamey eyes flickered open.

"Where . . . Wha's this place?" he said, his head spinning and eyes blurred.

"Yer safe," Gato answered. "This be my bed."

Jamey's eyes cleared some to see a small bare room with a lantern rigged in the center.

"A bolt got ya, passed straight through."

"Don't hurt much, but I feel limp."

"Ya lost some blood. The salt water and this will fix it, . . . bite this." Gato put the wooden handle of his knife between Jamey's teeth.

"Hold on," Gato said, pouring the liquor in the open wound.

Jamey groaned as the burning liquid dripped out the other end. The pain finally numbed as he looked up at Gato's expression.

"Wha's wrong?"

Gato smirked at the wonder of fate.

"If the bolt hit a finger over, the hole through your throat would have ended the game."

As Jamey slept, Gato relaxed knowing his options for gold still held.

*

It was strange, she thought. She had not seen him for two suns. Maria missed their accidental meetings and was beginning to worry. She decided she would make discreet inquiries this morn.

As she left the house, a mulatto messenger boy shyly handed her a message.

Dear Maria,

I had to leave suddenly, affairs of business.
I will see you at your premier.

Your friend, Jesse.

Maria felt much better as she folded the note and tucked it away.

CHAPTER 9

THIS WAS HER big day. Maria awoke, stretched, and then had a wonderful idea. She would organize a parade after siesta to create a festive spirit and make sure the whole of Santiago knew about her grand opening.

By the time the sun started falling, she had arranged everything. Under the fanfare of her *musicoes*, the decorated carriages started down the center of town flying banners of every color. For dramatic effect, the performers in costume rode and waved, throwing kisses to the crowd. Colorful streamers and borrowed flags matched the lively music against feather plumed horses. On the first float, Maria waved her excitement gaily dressed in a garish gown of scarves and sashes of scarlet red with bright white trim. The crowd cheered, children laughed, and dogs barked making her happier than she had ever been. This was her moment.

Finally, the grand opening was here. It was to be a glorious time in Santiago as the villagers crowded to be the first. In short order, all seats for the performance were sold with the rest standing full in the rear. The air hummed with excitement, wonder, and anticipation.

Jamey slipped backstage with Patch before the play began with a bouquet of flowers to wish her luck. His shoulder, still sore but healing fast, was forgotten as he introduced his friend. As nervous as she was, she noticed how strange they looked together. Jamey, tall and lean, was dressed in black but this time he wore a short cape lined in white. His high-calfed boots, brightly shined, matched a stiff brimmed sombrero with a white-feathered plume. His ornate silver dress sword was tucked discreetly beneath the cape and matched his silver-edged mask. The mask of dull black leather was shave cut making him more mysterious than usual.

Patch, she noted, also caught one's eye. Built like a bull, his broad smile narrowed his one slanted eye so much she wondered if he could see. His head, shaved smooth with the top knotted tail, was neatly braided and hung slick-black to his back. Loose clothing in tan with a bright green sash over the shoulder and around the waist supported his long curved sword in a decorated scabbard. Both were subjects of stares and comments as they found their front row seats just in time.

Maria hired the same attendant that announced the guests at the governor's reception and after a booming introduction, the stage curtains swung to the side. The crowd hooted and clapped and then quieted as the performance began.

It was a pleasant pageant based on adventures of settling new lands. Gay songs promising a happy ending discovering gold and romance thrilled the audience because it was something everyone secretly dreamed for themselves.

Maria's first song shocked Jamey. He was entranced as was the rest of the audience. Her voice reached out to every corner with a richness and beauty that shook his soul. Jamey fell in love with her at that moment. Her voice bewitched him as deep as the siren songs of mermaids tempting doomed sailors luring ships onto crashing rocks.

"Bravo, bravo!" he cheered, standing and clapping, spurring the audience to join him.

Patch watched and smiled knowingly.

The production continued and near the end Maria was singing her last song. Thrilled at the audience response, she sang from her heart as she glanced at the appreciative crowd, especially Jamey, who clapped the loudest, exhorting the crowd to standing ovations.

Then, a ruckus at the side corner almost broke her concentration. A table of rowdy sailors began singing loudly with her. Upset, she raised her voice as Jamey silently moved toward their table. Siding next to the biggest drunk, he leaned over, placed his hand on his shoulder, and whispered in his ear. As she sang on, she watched the drunk's face twisting in pain, his eyes wide with fear as he glanced up to catch

Jamey's stare. Patch stood close, wide-legged, arms folded, ready. The group quieted immediately and turned to the stage with rapt attention. As Jamey and Patch returned quietly to their seats, Jamey gave her a quick smile.

The performance was a rousing success. What a night, she thought. Everything was perfect. She would be the talk of the town. Maria guessed she was the most popular woman in Santiago. She loved it.

Disguised, he watched close with some curiosity. After witnessing Jamey quiet the drunks with just a word, he wondered if he was more than he pretended. It was clear he was an admirer of the *señorita*. It seems Francisco was correct suspecting it was more than a casual friendship. From the shadows, he decided he would test Jamey's mettle. Damon leaned over and whispered instructions to his aide, slipping him a small leather pouch of gold.

The aide quickly found the six causing the disturbance and filled their tankards with rum, listening to grumbles about their treatment. With gold coin pressed to their palms, he commented he was surprised men of their stripe could be put down by a single dandy. Their reputation, if not corrected, would be womanly in the morn. His comments worked them hot, wanting revenge, so he showed them where Jamey would be leaving backstage by the alley.

Worked to a fever, the six waited in the dark gangway. They would teach the masked freak a lesson or two and to be sure, they recruited six more from the ship. The biggest, who felt the stinging pain down his shoulder by the karate touch, vowed to slip his dagger between the ribs of the tall one.

After a few more thanks and congratulations, Jamey, Maria, and Patch slipped out the side door of the theater into the darkened gangway. As they headed for the street, the three were in good spirits when the dozen ruffians stepped from the shadows, blocking the way.

Jamey and Patch, without words, moved side by side, arm length wide. In the same move, Jamey roughly pushed Maria back against the theater wall.

"Stay here," he ordered.

Maria, pressing her back against the wall, watched the lantern light from the street silhouette the attackers as faceless black shadows reflecting silver blades.

Maria heard one mumble, "Ya mess wi us, ya die."

In a flash, she watched Jamey reach over his shoulder, drawing a long broad sword from his back as his cape floated to the ground. At the same time, his dress sword appeared in the other hand.

Patch, crouching like a wildcat, with his right hand, pulled a decorated sword from his back and a curved dagger in his other, held low. Maria, holding her breath, fumbled under her skirt for Pedro's old dagger strapped to her thigh. Hugging the wall tight, her blade ready, she whispered a quick prayer to God's mother.

Then, on some silent command, she watched Jamey and Patch move in a whirling dance of death and destruction. Jamey's pivoting plowshares threshed and cut their victim crops. Patch, as efficient, plowed his side. Screams turned to pleas for mercy as the attackers died one by one.

As Maria watched, entranced by the sight, she spied one attacker sprawled on the ground faking death. Suddenly, he rose up behind Jamey and lunged with his sword cocked to cut him down. Maria, without thinking, leaped through the air and landed on the coward's back, stabbing him in the neck, yelling, "You leave him alone."

Jamey, turning to her voice seeing her falling down on top of the dying man, grabbed her arm and yanked her to her feet. He pushed her behind him, content to let Patch finish the killing.

It was over. The three were left standing, huffing, looking at the crumpled bodies. Then, with a knowing glance to the other, they hopped over the lumps, ran to the street, jumped in their carriage, and raced off.

Meanwhile, DeSago's aide waited patiently, watching safely from across the lane and smirked with his cleverness. The sounds of the fighting were furious. Moments later, he was shocked to see the three emerge from the dark and race away in the carriage. Curious, he cautiously crossed the lane and crept into the alley, finding twelve dead men. He trembled at his failure knowing DeSago would not be pleased.

From the shadows, Gato, acting drunk, watched all.

Jamey and Patch accompanied Maria home. No one spoke. Maria's blood, still pumping hard, wondered how they both could be so calm. She had seen fights before, even deadly ones, but nothing like this night. The two fought cold and calm in a dance well known. The dim light from the street outlined their moves in a balanced rhythm beautiful to watch. It seemed almost spiritual as their avenging swords slayed their attackers.

Jamey escorted her to the door and cautioned her to bolt it tight.

"You were wonderful tonight," he whispered as he leaned forward and kissed her on the cheek.

Watching the carriage trot away, she felt the soft flutter of her heart from his lingering kiss. She now understood how all her problems were magically solved.

Unknown to Maria, Patch jumped from the carriage up the lane to take the first watch guarding her house.

Gato, deep in the shadows, was already in position.

*

That same moon, a storm battered sloop with two spent sailors tied up against the piers to the rear of DeSago's treasure ships. Orders were barked from a sergeant guarding the treasure ships and the sloop was quickly surrounded by a squad of marines, knives fixed. The sailors explained their mission and were immediately escorted to the governor's mansion and an audience with the Viceroy.

Moments later, Damon DeSago entered the room anxious to read the latest communiqué from Francisco on his secret mission to find El Raptor's lair.

*

When the sun dawned, Jamey and Patch outlined their final plans before Patch returned to Montego Bay. When the next squab from Jamey flew in, he was to shut down the fake mine and pay any workers.

Now, it was time for the second part of Jamey's plot.

*

"*Señor* DeSago, thank you for receiving me on short notice," he said politely with a short bow.

"*Señor* Ayala, the pleasure is mine. We appreciate your patriotism and the information on El Raptor. What business brings this sudden visit?"

"*Muy amigo* from Montego has sent urgent information from the shipwrecked Englishman," Jamey said, watching carefully.

"Information? I understood him to die," Damon quizzed, eyes narrowing.

"*Si*, he waited at death's door but by some miracle, hung onto life. He was in and out of his senses praising God. He is dead now."

"Speak up *señor*. What did he say?" Damon's tongue flicked with impatience.

"He mentioned El Raptor's hiding place on a small island near Tortuga."

"Tortuga! Humph, that information is false. My intelligence clearly places El Raptor on an island in the Exumas," Damon stated remembering Francico's intelligence report.

Jamey flinched, shocked, realizing Damon knew how to find their island.

"This makes me distrust your first information," Damon added, recalling the report his aide gave him about the fight at the theater. His nagging suspicion, which he always trusted, hinted something was amiss.

"But *señor*, I feel certain he spoke the truth. A dying man knows no lie as he views hell." Jamey said, desperately trying to salvage his story as fear seeped deep to the marrow of his bones.

Damon paced the room, quiet. He was no fool. He did not rise to his position without a deep suspicion of everyone and everything. It was the reason he choose Francisco for his special mission. He also dispatched his agent to Montego Bay to make inquiries on Ayala's mining efforts. The report stated there was activity and rumors in the village but all were secret. This, plus Jamey's fighting ability and strange looking friend, coupled with stories of shipwrecked English sailors, fueled DeSago's suspicions. It did not sit right. The information was slim to condemn but now with this conflicting information about Tortuga . . . He decided he would test Ayala further.

Damon said, "El Raptor's lair is named Whi—"

"White Bay Cay," Jamey blurted, almost yelling. "*Si señor*, the Englishman said the same, near Tortuga."

My God, Jamey thought, Damon knew. His knees felt like mush. His bile rose bitter. He began to panic. He must confuse DeSago, delay him. He must get away to send warnings to Patch and Jade.

"The Englishman knew the name of the island?" DeSago asked, surprised.

"*Si señor.*"

"And he says it is near Tortuga?"

"*Si señor.*"

Damon pondered this new information. The intelligence from Francisco and now the Englishman confirmed the name of the Raptor's lair as White Bay. However, Francisco placed it in the Exumas and the Englishman put it near Tortuga, hundreds of leagues distant.

Damon searched Jamey's blank face and continued slowly pacing. Jamey fidgeted, trying to think of a way to excuse himself. He knew Damon was deciding who to believe, his intelligence report or Jamey's lie.

Damon turned to face Jamey, deciding on one more ploy.

"I am convinced El Raptor is in the Exumas and confident our military will destroy them," he said as his snake eyes bored into Jamey for any hint of treachery.

"As you say, *señor,*" Jamey said, standing with no expression.

"I hope in some way my information has been useful . . . . I shall take my leave."

"Of course, *Señor* Ayala, you have been most helpful," DeSago said, returning to his oily nature.

Jamey almost ran to the door.

After Jamey's carriage left, DeSago sent for his agent, ordering him to follow and report.

DeSago trusted no one, especially one wearing a mask.

Jamey, when out of sight, whipped the team down the lanes, scattering people and animals. It seemed forever to reach his quarters, Finally, he pulled up in front, jumped out, and took the stairs two at a time. With shaking hands, he forced a deep breath to calm himself as he scribbled messages to Patch and Jade.

> **"Patch, Our enemy has found us. Return to White Bay with all speed. I will meet you there. Jamey"**

> **"Jade, Our enemy has found us. Evacuate or defend if able. We will be there in three suns. Jamey"**

Rolling the notes tight, he sealed them in the thin silver tubes tied to two of his best carriers. He rushed to the balcony and released them, watching them disappear over the distant hills, whispering a prayer they would arrive in time.

DeSago's agent reported.

Jamey raced around like a madman. He left a note of apology and the birthday gift he intended to give Maria that evening. Now he must depend on his landlord to make the delivery. Also, a quick message for Gato.

Throwing some clothes in a sack, he wondered how fast his sloop could make it to White Bay. He would be sailing alone in blue water in a boat designed for coastal work. He had no choice. Too much time would be lost sailing to Montego Bay forcing Patch and the Raptor to wait for him. He already had some provisions aboard and would grab fresh water at the wharf and go it alone. Nothing would stop him.

Taking a last check around the room, Jamey snatched his bag, flew down the steps and out the door into the waiting arms of DeSago with a squad of Spanish soldiers.

Across the lane, hidden in a shadowed arch, an old beggar watched close. Gato then faked limped away, thinking about profit.

chapter 10

FEELING THE EVIL, he reveled as he sniffed reverently the sweet smell of death, savoring the sour aroma hanging in the fetid air. The sulfured brimstone made him feel immortal as his eyes roamed around the cavern knowing his prince would be proud of his new lair.

His mind drifted remembering Saint Lucia, Holy Maiden and Bride of Christ, she of the stigmata. He shook himself. Why, he wondered, would she now come into his thoughts? Why? . . . In the devil's home? . . . Then, he smiled. It must be a sign . . . a message from *El Diablo*? Perhaps I am the same to my prince. Perhaps he will bless me with the stigmata. A rush of pleasure filled him as he examined his hands closely under the wall torches. The center of his palms felt hot. It could start at any moment, he thought, Lucifer's black blood pouring forth from his hands. It would be wonderful, miraculous. He might assist by cutting the skin to release the blood flow. He will be *El Diablo's* saint, prince of demons, spawn of the devil. He will be immortal.

He waddled like his cousin rats inspecting its hole. The small cavern was perfect except for some necessary enlarging at one end to hold the two iron cages. Next to them, sets of rusty wall chains were deeply embedded in the volcanic rock that faced his beautiful machines of torture, six in all, so his guests could anticipate their fate.

Over time, he tried and tested many types but these were the best. The Spanish chair, the water ladder, the pulley hoist, and of course, the rack. He was expert in their use as a great artist masters his brush. He tingled with pride knowing his talent and studied skill were dedicated to pleasing his prince of darkness, *Dear Lucifer.*

His favorite torture, though, was the dish, created by him. He was the master. Picking up the cast iron pot, he smiled as he remembered his first demonstration to his *familiares.* It was perfect.

As instructed, the *familiares* gathered around, circling him. He ordered a sinner stripped naked and bound tight, stomach up, to an oaken table. With a serious smile, he lifted two mice by their tails, jerking and wiggling, from a wire cage. He set them on her stomach and quickly covered them with the iron pot. Cast was better than hammered, he instructed. And rats were too big and messy.

As they watched, wondering his intent, he took a torch from the pit and carefully touched it to the bottom of the pot, heating the inside.

The mice, squealing in panic, tried to escape the heat by burrowing into her belly. Glancing at the soldiers shocked faces, he giggled.

The sinner, eyes bulging in pain, started screaming. Irritated with her noise, he stuffed a rag in her mouth so one could hear the mice chewing and digging.

"Remember," he instructed, catching every eye. "Just enough heat. Too much and the mice would die, not enough and they would not dig and bite."

The sinner bucked and jerked, eyes bulging in pain, moaning against the rag. He had to order a soldier to hold her still because her squirming almost ruined his lesson. Soon, though, the mice quieted and he knew it was finished.

"*Viola!*" he declared as he whisked the pot away with a chef's flair.

The mice were gone, leaving two small bloody holes into the belly.

"*Muy amigos,* our furry friends are now hiding in the cool tubes of the sinner's gut."

Giggling at their shocked expressions, he skillfully dug his thumb and finger in the holes feeling for the mice. The sinner, writhing and whimpering in pain, flushed his anger. "Stay still, you devil's whore, you will ruin the show." His fingers pushed and twisted inside her until, with a triumphant smile, he pulled them out by their tails holding them up for all to see. They were soaked wet in blood, wiggling and squealing, but alive and well as he released them gently to the cavern floor. Then, he looked hard at the soldier's faces, holding their eyes, knowing this lesson would never be forgotten.

Unfortunately, the sinner, staring blank in a stupor, died. What was her name . . . ? He thought, giggling crazy. Ah yes, another Maria. Her death, of course, prevented the burning at the stake, which he so enjoyed. But sometimes in the interest of knowledge one must suffer.

Tomás giggled like a hyena.

His laughter echoed throughout the eerie chamber as he thought of the mockery and the travesty he had wrought. For above him in this earthly hell was the church of God he purposely constructed on Satan's foundation. A more pure defilement could not exist. His chuckles settled to snickers as he continued scurrying around the cavern, puttering, letting his mind drift.

Since his arrival, he had been very productive with very little effort. The church and inquisition cave, now complete, hovered high above the village. Overlooking all, it made the peasants believe God was watching their every move.

Father Tomás left the daily ministrations of God's flock to two pious priests lodged in the village. There, the fools ministered a small chapel preventing prying eyes from his domain.

Tomás mastered the techniques of creating fear and superstition. It continually amazed him how religion yielded such complete control. In the four seasons past, the terror of his inquisition reached every hamlet and outpost in their Catholic world. He preyed on their mortal fear of God and damnation with pure evil efficiency thus allowing him to serve his own purpose.

His childlike chuckle mocked God as he recognized his own superiority. With his army of *familiares*, he arrested women named as God's mother and accused them of witchcraft. He then tortured them until they renounced and cursed their God. And for the final insult to the God that hated him, he burned them alive and sent their blackened souls to the gates of hell. This was his mission. This was his passion. Each burning at the stake was the mother who abandoned him.

Meanwhile, wealth poured in. The children of God wanted to maintain favor and assure the holy inquisition of their devotion. For gold tithes, he granted special indulgences and was now wealthy beyond his dreams. To ensure his station and favor, he made sure he sent generous sums to Rome and King Philip of Spain.

He decided to inspect the escape crevice leading out to the side of the hill. Standing on the carved ledge directly below the cleft lay one of his favorite places, his death pit. Here, tortured souls dying too soon were thrown to await the swoop of his ravens. Tomás looked up at them perched on the thick oak. He truly believed they were Satan's angels sent by *El Diablo* to serve only him. With limbs sagged, the tree was laden with swarms of the fat scavengers like rotten fruit, waiting patiently for their share of human carrion.

Spotting their benefactor, they cawed, beating their wings in excited anticipation. One of his joys was throwing a body in the pit not yet dead, watching it jerk and squirm while his angels picked and tore at the live flesh. Their pitiful screams echoing among the bones gave him some of his best fantasies alone in his bedchamber.

A tapping noise below disturbed his thoughts and he looked down at a lone raven picking the last meat from a skull. He watched with interest the dance between the crow and squiggling maggots, each wanting its share.

Satisfied, he breathed deep, savoring the stench.

Tomás sometimes wondered if he might be a vampire because he enjoyed the flavor of blood, even his own. Like the blood suckers, sunlight burned his eyes, forcing him to hide in his cowl. He enjoyed drinking blood from his victims in his black chalice, imagining he could taste their fear. He knew he was not a ghoul or a werewolf because he disliked the greasy sweet taste of human flesh. But blood tasted raw like sweet metal. It gave him strength. Yes, that must be it. On impulse, he touched his incisors, petting them. He was sure they were growing longer.

Sighing with satisfaction, Tomás returned to the cavern and glanced in the corner at the raven sheen of his pet perched shiny slick in the firelight. King of his kind, his man-length wings and marbled agate eyes understood only death and it was human meat he learned to crave.

He was Tomás' favorite black angel, the only one brave enough to enter the cave to wait for the best of the kill.

Tomás christened him his *Malo Noche*, (*he of the evil night*).

*

The obsession, forged over time, could no longer be denied.

El Diablo, his prince, once more appeared in his dreams standing before him with cloven hoofs. Below his clopped feet, a cushion of writhing serpents, coiling and sprouting fangs, hissed forked barbs of flame. Standing atop, *El Diablo's* leather scaled form, blackened red, loomed above wrapped in the swirling cape of his beast of fire, flicking and spitting, stabbing the air with blue-tipped needles of flame. His eyes glowed with dead empty holes as he raised his serpent scaled arms wide, reaching with clawed hands knotted in a fist, mocking the heavens, screaming, shrieking his hate, while his long slick tail whipped and wiggled like a tortured worm.

The stink of sulfur swirled and churned, burning Tomás' nose and curling his gut. Tomás fell prostrate before him trembling with rapture and fear as *El Diablo's* hellish cackle boomed in his head with a most important command.

"*Señorita* Aurora Maria Aragon must die a death of pain."

Tomás, quivered, twisting in a fitful sleep. He did not forget Maria was the woman wearing the shawl giving the condemned witches the beads. She was the one visiting God's church above each morn visiting her Jesus and his mother and, he was certain, to spy on him. She also tried to hide her true name by placing it second and because of her beauty she was surely one of God's favorites.

This evidence proved she was, without doubt, one of God's chosen ones. But, as he dreamed with a smile, he had found her out and Satan ordered her death.

Tomás murmured in his sleep and proclaimed, "I am yours to command exalted one. Your will be done."

He tossed, rolling in a night sweat near his rapture, his cock pulsing. He would destroy God's favorite handmaiden by forcing her to curse her faith. This would insult God more than all the others.

Tomás' body trembled in his sleep anticipating her suffering and as his body spasmed, his night scream haunted the evil air.

"God's bitch will die with the pain of all devils."

CHAPTER 11

THE CARRIER PIGEON arrived the next morn, four suns before scheduled, chilling him to the bone.

"Patch, Our enemy has found us. Return to White Bay with all speed. I will meet you there. Jamey."

A flurry of orders jumped the men to action. Excitement and energy renewed, they broke camp, loaded the Raptor, and dragged the floating camouflage aside. They would sail on the morning tide.

Patch visited Roseta late noon, his decision made. He would take her with him. He knew she loved him so the matter was settled.

*

But *señor*, you are not married," the father stated.

"Aye, but we will, soon as possible," Patch explained in his best Spanish.

Roseta and her mother waited quietly in the other room, ears pressed to the door.

"Well, you can surely wait just two morns. Our padre will marry you here."

"I am sorry, it is not possible. My ship sails with the dawn tide."

"Ship! What ship? I know of no ship." The father started becoming suspicious. Perhaps he was wrong about this Patch.

"You want to steal my daughter. No *señor*, NO! I will not allow it," he stated with finality.

Long arguments and discussion failed to change his mind. Patch started to force the issue but figured it would make matters worse. Dejected, he returned to the ranch. The father even refused to allow him to say goodbye to the woman he loved. He had no choice but to leave on the tide. Perhaps it was for the best. What kind of life could he offer her?

A sharp pain shot through Roseta's chest when her father turned Patch away. Panic and grief gripped her, her only chance for happiness, lost. Then, she remembered the fortuneteller's prophecy. *You will meet a man you will learn to love but you must be strong and ready to leave all behind.*

She fretted and cried until drained, but by the time the moon reached its zenith, she decided she must choose her own course. So, after the house was asleep, she stuffed her meager belongings in a cloth sack and slipped out the door. She would ride their old horse to the ranch and release it to return. As she quietly led the animal through the gate, she heard her mother's voice.

"Go with God, my daughter. May you find happiness."

Roseta turned with sudden tears and embraced her mother for the last time.

*

Never before at sea, Roseta thought it was very exciting. She ignored the furtive stares of the men, not caring what they thought. She was with the man she loved.

Two suns out found the ship becalmed, hung in irons with sails drooped like a wet wig. Patch, cursing the Gods, stomped across the afterdeck. Roseta wisely sat quietly next to Gara, who preened unconcerned. The crew gave Patch a wide berth, pretending to be busy, afraid he would turn his anger on them. One murmured there was naught to do if *Aeolis*, the wizard, stole the breeze.

The sea lay flat as a puddle and the tropical sun stared mean. Wet air sat thick and every scratch boomed like a shot. The empty pale sky held but one dark cloud off the starboard quarter and White Bay seemed forever away.

"Lower all jolly boats," Patch ordered. "We'll break our backs to the wind."

He would tow the ship to White Bay if he had to. Patch was over the side first to set the example. In half a hitch, four longboats, on command, dug their oars and the slacked towlines snapped taught, whipping water drops like a wet dog.

From the stern, he stood, shouting out, "To the bastard cloud, mates. God's breath is there fer sure . . . Hear me mates, ten crown each from mine fer yer best."

The men cheered as the oars slapped the sea. All hands pulled a good stick while the Raptor resisted like a mule.

"Give us a whistle, Jack. Let yer warble tempt a breeze."

Patch strained with the others, happy to burn his nervous worry. A quick glance over his shoulder showed they were gaining way. The cloud looked a league, maybe less.

"We got her arse movin mates. Les give a lively tune, Bill. Ther'll be no hen crowing this day."

Bill started low and soon all chanted along.

> "Towing here,
> Yehowing there,
> Steadily, readily,
> Cheerilly, merrily,
> Still from care and thinking free.
> Tis our life on the sea.
> Laughin here,

Quaf . . ."

The cloud grew close and darkened. Glancing over his shoulder, Patch spotted the first thin rain falling like a dirty veil a cannon shot away. The oars pulled tough and fast until finally wayward fat drops hit the still pond, plunking like pebbles, echoing tiny ripples to their own mystery tune. A slow roll of thunder quieted the men as they pulled with purpose, the bones of their back bent hard as a cat's paw rippled the surface, building a swell. Then, as soon, the squall hit, drowning the men's cheers, welcoming the cool rain, renewing their spirits.

"Back aboard mates," Patch ordered.

Tow lines slacked and all scrambled over the sides. The top canvas flapped and filled snapping like a whip while the crew jumped too, netting banging blocks and flapping sheets. The helmsman turned tight on a beam reach causing the course to crack like a cannon as it grabbed the wind.

Patch, with renewed hope, shouted orders to the helm.

"Two points up, Mister Speas. Watch yer luff. Les keep her clever, hey."

Patch stood planted, feet apart, hands on hips, feeling his ship come alive as Gara squawked the change in pitch.

"Gimmee a bright eye aloft. Bill boy. ...Gato, a gulp of rum for all hands for a job done."

Leaning the rail, Patch prayed silent they would arrive in time as Roseta, feeling his worry, moved beside him.

*

Ship's officers hunched quiet over the chart table in the fading light, Francisco scanning each man's face.

"You have your orders. Are there questions?"

None dared ask, tamely thinking the same. He who ships with the devil must sail with the devil. This was not soldier's work. There will be no honor here.

"*Bueno*, we attack on the morrow at the tick of the dead watch. Dismissed."

Francisco enjoyed being feared. As DeSago once said, it made one feel godly.

chapter 12

THE GUARDS HELD Jamey's manacled arms as he shuffled forward, dragging heavy leg irons. Stopping in the middle of the bare room, they released him and stepped a pace back letting him stand alone, shackled and defeated, head bowed in shame and regret.

He failed. If only he had killed the snake when he first saw him instead of playing this charade. Now, the murderer has won and his friends were in mortal danger. He gambled with their lives and lost.

The creaking door before him interrupted his thoughts. The familiar voice of his enemy burnt his ears as DeSago entered with an arrogant flourish of victory. He just finished an enjoyable fencing exercise and taught the maestro a trick or two. Still dressed in his custom fencing garb, without a sweat, he was followed by his dogged instructors and several aides. DeSago wanted to make certain those he commanded witnessed his power and reinforce his reputation as *El Serpiente*.

Still masked, Jamey, raising his head, defeated, met Damon's black eyes and smug smile.

Damon floated forward, his head arched high like an adder assessing its prey.

"Well, well, *Señor* Ayala, I see you are in some difficulty," he mocked, using his rapier as a walking stick and stopping in front of Jamey.

Jamey glared back, helpless.

"My agent informs me you have been acting very suspicious. After our meeting regarding El Raptor, you rushed home and released two messenger pigeons. Most interesting. I wonder why?" He loved to taunt. It was so enjoyable.

"Where were you sending the squab?"

Jamey stood straight, stone silent, meeting Damon's eyes with a dare.

Damon backhanded him across the face with his gloved hand, knocking him to his knees. Jamey caught himself and straightened, blood trickling from a split lip. The spark of hate renewed him.

"I think it is time to look under that mask to see what you are hiding," Damon said as he took the practiced point of his sword and caught the edge of his mask, flipping it off.

Damon stiffened, staring long in disbelief. The last Fallon stood alive before him. Somehow . . . somehow escaping the Spanish galley. As the events fell into place, he quickly collected himself.

"*El Diablo* smiles for it is *Señor* Jamey Fallon, my albatross . . . . So, we meet again." Damon smirked, relishing his double victory.

"I thought you long dead."

Damon's hate stirred, mixing with pleasure, knowing he would have another opportunity to torture the last member of the Fallon clan. His thoughts flashed back those many years to his father's death. He stood helpless before his father's body propped slack against the cold marble wall, his blank eyes glaring back, dry dead, his severed arms floating in sticky blood with his fingers still twitching. Damon idolized his father, imitating him in every way. No one in the castle guessed he was the son as he stood staring, forced to hide his rage, vowing blood revenge.

Now, Jamey's death would complete his oath.

Jamey, erect and defiant, was determined not to show defeat. His heart, though, sank low as the extent of his failure dug deep. The rest in the crowded room watched in morbid fascination as Damon played with his prey.

With a sweep of his blade, he turned to the group as he strutted around Jamey.

"*Caballeros*, the masquerade is done. I present El Raptor and my family's archenemy. You know of course the difficulties he has caused Spain but what you do not know is that his father murdered mine many years ago. I vowed revenge killing his father and all his family but for this last one," he said, stopping, pointing his steel at Jamey.

"This last, somehow escaped. But now God in his mercy has delivered him into my hands. This is a fine day."

Turning to Jamey, his eyes hooded as he took a step closer. His tongue gave a single flick as his venom-hissed whispers, thick with hate, burned Jamey's soul.

"Your God seems to have forsaken you."

Backing away, his voice rose for the benefit of his audience.

"Well now, what to do with this gift, ehh?" Damon teased as a black widow would her mate.

"What is the ultimate suffering and pain I could inflict," he said, stopping a breath from Jamey's face.

"I recall with fond memories the pleasant deaths of your mother, sister, and brothers. And of course, I remember the pleasure as I ripped out your father's heart" he mocked, smirking, reveling in Jamey's misery.

Jamey, red-faced, snapped with rage and lunged against the chains at the snake with every ounce of hate. Damon casually side stepped, laughing, watching Jamey fall on his face, humiliated.

Jamey crawled to his knees, sputtering, "If you were a man instead of a viper, you would fight me with any weapon you choose."

Damon smirked, "That certainly would be interesting but you would die too soon."

His foil whipped through the air directing the guards to lift Jamey to his feet.

Damon strolled back and forth with great drama seemingly pondering his fate. Jamey glared, thinking if he had a free hand for just a moment, he could kill this serpent. Cut its head off and watch the body death twitch. Just one hand, just for a moment . . . . But he knew it was not to be.

Damon stopped, signaling the guard by the side door.

"Ah, I have it. I will hand you over to my friend. It is obvious you have lost your soul and my Christian duty dictates I help all sinners."

Damon's sniggering laugh chilled all in the room.

The door opened and the guard ushered in Father Tomás. Always prepared, Damon had summoned him when he left to arrest Jesse, positive he was in league with the Raptor. Now, finding Jamey and the Raptor as one, he would enjoy the priest's ministrations all the more.

"Ah. Father Tomás, welcome… Thank you for coming on such short notice," Damon's voice sing-songed, thoroughly enjoying his dramatics.

Tomás waddled forward, wary, not knowing what to expect. He did not appreciate the forceful request of the guards advising him to accompany them to the governor's mansion. Now, seeing *Señor* Ayala chained without a mask and no deformity, his interest piqued as he returned Damon's greeting.

"*Señor* DeSago, always a pleasure. How can the church of Christ be of assistance," he replied just as slippery.

"Father Tomás, I have here, El Raptor, the plague of our waters and a spy pretending to be our friend."

DeSago looked at Jamey with a slick grin, his tongue giving the smallest flick.

"Also, friend Tomás, because our God has smiled on me, he has delivered the son of the dog that murdered my father. He is an apostate and I fear for his soul."

Damon's smile turned cruel.

Tomás, now understanding why he had been summoned, felt a rush of pleasure surge through his body. El Raptor was his to torture and his name, Jesus Christabel, the same as God's son, made his task even more enjoyable. *El Diablo* will be pleased.

Tomás stood hooded as usual. The silent observers of this drama watched his stumpy body as glimmers of light from draped windows glowed his pale skin between the shadows. Knowing his look, they still drew back in fear when the light reflected from his evil-colored eye.

"I release him to your capable care. I ask the holy church to do its duty and purge this man of his demons," he said, starting to turn away but then hesitated.

"Oh, also, his true name is Jamey Fallon."

DeSago looked at Jamey with lips curled tight against his teeth in a final sneering smile.

Hearing the name, Tomás turned toward the chained man in confused shock.

"*Perdón, Señor* DeSago, you say his surname is Fallon?" Tomás asked, his mind spinning in anticipation.

"*Sí*, he is known to you?"

Tomás thought fast.

"The name is familiar but I know not where," he said, forcing down his excitement.

"Of course *Señor* DeSago, my good office will handle this matter. Our holy inquisition has never failed."

Tomás turned to Jamey, pointing an accusing finger.

"This heretic, Jamey Fallon, will willingly confess his sins and ask his God for forgiveness . . . before he dies."

Tomás returned Damon's vermin smile. He, too, was enjoying this game.

"He is yours, friend Tomás," Damon said, turning his back with a dismissive flip of his hand.

"I must sail on the morrow tide to Spain."

Tomás ordered his church soldiers to seize Jamey and as they marched away, Damon fought the temptation to just sink his rapier in his chest and be done with it.

"Ho, one moment, Father Tomás."

The priest halted his group and turned.

"I want *Señor* Fallon to know I will entertain *Señorita* Aragon the same as his friend, Clarice," he said, smiling with pure pleasure, watching Jamey's tortured face.

"Ah, I see you remember . . . Take this cur from my sight."

Tomás smiled with a wiggling joy hearing Jamey and Maria somehow connected as Damon's jackaled laugh echoed through the empty corridors, searing Jamey's soul.

Damon wished he could delay his voyage to witness Jamey's suffering. He sighed a little regret realizing he must leave at high tide to allow his ships to float over the harbor sandbar. It was sail on the morrow or delay another full moon. No, he would leave on the ebb no longer concerned about Jamey, confident the priest would relish his duty. He would enjoy the full report when he returned.

Damon chuckled, floating to the next room thinking of the information he purchased for thirty pieces of eight.

"Let me see, I have just one other matter to dispose of."

*

He wept in ecstasy, never before so excited.

"Thank you, God Diablo. I am yours forever," he muttered, thinking this was far better than his first kill, the young Maria when he was a boy. This surpassed all the rest put together. Lucifer truly blessed him.

The *familiars* dragged Jamey to the cave and chained him to the wall. The dank smell of the cavern mixed with rotting blood forced him to breathe through his mouth to keep from retching. With a wave, Tomás dismissed the guards and stood silent, studying Jamey's face. His curious gaze imagined the features of another man.

Jamey stared back, disheartened, but defiant. The priest looked strange with his discolored eye circled in rheumy rings. It seemed no sun ever touched his sallow sticky skin leaving it looking like raw meat left soaking in water. It was putrid, leprous, diseased by something evil. A sudden shiver trembled him realizing Tomás looked like a white devil.

"Your name is Jamey Fallon?"

"*Si.*"

"Your father is Thomas Michael Fallon?"

"*Si.*" Jamey answered firmly, wondering how this priest knew his father's name.

"He is dead?"

"*Si*, DeSago murdered him." Jamey glared back.

Tomás went quiet, weighing this wonderful information as he moved toward Jamey's face, examining him close, feeling his hate boil.

"Well brother, we finally meet," Tomás stated with evil glee.

Jamey's eyes narrowed. "What are you saying?"

"I am your older brother, or half brother, from Spain. Did our cur of a father not mention me?"

"I know of no brother in Spain." Jamey thought he was mad.

"Oh, I am your brother, a bastard, but your brother. Our father sired me with a bitch when he was a soldier in Spain. Then he and my whore mother abandoned me. They left me with an old man and woman who beat and tortured me until I killed them."

Spittle dribbled as his rage grew.

"My name is *Tomás Miguel Fallon-Costa*, or in your language, Thomas Michael. I am named after our father. Costa is the name of those that beat me. Yes brother, my name is Thomas Michael Fallon," he said, giggling like a child with his favorite toy.

Jamey's mind raced. None of this made sense. All his father's adventures, told to him and his brothers before the hearth, never hinted of any liaison. But this creature did have his father's name. Jamey's mind searched. He guessed his father, when young, had many dalliances but knew he would not abandon his child. He remembered how his father loved him and his brothers and adored his wife and daughter. No. He knew his father could not have done this.

"Well brother, you have no words?" Tomás asked as he picked up a rusty dagger and slowly moved towards Jamey's throat. Jamey twisted away as Tomás jabbed with the point, nicking his neck. Jamey winced back, leaving blood trickling from the cut.

"Do not worry, brother, I will not kill you yet. You will beg me for death soon enough," he said, giggling again.

Tomás shoved his hood back showing Jamey his repulsive face. His skin, fly wing thin, was stretched drum tight sure to split at the slightest touch causing his flesh to fall away to the bone. Purpled veins, spider webbed and weaved like a veil, seemed all that held him together. Jamey shivered at the evil.

"I have dreamed of killing our mother and father forever. I confess it is as good to have you," he said, grinning with perverted happiness.

"You will die, Jamey Fallon, but first you will suffer. You will feel all my pain."

His vile eyes hooded and glowed in the candlelight as he decided Jamey's fate. He would use the torture dish. It would be perfect.

Tomás sniggered, turned, and waddled away. Jamey watched him leave knowing he was insane and demon-possessed.

"Caw! Caw!"

His Black Angel's final word sealed his doom.

CHAPTER 13

SHE WAS WORRIED, a full season plus had passed. They were away far longer than ever before. Even the regular messenger birds did not calm her fear.

White Bay Cay was finally complete and Jade and Montaña were justly proud of their island. The great house stood grand on the cliffed promontory commanding a view of the entire island and surrounding seas. Completed battlements with heavy cannon watched over all, warning any enemy. Below, the small harbor sheltered a cluster of small craft providing support for fishing, moving supplies, and coastal security. At the far end, the watchtower protected the only deep channel and provided its own impressive landmark.

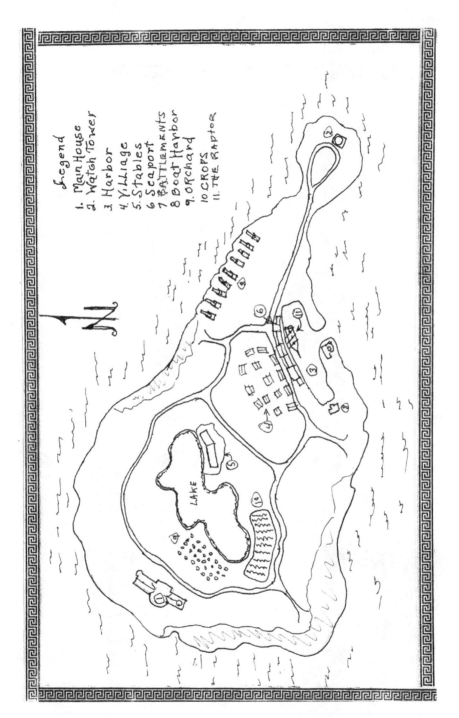

White Bay Cay----El Raptor's pirate island.

Watch tower at eastern edge of White Bay Cay.

The great house on the western bluff of White Bay Cay.

Crops and fruit trees next to the stables were neat and tidy promising generous yields. The small village behind the harbor circled a newly completed chapel with its own bronze bell creating a sense of community. Families and workers were content and treated fairly as they warmly greeted Jade and Montaña during their daily patrols.

Jade smiled, wondering how strange they must appear together. She was hardly taller than his hounds and less than a hundred weight. Montaña towered over her and was most thrice her pounds. Together, they surely made an odd pair but she loved him. He was solid, comfortable, and dependable as she. His good nature and friendly smile, combined with his fierce loyalty to her, cemented that love.

She did toy with the idea of Montaña for a husband. He would be sure and true. She wanted babies, but shuddered knowing his would be too large to bear. But then, she sighed, she did not love him that way.

Jade enjoyed her solitude but was lonely, yearning for something more. She needed to be loved as a woman. Her dreams and fantasies of Jamey were not enough anymore and thoughts he would never be more than a friend visited more often. If he would make love to her just once he would be hers forever because the depth of her passion and her animal desire ran deep. She dreamed often of them together only to wake frustrated in a sweaty sheen with only her fingers for relief.

Sometimes she wished Jamey would catch the fever again so she could have him alone and tend him. She now understood a few things more after asking careful questions of older women. Her sudden blush turned to a smile, remembering their last day in the ship's bunk.

Her body flushed hot remembering the thrilling throbs through her body. A tiny giggle escaped as she thought it was rather like milking a cow, only backwards, but much more enjoyable.

Not a bad fever, Buddha, just enough so I might have him to myself for awhile. Her mind, curious, knew there was much to learn and explore. She missed the pressure of his naked body against hers.

"Just a little fever, Buddha, I promise I will be very good," she whispered, wondering how it would feel with him in her, hopefully soon.

*

The night, bat black with a ghost mist, hugged the still water and every tick sounded like thunder. The lieutenant's stomach churned, his eyes straining against the vapor of the sea. The pirate island invisible in the purple haze.

"A demon night, sure," he mumbled. "Floating thick in this rotting sea."

They drifted with the current not wanting to use the cloth wrapped oars for fear of making the slightest sound. He cursed his duty as time crawled.

Finally, at last, the longboats dug into the slushy shore and the marines, silent, climbed over the side to the beach. Hushed, they formed in assigned squads and with a single hand signal, moved out to take position like skulking hyenas.

The lieutenant cursed himself, trying to block his thoughts. The legends told, sworn by the cross to be true, were many. The worst was El Raptor commanded the weather, the beasts of the deep, and a sea dragon roaring fire protecting all that was his. The lieutenant whispered a silent prayer he was not here this night. He would rather jig with the devil.

Sniffing the air, he stared at the dark. *It was a demon night sure.*

An absent moon and graveyard fog veiled their movements as they crept with nary a sound. The lieutenant now knew the padded canvass wrapped over their boots was a good idea.

Captain Francisco Vargas paced the aft deck, edgy and anxious. He spent the past quarter moon planning tirelessly for this moment and now all he could do was wait. He reviewed the past events while he paced. *Señor* DeSago chose him for this mission above all others and he vowed not to fail.

In a secret briefing with Francisco before he sailed, DeSago traced over the charts knowing the Raptor must have a base for supplies, food, and repairs. A study of the seas and the location of every pirate attack convinced him the den was somewhere in the area he had circled. With Francisco patrolling the area collecting bits of information, he could narrow the search area and locate the Raptor's sanctuary. Once located, he was ordered to destroy and kill everyone. Francisco would never forget the venom in DeSago's words as his snake eyes zeroed on his, the command clear, no one was to survive.

Francisco had cruised the area disguised under a neutral French flag, intercepting every small vessel on some pretense. All aboard were carefully interrogated for any scrap of information about EL Raptor and its base of operations. After stopping eight small boats, six gave with some encouragement, various facts, which when evaluated, pointed to the location of the pirate island. Melding other knowledge, he now knew the size of the island, the population, the number and type of buildings, the warning systems, their defenses, and the time sentries were relieved.

Although pleased with the intelligence, to be certain, he assigned three of his men in one of the captured fishing boats to sail within half a league of the island, anchor, and pretend to fish. Disguised, the three verified much of the intelligence with their telescope.

Satisfied, Francisco dispatched one of the captured sloops to report their success to DeSago. Regrettably, the rest of the boats were scuttled and the men killed. Such were fortunes of war. Secrecy was paramount and could not be compromised if they were to be successful.

Unfortunately, as of two tides past, their information determined the Raptor was not docked in the island's harbor. Francisco weighed waiting for its return but decided he dare not delay any longer. He could not ignore this moonless night and DeSago's orders were to destroy everyone at the base, not sit around and wait for the pirate ship to return. If luck smiled, he thought, the Raptor arrived since his last intelligence. *If luck smiled.*

Francisco marveled at DeSago's deductions and planning, which so far was flawless. Now he, Francisco, would execute the final operation and reap his reward of wealth, power, and Maria.

Just then, a block banging a mast shook his dream and he turned to his first officer.

"Lieutenant, the north star angle." he ordered.

The lieutenant raised his quadrant and reported, "*Capitán*, thirty-six degrees, heavens are clear."

"Lieutenant, one eye to the hour glass, mind you."

"Aye, *capitán*."

The attack would begin when the angle of the North Star to the earth reached forty degrees, which by his calculations, would be about four hourglass twists before dawn.

He complimented himself on this part of the strategy. He agonized over the sneak attack knowing it was imperative all squads strike at the same time. Since they would be separated and positioned over the island, communication was impossible to ensure perfect timing and coordination. A powder shot or flare would alert the sentries, stealing the surprise, so he issued each squad a lifeboat quadrant with a brief lesson on measuring the North Star. He instructed all squads it was imperative they be in position to attack when the star rested at forty degrees.

"Another sighting, lieutenant," Francisco ordered, stomach churning.

"Forty degrees, sir," the lieutenant shot back.

"Why hasn't the attack begun?" he whispered to no one.

Before launching the longboats, he moved the ship within a league of the island. He was close enough to hear gunfire over the still wind, but it was quiet as death. He began to worry something went wrong. What did he overlook? Fear itched the center of his back as failure and DeSago's wrath flashed through his mind.

Suddenly, a powder shot and bonging bell drifted over the ink-black sea, inspiring a relieved breath.

*

Satan's fate smiled. Total chaos, fear, and panic struck the residents of White Bay. Over sixty of the total eighty-two inhabitants were tradesmen and workers with no experience at arms. The remainder with long careers in various wars were older and soon overwhelmed. Most were slaughtered in their beds. Men, women, and children were cut and chopped with blades and axes until one old salt got a shot off. Dogs still alive howled as the bronze bell tolled and death swooped over the island.

Montana's small quarters sat on a low knoll above the other cottages. With the shot, he charged out the door, his two mastiffs ready. Seeing the mayhem, he stormed full run into the Spaniards, war hammer high, whooping his ancient Maya battle cry. In a flash, twelve enemy lay dead from his hammer and the killing jowls of his mastiffs. The three attacked in a blood rage, numb to the saber and arrow wounds as the enemy died one by one.

Finally, the dogs fell, their injuries mortal. Seeing them drop, Montaña, bleeding from a leg wound and a ripping cut to his ribs, bellowed his rage, death in his glare. His eyes found their leader, screaming orders, and he stalked toward him, possessed.

The Spanish lieutenant, crazed in the blood lust, turned just in time to see the brown giant reach for him. He tried to dodge away but was too late. He felt Montaña's meaty hands clamp like a vice around his head, lifting him off the ground. As their eyes met, he was conscious of his last thought, *a demon night, sure,* just before his skull squashed like a melon.

Tossing the limp hulk aside, Montaña, gravely wounded, suddenly remembered Jade alone at the compound and fell back, running up the hill to be at her side.

At the first shot, Jade sprang from bed to the parapet. Spotting the fires flaring amid the distant screams, her heart doubled its beat. Racing back to her quarters, she buckled on her dagger, grabbed Jamey's short bow and full quiver, and headed to the compound gate. She had been practicing with the bow to surprise Jamey and now cursed herself for not training at night.

Once outside, she noticed the slippery shadows of Pan and Thers as they sensed the intruders and moved silent as death, crouching below the wall. They hunted as one and they would simply kill the intruders silently and skillfully as their ancestors. They were ready to work.

The double gates, braced by a beam, boomed and banged from the attackers trying to breakthrough. The gates groaned and shook, but held. Jade and her cats waited. Next, muffled noises of ladders scuffled against the compound wall mixed with clanking swords and hard orders.

"Kill every soul you find, from babes to bitches."

Jade's senses, tuned tight, heard the order and turned her fear into cold resolve. No longer the timid slave of old, she would kill every living thing that scaled the wall.

Her cats snarled just once as the Spanish squads started swarming over the ledge. As each man dropped to the ground, he was met with slashing black fury. Pan and Thers killed the first five almost without a sound, slashing throats with one swipe of their dagger-long claws. They pounced on backs severing necks and spines with a rending tear of their jaws. They ripped out bellies and guts, disemboweling the shocked marines.

At the same time, Jade sent silent arrows into the chests of three mounting the top.

The assault stopped. She could hear hushed sounds on the other side. Jade figured with the first eight killed outright, they were changing their plan of attack.

Jade and the cats, still, with ears sharp, listened close, waiting.

Then, a sudden sound whipped her around to face a large shadowed figure. Going for her dagger, she gulped a relieved breath. It was friend Montaña limping badly, bleeding from a body slash plus two arrows sunk deep in his thigh and shoulder, both snapped at the root. Words were not necessary as Jade welcomed him with a hug, wrapped his injuries, and stood by his side, ready for the worst.

The cats ignored him, watching the wall, knowing it was their mistress' friend. He stood by her side holding a double long sword in one hand and war hammer in the other. The four friends stared silently at the wall, waiting for the enemy's next move.

Outside the wall, the Spanish squads assigned to attack the great house were unsure how to proceed. The intelligence was specific. During night hours, a single woman house servant occupied the compound. That information was obviously wrong. Every man over the wall was dead. One of the marines, jumping back from the top, reported, eyes wide, that black shadows killed them, swearing it was an evil spirit of some kind.

Another marine, wide-eyed, said he heard the devil snarl.

The sergeant, deciding he needed more help, sent a runner. Within a quarter glass, all the remaining marines huddled below the outer wall, waiting for orders. A fast count totaled fifty three.

A corporal from the squad that attacked the village reported. "Twelve are dead, *sergento*, killed by a screaming brown giant protected by wolves. *Sergento*, he was not human, arrows and sabers could not stop him." He crossed himself. "I watched the lieutenant's eyes bulge from their sockets as the Goliath crushed his head, popped like a plum . . . Then he vanished, like an evil spirit," he finished, half whimpering, crossing himself again.

The sergeant listened with seeping dread. The corporal's report, added to what happened at this wall, meant evil forces were at work on this damned spit of land. As the only officer left, if he retreated, he would face the wrath of his *capitán*. He felt his hands trembling. He decided he would rather fight the black spirits. Surely, fifty-three at once would win the day.

Another quarter-hour sifted, no sound from either side

Then, with a roar, all squads scaled the wall. They hurtled in masse, howling their Spanish battle cry to frighten away the black spirits. Most died as they hit the ground inside the compound. The four defenders moved like a killing machine, slashing, biting, stabbing, and cutting in a whirlwind of destruction.

But the enemy numbers were too great. Eighteen remaining marines confronted the four as they backed slowly toward the house, waiting for the final charge. Jade and Montaña, standing side by side with Pan and Thers, crouched close in front. Ready.

On the sergeant's command, the marines charged with swords and lances.

Time stood still.

Jade and Montana fought as one, each covering the other. Pan and Thers, the same, bit, chewed, and raked the enemy as they forged ever forward. First, Pan crumpled with a lance through his throat. Seeing her mate fall, Thers went into a killing rage of blurred fury, snarling her grief. Five more marines met Satan before she finally collapsed with a dozen wounds.

Jade's tears flowed watching her pets fall and her anger turned cold. She fought as her brother had taught. Hand to hand, twisting and leaping with lightning speed, sinking her dagger in throats and groins. Montaña, severely wounded, cut, smashed, and choked with bare hands. Any part he touched he crushed, snapping arms and necks. Six remaining soldiers fell back, stumbling over their dead.

Jade, huffing, barely noticed the bows in the black night. As her mind understood, she yelled a warning and threw herself in front of her friend as two arrows sunk deep in her chest.

Montaña reached to catch her as she slid to the ground with a last dying sigh.

At that instant, on the quarterdeck, Francisco felt the chill of his own death.

Montana, tears falling, rose to his full height and roared his sorrowed pain. The six remaining marines, seeing his grief, knew they were dead men standing.

Montaña charged, his black eyes mean, as three arrows hit his bull chest. Feeling his death, his crazed attack continued, slaughtering the six without mercy.

It was done. *Capitán* Francisco Vargas had completed his mission.

Jade's soul could finally soar like an eagle.

*

Francisco paced the deck. Where were his marines? They were a full glass past due. Dawn was near with no sounds from the island for at least that long. Something was wrong. Maybe they fell into a trap. Doubts and failure again creeped into his mind.

"Ship's boat approaching, *capitán*," the lieutenant reported.

Francisco ran to the rail as the longboat scraped the waist and sailors rushed to help the lone man aboard. Wounded badly, he was first taken to Francisco to report. The ship's officers listened to a story they could not believe.

All the marines, but him, were dead. The surprise attack went as planned with the killing of everyone in the village but the squad assaulting the great house was repelled. They sent for reinforcements from the village and once there, formed up outside the wall and on command, launched a mass attack with over fifty men. As they scaled the wall, most were killed by a giant and a female child with two huge black cats. He was the only one to survive. He whispered he had never witnessed a slaughter so complete by so few. He was sure as he stood before his captain trembling from fear and pain, the great house was protected by evil spirits with unholy powers.

Francisco was shaken. All his men, dead! He made the marine repeat the story. Francisco had deployed six squads totaling sixty-six men and over fifty were killed by a girl child, a giant, and two cats! Impossible.

*

As the sun struggled against the night mist, Captain Vargas set sail wondering about the many legends of El Raptor. Like an evil spirit, he suddenly appeared from nowhere wreaking his destruction. Francisco felt a shiver and ordered topmasts to keep a sharp eye.

"No one will believe this tale," he whispered to the wind.

Captain Francisco Vargas and crew failed to notice the small white hawk following them to sea.

As the early sun calmed him, Francisco sighed with self-pleasure, saluting himself on a successful mission that would ensure his reward. Standing the aft deck, he welcomed the new day, watching the rising sun glitter over the rolling sea as a stiff breeze filled the sails. He ordered course change to intersect with DeSago's treasure fleet and started below for some well deserved sleep. Damon would be pleased.

Descending the quarterdeck ladder, he stopped short. The sun suddenly vanished, the wind stilled and night ruled. A razor moon, made for cutting, hung like a silver sickle casting a dreamy pall across the heavens. A needle shaft of wind made him shiver as he watched the sky turn wine-dark, tinting the sea the same. Puzzled, a sudden screech pulled his eyes to the sky to a snow-colored hawk hovering in the still air like a single star. It starred only at him.

With his ship becalmed and sails slack, sudden fear shook his soul. He ran to the rail and looked down in the eerie light at a purpled sea, flat as a sour pond. The stage was set as he heard the crew, whimpering and standing frozen, waiting like an expectant audience.

Again, the hawk screeched and a blistering lightning bolt cracked across the sky like a jagged skeleton, announcing the start of the grand performance.

Stunned, Francisco watched a multitude of sharks, like an opening act, slowly circle the ship in an eerie dance. Blade fins sliced the glass-flat water like a knife as their shadowed bodies undulated in rhythm like fat snakes. Then, a snort drew his eyes at two massive sperm whales sitting high in the water a cannon shot away flanking each side of his vessel. Jonah's for sure as their gray bullheads raised like islands from the slick sea. The ship, in doldrums, sat creaking with shrouds sagging as Francisco and crew waited, mesmerized, wondering their fate.

The white hawk, hovering in the windless sky, would direct her cast like an avenging angel.

So, with a dip of her wings and a commanding shriek, a fountain of water on cue spewed from the blowholes of the gray leviathans as they dove to the deep. The world stood death still as they sounded and time dragged forever. Then, like crashing cymbals, the monsters breached in unison and started toward the ship. From the heavens, low thunder rolled the beat as they swam faster and faster, churning a frothy wake, plowing the blood-colored sea, bent on a collision course.

The sailors fell to their knees sobbing their lament, crossing themselves, as the whales, looming abeam, slammed into the ship's sides cracking it like a Christmas walnut. Francisco heard the snap of the ship's spine as the stoved timbers splintered and caved, letting the sea pour into the hold. He stood frozen, staring at the staid hawk, wings wide in the still air, in awe of the power of God's revenge.

Knowing his death, the corner of his eye caught the movement of the first tentacle feeling its way over the rail. Francisco's mind went

numb as the root-like appendage, thick as a tree, with suckers the size
of his head, slithered like a snake toward him. Dazed, he watched the
slimy tentacles as the magnificent bulbous head of the sea monster
came aboard, searching for prey. The boneless blob was massive, with
flat yellow eyes, and was sure the star of this drama of horror as it slunk
forward, its stems squeezing hapless sailors like its anaconda cousin.
Its huge parrot beak, opening to a vile stench, chopped and swallowed
bodies while its tentacles slithered, searching for every sinner.

Francisco's shoulders slumped in defeat, submitting to his fate as
a tentacle gently circled his middle like a lover's hug. As he was lifted
off the deck, he looked down at the maroon sea. The sharks, floating
still, faced the ship with fins in ranks like soldiers at attention. He felt
the hug tighten, curling him ever higher as he imagined the gray killers
below panting their pleasure like a dog waiting for a tender treat.

Then, heaven's avenger tossed him in the air, flailing like live bait
before plopping into the bloody water like a bobbing cork to watch
the last act. Cracking timbers filled his ears as he watched the sea blob
squeeze his ship in half to drag to its home at the bottom of the ocean.
The bubbling froth of the ships last breath held his eyes as the monster
climbed atop, triumphant, a tentacle raised for a final bow.

Suddenly, the air stilled as he floated, not moving, waiting for the
next act of his final destiny. He looked to the sky at the still present
hawk staring at him and feared for his sinned soul. Echoing around
him, wailing cries of eaten sailors sang the final chorus.

His fate was sealed.

His leg went first, ripped off at the knee. Shock and pain glazed his eyes as he flailed and splashed wild. His eyes, wide with fear, watched the razor fins slice the syrup sea in closing circles. His arm went next, crunched clean at the elbow. He knew the slick shadows savored every bite as his trembling lips muttered for mercy. Terrible stabbing pain filled his body as he heard the sea witch's siren song of death calling his soul, willing it to hell. Then, at last, he felt the last gnawing bite across his belly and slipped beneath the surface.

A final stark white bone of lightning clapped with thunder split the purple skin of the sky in a saluting finale announcing the end of justice's production.

The pretty white hawk dipped its wings and with a soft peal, swooped a pleasing loop and flew to the horizon.

Then, on cue, the early sun bloomed, warming the light blue sky that matched the gentle sea. It would be a beautiful day.

chapter 14

"WHAT A WONDERFULL morn," she mumbled, stretching with a yawn.

Maria slept late, waking to a cool breeze billowing the curtains. She lolled around, reveling in last night's triumph. The fiesta, the parade, and of course her fantastic performance. She must be the talk of the town. Perhaps she will be invited to the Spanish court. Perhaps . . . her dreams whirled in fantasy.

After a cool bath and light breakfast, she wandered to the village square in a fashionable dress just in from Cordoba. Delicate beige trimmed in a darker Spanish lace around an open collar, the lace trim trailed seductively between her full breasts finally wrapping wide around a tiny waist. The skirt, with only one petticoat, but full, hung to the ground covering soft brown sandals. Her fan and parasol matched the same lace trim, but it was too warm for gloves.

Maria, feeling kitten frisky, strolled along and was greeted by everyone she passed. Her ebony hair highlighted goldish eyes under a matching brimmed hat. She felt pert and pretty, every bit as modern as the fashion drawings she viewed in the shop.

She contrived to look special thinking she would accidentally meet Jesse. She frowned at the thought wondering about her feelings toward him. She would admit she enjoyed his company. He made her feel special and safe even though her stomach tickled, an edgy tickle, every time they met. She wondered why.

Sitting on the public patio sipping her drink, she pursed her lips with a slight frown, wondering. He didn't seem to be anywhere.

She casually walked past the places where they had met before without luck. Many a passersby continued to stop and praise her on her debut but now she was disappointed. She looked forward to sharing her happiness with him, realizing she missed his company.

His good cheer and laughing eyes lifted her spirits and his teasing made her feel important and loved. She frowned. She didn't mean it that way. Maybe love like a brother, yes that was it, a brother. With a sigh, she left her coin and headed home.

As the shadows grew long, Maria changed into comfortable clothes and lounged on the shaded veranda at the rear of the house. Her mood turned melancholy, wondering what she would do after yestereve's success. How does one top that?

A knock at the door interrupted her thoughts. Moving to answer it, she thought it might be Jesse and decided to be angry with him. When opening the door, she was met by a mulatto messenger awkwardly handing her a huge bouquet of mixed flowers and a small package with a sealed note. After rewarding him with a small coin, her spirits soared again as she returned to the veranda with her prizes. Well, maybe I will not be angry after all, she thought, smiling.

The letter was from Jesse.

> Dear Maria,
>
> Please forgive me. Fate has called me away for a time. I sincerely regret not seeing you on your special day. I had planned a certain accidental meeting.
>
> Happy birthday.
>
> Please remember me with kindness.
> Your friend,
> Jesse

Maria read the note twice, suddenly sad again. She absently placed the flowers in a vase and returned to the day couch to open her present. As she drew out the fine gold chain, her breath caught as she admired the Catholic medal attached. Pure gold banded in silver, the intricate deep relief depicted the Virgin Mary holding the baby Jesus with a small ruby at the crown. It was beautiful.

Her heart fluttered, reflecting on his thoughtfulness and caring. As she admired its artistry, the medal slowly turned in the fading light illuminating the engraving on the back. She tenderly laid the medal in her palm and whispered the message.

"If only what cannot, could be. Jamey"

She sat quietly, weighing its meaning, finally admitting she was afraid to know. Somehow, it frightened her. Stupid engraver, she thought, as she tucked it away for the night, he did not spell Jesse correctly.

Maria tossed and turned all night with crazy little nightmares, all of them involved danger to her friend.

The next morn, she rose early, shook off her fears and decided to spend the day at the clinic to get her mind off Jesse and what he meant to her.

As she walked down the dusty lane, four soldiers suddenly appeared, blocking her path. The young sergeant, with much apology, informed her they were here for her protection with orders to escort her to the governor's house.

"What for *sargento*?" she asked, surprised.

"I again apologize, *señorita*, but I was not informed. My orders were to find and escort you."

This was highly unusual and Maria became alarmed.

"Well, *sargento*, thank you for the message, but I can manage without the escort," she stated firmly.

"I must insist, *señorita*. It is my duty," he said with a fake smile, holding her eyes as he waved his hand and signaled, causing a carriage to roll up beside them.

The trip to the governor's house was tense. No one said a word and the few questions she asked received replies without information. Maria became worried thinking it might have something to do with Jesse and why she had not seen him. Or, most likely, it was the governor or maybe the viceroy wanting to honor her in some way because of her successful event. That must be it. She was sure. She should not worry.

After finishing the thought, she absently brushed her dress to make sure her dagger was still there.

The ugly misshapen peddler, Gato, watched all from his fruit cart.

*

She didn't like the looks of this. Her intuition nagged at her. Something was wrong.

"*Per favor, señorita*, be seated. *Señor* DeSago will be here *uno momento*. He sends his apologies," the aide said, rattling on in his polished training.

"May I pour you some tea?"

Maria was nervous, sitting stiff and straight. Maybe they found out she was an imposter, just a poor farm girl. She started to fidget but held a composed expression.

"No, *gracias*," she answered calmly.

She was sitting in a small receiving room with two doors and very high ceilings. There were two arched windows with the hot sun mostly blocked by purple velvet drapes. Ornate cornices and moldings at every corner's edge matched the richness of a wool oriental carpet. She noticed the room was finished with heavy furniture placed in groups to allow whispered conversations.

Turning at the creak of a door, she watched Damon enter with a commanding presence, in complete control. He floated toward her, his thin lips curled in a satisfied smirk. After handing Jamey over to the good padre, he felt invincible. Now he would conclude this charade by determining how *Señorita* Aragon fit this puzzle. His spies kept him informed of their friendship and frequent encounters, plus, now, possessing the information bought by his thirty pieces of eight, he suspected betrayal. He toyed with the thought of accusing and bullying her but decided to be patient. He would move slowly, toy with her, trap her.

He wondered if they were lovers, if she was part of the plot.

"Ah, *Señorita* Aragon, thank you so much for coming so quickly," he said with his slippery tongue, sounding sincere.

"I did not have much choice, *señor*. Your guards practically arrested me," she said, deciding a little indignation might help.

"What is this?" he said, feigning surprise. "I must apologize *señorita*. My guard was sent to deliver a personal invitation. He must have misunderstood my directive... He will hear of this, I assure you," he said, sliding over to the teacart.

"May I serve you tea?"

"*No, gracias, señor*." Maria knew he was lying.

"Please, please, you must call me Damon. We are friends, are we not?" he said, all smiles, turning on his charm.

Maria just nodded, not offering the same liberty.

Sensing her wary manner, Damon snickered to himself.

"I was impressed with your performance the other night. All of Santiago is talking of your triumph."

Damon casually took a seat across from her and poured himself some tea.

"Finally we have some culture and civility."

Unarmed, he wore a scarlet suit, satin, buttoned high with a frothy collar. Although the day was humid, he felt cool as usual. His slick beard, thin sharp, matched his black eyes as they savored its prey. His tongue flicked for just a taste. She was beautiful and it had been some time since the last.

Maria started to relax allowing herself to breathe. It was as she suspected. He just wanted to praise her performance. Perhaps the sergeant did confuse the order. Maria accepted a cup of tea and allowed herself a small smile.

DeSago, watching her reaction, thought how clever he was. "Do you plan more performances?"

"Not for awhile. I will be spending more time at the clinic."

"What a pity . . . . I mean your performances, of course. But perhaps I can help with your clinic in some small way," he said, smiling thin.

"Gracias *señor*, we would be grateful for your support."

"By the by, did you hear the good news?" he mentioned casually, sipping his tea, watching close.

"What news?"

"We captured El Raptor."

Her eyes opened wide. "Really! How wonderful. Now our shipping will not be molested."

She was genuinely pleased.

"*Si*, he was in Santiago all this time under our very nose."

"In Santiago, *aqui*?" she asked, surprised.

"*Si*, in fact, I believe you know him," he casually continued.

"Me? How would I know him?"

"Well, El Raptor is also *Señor* Jesus Ayala."

Maria's eyes popped wide in shock, her jaw dropped. She was speechless. He knew then, Jamey had fooled her also.

"You look surprised, Aurora?"

"*Por Dios*, Jesse, it cannot be. He acted a friend, he . . . he . . ."

She couldn't think straight. Her teacup rattled in its saucer.

"Well, never fear. He has been arrested and is in the custody of Father Tomás."

Maria was stunned. Nothing made sense. Jesse, a spy? Jesse was El Raptor? The scourge of Spanish waters. He is a *pirata*? Her mind, racing, was numb at the same time. It could not be true.

"Are you certain?" she asked timidly.

"*Sí*, he has confessed. The mask just hid his face. He is not deformed in any way," Damon said, taking a sip. "We caught him sending secret messages. There is no mistake."

Maria just sat there staring down at her teacup. She suddenly did not feel well. He might think me involved because of Jesse's friendship. She wanted to be away from here and away from DeSago. Her stomach, turning, threatened to heave. She must leave.

"*Señor*, this has been quite a day. I thank you for your kind words about the pageant but I must admit the news of *Señor* Ayala is very upsetting. To think someone could betray and fool us so completely . . ."

Maria stood and started toward the door.

"Well, I will take my leave. You must have much to do."

"*Sí*, affairs of state are always pressing. When I return from Spain I will look forward to a much closer friendship. You are very beautiful . . . Aurora."

Seeing his salacious smile, Maria felt her skin crawl.

Stepping faster toward the door, she said, "Thank you for your hospitality. I will notify you of future performances."

Damon ushered her to the foyer convinced she was not involved with Jamey. He snickered knowing he destroyed any attraction she might have for him. She was beautiful and now vulnerable. Perhaps he might pursue her when he returned. Expose her first. Break her spirit. Yes, he might do that. Francisco can find another. It had been awhile since he enjoyed female company. It would be enjoyable . . . hearing her scream.

He sent for one of his spies.

While Maria was escorted home in Damon's carriage, her mind tumbled in confusion. Jesse, her friend, an imposter, a traitor, it was too much to bear. She took a deep breath of fresh air to clear her head and erase DeSago's suggestive comments. Shivering, her mind flashed on his slick manner, treacherous, like a jungle viper.

Was it true? Was Jesse a traitor? Was he just playing her for a fool? He was the only man besides Pedro she learned to trust. It just did not make sense. He had helped her. He defended her. He was a gentleman. He was her friend. He was so sincere. No, she knew her feelings were right. She knew in her heart he could not be the man DeSago accused.

She felt tears rolling down her cheeks.

Finally home, Maria dismounted the carriage and walked to her door deep in thought when a beggared figure, touching her sleeve from the shadows, whispered, "*Por favor señorita*, I must have a word."

Maria jumped, her heart pumping. "*Por Dios*, what . . . !" She stared back, on guard.

"Gato, you can speak?"

"*Si señorita.* We must talk."

Maria stepped back, frightened and suspicious. "What treachery is this, sir. What are you now?"

"Do not fear," he said low, glancing from side to side.

"I am in the service of *Señor* Ayala. He has been arrested."

"I know, charged a traitor and me almost with him. Faith, seeing your trick, I suspect them right," she snapped back.

She had enough of treachery.

"*Por favor*, a few moments of your time *señorita* and all will be clear."

Maria looked at his ugly face and saw real worry. Although frightened, she relented, and led him to the side by the carriage house, away from prying eyes.

Alert, but nervous, Gato told her everything he knew that would help his cause; Jesse's deep concern for her; Gato's assignment to protect her; the elimination of the gang of toughs; the sudden cooperation of her supplier; the mysterious investor; the defeat of the troublesome drunks; the killing of the attackers after her performance. He invented several more for good measure.

"I am in his service and must do what I can. But this is sticky business and above my head. Can you help?"

Maria stared back, silent, for a long time, all of the events jumbled to complete confusion.

Finally she said, "I will think on the matter but all seems lost for him. What a mess. I cannot see any path open." She paused.

"Let me think on it awhile."

Pacing her room, her thoughts were in turmoil. But what of it, she thought. What will happen to him now? How do I know Gato speaks the truth? These matters were too heavy for her. She did not know whom to believe. *Por Dios, Señor* DeSago is the viceroy. Father Tomás, a man of God. She paced back and forth thinking there was no way to save him. "*Por Dios*, he is a prisoner of that dreadful priest."

Maria remembered meeting Father Tomás at the governor's reception and her shock when she saw his face and evil eye. It was difficult to believe he was a man of God. Maria did not know which way to turn. She had heard all the rumors of the holy inquisition and was the one that pressed rosaries in the hands of the condemned women, but what could she do now. Maria prepared for bed and a sleepless night.

When the moon topped the heavens, she awoke with a start. Her dream and her heart taught her to judge a man's actions, not his words. Jamey had proven his friendship and deserved her help. She dreamed a plan, daring and risky, but the only chance. If she did it right, it would work. If not, she hopefully could act innocent, praying she would not be searched. The decision made, she stared long at the ceiling planning the details, over and over, and then once again before falling into a fitful sleep.

That same night, under a round moon, DeSago's spy vanished forever, wearing Gato's necklace.

chapter 15

GATO STAYED OUT of sight, following from a distance. His charge was still to protect her. He guessed she was probably going to church to ask for guidance. He was at a loss. This difficulty was way beyond his talents. He hoped the *señorita* could help, even in a small way. If she could just find him, he would do the rest. Why he was sticking his neck in this noose, he couldn't figure. It made no sense. The game was up. He should just save his own hide as usual. As he plodded forward, his mind continued suggesting he flee but his heart moved onward, praying to any God for the best.

From the bushes, he watched her enter the church like she had many times before. Familiar with the area, he scouted, noticing more church soldiers than usual standing post. Sliding along a shadowed wall, he cat leaped to the ledge and peeked inside. It was the same. The chapel was empty except for Maria kneeling at the altar before the Virgin Mary. He hoped she would ask her to help him. With a sigh, he settled deep in the dark alcove for the usual wait, vowing to press his cause again when she left.

The soldiers patrolled below, a spit away, laughing at old jokes. He wondered why God's church needed soldiers? Some faith.

What's that? He thought, suddenly alert. One said *Raptor*. Gato belly crawled along the ledge, ears perked, listening close. He heard right, his captain was being held here somewhere. His anger flared at their jokes about his torture. He would like to see their expression with their throats cut. It was strange, he thought, for the first time since a young man, his heart cared for another. He would keep a sharp eye and hope for the best.

Juan also watched Maria every time she visited, observing quietly from a shadowed corner, admiring her devotion as she knelt in prayer. With her head bowed before the Virgin Mary, the church seemed again like a holy place. Her faith reminded him of his wife and daughter. She was the kind *señorita* giving them rosaries for comfort before they were sacrificed. But deep down, he knew her faith could not exorcise the evil that devil priest had wrought.

He also watched her close because on an earlier visit he spotted Father Tomás, lurking behind the altar, spying on her. Now, Juan peered hard at the shadowed altar and spotted Tomás again, peeking. Even now, his perverted spying as Maria innocently prayed to her saint made his stomach turn with hate, a trembling hate that consumed him, the only relief the death of the murderer. Soon, his beautiful wife and daughter would be avenged.

The church, small but ornate, received the filtered rays of light through the stained glass and cloaked the air with deceiving reverence. Juan could not comprehend how God's holy place could hold this malevolent devil without retching. He agonized over the contradiction on many sleepless nights finally realizing it was beyond his reasoning. As rays of light crossed Tomás' cowled face, his spittle dribbled down in a sneering smile. Juan knew Maria was in mortal danger.

Yestereve, before the moon, Juan observed the soldiers drag another poor soul to the cavern. He wondered what sin he was charged because the priest usually tortured women. Women named Maria, for reasons, as yet, he did not understand. He recalled just a short time ago, observing the priest's crazed ranting in the sacristy screaming as he shook his fists at the statue of the Virgin Mary. Tomás ranted with vile curses and spit on the statue. Shocked, Juan crossed himself, hearing the blasphemy, fully expecting God's thunderbolt to strike. But, it did not.

Then, Juan thought of Michael, the Archangel, and remembered it was his task to mete God's justice. He smiled, welcoming the mission.

Juan had been vulture patient, working, untiring, gaining the priest's trust or better, indifference. Juan acted the old slave, always keeping his head bowed and eyes low, meekly proclaiming the priest his master. But Tomás, wary as a rat, was always guarded by two of his best. It was impossible to get close enough to plunge his dagger to the hilt. But now, finally, after two seasons of cleaning and working in the church, Tomás decided Juan was not a threat.

Juan smiled, knowing his patience was rewarded at last, allowing him to send the priest to hell.

Maria stood and genuflected, breaking his thoughts as he watched her tiptoe toward the alter.

What was she doing? He thought, suddenly worried. She always kneels a half glass before the Virgin's statue and leaves. Now she is snooping around apparently looking for something.

Juan slipped deeper in the shadows. Knowing Tomás was also spying, he watched her trying the doors and checking behind the drapes. What was she doing? He held his breath as she stopped before the last door. *Por dios,* she found it, the entrance to the cavern. As she glanced over her shoulder, he watched her slowly open it and disappear below. He almost shouted a warning but something told him to wait. The time was not yet right. Juan knew two guards were always stationed at the end of the narrow shaft. There was no way she could get past them. Why was she doing this? Why now? Did she know about the prisoner below?

Just then, Tomás stepped from the shadows, following her. Juan feared the worst. It was time to act..

Maria was terrified but she must try. She wrestled with the problem all night, finally deciding she must help her friend. When DeSago told her about Jesse, she could not believe it. Her friend Jesse, *El Raptor*, the scourge of the Spanish Main? It just did not make sense. They have falsely accused him and she must help as he would if positions were reversed.

She spent a full hourglass dressing for this foray. Her exact plan did not go further than finding Jesse. After that, depending on their fix, they would have to depend on their wits to escape. To allow quick movement, she strapped two daggers to her thighs, one on each side under a single petticoat dress. The hard part was tying the cutlass down the bow of her back. But luck smiled, the curved sheath fit her arch perfectly and with her long hair and black mantilla, she was able to hide the bulky hilt at the base of her neck. Finished, she inspected herself in front of her looking glass deciding she was very clever. Lastly, on impulse, she threw some clothes and personals in a sack and tossed them in the carriage.

As usual, Maria visited the church at the same time kneeling in the same pew. But then, instead of leaving after her prayers, she looked carefully around the chapel making sure she was alone before tiptoeing to the altar hoping to find the entrance to the inquisition quarters. She had heard many rumors including the one that it was the top floor of hell, held closed only by God's church. So, she guessed it must be by the church somewhere because Father Tomás and the soldiers lived here and rarely left.

Poking silently around, she tried several doors, some locked, some not. The last door, the heaviest, creaked from hinges rusted from the damp air below. Its graveling squeak echoed like an un-tuned viol throughout the beamed ceilings of the deserted church.

Maria froze rabbit still, listening for any sound she had been found out. Nothing. She allowed herself a relieved breath as she peered down the steep narrow stairs carved through solid granite, lit only by alcoved candles.

This must be the way, she thought, feeling it in her bones. Frightened as never before, her stomach churned and her ears felt her drumming heart as she slowly descended the dim-lit stairwell. As she crept, every tiptoe sounded like drums. At last, an eternity later, she reached the bottom, peeked around the corner and her shoulders slumped in defeat. Two armed soldiers, half-dozing, stood guard in front of a wall of solid bars.

Tomás smiled with glee, forcing himself not to giggle as he left his dark corner and followed silently down the cavern stairs. He could not believe his good fortune. Satan surely loved him for he delivered the witch right into his lair. It was perfect. Feeling his cock wiggle, he tiptoed behind her and watched her peek around the corner at the guards.

Then, Maria felt a cold chill prickle the nape of her neck.

"*Señorita* Aragon, what a pleasant surprise," Tomás whispered, a breath behind her, his grin slanted.

Maria yelped and jumped a pace, scared silly. Her heart thumped like a fist as her hands covered her chest, trying to catch her breath.

"I, I, I, was looking for you padre. You frightened me," she stammered, her mind racing for more excuses.

The two guards snapped awake and jumped forward at attention. With a wave of Tomás' hand, they seized her arms, holding her fast. She stiffened, but submitted for fear they would find the hidden sword.

"Well, you found me, witch."

"What is the meaning of this?" she said, trying to act indignant.

"What are you doing, sir?"

Pulling back his hood, his smirk turned wicked mean.

Maria shrank back in fear as the candlelight flickered over his sallow face and rheumy eyes. One cold black and the other devil white sat deep under shaved brows. Cotton thin hair sprouted a thimble high, topping his moon round head plopped on fleshy rolls of neck fat. He thrilled at her reaction to his fiendish appearance believing he looked more like the Prince of Darkness with every night's turn. In fact, he was certain he felt his tailbone growing and two noticeable pointy knobs were forming at the top of his forehead. He was sure of it.

As Tomás leaned close, the stink of his breath roiled her.

"Throw God's bitch in the cage next to my brother."

The cave's stench was as bad. She forced shallow breaths as she was dragged to the hanging cage and stuffed inside. Still stunned, the slamming clank of the cell door echoing sharp through the chamber snapped her mind clear. Surprised, she suddenly calmed, her mind buzzing, working to figure an escape. *Pedro's training.* She prided herself for keeping a clear head in a tight spot. There were many when she was with Pedro. Never panic, he taught, afterwards, maybe, but not during. The snap of the padlock centered her mind as Tomás dismissed the guards.

As they walked away, they chuckled, muttering vulgar comments about the padre having fun with this one.

Tomás stood quiet, facing her, his pudgy hands folded, hiding in the cuffs of his robe, appearing pious. He grinned his triumph, anxious to begin her trial. As he stared at her, he imagined all the many tortures and pain he would inflict, when suddenly, his eyes narrowed in satisfaction, feeling his sticky emission dribble down his leg. He smiled, sated.

"Why are you doing this?" she asked.

Still settling from his rapture, he huffed, impatient, replying calmly like a bored professor.

"Because, you are named the same as God's mother and therefore, his handmaiden. Therefore, all those named Maria are Satan's enemy. Therefore, since God favors you, Satan demands your death."

He paused, looking at her, thinking her dull, the reasoning so obvious.

"Since I am Satan's prince, those named Maria are my enemy. My mother, who threw me away, was named Maria. The first that I loved, who shamed me, was named Maria. The woman who beat me as a child was named Maria. And, of course, you are a Maria. Your suffering and death will be special."

Rattling on in a bored voice, his eyes gleamed pure evil.

"You tried to deceive me by putting your name second but I found you out. You gave comfort to other condemned witches named Maria. God made you beautiful so I know you are one of his favorites. My prince, *El Diablo*, has bestowed this honor on me to insult God through your pain and torture."

He paused and smirked, enjoying the shock and fear in her eyes.

"It is all very simple if you just reason it out."

Then, coming alive with excitement, his eyes bulged with pleasure, proclaiming, "This time is my triumph, the best of all."

He pointed with flare to Jamey.

"See this hanging on the wall? He is the son of the father who abandoned me as a newborn. But with you, he is now nothing. You are *especial*. You will be my crowning glory, a worthy sacrifice and God will surely scream."

Thick yellow spittle dribbled down his chin making her skin crawl, realizing he was insane.

Giggling, Tomás turned and waddled away, anxious to retire to his bedchamber and cut himself. He trembled with anticipation.

Maria watched him turn the corner, heard a clank and another lock snap. Tomás muttered orders to the guards and their cruel laugh echoed through the chamber. This was the most excitement since they tortured and burned the mother and daughter.

The cavern fell silent. Maria took a shallow breath and looked around. The rippled glow of candles made it difficult to see clearly. The only other person in this hellhole was a man hanging, chained to the wall. With his head slumped, he looked unconscious or dead. Did that monster say it was his brother? She wondered where they held Jamey. There were no other cells she could see. The smell rumbled her stomach reminding her of a dead cow she and Pedro found on the road, bloated and burst from the sun.

Scurrying sounds in the shadows turned her around with a shiver. Small fat shapes flitted in the corners, squealing, excited over fresh meat. In front were machines of some sort. She decided she did not want to know their purpose. Past them, stood a smoldering bricked fire pit, stoked low, but fired hot with various metal tools poked inside, glowing black-red. A witch's cauldron, boiling pitch, hung low but was levered aside. The fire glow rippled spirit shadows as thin trails of smoke curled to the cavern roof, wafting to a crevice seeking escape. Her eyes, searching for any advantage, noticed the drifting smoke seeping through the narrow cleft.

Maybe a way out?

Every sound echoed, the softest scratch sounded like a scream in the hollow hall.

"Caw, caw, caw."

Maria jumped and twisted toward the sound.

Tomás' black angel, stretching his wings on his perch with raven agate eyes, stared back, bitter and cold, reflecting off the fire glow. She shivered and forced her eyes away, turning her attention to the half dead soul hanging Christ-like from the chains on the wall.

Her mind raced as she called to the man.

"*Señor, señor,* wake up," she whispered as loud as she dared.

Nothing. He might be dead. She stretched her arm through the bars and grabbed a pointed twig off the straw floor. She jabbed him and his head turned a bit, moaning. Nervous, she glanced around, listening, and jabbed him again, harder. He jerked and snapped his head up with blue-eyed defiance. Maria's breath stopped in shock. It was Jesse without a mask. No scars or deformity, but it was Jesse. She would recognize those eyes anywhere.

DeSago spoke the truth!

Her mind tumbled, nothing made sense. She suddenly felt the fool. He must be El Raptor. He lied to me. He tricked me. She felt crushed, low, like someone kicked her in the belly. Real pain, like no other, pierced her heart. Tears welled, rolling down her face as uncontrolled sobs choked her. He betrayed her. Now look at the mess she was in. She was alone with no one to help her. She fell to the floor of the cage and curled in a ball, sobbing, shuddering uncontrollably. She couldn't stop.

A while later, her dream cries jerked her awake. She looked around slowly, feeling sorry for herself. Time slipped until finally anger was born and grew hot. Pedro appeared in her thoughts, her only friend, his words clear. *Remember Maria, a stout heart wins the day.* With that, she wiped her tears, sucked a deep breath, and scolded herself to stop being a baby. I will show him. She swore. I will pretend to be fooled until he helps me escape. Then, I swear, he will pay for his treachery.

She poked him again, really hard.

"Jesse, is it you?"

He jerked back again, his eyes squinting against the dim light, wondering if he was having delusions.

"Maria?"

"*Si*, it is me."

"*Por dios*, why did they arrest you?"

His mind was still fuddled.

"I came to help you but was caught."

"Oh no, not you."

His heart sank knowing he sentenced one more friend.

"Shhh, lower your voice. Can you walk?"

"*Si*, I think so."

Pulling her dagger from under her skirt, she went to work on the barrel of the padlock with the needle point knife. She gave silent thanks to Pedro for teaching her his trade. She was not near as good but good enough.

A moment later, Jamey was amazed to see the padlock pop open. Carefully opening the door to her cage, she winced at its squeal like a dry wagon wheel. After another quick look around, she jumped to the floor and silently moved next to him, attacking his wrist shackles. Leaning close, he felt her warmth and female smell. Stretching on tiptoes to reach, her breath tickled his arm and he started to come alive with hope. If he could get free, he would fight to the death to save her.

Off balance, she jabbed at the keyhole, intent, tongue peeking from the corner of her mouth. She thought she almost had it when everything went black and she crumpled to the floor.

Tomás stood over her with a club giggling like an idiot, watching Jamey strain against his chains, hate burning in his eyes.

"Ah, I see brother. You still have some spirit."

He giggled again.

The guards hoisted Maria's limp body and chained her to the wall next to Jamey. Tomás waved them away. He wanted to enjoy this alone.

His eyes held Jamey's as he waddled close to Maria. Then, with a taunting smile, he slowly licked the side of her face with his sticky tongue, sneering in delight at Jamey's torment. He leaned over, holding Jamey's eyes and started moving his hand slowly, ever so slowly, up her thigh under her skirt. He loved this mental torture.

Crazed, Jamey growled his loathing, cursing and screaming at Tomás to leave her alone. Wildly yanking and twisting like a trapped animal, the shackles cut deep into his flesh. Tomás snickered, slowly moving his hand further up the inside of her thigh. Jamey, hysterical, cursed and screamed, his loathing crazing his mind.

"Master."

Startled, Tomás whirled around to see Juan meekly hunched with rounded back, feigning submission.

"What do you want, you maggot?" Tomás spit with contempt, furious for disturbing his pleasure.

"A message, master."

Juan humped lower, eyes down with stretched out arm, holding a folded note with a wax seal.

"Get away, you worm. Give it to the guards... Why did they let you in?"

"Master, it is for your eyes only." Juan cowed, curling lower, watching close.

Tomás, grunting his anger, stepped toward him, snatched the note and started to kick him away.

Juan pounced like a lion with amazing speed. A man reborn, he grabbed Tomás and punched and pounded his fat face with every ounce of his anger. Juan was never so happy as he was at that moment. Tomás crumpled to the ground with a bloody mouth looking up at Juan in shock and pain, whimpering, teeth broken and sticking through his lips. Dazed, he blubbered, spitting blood as Juan savored the fear in his eyes.

Then, a yell from Jamey sobered him. Quick, he jammed a dirty cloth in the priest's mouth, bound his hands and feet, tore the keys from Tomás' robe, and freed Jamey.

Done, he tossed Jamey the keys and returned to his prize, reveling like a child with a new toy. It was a gift he prayed to God with all his strength. Just then, he felt the spirit surge of Michael, the Archangel, fill his heart.

Finally, God's justice would be served.

*

Jamey unshackled the unconscious Maria, cradling her carefully to keep her from falling. It was then that he felt the hard metal blade against her back. Pulling the cutlass free, he marveled at her cleverness.

"Now to get away," he said, determined as he looked around the cavern.

Then, remembering Tomás, he stepped toward him, blade ready, his death sure. Juan, seeing his killing eyes, grabbed his arm.

"No *senõr*, I beg you. He is mine. He burned my wife and daughter at the stake. I have lived only for this moment. Please allow me my revenge. He must not have a quick death."

Jamey hesitated, seeing the pain and resolve in Juan's eyes.

"He is yours, then. How do we escape this den?"

"I poisoned the two guards at the gate but you must go this way because of the other soldiers." Juan answered, pointing to the crevice in the wall. "Follow the tunnel outside and circle around. I put the *señorita's* buggy behind the grove of ravens. Leave now, run, I promise you God's justice."

Jamey didn't argue. His first priority was getting Maria to safety. Hefting her limp body over his shoulder, he headed for the narrow tunnel, cutlass in hand.

His smile joyous, Juan turned toward the struggling Tomás. The priest's beady eyes bulged in fear like a squeezed rat, mumbling against his gag. Juan lifted him to his feet noticing his body was soft like rotten fruit, his odor as bad. Ignoring the smell, he drug him to the fire pit, dreaming of this moment, plotting for this moment, planning for this moment, perfecting every detail.

Moving with purpose, Juan bound him to the cross-like timbers mounted next to the torture machines. He hummed a merry tune, taking his time lashing each arm, stretched full out. Then, he tied each leg firmly at the base, spread apart, unlike his savior, Jesus, and split the robe to his knees. Finished, he stood back as the glint of his blade mesmerized his gaze, overflowing his anger. Staring at the steel, dreamlike, it seemed to move on its own toward the priest's fat gut.

Tomás, watching Juan's crazed eyes, squirmed against his bonds, moaning.

Juan's eyes lifted to his captive's unearthly orbs and shook the urge away. Smiling crooked, he sheathed his blade and gently pushed Tomás' hood back to behold pure human depravity. Cocking his head, studying, he examined the priest's face and his devil eyes, trying to understand why. But then, he turned away, resigned, knowing he never would.

Next, he gathered straw from the rock floor and formed a mounded trail sandal high about three men long leading to the cross. Taking his time, he shaped and patted it snug, making sure it was perfect. Last, he found a stubby candle, lit it, and placed it at the start of the straw wick.

Pulling a stool close, he sat by the flickering candle. He was serene, completely at peace as he patiently waited. He made sure he secured the iron gates with his own clasp locks so the soldiers could not interfere with his pleasure. He wanted to enjoy every moment of Tomás' misery and pain. As the candle melted lower, he watched Tomás' eyes understand his fate. Juan remembered the same terror in the eyes of his loved ones.

Then, with a flat whisper, he told Tomás who he was and the pleasure he would feel watching him burn.

Tomás squirmed and groaned against his bonds as Juan relaxed, enjoying the moment. The candle, burning slow to the floor, reached the wick, and both watched the first flicker dance to the dry straw.

Juan slowly rose, walked over to Tomás and removed the gag.

"I want to hear you scream."

*

Jamey broke from the cave to sunshine standing on the ledge above the death pit. Gagging at the revolting stench, he stared down at piles of bleached bones and skulls. Shaking it off, he adjusted Maria's weight over his shoulder and carefully circled around the edge, his blade ready. Rounding the corner, the startled ravens took to the air in a flapping rush, shrieking their angry caws.

Hearing the din of the flock, the *familiares* ran toward the oak and spotted Jamey sneaking toward the carriage.

The *sergento* yelled, *"Alto, alto, cabrone,* in the name of the holy church."

Jamey turned at the order with a curse and dumped Maria ungracefully to the ground as all his rage toward DeSago, Tomás, and this evil place exploded.

With the carriage at his back, he crouched low, sword cocked with killing eyes. The soldiers slowed seeing Jamey's stance and approached careful, fanning out like a crescent moon. Jamey's mind clicked calm, eyes cold. He would not defend, he would attack.

Sneering, he charged them full run bellowing his father's battle cry. Leaping toward one, he feinted right, slashing left across a soldier's throat. The soldier froze, eyes wide, not knowing he was already dead. Twisting, Jamey snatched the falling sword and faced the others with both blades singing their death song. The next soldier lost his head. Another, eyes-wide, froze, watching the head topple as Jamey's cold blade pierced his heart. The six remaining backed away in fear. Jamey, wanting more death, spotted the other squad of white crosses sprinting toward them and halted his attack. He cursed his luck and backed up to Maria's body to protect her.

At the same time, Gato was slouched in the shadows at the church patiently waiting for Maria. Time moved turtle slow and made him uneasy. He sensed something was about, but what? He puzzled why that old man moved Maria's carriage around the side by the grove. Shrugging, he settled back and sucked a deep breath, forcing the patience of his feline cousins.

The sergeant's yell jerked him alert. Hearing the clank of armor, he peeked over the ledge and spotted the squad running, swords drawn, around the corner of the church. He quick counted nine, with the sergeant, who hailed another squad adding eight more.

Cat paw quiet, Gato dropped to the ground, stalking low to the corner and peered around in time to see the soldiers fan out around the captain with the *señorita* over his shoulder. Jamey was surrounded. He watched Jamey drop her to the ground and turn to face his attackers.

"Nine against one", Gato mumbled.

Even the captain's skill could not prevail.

He looked on in turmoil. Experience told him not to meddle. Let events take their course. Besides, he reasoned, he was poor with the sword and would be of little use. The garrote and the stiletto were his specialty, which did not fit this fight.

He watched Jamey quick kill three, which stopped their attack. But, he was trapped as the rest waited for reinforcements. Gato watched the other squad, blades ready, join the others. He knew Jamey was a dead man as he watched him, crouched, defiant, standing over Maria's slumped form. Gato thought she might already be dead, but then, he saw her arm move.

He charged forward. His heart decided while his mind cursed his folly. In a flash, he dove through the pack of soldiers, scooped up a dead enemy's sword, and joined Jamey's side.

"Welcome Gato," Jamey greeted as he huffed with sweat, relieved to see a friend even though he knew it was a fight they would lose.

Gato nodded with a sly grin.

The other squads formed up, reinforcing the six. The sergeant, cocky with his numbers, barked his orders.

Gato whispered, "I will hold them. Take the *señorita* to safety."

Jamey looked at him in wonder.

"No friend. We will stand together."

Gato stared straight into Jamey's eyes and said hard, "*Capitán*, if you value my service, you will save her life."

Then, he whispered, "*Adios, amigo.*"

Before Jamey could argue, Gato snatched up another enemy sword and charged the band of soldiers, full bore, screaming like a banshee. Disappearing in the mob, he jumped, tumbled, dodged, swinging both swords like a wild cat. He flitted around, like a bottled moth, whipping both swords as fast as he could, hitting mostly air. The soldiers, shocked at the move, yelped and hopped around trying to get out of his way.

Jamey hesitated, but then quickly lifted Maria, placed her in the carriage and climbed aboard. He whipped the team's rumps as a soldier tried to climb aboard. Jamey kicked him in the face and he hit the ground just as the rear wheel rolled over his gut. Jamey heard his death scream as he slapped the reins and galloped away. As he glanced back, he watched Gato slump to his knees surrounded by his killers. Jamey cursed fate, knowing he lost a good friend.

"*Adios, mi amigo,*" he whispered.

Gato felt the blade pierce his chest and sighed, sinking slowly to his knees. Watching Jamey escape, he quieted with a smile of peace. Then, slowly raising his eyes, he beheld the enemy faces and for the first time in his life, his soul did not hurt.

He welcomed the second sword thrust.

Jamey's sloop, docked tight, was ready and waiting.

"White Bay, here we come."

chapter 16

IT APPROACHED SNAIL slow. As he watched with fascination, it seemed to linger at first with no purpose. It meandered, sauntering from side to side, then stopped, flaring high like a wild beast raising its head to sniff the air. But as an animal, it crouched low stalking towards its prey. Tomás watched it creep toward him with slow purpose, sure of its hunt. He shivered cold, anticipating the pain while mesmerized by its pure blue and gold beauty. Its wild power crackled a warning as it marched to its destiny.

He cried, whimpering, "Why me, Demon master? I, your trusted *generale.*"

But he knew why. This was the essence of *El Diablo,* the master betrayer. He should expect no less with failure for did he not do the same?

The liquid fire continued its slow trek, sure of its kill, deciding which part to devour first.

Tomás squirmed and jerked against the bonds as the first licks reached his sandals. The flames, tentative at first, flicked its tongues, like a lovers lick, for a first taste. Savoring the taste, the beast decided to flare and squirted between his toes, which bloated and boiled, popping open its juice, fueling the burning heat.

Stabbing needles shot through his body as his first shriek of pain came as an eerie wail of an infant's cry. He peed himself. It dribbled down his legs. His screams, unending, echoed through the cavern..

The beast merely hissed at his puny attempt as his wailing cries echoed through the crevice and outside, filling the air with his torment. His howl startled the last coven of ravens and they took to the air. The flapping and cawing din of the flock speckled the sky like cowardly black angels forsaking their master, fearing their fate.

The slithering flame commanded his watching as his legs cooked red and split open like a roasted pig. His greasy meat stoked the amber flow, crackling and spitting like smacking lips relishing a flavor, tempting its appetite. The inferno continued climbing slow and relentless, enjoying every move like a curious bug with its fiery antennae, flicking to and fro, looking for the best to consume.

"*Por Dios*, the pain," he cried, begging for death.

He could not grasp why he was still conscious. But then, he realized old Beelzebub would decree he must see and feel all. Satan, the foul fiend, knew fire was Tomás' only fear. It was the perfect torture, created only for him. Dread circled his soul as his white devil eye watched the fire slowly eat him, its untamed nature bewitching, beholding tiny demons dancing with joy on every fire tip. Crazed, his unending wails turned to whimpering squeals as he squirmed and trembled, jerking against his bounds.

The fat-kindled fire lunged to the hairy patch between his legs, crinkling the kinky hair as his tiny member withered further to hide. His guts boiled pushing heated breath past his whining cries of pain so intense it touched his black soul.

At last, *Diablo's Beastia,* deciding to tease no more, began to devour its meal. His pudgy fat crackled like bacon, burning a whiff of sick sweet and the sour stink of human flesh. His body twitched, shivering cold as pointed barbs reached up his nose. Fighting for breath, he sucked tongues of flame swirling in his gasping mouth and jerked back, exhaling, his nostrils shooting flames like dragons. Then, his corn thin hair ignited, bursting in an orange ball of pointed plumes.

The devil's mask was complete.

Tomás, Satan's lover, was wrapped snug in his prince's cloak.

As he died, his eyelids melted, leaving his bulging two colored eyes to view his sins. His final screaming death cry announced its justice as he realized his soul would suffer this pain for eternity.

He cried out, bleating his last words of shame, "Mama! Mama! Mama!"

The beast consumed its meal and satisfied, simmered to rest. Tomás' blackened shell hung shriveled and brittle, curled like a poked shrimp, offering itself to the endearing darkness of hell.

The Dark Angel, his *Malo Noche,* perched in the corner, watched all, curious, with steel agate eyes. Then, with a simple, *caw, caw,* he flew from the cavern disappointed he would not taste human flesh this day.

Juan slowly rose and stood quietly in front of the cooked body. His anger drained like lanced poison, remembering his promise to his wife and daughter. Finally at peace, he turned his back on that which cursed him and slowly climbed the narrow staircase for his final chore.

He absently poured the lamp oil, wetting the oak floor and watched it seep through the cracks, soaking the altar. Murmuring a short prayer, he touched the candle flame to the wood and watched it flair.

Making the Sign of the Cross, he slowly walked out the double doors glancing over his shoulder at the stream of fire flowing smoothly over the planked floor like devil's gravy. As the flames roared, destroying the evil dwelling, he thought its power actually beautiful.

The fire bell tolling from the village sounded strangely like singing angels, rejoicing. Juan sighed, his soul finally at rest.

chapter 17

TWO LEAGUES DISTANT, Patch sighted through his telescope and spotted the thin trail of smoke. He knew he was too late.

The hourglass sands sifted damp slow before they guided the Raptor into the quiet harbor of the dead island. Jumping to the dock, ghostly silence met them. The buildings seemed little damaged with a few small fires smoldering their last as Patch and crew realized the extent of the disaster. Dead bodies of their comrades and loved ones strewn about were starting to bloat under the morning sun. Women and children, still in bed, were found chopped and hacked by the heartless killers, shocking even these hardened men of the sea.

After orders were given to search for survivors, Patch sprinted the hill to the great house. Silently cursing the fates, the condition of the bodies at the wharf told him the attack was last night. Huffing, he reached the wall surrounding the compound and found the huge metal planked gate standing open. Fearing the worst, he rushed inside hoping for a miracle his heart knew was not to be.

Puffing, out of breath, he stood frozen, staring, with mind blank at the killing ground. Scores of dead Spanish marines lay sprawled around in unnatural positions. Swallowing hard, his eyes slowly lifted toward the house. Montaña, dead, was sitting propped against the wall holding Jade gently in his arms. Curled in her protector's embrace, she was like a sleeping child, beautiful and innocent even in death. Her lifeless pets lay at their feet, still on guard, facing the slaughtered enemy.

Tears rolled down his face as choking sobs shook his body. He fell to his knees and lifted his face to the heavens, howling his despair, cursing Jade's God.

The Raptor's crew did their duty. Each family was buried in a private grave and the old sailors were buried at sea, fulfilling tradition. The enemy dead were dumped in mass graves.

Alone, Patch prepared his sister's resting place at the highest point on the brow of the island overlooking the sea. After wrapping her body carefully in white linen, he gently lowered her on the cool earth between her two pets. He dug a separate grave for friend Montaña, just in front, to remain on guard.

As the sun bowed low, he patted and smoothed the last covering of damp earth with his hands. Then with a sigh, he rose slowly, still numb with despair, staring at the small unmarked mound. Finally, he whispered a last promise and turned away, pledging equal retribution.

He must find Jamey.

CHAPTER 18

ARIA PEEKED WITH one eye. He was at the tiller gazing at the sky. He looked wild with his bronzed chest showing from an open shirt tucked lazy in dark trousers. His familiar knee high boots were scuffed and wind-blown hair fluttered across his squinting eyes. As he turned, checking the wind, she noticed the sheathed rigging knife hanging from a wide leather belt. She watched him adjust the canvas sail and wondered who he was.

She lay there in some comfort, not wanting to move. Her muscles ached and her head hurt. As her mind cleared, images of the recent terror crept into her thoughts. She shivered, remembering the horror when that evil priest took her to his cave and locked her in the cage.

Wondering why God would allow such evil to exist, she remembered Pedro's warning. *Remember Maria, Satan holds the heart of many.*

Acting still asleep, she wondered where they were and who this stranger was pretending to be her friend. I must keep my wits till I can escape, she thought. She shifted to a more comfortable position and felt a wincing pain on the back of her head. Touching the spot tenderly, she felt a knot big as an egg.

Peeking again, she caught him watching her with a gentle smile.

"*Hola, buenos tardes,* how do you feel?"

"My head hurts," she grunted.

"I'm not surprised. You were hit hard."

"Where are we?"

"On a boat in the middle of the ocean."

He has stolen me, she thought, feeling anger rather than fear. Shifting her leg, she touched the dagger still strapped to her thigh and felt better.

"Where are you taking me?"

"To a safe place."

Relaxing a touch, she sat up and looked around as huge swells rose and fell in a relentless rhythm. Suddenly, the sloop dipped in a deep trough and her eyes went wide, seeing a solid wall of water, house high, over her head. The next moment, they rode to the top, ready to fall. Frightened by the rolling and pitching, she panicked, never before in a boat much less the ocean.

"Hold the boat still," she ordered. "I think we might turn over."

"We're fine," he laughed.

"It is not funny. I cannot swim. You put me back on land . . . I do not feel well."

She rested back on the canvas, facing him.

He seemed in perfect control. Looking around, she spotted her bag and one other sitting against a mixed sack of food. Thinking of food made her stomach turn. Deciding she did not like boats much, she curled on her side, her head still fuzzy and fell back to sleep.

A while later, with one eye, she peeked again at this stranger. He was tall, not good looking, but handsome. His laughing eyes and ready smile made him hard to dislike. She remembered Pedro's voice, *know your enemy.*

"Your name is not Jesse?"

"No. Jamey. Jamey Fallon."

"So you are not Spanish?"

"No."

"But you speak Spanish."

"*Si*, my mother taught me."

"You are English?"

"No, I am Irish."

"Irish? What is Irish?" Maria never heard the word.

"Irish is like . . . Spanish."

"So you are Spanish," she concluded.

"No, no, I am Irish. It is a people like French, Spanish, English."

"Oh." She sat quiet, thinking.

"Are all Irish like you?"

"Well, most are not as handsome," he smiled, catching her eye.

"Humph." She quieted again for a moment.

"Are there Irish women?"

"Certainly, how do you think we make Irish men," he teased with a smile.

"Do not make fun of me," she said, her eyes flashing lion gold. "I do not know these things. I never heard of Irish."

She calmed, becoming quiet again, thinking.

"I see you are not deformed," she stated.

Jamey's hand went to his face. "*Si*, it feels good to be rid of the mask."

"Are you El Raptor, the *pirata*?"

"Raptor, *Si*, but a privateer, not a *pirata*. I take from the Spanish what they steal, for England."

"It is the same to me."

He decided to let her ask questions at her own pace instead of trying to explain the whole story, which even to him was confusing.

"I liked the mask. It made you look mysterious," she said absently, remembering her friend Jesse.

"But now I am handsome," he laughed.

"Humph." She quieted again.

"Do you hate the Spanish?"

"Some I love, some I hate," he quipped.

"Humph, do you have an Irish woman?" She couldn't resist.

"No." He smiled soft as their eyes met.

Maria lay back with a quiet sigh realizing she had been holding her breath. She had all the answers she needed for now. She did wonder what he was going to do with her and she wondered why the thought excited her.

Jamey watched her resting on the crumpled canvas.

Her skirt, pushed high on one side, showed a tanned thigh, tempting his thoughts. He would never tell her when he was putting her in the boat, still senseless, the top of her torn dress accidentally fell, freeing her firm breasts, round and beautiful. As he quickly pulled the top up, her nipples pinked and perked hard.

She was beautiful and he loved her. She probably hated him because he was not who he pretended to be. He had lied and was the enemy. Maybe she was even afraid of him. He vowed to do whatever he must to win her.

Jamey no longer wanted to be her friend.

As the sun wore on, the small sloop, moving steadily north, sagged some but cut the sea slick like a skimming swallow. Although making good time, their capture and escape cost a full sun. Jamey worried about everyone on White Bay, especially Jade, and whispered a small prayer Patch arrived in time.

After endless questions, Maria decided to bide her time until they reached land. At ease on the sea, he had the upper hand. She would act resigned to her fate, waiting to act on her own terms.

She was fairly comfortable except for being in the boat. Her stomach was always queasy and there was no privacy, which embarrassed her. Deciding to change her torn dress, she started rooting through her bag. Watching her, Jamey told her dresses were not fit for small boats and threw her a pair of his pants. She frowned, knowing he was right but didn't much like the idea.

"Do you want me to turn around?" he teased.

"But of course, *por favor*. I assume you are still a gentleman."

Smiling, he turned his back but an irresistible urge made him peek and it was just at the right moment. Maria stood with her back to him completely naked, her legs spread to keep her balance as she wrestled with the clothes. The moment's glance seared her image in his brain.

Her flawless back, swaying in a graceful slimming curve, widened to a perfectly round rear. His mind's eye remembered her feminine hips flowing to long legs and his breath stopping as she bent, exposing the shadowed hint of her sex. Jamey's blood stirred as never before.

He definitely did not want to be her friend anymore.

Maria also peeked when Jamey changed and felt a soft blush and a tickle of desire flow through her body.

"Where are we going?"

"To our island. White Bay Cay."

"What is there?"

"My friends and my home."

"Your friends, they are Irish?"

"No, they are from Asia. His name is Patch and his sister's name is Jade."

"Ah, I remember this Patch," she said, thinking a moment. "Jade? Jade? That is a name of a gem, no?"

"*Si*, I gave her the name because of her pretty eyes."

Maria became quiet.

"Is this Jade married?"

"No, she is nine years less than me."

"How old are you?"

"Twenty-six, how old are you? You just had a birthday,"

"Maria paused in thought. "I am eighteen, a year older. I think this Jade must still be a child," she concluded.

Jamey laughed and Maria's temper flared, eyes speckling gold.

"Why you laugh? What is so funny?" she said with a huff and then sat silent for a time.

"Is she pretty?"

"Who?" Jamey acted dumb.

"This Jade!"

"*Si*, she is beautiful," he responded innocently.

"Humph." Maria lay back against the duffle and turned her back.

"Maria," he said softly.

She turned and faced him.

"But you are more beautiful."

Maria curled on her side, suddenly warm, with a smile and a happy heart.

Sleeping hard that night, she woke, feeling well. No headache and her stomach felt calm. Playing asleep, she peeked again at Jamey. He was looking to the sea.

He was lean, almost thin. Carved muscles sculpted his wide shoulders and narrow hips. His open shirt showed sun blond hair gathering to the middle, then traveling down past his button, then flaring again disappearing below the rim of his pants.

He suddenly turned, catching her stare, and smiled.

Blushing hot, she lowered her eyes under veiled lashes, feeling a strange tingle low in her belly. She wondered if he guessed her thoughts. Blushing again, she rested back, pretending to sleep.

When the sun was high, Maria pushed up and stretched, looking around at the wet desert. The sea was calm and she wondered how much longer it would be before landing at Jamey's island.

"I want a bath." she announced.

"Jump over the side."

"I cannot swim."

"Tie this rope around your middle."

Another idea she did not like very much.

"It's okay. I will watch you," he said.

Maria started to wrap the rope around her waist.

"Well, you have to take off your shirt and pants."

"You will look."

"No, I promise." Jamey said, turning his head to prove his chivalry.

Maria turned her back, watching him from the corner of her eye. Quickly stripping her clothes except for her chemise, she quick tied the line around her waist and scrambled over the transom so he wouldn't see.

"Aieeeee, it is freezing!"

Jamey laughed as he luffed the sail and snugged her line tight at an oarlock.

It was scary not feeling the bottom so she kept one hand on the rope refusing to think about possible sea creatures beneath her. But soon, she started splashing around enjoying the refreshing water.

When he helped her back on board, the wet cotton melted around her breasts, outlining her hard nipples.

"Stop looking!"

Chuckling, he handed her a skin of fresh water to rinse away the salt. Later, after a hard tack and biscuit breakfast, he taught her how to adjust the sails and sheets. He needed some sleep.

"My turn for a bath," he said.

He dropped the sail on a flat sea, stripped off his shirt and boots and dove overboard. Watching him swim around the boat, she envied the way he moved through the water with long smooth strokes.

"You swim good," she said.

"I'll teach you."

Climbing back aboard, he asked her to turn around.

She did but she peeked.

He stripped his pants and while climbing into some dry, she suddenly had an urge to bite his bare bottom and grinned at the wicked thought.

By the end of the second sun, they shared the story of their lives. Jamey told her about the death of his family, his search for the killer, the galleys and his privateering. She now understood his game with DeSago. He explained Gato's mission to protect her in Santiago and how he sacrificed his life for them. Maria eyes welled with tears remembering the little man, her guardian angel. She would pray for him every night.

Her heart proved true. Jamey was her friend, like Pedro. He was an enemy of Spain, which still confused her but he saved her from the priest who was in league with the viceroy. No, he proved he truly was her friend. She also knew she could never return to Jamaica.

When it was her turn, she told him about her childhood and drunken father, her adventures with Pedro, and all her pretense and success in Santiago.

As dusk announced the stars, he leaned against the transom watching her doze while she absently ran her tongue slowly over her dry lips. His blood stirred as he remembered their time together in Santiago.

"I forgot to thank you for saving my life," he said.

Maria, opening her eyes, looked back at him. "It was you who saved me."

"I mean at your *teatro* when you jumped on the *cabron's* back."

Maria quieted as memories of her grand opening flooded her thoughts.

"I think I will nickname you *Muscles*," he said thoughtfully.

"Muscles? You mean like muscles?"

"*Si*, I give all my friends nicknames."

Her eyes flashed. "Ho sir! You think me a man?"

His grin teased. "Just little muscles."

"Ho sir, how unflattering you are."

"Tiny muscles?"

"No! I do not like. It is a name for men."

Jamey laughed and Maria's temper flared. Humph, he calls me Muscles and her Jade, she thought. And I am just a friend to him. Suddenly, feeling hurt, she turned her back, hiding her starting tears.

Jamey didn't know what he did wrong.

"I am sorry, Maria. I was teasing. I promise not to call you muscles."

That wasn't the problem.

Twilight painted the sea a dreamy hue. After two suns without sleep, Jamey was exhausted and his eyes kept drifting closed. He knew he wasn't thinking clearly and might veer off course. Calling Maria to his side, he taught her how to hold the sloop against the stars. He set the canvas and tightened the sheets while she concentrated staying on course. He laid back smiling at her determination and was asleep as soon as his head touched the canvas.

The moon rose glowing its night magic and Maria, feeling its pull, let her thoughts drift to Jamey and their adventures. The soft night and gentle sea set against diamond stars mellowed her mood as she wondered about her feelings. Watching him curled asleep, she suddenly ached to lie next to him and feel the press of his body against hers.

The full night brought Jamey many dreams as he tossed and turned. As dawn came near, his deep slumber brought forth a dream of a soft kiss from Maria. The vision was so real, feeling her soft parted lips as his tongue slowly searched between them. He sensed a moment's hesitation at the intrusion, but then she pressed her body against his with a soft urging moan. His tongue probed deep, tasting her surrender.

Moments later, his eyes drifted open with Maria's face close to his, her hazel eyes smoky with desire.

"Time to get up," she whispered.

Jamey yawned and stretched, still sensing her taste and the press of her lips. That was a very real dream, he thought.

"I slept hard . . . How was the night?"

"Long, much long."

"I had a bunch of dreams," he casually mentioned as they changed positions. "The last one was wonderful," he said, grinning, catching her eye.

Maria turned away, beet red. Jamey wondered why she was so quiet while they ate their meager breakfast.

Later, spotting jagged headlands in the distance, he knew they would unite with Patch and the Raptor before long.

Jamey spotted the jagged headlands in the distance.

chapter 19

"SAIL HO, TWO points off larbard bow.

Patch stepped to the rail and stared at the empty line between sea and sky.

"Wher away?" he yelled.

"Two points it be off larbard, low sail," the topmast repeated.

Patch caught just a glimpse as the sea swell lifted the small boat high. He knew it had to be Jamey. Smart orders to the helmsman brought the Raptor's bow head on to the sighting.

It worked as planned. They agreed if ever separated, the last ditch was to wait between these two known visible islands, limiting the passing distance, ensuring one sighting the other.

Before leaving White Bay to find Jamey, Patch assigned a contingent of twelve men with land skills under a ship's officer to repair any damage and recruit tradesmen with families to resettle their island.

Patch, plagued with conflicting emotions, dreaded telling Jamey of Jade's death and the fate of their island. But, he was happy to find his friend. There was much to catch up on. It would be a long night.

He berthed Roseta in Jade's cabin, thanking the Gods she was at his side. Not since a child had tears ever fallen, especially in the presence of a woman. But with Roseta's love, he felt safe in his mourning and his love for her grew even deeper.

A double sandglass later, Jamey's sailboat slid against the Raptor's waist. Tired and weak from their ordeal, Maria and Jamey were hauled aboard by sailored hands. Maria, embarrassed by her appearance, was whisked away to Jamey's cabin and orders to fetch Roseta with soap and water.

Jamey and Patch greeted each other with brother hugs and smiles. He told Patch to change course immediately to east, southeast and although exhausted, pulled his friend away from the crew wanting news of White Bay Cay.

Patch looked long at Jamey, face suddenly drawn. "Jade is dead. They killed all. I was too late."

Jamey froze cold. His gut knotted as his legs buckled, falling to his knees. His mind flashed back to his family's deaths. It was hard to breathe. His worst nightmare came true.

"My God, Patch. My God, it cannot be true. Tis . . . tis too much to bear."

Jamey collapsed to his haunches, burying his head in his hands. Sobs shook his body. Patch tried to help him up and take him below, away from the eyes of the crew, but Jamey pushed him away.

"Gato, also, is dead because of me."

Rising, Jamey jumped to the rigging. He scrambled, numb, to the topmast and sat cross-legged, alone, gazing, unseeing, at the horizon. Filled with disgust and shame, he could not face another. His body felt heavy and thick. His lungs ached with an invisible weight crushing him down. Choking sobs sucked his breath. He couldn't stop. It seemed everyone close to him died.

The hot bath felt glorious. Maria sat in the small wood tub, knees up, buried in the hot water while Roseta straightened her clothes from her hurried sack. With no female companionship for days, Roseta talked as fast as she could while Maria laid her head back, letting her body enjoy the soaking. Finally, the water cooled and after drying off, she slipped into a smock as Roseta turned to help with her hair. With her first close look, Roseta gasped in surprise.

"*Madre Dios*, it is you, the fortune teller."

Maria stiffened as her past flashed through her mind.

Excited, Roseta said, "Do you not remember? You told my fortune in Montego Bay."

Maria was trying to think fast.

"It came true as you said. I found my man and now I am here."

Maria sighed with relief as a faint memory returned.

Roseta, excited, continued her chatter, telling Maria everything that happened since as she finished Maria's hair with a red ribbon.

"Is he your man?" Roseta asked.

"Who?"

"The handsome *caballero* in the boat."

Maria quieted, thinking about the question. Was Jamey her man? Did she want him to be? After all they had suffered together she still barely knew who he was, except Irish and a pirate.

"I do not know," she said thoughtfully.

"This a very pretty medal in your bag," Roseta said, handing her Jamey's gift.

Maria cradled it in her palm and whispered the inscription.

"If only what cannot, could be. Jamey"

Was he wishing for something impossible? Was he wishing for me but knew we could never be together? The only thing she was sure of was the engraver did not misspell Jesse.

As Roseta jabbered, Maria's thoughts drifted. What was to become of her, a poor peasant girl from the jungles of Jamaica?

The sun grew long. Food was brought to the women and Patch checked on their welfare, introducing himself again to Maria. He was unsure what she meant to Jamey since only meeting her that once at the pageant. When he saw the look on Jamey's face during her performance, he remembered teasing him royally. Then there was the fight in the alley. What a night. He was struck by her courage when she jumped on the attacker's back that was going to ambush Jamey. She was a tough little lady. She and Roseta were much alike.

"Where is Jesse, . . I mean Jamey?" Maria asked.

"He need time by hiself. I give him bad news."

"Can I know?"

"His friend, my sister, Jade, was murdered." he whispered low, dropping his eyes.

Maria drew her breath, covering her mouth in shock.

"*Por Dios,* I am so sorry."

Patch, suddenly self-conscious, excused himself.

Later, Maria and Roseta climbed on deck for some fresh air. Both were an unusual addition on the Raptor. Leaning on the taffrail, watching the orange sun fall, Maria looked aloft at Jamey sitting alone in the crosstrees. Worried, she wanted to go to him.

Both were dressed in long linen dresses and sandals, no powder, rouge, or jewelry, except Maria with Jamey's amulet. Their hair loosely was tied back to take advantage of the cool breeze presenting two lovely women pleasing to the eye.

"Why not? I can do it," Maria muttered to herself.

"What did you say?" Roseta asked.

"Nothing, *perdón*, I will be right back." Maria started below deck to change into Jamey's breeches. Perhaps improper, she thought, but she intended to climb the rigging to check on her friend.

Just then, Jamey started his slow descent and when he stepped to the deck, Maria shyly went to him to say hello and express her sympathy.

He looked terrible, still worn and dirty from their sailing ordeal. Seeing the grief on his face brought tears to her eyes. He looked lost and defeated.

"I heard of Jade. I am so sorry."

"It is my fault she is dead. I killed her," he said, his voice choking.

"But you were in Jamaica with me."

"If DeSago felt my knife when I had the chance, instead of waiting, she would be alive to see this day. I am to blame."

Maria stilled, seeing his suffering, not knowing what to say as she felt the depth of his sorrow.

"She was my friend. I loved her and I killed her."

Tears welled full in his eyes.

Then, Patch appeared, put his arm over his shoulder and led him below.

Patch moved the women to Jamey's cabin, put Jamey in his own, and he took Jade's. Once below, he popped a cork on two and spent a double sandglass getting Jamey three sheets before rolling him in the bunk, hoping for the best come daybreak.

*

The following morn the ship's cook informed the ladies breakfast would be served in their cabin in a half glass. With their permission, the captain and first mate would join them.

Both women hurried about excited over seeing their men. In a flurry, they double checked their appearance and pasted the cabin with a women's touch. Maria checked to make sure Jamey's medal hung outside her dress.

A quick rap and they were in. What a change. Both were straight and handsomely outfitted. Jamey looked a new man. His face, still drawn with a hidden sorrow, was also a face with purpose and a plan. For a moment, the four stood looking at each other in awkward silence until Maria took control.

"Welcome sirs. Thank you for your company," she formally announced, smiling.

Both men broke into grins, suddenly at ease.

Breakfast was wonderful although no one could taste the food. The four were like youngsters discovering the opposite sex for the first time. But after much conversation and laughter, things were soon back to normal.

Jamey loved the way Maria laughed and the way her eyes danced in the candlelight. He noticed the medal at her neck and thrilled as she lovingly fiddled with it.

Too soon, the men excused themselves to their duties leaving the women to straighten and gossip over the conversation discussing what the men meant about this and that.

On deck, one of the crew handed Jamey a letter sealed in wax with his name neatly addressed. He reported it found in Gato's locker. Per the custom of the sea, his gear was divided by dice and the letter was found at the bottom of his sea chest. With a questioning look toward Patch, Jamey slit it open, wondering what to expect.

"Captain Fallon, If you have this letter, I am dead. If I have served you well, I ask a boon .

"Wha's this? Patch," Jamey said as he read. "That rogue has a daughter . . . in France . . . a village named La Rochelle. Can you believe . . ."

"Tha's a wonder," Patch said. "Though I hope she favors the mother, poor thing."

Jamey continued reading. "He asks if any wages earned be sent to her . . . her name is Monique . . . she is age six . . . mother is Annette . . . he sends his love . . . he signed the letter . . . Andre Botac."

Jamey folded and slipped it in his pocket.

"You know, when last we spoke, he sounded the schooled man." Jamey patted his pocket, saying, "This writing is learned . . . The rascal fooled us all."

"It be a surprise, alright, he would die with honor."

"Well tis sure his family will not want. Hear me Patch. If I fall, you see to it."

Patch nodded.

As the sun fell below the yardarm, they huddled around the chart table until lanterns were lit, planning their next move. Jamey calculated the Raptor's course and speed against DeSago's convoy and figured with any luck they would intercept them in three suns about a hundred leagues east of Tortuga. That left just three suns to train for an almost impossible battle.

The Raptor, a small brig, would face four Spanish vessels, two of which were first rate war-ships carrying one hundred and four cannon each. Just one measured twice their might. The Raptor's one hundred and fifty men against six hundred did not count the two treasure ships also equal to any fight. Like a dagger dueling a cannon, the odds were best for the devil.

When finally leaving the cabin, Patch and Jamey sealed a plan, which both agreed might work. Their first task, however, was to see to the safety of the women. To that end, they serviced the sloop and assigned two old salts to escort them to Tortuga.

As expected, Maria and Roseta wanted to stay, promising to remain below during the fighting, insisting they could care for the wounded. Both were worried Jamey and Patch would be killed.

Maria wished he would just forget the past and live his life with her. Her heart finally convinced her brain she was in love and was frightened she might lose him. She would have to confess her feelings as they were to leave on the small sloop on the morrow.

That night, under a sharp crescent moon, Jamey and Maria relaxed by the gallery window in his cabin, gazing at the phosphorus sea trailing the ship.

Finally, with a sigh, she broke the silence. "I do not want you to go."

"I have to," he said.

"I must avenge my parents and Jade. I will have no peace till I do."

"But what if it goes badly and you get killed?"

"Well. I will try hard not to."

"It is not funny. What am I to do without you?"

Her big eyes filled with tears as Jamey turned her toward him.

"And what would I do without you," he said, looking deep into hers.

Without thinking, they were in each other's arms, their lips touching soft, then demanding, saying all without words. Maria's body pressed in a perfect fit against his, melting, becoming one. His tongue probed gently, then hungrily as she moaned her desire and surrender. Jamey's body trembled, tasting the scent of her craving, firing him to the wild madness of the chosen lover.

His hand circled her breast hard and pleasure shot through her body as his other slowly caressed slowly down her flat belly. She moaned as he cupped her mound, causing her legs to go weak from the pleasure. Then, sweeping the chart table clean with a whisk of his arm, he picked her up in complete command and gently laid her back. His eyes held hers as she followed his movements, not knowing what to do, her body demanding fulfillment.

His eyes locked in want as he moved between her legs and yanked her bodice down. Her firm ivory breasts, with tips hard pink, made his mouth water. He bent, taking one in his mouth, rolling his tongue around the edge, nipping the hard nub.

Maria welcomed the sweet pain, her body aching for more. He pushed her peasant skirt to her waist and in one movement, her undergarment was gone. He spread her legs and petted her wet sex.

Instinctively, Maria raised her knees and opened herself wide, her head rolling back in wanton abandon. Her hips, lifting in rhythm, matched his stroking hand as her baby moans pleaded for more.

The lamplight flickered gold as Jamey, spellbound, looked with glazed eyes at the dream nymph born just for him. Then, with a groan, he held her legs and plunged full and deep. Crying her welcome, her body hungrily held and sucked at him, her animal passion unleashing its abandon. Her sex begged and reached for all, quivering, feeling his thickness to her belly.

Jamey lost control, sensing her wild need as his hammer thrusts dove into her Eden. His body stiffened for its ultimate release, when suddenly, Maria's bursting spasms wracked her body in ecstasy, convulsing over and over. Jamey exploded, draining his heart, his surge matching her every milking suck.

Finally, their pulsing rhythm faded and Jamey gently tucked her in his bunk. He stood a moment as the candle-glow bathed her beauty before curling next to her, joining her sleep.

The lover's night passed with gentle tasting and touching, exploring and discovering each other's pleasure.

*

Jamey rolled over at the sound, opening one eye, seeing her from the side. Maria, bending over, was slipping into a white chemise, barefoot, with her dark hair hanging loose, tempting him with her innocence.

"Well, good morn, *beliza mia*," he said, using his rascal smile.

Maria turned to him without standing, her tussled hair falling lazy across the side of her face. Her big tawny eyes met his with a sultry power, stirring his soul.

She straightened and faced him, legs apart for the roll of the ship. With hands on hips, she cocked her head and wild hair fell over one eye as her parting lips, pouty and wet, beckoned him. Her innocent earthiness demanded he have her. His eyes roamed lower as the borning sun shadowed her through the thin cotton, outlining that special place. His body turned hot.

Seeing his look, she smiled.

"No more. No more for you. It is late," she stated firmly. "People will talk."

Then, she was beneath him once more, ready and hot. She spread herself, wrapping her legs around his waist, urging him with pumping hips. Jamey took her fast, impatient, plunging in abandon. In moments, they stiffened, Maria burying her head into his neck, shuddering her peak with puma moans. Wanting all of him, she pulled him flat against her naked body and Jamey felt her milking with every thrust as they both embraced *le petite morte*.

*

It was time. The small sloop bobbed against the ship's waist, tied and ready. The Raptor furled her sails, drifting still in the water ten leagues offshore Tortuga. The two old salts finished loading the women's bags and turned to assist them into the boat. No words were spoken as the women stepped past the rail with wet eyes. Jamey and Patch steadied their arms as their sandals felt for the rungs.

Maria turned, looked up into Jamey's eyes and whispered, "*Vaya con Dios* . . . please come back to me."

Jamey and Patch watched the sloop melt across the horizon as the Raptor set full sail, racing to overtake DeSago.

chapter 20

GARA WAS ALOFT. Jamey calculated they would intercept DeSago's ships on the third sun. This was the fourth and still no sign. He poured over the charts again, checking everything for the tenth time. Under Patch's inspection, the crew trained double and was never more ready. Jamey and Patch briefed them carefully on the battle tactic and every man's duty. All knew timing would determine the victor.

Jamey ordered the ship's carpenter and sail master to rig and bend the largest spare main yardarm and mount it on the top rail of the sterncastle. The foot ends of the sail, at the clue cringle, were weighted with two cannonballs in quick-laced pockets. When finished, hands lashed it hanging off the aft rail ready to release on command to fall in the water.

As planned, when dumped over the stern, the spar would float and the large sail would play out full with the bottom ends of the sail sinking with the cannon ball weights. The contraption had lines, each about eighty meters, tied fast to the four corners. The opposite ends were knotted together to a fist-thick hawse and the slack carefully coiled on the aft deck. The bitter end of the hawse, led forward, was lashed snug to both the aft and main mast.

All was ready. No enemy sighted.

Jamey watched Gara till his eyes stung. The skies were clear so he figured Gara could see forty leagues in all directions. He started to worry, reviewing the facts, afraid he plotted wrong.

He knew DeSago had to sail from Santiago harbor the morn after his capture to catch the high tide for the deep laden treasure ships. When he escaped with Maria in the sloop, he took note that all four vessels were clear of the harbor. He knew they couldn't make more than eight knots, especially in convoy. His added insurance, fraying the rudder hawse lines the night the bolt hit him would delay them at least a full sun. He was at sea three with Maria before meeting Patch and one was lost as captive of Father Tomás. With the Raptor's speed through the water at twelve knots angling south, southeast, DeSago had to be in this general area.

Doubts plagued him. Perhaps DeSago decided to alter his course? No, that didn't make sense, he would insist on the fastest route. Perhaps he didn't leave after all. Maybe he turned back because of the rudder problem. No, he would not anchor another full moon waiting for high tide. He had to be out here somewhere.

Jamey's mind pondered the facts without end when he glanced again at Gara and spotted what he had been praying for.

Gara was stretching into his elongated soaring circle.

"He sees em, Gara's got em," he yelled.

Patch looked to the sky still not able to understand the eagle's silent message.

"Change her head to south-east by east. Patch, two bright lookouts to the peak."

Jamey's excitement quickly spread through the ship.

"A sharp eye, now."

By eventide, they sighted the skysails of the convoy tipping the horizon on a steady course. The battle would commence on the early morrow. No salt aboard the Raptor would sleep this night.

At dusk, Jamey leaned on the stern rail watching the sun fall into the sea and imagined the distant sizzle as the ocean doused its flame. Speckled stars of the night chased the pink hue of twilight as he thought of the impending battle. A thin silver moon, curved as a reaper's scythe, foretold the morrow's death.

"At last this will be the end of it," he whispered, remembering his family and Jade. His heart calmed, praying that fate would serve justice and revenge.

The early sun born from the sea belied a day of death as the Raptor swiftly closed the distance to the hunted ships. One league off their stern, Jamey's telescope spied their signal pennants, flipping back and forth, relaying orders to prepare for battle. The wind was crisp, due west, and as he guessed, the warships fell behind the treasure ships to intercept him.

The war galleons floated close holding twenty rods between. This battle tactic forced an attacker to swing either larboard or starboard. Any attempt to run the gauntlet through their middle would be suicide. Mounting fifty-two cannon on each waist, a ship cutting between would be blasted with a cannonade of a hundred plus at very close range. The Spanish first-rate warships were the largest afloat compared to just eighteen cannon on each waist of the Raptor. It would be certain suicide.

The Spanish, shortening sail, were content to wait, relishing the fight. Reduced speed also stabilized their decks providing greater accuracy. Scanning the field with his scope, Jamey was surprised to see the treasure ships also slip slow in the water instead of running while the warships engaged him. They hove too, most three furlongs distant, anxious spectators, he knew, wanting to witness El Raptor's defeat.

The Raptor closed quick at twelve knots, all sails cranked on. Gara scouted from above while bagpipes wailed their death dirge with the Raptor's ensign flashing their intent. A furlong from the enemy, the war drum began, booming an incessant battle beat as gun crews stood ready.

Jamey, giving a last look aloft, measuring sail and wind, noticed a white falcon circling with Gara.

"Patch, look aloft. A white hawk soars with Gara."

Patch peered at the sky, cupping his hand to block the sun. "Ehh, where from? Strange fer here. Ther be no land near."

"'Tis an omen, sure."

"Aye, but for good or the devil."

Jamey held his eyes to the white hawk, not knowing why, when, suddenly, a force flowed and shivered him. At that moment, he sensed a communion, they were as one. Surprised, his memory flashed, remembering his time as a boy sitting at the hearth, his father telling a similar tale while soldiering in Spain. It was the same, he was sure.

"Jamey . . . Jamey! whers yer mind? Patch asked, wondering, following his eyes.

Jamey snapped back, forcing his thought away.

He turned his attention to the enemy, raising his telescope to scan the decks of the war ships. As expected, he spotted enemy crews charging cannon on their outside circle while ship's officers, standing the fore decks, measured Raptor's approach through their scopes. He knew they wondered which side he would swing to and imagined the crew marking wagers, hoping it would be their cannon to claim the ten stones of gold. He sensed their smirks, knowing they out-manned and out-gunned them ten to one.

The Raptor sailed bow on, stunsels full out. The enemy officers, scopes tight, became anxious knowing the Raptor must change course.

But the Raptor's run continued forward on a broad reach, close-hauled, full and bye, plunging through the sea, ever forward.

A hundred meters out, the Spanish realized the Raptor intended to run the gauntlet. Frantic orders barked from gun captains and flag signals flew as enemy crews scrambled to receive the Raptor on its suicide course.

The Spanish officers, eyes to their scopes, could not believe Raptor's action. It was too good to be true. They would hit him with a full barrage at close range, blowing him out of the water. With emergency change in orders, Spanish crews jumped too, yanking block and tackle to get all cannons run out and primed, anxious for the first shot.

"Stand ready to release the spar on my command," Jamey ordered as his crew stood braced with two handed axes.

Seventy-five meters from the bow of the war ships, Jamey could see and feel the hungry enemy. Fifty meters, the Raptor was flying beautiful in the wind, healed tight.

The Spanish commodore grinned and turned to his captain.

"*Bueno*, the cutthroat will run the dirty lane. He cannot bring his cannon to bear slipped that far over. His gunwales are awash and every plank in his bilge is ours . . . . The fool has sentenced his ship."

"Drop the spar . . . NOW!" Jamey shouted, hearing the axes whack and the heavy spar hit the water. The coiled hawse line payed out whizzing through the stern rail. With the opposite end lashed tight, the ship's masts seemed to lean forward expecting the coming jolt.

Seconds before the Raptor drew between the bowsprits of the enemy ships, the Spanish ordered their cannons to fire in a timed salvo. Calculating the length of the fuse and the speed of the Raptor, the fuses were lit staggered to fire when the Raptor sailed past.

One hundred and four cannon were torched with perfect timing but the Raptor was not there. From twelve knots, she went to dead stop, sails full bloomed. The spared sail dropped in the water tied to the hawse line and knotted to the masts braked the ship so quick, Jamey and crew pitched forward, some falling to the deck.

The sea sail, blossoming full in the water, created an immovable force and the Raptor was like a dog coming to the end of his chain. Jamey chuckled. It worked better than planned. The thick hawse tightened and twanged like a bowstring while the two masts groaned their resistance.

All one hundred and four Spanish cannon blasted the other. Screaming attempts to cease-fire were in vain over roaring cannon explosions and excited gun crews. Spanish commanders, in shock, had bombed their own ships with systematic destruction.

After the Spanish fore guns fired, Jamey ordered the hawse line chopped free. With sails still full of wind, the Raptor shot forward between the wrecked warships so close, Jamey could hear the officer's frantic yells and the screams of dying sailors. After the devastating bombardment, both ships in splintered ruin were out of action.

With eyes hard and cold, Jamey surveyed his targets and gave the order, "Pay em in iron, lads."

Spanish crews, in complete chaos, watched helpless as the Raptor sailed down the center, every cannon thundering, carefully felling masts and rigging with chain and ball. The Raptor's crew rearmed in a flash, fired the hole, and again their cannon roared, belching heavy ball centered at the stern water lines. The barrage tore away rudders and opened gaping holes in the hull between the water and the wind, promising both ships a slow death.

Both warships would sink before nightfall. The Raptor's crew, hurrahing their victory, suffered not a single hit.

In the distance, the two treasure galleons watched in horror. The Raptor must truly be in league with Thor to full stop in the water under full sail. It was an impossible feat. El Raptor surely controlled the pirate wind.

Confusion reigned on both treasure ships. The Captains, confused, were unsure what orders to give as they watched the Raptor's sails grab the breeze, bow digging deep and closing fast.

Before the battle, *El Serpiente* stood smug and sure, scope to his eye, waiting impatiently for Raptor's defeat. He trembled in anticipation anxious to witness the Raptor blown out of the water. Failure was impossible. Damon was already planning a suitable reward and celebration for his ship's officers for their victory.

Now, he stared in shocked disbelief. His rage so intense, he thought he might die. His fury and impotence raged, watching two of Spain's greatest warships destroyed in such a manner. It was too much to bear.

Damon's blood burned hot, his mouth began frothing as he mumbled incoherently. A part of him tried, too late, to regain control. Something had snapped. His body trembled numb and cold, his madness centered on revenge at any cost. He would gladly gift Satan his soul for Jamey's death.

The Raptor approached the treasure ships, sailing a lazy circle as wolves would a stag, taunting them a culverin shot away. Raptor's war drum, beating a rumbling cadence, stopped and silence sucked the air. Then, bagpipes piping the *Irish Death March* mourned over the wind, wailing, announcing the Grim Reaper.

Spanish crews cringed with dread to the marrow of their bones, lamenting their sins, waiting for the worst.

Gara and the white hawk continued to soar. The Raptor's blood flag warned mean.

"Hand me the long bow, Patch."

Jamey sat on the deck and rolled on his back, bracing the bow staves against both feet. The man-length arrow was nocked and drawn hard and full to its barb, ready to loose on Patch's order.

"Ready now, she be comin back." Patch said, watching the balance ball return toward center.

"Fire," he shouted.

Jamey let the shaft fly, quick nocked another, and when the ball hit center mark, sent it on its way.

The first arrow struck the forecastle on the first treasure ship. The other arrow hit the second, burying itself in the neck of an unlucky sailor. Attached to each was a message wrapped around the shaft.

"Fight and die—Yield and live, El Raptor."

Jamey wanted to salvage the ships to transport the treasure. He was certain Damon was aboard to protect his hoarded riches and would wager his share it was the *Angelica*, the largest. His heart bumped a notch knowing they would finally meet face to face, one last time.

"Drummer, start your beat," he ordered.

The Raptor's battle drum boomed a hollow cadence attended by the bagpipes, sounding like God's final judgment.

The Spanish captains on each ship read the ultimatum and called a hurried conference with ship's officers. All agreed it was foolish to engage based on what they observed. El Raptor's reputation of sparing those who offered no resistance was well known. This was not their gold and to die and still lose the gold was foolish. The decision was clear.

The *Cortina* struck her colors first. The Raptor closed and under its protection, launched two long boats with boarding crews to secure the vessel.

Scanning the decks of the *Angelica* with his scope, Jamey's heart doubled as DeSago's image filled the lens. His jaws knotted and he flushed hot watching Damon pacing the stern deck, flailing his arms, screaming at the officers.

Jamey smiled sure. Fate would finally allow justice to be served.

Ignoring DeSago's ranting, the Captain of the *Angelica* gave the order to strike the colors.

"*Capitán*, hold there! Damon ordered.

"As Grand Viceroy, I relieve you of command."

Shocked by the order, the captain turned and faced him.

DeSago continued, "You will strike your colors only after you prepare a surprise attack when the Raptor boards, not before. Keep your marines well hidden. A thousand gold pieces each for Raptor's death."

The captain stared back in disbelief.

"But *señor*, striking the colors announces our surrender. An attack after is without honor."

The ship's officers stood close in support.

"Honor! You fool. Honor for the Raptor?"

Damon's snake tongue flicked, his hooded eyes bore into the captain's. "You heard my order, *capitán*."

The command was given and two squads of marines stood at attention, flintlocks at port arms as Damon stalked down their rank, tongue flicking, staring slow into the eye of each, burning his order deep.

"Raptor's death or yours," he hissed.

Every man shivered. Damon's black eyes held theirs, pleased with their fear as his lips, tight with a sneer, cradled his flicking tongue.

The squad sergeant ordered the men hunkered down, hidden behind the bulwark. On Desago's order, they would rise as one and assassinate Jamey when he boarded.

The *Angelica* lowered their flag and the Raptor slowly closed, grappling hooks at the ready. Jamey kept his glass locked on DeSago.

"I don like the looks," Patch said.

"Nor do I. They look too calm."

The Raptor eased closer.

"They too quiet. They wait too stiff."

"Aye," Jamey answered, then ordered, "Stand off, helm. Patch, keep us away till my order. Get slingers aloft. Load two twelve's with scrap."

Jamey cupped his hands, hailing, "*Capitán, Angelica,* our cannons are primed. Show all hands or we will fire."

The Spanish captain stood frozen in disgust.

Damon's rage exploded as he screamed, "Kill Him! Kill Him! Fire, FIRE!"

The nervous marines jumped up, firing wild.

Jamey smirked and ordered the shrapnel shot into their ranks.

The Spanish captain watched helpless as his bulwark exploded in deadly splinters leaving his marines moaning in their blood. Furious, his eyes flashed at Damon's and saw his wild expression, his mouth foaming in madness and ordered him taken into custody and locked below. Immediately, he ordered the white flag raised.

Soon, the Raptor laid alongside with Jamey the first to swing over the rail.

He looked a sea hawk with high leather boots and black trousers. His white bloused shirt, open at the collar, was loosely tucked. His hair, long to his shoulders, was tamed back with a red headband accenting steel blue eyes. His father's broadswords crossed on his back with daggers at the waist and sheathed on his boot, cowered the enemy. With two whips coiled at his belt, he was the complete warrior.

Patch and boarding crew immediately followed. Both issued practiced orders to secure the ship as Jamey presented himself to the captain, accepting his sword with a short bow.

The ship was theirs.

"*Capitán*, where is *Señor* Damon DeSago," Jamey inquired calmly.

The Spanish captain, surprised El Raptor knew of DeSago, wondered if sorcery sat on the pirate's shoulder.

"*Señor* DeSago is in my custody, *Capitán* Raptor. He has suffered a mental collapse and had to be restrained."

"Bring him here, now," Jamey ordered.

The captain started to hesitate but then gave the order. Moments later, *El Raptor* and *El Serpiente* stood face to face.

"You! You!" Damon sputtered with rage, eyes bulging. "Why will you not die?"

Jamey watched close, seeing evil incarnate.

"You know who I am?" Jamey asked.

"*Si! Si*! I curse God for allowing you to live. I would give my soul to *Diablo* for your death," he yelled, hissing through locked jaws and flicking tongue. His rat-black eyes glared in fury as his forehead vein bulged like a welt ready to burst.

The Spanish captain flinched. "You blaspheme *señor*."

Jamey's cold gray eyes bore down. "I understand you are trained in the art of the sword."

Damon's eyes narrowed. "*Si*, I know the sword."

"Then I challenge you, Damon DeSago. A duel to the death. Let God or the devil decide."

Patch grabbed Jamey's arm. "Nay Jamey, jus kill the scurvy snake an be done with it."

Jamey's eyes never left Damon's. "No, honor must be in my revenge when he kisses my steel. Clear the deck Patch."

Patch, knowing no argument would change his mind, reluctantly ordered everyone to stand back and clear the mid-deck.

"Cut the snake loose, give him cutlass and quillon," Jamey ordered.

Damon smirked. The cutlass and short sword were his favorite. In his hands, victory was his.

Jamey stepped into the ring crossing his arms up behind his neck and grasped the hilts of his father's swords. As they escaped the caved scabbards, the cold steel hissed their warning.

Damon, with his blades, once more felt in control. Balancing the heft of the steel in his hands, he stared at Jamey with red-hot hate and turned away, calm, flexing, seeming to take his time, waiting. Jamey turned to move to the opposite side of the circle.

Suddenly, without warning, the cobra whipped around charging with his fanged blades, seeking flesh. The sneak attack caught Jamey off guard as he dove to the side, but not in time. Damon's cutlass cut deep into his left arm.

Patch jumped forward at the cowardly act, katana held high, determined to kill Damon and end this charade.

Jamey, stunned, waved Patch away as sharp pain shot through his arm. Damon, spun around and lunged, forcing the attack. Again, Jamey, off guard, dodged at the last moment as Damon's blade sliced across his thigh.

Jamey fell to the deck and tumbled to his feet with moves taught by Patch, his eyes blurred from the heat of his wounds.

Then, Damon calmly stopped, glaring at Jamey with a snarling smirk, his hooded eyes snake sure of its prey. Seeing Jamey's wounds, he would now take his time, toy with him, punish him, his death certain.

Jamey fought to recover. Badly hurt with gashes, he not yet swung one sword. He watched Damon slowly advance with his thin smile peeled tight against his teeth. His tongue flicked like a viper, tasting the kill. Jamey reached deep for strength.

They came together as two stags, blades crashing against the other in blinding, ringing steel. Damon's thin whipping strikes and thrusts matched Jamey's slashing sweeps and chops. Power grunts matched each thrust and parry to the beat of a tune named death.

Damon broke away, surprised at Jamey's skill. Jamey, sucking for breath, stood weak with a slash across his cheek and a slice across the belly. With his leg and arm gashed, blood soaked his clothes from his pounding heart. He tasted warm blood, like liquid metal, and swished his tongue, spitting a glob of red as he shook his head to clear his mind. Staring back at Damon, he felt his legs start to buckle and leaned against the rigging, bracing himself. His swords felt like sledges as he looked down at his wounds, eyes blurred.

For the first time, his confidence faltered, weakness flowed over him. Damon had not one wound. Perhaps the devil will win this day, he thought. He glanced at Patch starting toward him and waved him off.

El Serpiente's tongue, giving the slightest flick, tasted victory and whispered hard, "The hawk's claws are no match for the serpent's fangs." Damon smirked, mocking, his venom vile. "Your death will taste sweet."

Damon's words cut deep into Jamey's heart. He stared into Damon's eyes remembering the tortured deaths of his family and his friend, Jade. Before him was the evil responsible. Damon's vile face burnt his soul.

Reaching deep, Jamey huffed for breath and felt his mind click.

Jamey, the warrior, pushed away from the rigging, planting his legs tough to the deck, his flint cold eyes bored with a single purpose.

Damon saw the change.

Jamey advanced, his two broadswords whirling their dance. His blades wheeled at blinding speed around his stone cold gaze of this destiny, this final mission.

Damon viewed his death in Jamey's eyes. He was going to die. Backing against the bulkhead, he threw down his swords and fell to his knees.

"Please, please, do not kill me. I'm sorry, I'm sorry, *señor*. I was not in my right mind. Have mercy," he pleaded, sniveling.

"*Por Dios*, spare me, spare me."

He begged with outstretched arms and tearful eyes, rocking back and forth on his haunches.

Jamey halted his blades, looking down at Damon, off guard by his actions.

Damon, seeing his hesitation, pleaded, "*Por favor, señor*, have pity. I was demon possessed. Let me live, I beg you," he wailed, lamenting like a scourged sinner. He thought it was his best acting yet as he watched Jamey falter, weighing his pleas.

Damon smiled to himself. *El Serpiente has tricked the mighty Raptor.* Playing the role, he continued pleading, begging for mercy, as one arm slipped toward the hidden dagger in his boot.

As Jamey turned toward Patch, DeSago, flashing his blade, lunged at Jamey's belly.

Jamey, sensing the movement, continued his turn, pivoting, raising his broadsword high and hacked down. His blade fell like a guillotine, cleaving both of Damon's forearms clean with the single blow.

Shocked, Damon fell back on his hind legs, unbelieving, staring at his hands and arms lying on the deck, fingers still twitching as blood squirted in spurts from his arm stumps like his father long ago. Then, slowly, lifting his eyes to Jamey, he beheld his own death.

Jamey's pale eyes zeroed, cold as northern ice, his whisper hard, "These are the swords that sent your father to hell. He waits as you watch yourself die."

Jamey turned and walked away ignoring *El Serpiente's* bellowing screams of defeat.

Just then, Jamey and Patch, hearing a pealing squeal, looked to the sky and watched the pretty white hawk dive to a flying circle, tipping its wings, and disappear into the sun.

chapter 21

PATCH ASSUMED COMMAND while Jamey's wounds were tended. One treasure galleon was released to the Raptor's crew choosing to return to England with their share of riches and deliver the queen's portion. Angelica's treasure was loaded on the Raptor and stripped of all cannon before command was returned to the Spanish Captain to save survivors from the sinking warships.

As promised, they were left with all masts and sails to allow a safe voyage to Spain. The Spanish captain requested DeSago's body for burial. Patch thought the request unusual but saw no reason to deny the petition.

At dusk, the Spanish ship set sail for Seville. Some leagues away, making sure the horizon was clear, the captain ordered DeSago's body wrapped in linen soaked in salt to preserve as best they could. There were those in Spain who should witness the manner of his death.

*

The Raptor sailed into Tortuga bay triumphant and tired. Deck hands clewed the sails as topmast men scrambled aloft to lash canvas snug against the spars. The bower anchor, dropped to the ocean floor, rattled chain through the hawse measured seven times the depth. After the flukes sunk deep, the bow swung to the tide and a kedge was set off the stern for good measure

Jamey and Patch watched from the rail content to let the second mate do the honors.

Although seriously wounded, Jamey felt the relief of victory with the death of DeSago. A fortnight had passed since they watched Maria and Roseta sail away over the horizon. It seemed a century and both were impatient to go ashore to see their women.

Long boats were launched but hauling Jamey over the side was no small feat with him yelping in pain. He needed a crutch for the leg wound and the arm was slinged. His middle was wrapped tight and a fat bandage covered the slash on his cheek. The ship's doctor, also the cook, did a fair job even with the face stitches. Jamey didn't remember much after drinking a half tub of rum.

Maria and Roseta fidgeted, anxious, standing on the beach watching the longboats draw near. Both wore new dresses, one blue, the other yellow, with matching hats and parasols, the latest fashions from Paris that drew stares of admiration and envy from passing men and women. Maria and Roseta took no notice straining for the first sight of their men. With hands cupped over her eyes, Maria spotted Jamey and tears welled, seeing him slouched and covered in bandages.

Finally, the launch slid into the sand and the men were in their arms. Jamey winced with her squeezes while scores of questions were asked all at once.

By the evening meal, they were settled in the rented house with a bath and clean clothes.

After a hearty meal with celebrations and laughs, the men filled their glasses, stood serious, and called the table to attention. Maria and Roseta, glancing at the other, wondered their intent. All went quiet as Jamey and Patch cleared their throats. Then both, feeling the drink, took a deep breath and declared, glasses held high, their intention to marry them on the morrow with a real priest before God and the world.

The table quieted again. Maria and Roseta exchanged glances and erupted with laughs and tears, jumping up for more hugs.

The women, of course, already discussed this possibility at great length, making some preliminary plans just in case. Wedding dresses were purchased, a vendor found to provide fresh flowers on short notice, and a visit with the local padre to make sure he was available.

The moon full, retiring to their rooms, Jamey's pain was numb from the wine but he was not very mobile. Concerned about his ability to make love, he became self-conscious knowing his limitations. Maria sensed his worry as she led him to their bed.

"Just lay back and be still," she whispered shyly.

She made him comfortable, propping his back with pillows, and lit several perfumed candles.

He started to say something but she gently shushed him as she backed to the foot of the bed.

Their eyes met and held as one. Smiling tenderly, she slowly started disrobing, never taking her eyes from his. Her clothes lazily peeled off in natural movements, teasing him with anticipation. Her lips parted in an earthy pout as she wetted them with the slow tip of her tongue. Jamey could taste her essence as he watched, mesmerized, by the raw seduction of her sex. His body trembled with desire as she raised her hands and unpinned her hair, letting it fall thick against her shoulders, veiling her face in a natural tease.

Maria felt naughty, wanting him to see her naked. Sensing his desire, she cruelly lingered, letting each piece fall slowly, humming her favorite love song. Her hips swayed to the tune while candles waved their golden light over her body in a fantasy glow. Her gold-green eyes held his with love as she tossed her hair and spread her legs for a teasing moment. Her body tingled, feeling his eyes drink her in. Then, with parted lips, she crawled slowly toward him. He reached for her, smelling her need.

"No, just stay still. I will love you tonight."

Her caress was sweet torture.

Opening her eyes at first light, she turned to see him lying on his stomach, arms folded, cushioning his head. Remembering last night, she smiled wicked with love at his soft sleep.

Thinking of their time in the small sloop, she couldn't resist. She slid the cover back and nipped him hard on his bottom.

Jamey yelped and twisted over, seeing her impish grin.

"You bit me," he said, surprised.

"I wanted to since the small boat."

"You peeked?"

"So did you."

Maria straddled his hips as he turned fake serious.

"No, not with these," he said, pointing to his eyes. "I have an eye in the back of my head."

Sitting back, she cocked her head with a questioning look, wondering if it was true. He looked serious. Curious, she leaned forward to check the back of his head. Maybe he did, she thought, she did not know these Irish... This one was tricky.

As he planned, when she leaned forward, her breast pushed close to his mouth and he nipped her nipple.

Maria jumped back. "Ohhh, . . . you devil."

"Well, you bit your favorite spot."

"That was different," she said.

"Why?"

Holding his eyes with hers, she leaned toward his mouth.

"Because, . . . I want more," she whispered.

He became lost in the aroma of her desire.

Later that morn, two happy and spent men excused themselves after breakfast, hurried to the village to visit a jeweler, the church, and a stone cutter.

That same eventide, the moon glowed the sea silver as the padre performed a quiet double wedding ceremony, his first. The men, clean and straight, stood stiff, suddenly frightened. The women, Madonna's in their wedding costumes, were never happier. The final blessing brought laughs and tears. It was a perfect time.

Later when alone, Jamey handed Maria a small gift, simply wrapped. Excited as a child, she opened the velvet box and brought forth a teardrop pearl, plump as a fig, its luster soft as moonshine. Her breath caught, never before seeing anything so beautiful as it hung, delicate in its own gold cradle, crowned by a fiery ruby.

Holding it gently from its chain, she admired its changing hues under the moonlight. Love tears fell as it slowly twisted, revealing the message engraved on the back.

"If only what is, will forever be. Love, Jamey."

Her heart overflowed. She couldn't speak. Falling into his arms, he held her, feeling her tremble with the depth of her love.

He whispered softly, "I want to take you home."

The next morn the Raptor set its course to White Bay Cay.

*

After seven suns melted into the sea, the topmast hailed, "Land ho! White Bay."

Excited, Maria and Roseta rushed to the rail, standing on tiptoes, watching the misty headlands slowly appear through the early sunrise. Anxious, they chatted away as their island home magically rose from the empty sea.

A sandglass later, the Raptor was snugged at the wharf and greeted by everyone on the island. Earlier, a crisp spring rain freshened the air, scrubbing away the dust, glistening the island with smells of green growth. The buildings, fully repaired with paint glossed new, made their welcome special.

Jamey and Patch became suddenly quiet as they helped the ladies ashore. Jamey's first glance was to the bluff and the home Jade, Patch, and he shared. He took Maria aside.

"I must be alone for awhile. Patch will give you a tour of the island."

Maria, feeling his sorrow, knew this was his first time back since his friend's death.

"I know," she said. "I will be waiting."

She hugged him tight, kissing his cheek.

Jamey started toward the cliff, crutches gone, using a walking stick. His arm was still bandaged, but not slinged, and a light dressing covered his cheek. He trudged forward, limping hard, with silent thoughts and a heavy heart. The headstone burden slung over his shoulder hung heavy in a sack. He marched alone with the Christ load on this overdue pilgrimage, the pain of his wounds, his penance. Each step brought memories of Jade's beauty and her shyness that hid a deep passion behind gem-green eyes. He always knew she loved deep with absolute loyalty, never asking anything in return. He also knew she loved him more than a friend and he silently cursed himself for denying her wish.

At last, he stood, head bowed before her grave, a tiny mound on the earth. A physical pain hit his chest as grief filled his heart. Unable to hold back the tears, his breath caught as he surrendered, sobs shaking his body, regretting forever his sin.

Then, as time flowed, a gossamer breeze surrounded him. Gathering himself with a sigh, he unwrapped the headstone and carefully placed it at the head of her gravesite. He stood back with wet eyes and read the chiseled script.

JADE

Beloved Friend and Sister

May Your Spirit Finally Soar

As he whispered, "I'm sorry," he heard a soft peal and raised his eyes to see a pure white hawk just above the headstone. Smaller than most, but perfectly formed, she floated with wings full on the still wind. Gazing in wonder, he looked into her jade eyes and as they held him, forgiving, a sudden wave of peace filled his soul. A relieved smile formed as he watched her tip her wings, floating ever higher, then diving to a happy loop, yipping sweet squeals. Then, she soared high, as it was meant to be, finally gliding over the gentle sea.

Jamey, watching her disappear, lifted his face to the sky and whispered, "Thank you Buddha, for honoring her."

When he returned, Maria held him in a loving hug. He was finally at peace. All the ghosts and guilt were gone. Maria, feeling his renewed spirit, looked into his smiling eyes, loving him even more.

Holding her hand, he led her up the hill to the great house.

"Let me show you your new home."

*

Close by, a pure white hawk coasted on the wind.

epiLoGue

Dear Clarice;

I pray this letter finds you well as it bears good news. Earth's Satan is dead. Damon DeSago was executed on September 18 of this year for his crimes. You, your family, and mine have been avenged. I have finally found peace and wish the same for you with every happiness.

Your friend,

Jamey

Clarice sat still, staring at the letter with blank thoughts. She was numb, floating, nothing touching her body in any way. She sensed a small simmering spark, deep within, but could not call it forth. Her emptiness seemed forever.

She finally stood and slowly continued packing. They were sailing in a fortnight to the new world.

*

Ma Cherie, Monigue;

We have never met but we feel we know you. Your father was a dear friend and we are writing for him. Sadly, he was killed on August 23rd, in a battle. He died with honor saving our lives. He was very brave and wanted you to know he loved you very much. He will be watching you from heaven and wants you to grow strong, study hard, and be happy.

We will come and visit you soon. You are part of our family now.

Kindest regards,
Maria Fallon

Monigue sat bravely on the hard chair, her little legs dangling. Fat tear drops rolled from her big brown eyes as she whispered softly, "I will poppa, I promise."

The stiff suited solicitor, noticing her unusual beauty, handed her mother a document with a financial accounting.

Little Monigue was now wealthy.

*

Dear Maria and Jamey

It is hard to believe a full Christmas has passed. Patch
and I pray you are well. My time is getting close but I know
all will be well. A fortuneteller told me so.

It is hard to believe Joshua is already two years old. The
shipyard is growing. Patch is working hard and is proud.

We like this new world. Please visit soon, we miss you.

Friends always,
Roseta and Patch

*

Dear Roseta and Patch;

Tis a girl, feisty and pretty as Maria. We have named her
Corina Maria. We are blessed. An English captain stopped at
our island and presented a medal from the queen for services
to the crown. It has a white hawk over a two-headed raptor
under the royal crown of England.

One wonders how they knew?

No other exciting news except the Raptor was sold and
replaced with a smaller ship named the Dolphin. She is a
beauty like our new daughter.

We will visit as soon as possible.

Friends always,
Maria and Jamey

*

Señor Carlos DeSago;

We regret to inform you of your brother's death. *Señor* Damon DeSago's remains are in Seville at Cielo Puerta, 336 Liano Avenue awaiting your instructions.

With much sympathy,
Almirante Angel Sobor Rios

Carlos stood alone in the candled sacristy. The flickering flames heated his dark mood as he stared at his brother's shriveled corpse. His eyes bore close with intense concentration to never forget any detail. Damon's body was small and withered, his face still frozen in horror as it was the day of his death. It was difficult for Carlos to remember this was the same tall strong brother he loved, the last of his family.

As he kneeled, Carlos's hate started bubbling deep. First his father and now his brother murdered. He whispered bitter low, "Jamey Fallon will die. His family will all die. The DeSago family will be avenged.... This I vow before God and all that is holy."

Carlos crossed himself as he raised his cold eyes to the crucifix above Damon's casket.

***

THE SAGA CONTINUES

9 781664 197596